zombabe

I. S. Belle

eBook ISBN: 978-0-473-65665-2

KDP Print ISBN: 979-8-363-41195-3

IngramSpark Print ISBN: 978-0-473-65664-5

content warnings

Hi everyone! I want to give people a heads up for some of the content so they can opt in or out at their leisure. Stay safe, folks.

Content warnings: violence, murder, cannibalism, generational trauma, addiction, racism, Nazis, cops, guns, mentions of school shootings, mentions of sexual assault and pedophilia, parental abuse, homophobia.

And while I have you here, a relevant fact: people who experience auditory hallucinations are much more likely to be the victims of violence than the perpetrators of it.

To everybody who wanted Jennifer and Needy to ride off into the sunset at the end of the movie.

Who knows upon what soil they fed
Their hungry thirsty roots?
—— *Christina Rossetti, Goblin Market*

prologue

BULLDEEN WAS DYING.

For a long time, this place was a dump in rural Maine. The dump was cleared away during the 1860s, and the town of Bulldeen began. None of their crops survived that first winter. The next attempt clustered closer to town and held on long enough to harvest.

The changes crept in slowly, at first. People grew irritable, as was to be expected in those dire circumstances. Nobody was surprised when irritation turned to violence. After a few decades, the townsfolk started to sicken en masse. Kidney failure, seizures, brain damage.

An official diagnosis wouldn't come for generations, but the farmers knew then that the dump had turned the soil toxic. Everyone had eaten the slow poison, and so they made plans to start again, somewhere pure.

Then, in 1892, a miracle: a newcomer they would come to know as Founder Jim crafted a strange plant mutation he dubbed thornfruit. It thrived on the poison, sucking it from the soil and storing it in its stem. The fruit itself was sickly green, dangerously spiky, and disgusting. But it grew fast, and was safe to eat. For two years, it was their main food source. In

1894, it was discovered by a skincare company who ordered it by the boatload. The flesh of the fruit would be a key ingredient in moisturizers worldwide over the next century. Suddenly, the town glimpsed survival. An economy grew up around their miracle fruit, everybody ignoring the simple truth: this was a temporary fix. Thornfruit couldn't grow anywhere else. Many had tried to force it, but thornfruit thrived solely on Bulldeen poison, and there was a finite amount. When the last drop was leached from the soil, all those crops were going to rot. And Bulldeen would rot with it.

Henry "Babe" Simmons had never stepped foot outside of Maine. Two weeks before graduating in the class of 2003, he went over to watch TV with his best friend, Eugene "Dude" Marsh. Halfway through an impassioned argument about sweet breakfasts versus savory ones, Dude unknowingly gave him an Almond Delight chocolate bar containing traces of peanuts. After two squares, Babe's throat started to itch.

"I'm fine," he said, when Dude asked why he was clearing his throat so hard.

Thirty seconds later, his windpipe swelled shut.

He spent his last moments on his back, lying on Dude's carpet. In a pleasant moment at the end, he felt his panic subside, awash in endorphins that turned the world into one big, glowing aura. His hearing fizzing out and his vision pinholing, the world narrowed to his best friend's face swimming over him.

Dude was crying. Babe had never seen him cry before. It was beautiful.

"Babe," Dude begged.

Babe opened his mouth to answer, but lost consciousness.

The paramedics charged into the room to find Dude pumping desperately on his chest, blowing into his cooling mouth. Thanks to the CPR, Babe had two broken ribs. He had been dead for twenty minutes.

This was a Wednesday.

On Sunday, he came back.

chapter
one

THE DEAD THING opened its eyes. It was lying in a narrow box. Dirt above. Dirt below. The dead thing sniffed, scenting a heartbeat racing above the surface. It clawed at the box until the wood shattered. Heaved its body up, up, up through the suffocating press of the earth until its hand touched warm air.

Another hand grabbed it and pulled. Two more yanks, and the dead thing—no longer dead—crawled out onto the grass.

"Hey," said the boy attached to the pulling hand. "Are you—"

The thing previously known as dead lunged, knocking the boy onto his back. Its thoughts were a frenzy.

dirt growl hungry

"Babe."

hungry hungry hungry

"Babe, if you're gonna eat me, can you quit dragging it out? The suspense is killing me, man."

skin against nose press teeth skin tremble

"Henry."

meat fresh meat henry he never calls me henry

Babe woke up. He stared down at Dude, who had given

them both nicknames in first grade. Best friends had to have matching nicknames.

Babe blinked once, twice, until Dude came into focus. Dirt dripped onto Dude's pale forehead. It was hot, both boys sweating through their Sunday best. They were seventeen years old. Babe had just crawled out of his own grave.

A wave of hunger made Babe shudder. Beneath him, Dude winced.

Babe sat back on his haunches. His mind reeled, memories shoving blearily into place.

"It was an almond bar," he blurted. "I checked. It didn't say *anything* about peanuts!"

Dude blinked up at him with heavy eyelids. They drooped more each year. One day, he'd need surgery to pull them back up. The townsfolk didn't know this. Most of them thought he was constantly stoned.

"I called the company," Dude said. "They're going to put a warning on the wrapper."

Babe wiped the dirt from his pink cheeks. He shook.

"Did I..." He couldn't finish.

Dude nodded.

"You brought me back?"

"Worth a shot." Dude adjusted his tie with a slow, sure hand, not looking away.

"Huh?" Babe climbed off Dude onto the yellow grass. He pushed himself to his feet, trembling hands brushing at his dirty suit. He had vague memories of shattering wood under his fingers, which should have left massive splinters, but both fingers and fingernails were unharmed. He looked around. They were standing in Bulldeen's only graveyard, tucked into the side of town between the sewer district and the hills.

"I thought this was all fake," Babe heard himself say. "The

stuff they say about Milly Hart coming back and...and Anna's great-grandma, and...It's real?"

"Looks that way," Dude said quietly.

Babe shoved his blonde hair back from his forehead. It flopped back into his face, pasty with sweat from the heat and the climb. "This is ridiculous," he croaked. "This is insane. This is a really weird prank. I'm not—I can't—"

But he remembered choking, the darkness overtaking him as his air ran out. And he remembered the darkness of the coffin, the lurching climb up to the surface. He remembered Dude's face, so close, those beautiful brown eyes, wide and wet—

Babe turned to find Dude still sprawled on the ground, gazing up at Babe in something too close to wonder.

Babe swallowed. He had no idea how to deal with this, but Dude was familiar. Easy. He held out a hand, trying to keep it steady. "Are you gonna get up or are you growing roots?"

"How are your ribs?"

Babe frowned, fluttering a hand against his torso. "They're fine. Why?"

"Nothing." Dude pushed himself up, wobbling.

Babe moved forward to steady Dude, and his hand came away bloody. He rubbed it between his fingers. "Is this fake?"

Dude checked. "My fake blood is darker than that."

Babe grabbed Dude's right hand. A deep slice dripped down the palm.

"Who cares about your prop stuff? You're hurt!" Babe dug into his pocket and pulled out a handkerchief, dusting off the dirt crumbs. He tied it around Dude's hand. It was hard. He didn't have his glasses on.

"Darn it," he muttered to himself, as the knot slipped away again. Somehow, he was glad. Easier to focus on tying a knot than the fact of his own death.

Dude reached into his own pocket and pulled out Babe's glasses, trying to unfold them with his good hand. "Here."

Babe took the glasses and slid them home. The world had edges again. The sky was bloody. Sunset in Bulldeen. It would be a ten-minute walk through the sewer district, then another half hour across town until they reached Babe's house in Bull's Head.

"Thank you." Babe secured the knot.

Dude flexed his fingers. He cleared his throat. "This is *not* to Boy Scout standards."

"So what?" said Babe, who had tied it like a shoelace. "A knot's a knot. You aren't bleeding out."

Dude sucked in air through his teeth. "I don't know. With the state of this knot, it'll fall off in a couple minutes."

"It's tight." Frustration leaked into Babe's voice through the numbness. Old habits. "It's a tight knot!"

"But not a Boy Scout knot. Remember what Scout Master Harwin said—"

"Don't lecture me about Scout Master Harwin. You whispered everything he said in a dumb voice and got *me* in trouble for laughing."

Neither Babe nor Dude cared about knots. They didn't care about Scout Master Harwin. But those two could argue over everything, and they often did. The week before, they'd spent three hours debating mustard versus ketchup on hot dogs. The answer (mustard) didn't matter. What mattered was how much fun they had winding each other up. Thirteen years of friendship, and they had arguing down to an art. To the rest of the town, Babe was overly kind and polite, while Dude was relaxed in a way that bordered on apathy. Around each other, their voices would rise and roughen. Even their best friends, Jules and Anna, couldn't generate the effect they had on each other.

Dude raised a finger to scratch his cheek, smudging blood next to his nose. Babe trailed off mid list of Dude's Boy Scout offenses. They were standing in a graveyard, Babe's grave desecrated behind them. Dread gnawed at Babe's beating heart.

Dude looked up at the sudden silence. He was five-foot-three in boots. Babe had hit a growth spurt in freshman year that had carried him to six feet.

"How long—"

"Your funeral was this morning." Dude still hadn't taken his gaze off him. He was barely blinking.

Everything felt unreal, like Babe had opened his eyes into a dream. A wave of hunger rushed over him and he clenched his fists, breath hissing through tense lips. For a second, Dude wasn't Dude, just some warm, ripe thing to sink his teeth into—

"Babe?"

—and then he was his best friend again. Babe brought up an absentminded hand and scratched at the back of his head, which was home to a strange itch beneath his skull.

He swallowed, felt the saliva suck back down his throat. The resurrection stories in Bulldeen did not mention hunger. They mentioned a price. They did not specify what had to be paid, but Babe had been raised on these dark fairytales, and he knew how every one of them ended: more death.

"Dude...what'd you *do*? To bring me back?"

Dude shrugged again. "Don't worry about it."

Another swell of hunger. Babe swallowed and swallowed, dread thick in his throat along with the spit, foreboding in his veins. *What happened to me? What am I?* He squeezed his eyes shut. When he opened them, Dude's expression had changed, a minute flicker that only Babe would be able to notice. Relief to worry.

"What is it?" Dude asked. He was being so sincere he was

freaking Babe out. Dude didn't show this side of himself much, not even to Babe. There was always a dry joke, an air of cool casualness. All that was gone now, his eyes wide as they could get with those drooping lids, gleaming with a worrying amount of wetness.

"Don't worry about it," Babe croaked. Another swallow. He'd never been hungrier in his life. He breathed in deep, tried to numb himself again. He was good at that.

"Right," Dude said slowly. Then, finally, he made the face Babe had been waiting for. This was his *I'm going to make a joke to diffuse this tense situation* face: a wry twist to his mouth, gaze averting as his mind whirred to come up with a wisecrack. It took longer than it should.

"If I have to suffer through the last two weeks of school, so do you."

Babe blinked. Right. School. He gasped, gripped at his dirty suit. "Oh, God! My dad must be—"

"Mmm-hmm," Dude said. He nudged a rock out of place with his foot, examining it. "Yeah, he was...we should probably..."

"Of course," Babe said, panic for his dad overtaking every-thing else.

They started out of the graveyard. Babe was so busy stressing about his dad that he didn't notice Dude glancing back into the graveyard. Dude scanned for a second, but nothing moved. The thing he was looking for wasn't there. It was already ahead of them, and moving very fast.

chapter
two

STRANGE THINGS HAPPENED IN BULLDEEN. The townsfolk tried not to pay attention.

A group of the first thornfruit workers went slowly insane in 1893, and the townsfolk left them in The Parrot, the town's grimiest bar, to hiss about whispers in their heads and barbs under their skin. When they were found frozen to death in the fields the following winter, their scratched-up corpses were quietly buried, and a sign was put up for more workers. Five able-bodied men were out in the fields the next morning. If those workers heard the occasional sharp murmur when no one was present, if their skin itched as if something was trying to emerge, they kept quiet about it.

The explosion at the school was a faultless tragedy. No one could have predicted the boiler would burst in 1938 in the middle of a school dance. Four teachers and two dozen students were killed—half the student body. Back before the elementary school was built, both teenagers and small children were in the same building. Out of the two dozen students killed, most of them were under ten.

Graves were dug. Graves were filled. Families grieved and drank and showed up to work on Monday.

1940, the shootout in the middle of town square. 1965, the town hall burning down with people inside. Rubble was cleared away, bodies taken to the morgue and then to a hole in the ground. Bible verses were read. Dinners were prepared and eaten, dishes washed and put away, covers pulled over heads.

And then there were the resurrections.

If any of these things were talked about, it was in a whisper. Strange and terrible things were often whispered about.

In the long-gone summer of 2003, one of those strange and terrible things was Hunter Creel.

As Dude and Babe rushed home, Hunter Creel prowled the edges of the sewer district with his cronies. He had havoc to cause—cars to steal, people to harass. Kids, adults, it didn't matter. Everyone had a sensible amount of caution around Hunter.

He was scoping out an abandoned house when he noticed people at the end of the street. He glanced. His friends didn't pay attention, kicking a rock between them: Brian "Buzz" Kettering, a neo-Nazi who liked to joke about school shootings, and Moe Stafford, who had been okay until sixth grade, when he'd realized he wanted people wanted to avoid him for being an asshole rather than a loser.

Hunter stopped in the middle of the street. Buzz stopped behind him. Moe continued on obliviously, still kicking the rock, until Buzz called, "Hey, dipshit."

Moe spun. He frowned, honing in on their leader's confusion. "What'd you see, Hunt?"

"Dead man walking," Hunter said, pointing. He wasn't scared. Not shocked. Just a vague curiosity. It was definitely them—two of what Hunter had long called *the dead freaks.* So often he'd left them with a menacing *you're dead, freaks*. Dude's weirdly muscled, weirdly short silhouette slouched beside the lanky form of Babe Simmons, who wasn't dead. No, Babe was up and walking around, dirt-smeared and wearing the suit he'd been buried in. Hunter assumed he'd been buried in it. He hadn't gone to the funeral. Babe and Dude crouched over a public water fountain, Babe rubbing water over his face and stepping back for Dude to do the same.

Moe laughed nervously.

Buzz muttered, "What the hell? Do we jump them?"

Hunter opened his mouth to say yes, they should. On the first syllable, something flickered in the back of his brain. Not quite a whisper. An itch.

"Not yet," he said.

Moe squirmed. "You don't think..."

"Who cares," Hunter said, and spat in the road. He'd never bothered with those wild stories that got whispered about back in grade school. Now that he was confronted with one in the flesh, it didn't faze him. Just another messed up thing about Bulldeen.

He started back the way he'd come. Buzz and Moe followed, kicking the rock back and forth. They didn't get up to much trouble that night, other than shoplifting boot polish and rum from the Shop N' Save, and stealing a homeless man's shoe while he slept. But Hunter found himself grinning, a sharp grin that twitched whenever he tried to think about the reason for it. The reason, if he didn't think too hard, was this: tonight was the start of something. He was sure of it. He threw Leroy Child's shoe on top of the Shop N' Save, and sauntered down Main Street, gray eyes alight with victory that was surely on its way.

He whooped, and his friends whooped with him. Both were confused by this elation brought on by a very normal summer evening of shoplifting and bullying a homeless man for no reason, but neither of them questioned it. The night was young, and so were they. Hunter was grudgingly eighteen, Buzz was a happy seventeen, and Moe was straining on the tail end of sixteen.

They would not get any older. In three weeks, all of them would be dead.

chapter
three

BABE CONCENTRATED on putting one step in front of the other as they walked through the town square into Bull's Head. It was better than focusing on the gnawing hunger.

As they passed the town halls—the one they used, as well as the empty patch of brown grass across the street with a plaque, commemorating the people who had died in the first hall that had burned down—Babe had to come to a stop and clench his fists, clamping his teeth so tight, it made his jaw throb.

"What is it?" Dude asked.

"Nothing." Babe gritted his teeth. Whatever was happening, the best option was to ignore it and hope it would go away. That was how he dealt with everything he didn't know how to handle. It had worked so far.

Dude stood next to him, waiting. He didn't touch him, which Babe was grateful for.

Eventually, Babe unclenched. They started walking again. Babe resumed his exhausted, tight stride and Dude tiptoed along the drains. Dude had been informally training to be a stuntman (and propman) since he was six. This involved being able to balance on anything. It also meant that when he did fall, he could do it without hurting himself. He'd done a lot of falling to achieve this.

"Hey," Dude said, as they passed the closed-down movie theater, Bull's Flicks. "After this, let's go over and see Jules and Anna. They'll want to know."

Babe nodded.

Dude ran a hand through his dark hair, which was stuck in perpetual bedhead no matter how much he smoothed it down. "They're both at Anna's."

They passed The Horn, one of the three local bars, in silence. They passed the Shop N' Save, the only grocery store in town. They passed the police station and the bakery and the butcher's, Miss Petty's tailor shop, and the video store which doubled as a shoe repair shop.

They were just entering Bull's Head—the nicest suburb in Bulldeen out of two whole suburbs—when Babe tensed up with another shock of hunger.

He took a deep breath and tried to focus on the world around them, the streets leading to suburbia. "Why aren't *you* at Anna's?"

"Girls need their girls' night," Dude said. He went to kick a rock.

Meat, a voice whispered in the back of Babe's head. Not hunger, just awareness. *Tiny meat.*

"Wait!"

Dude's kick stuttered. His leg swerved to the left. "What?"

Babe bent down to pick up the snail Dude had been about to kick.

"Oh," Dude said. "Sorry, little buddy. Almost smooshed ya."

Babe dug in his pockets. He always carried a tiny pair of scissors, a Ziplock bag of dog treats, a Ziplock bag of cat treats, and an energy bar. Sometimes he carried an EpiPen, but before this week, he'd never been in a situation where he'd needed one. If you don't use something for long enough, it's easy to believe you don't need it.

Babe's pockets, of course, were empty. The funeral director hadn't packed them with his usual inventory. He picked up a nearby rock and coaxed the snail onto it, then straightened up and headed for a yard.

Dude stayed where he was, kicking pebbles after a close examination to make sure they were really pebbles. "Is he okay?"

"I think so," Babe said.

This was something they shared—a love for animals, small or large. They only differed when it came to insects. Babe hated them with a passion, refusing to go into a room that had a spider in it. Dude, however, was perfectly happy sliding the spider under a glass and letting it free outside. He'd even talk to it as he carried it out. *Gonna take you to a safe place, alright? I hope you like it out there. Your own little spider kingdom.*

Babe didn't bother talking to animals. He locked that talk in his head.

He couldn't be bothered saving snails right now, but Dude was there, so he kept those thoughts quiet as he went over to a yard and searched for a dandelion. Other than thornfruit and struggling grass, the only thing that grew in Bulldeen now was weeds. He stretched over the fence to place the snail down gently.

Dude kept kicking rocks. When Babe did stuff like this, it triggered an ache in Dude so intense he couldn't look directly at him.

Babe wiped his hand free of snail slime. "Sorry, what were you saying?"

"I'm going over later. I was there earlier, I just...went for a walk."

"And came back with your dead friend?"

"Not dead," Dude said, and it was almost casual. It was only thanks to the years of knowing him that Babe could pick up on the sharp edge.

"Not dead," Babe agreed, and touched his own wrist pulse. *Ba-bump. Ba-bump.* Echoing the rhythm, two pulses of hunger hit, one after the other. Babe clenched his teeth, closed his eyes and rode it out.

As if to join in the beat, Dude began to whistle. He had a gap between his two front teeth that made him the perfect whistler, loud and clear and always in tune. The whistle continued softly, coming nearer to Babe and then stopping.

Babe opened his eyes. Dude stood within arm's reach, watching him in a way he'd deny was anxious. Confused.

You don't know what's happening to me either, Babe thought. It was a lonely and frightening concept. He tried to remember the schoolyard gossip about Milly Hart as they walked the two blocks through Bull's Head to Babe's house. Milly was a strange one. She never talked about how her mother died.

Babe lived in a neat one-story surrounded by brown grass, one of the eight non-contaminated lots on the block. The toxicity in the soil had seeped into the wood and brick of many Bulldeen houses. This triggered a mass migration as people were forced out, the houses slapped with signs warning of poison and left to rot. It was worse in Bull's Head, every second house getting closed off. Some of the evicted had left for brighter horizons. Most of them had stayed, moving back into the sewer district they had tried so hard to escape.

The Simmons family were spared from the cull. They had lived there since they arrived in 1902.

Babe and Dude went up the short driveway lined with

generations-old pebbles. Babe knocked on the strong wood. Dude gave him a look.

"What?" Babe said. "I can't just barge in. He might have a heart attack!"

"He might have one anyway."

Footsteps. Babe braced himself. He should be glad. He got to spend more time with his father. Who wouldn't want that? He pulled a smile up, making sure to only show his upper teeth. His father disapproved of Babe's crooked lower incisor, and also of Bulldeen's only dentist.

The door opened a crack, allowing Ryan Simmons a sliver of the outside world—a sliver that only included Dude.

His eyes narrowed immediately. Ryan was skeleton gaunt with a narrow pencil mustache.

"You," he hissed. "I told you to *never*—"

"Uh," Dude said, blinking rapidly, gesturing at Babe on his right.

"How *dare* you." The door opened further. The world widened.

"Dad," Babe said, but Ryan had already noticed. His breath stuttered, eyes blowing wide, pallid face losing any of the pink it had to begin with.

Babe waved. "Hi. I'm *really* sorry, I know this must be—"

Ryan lunged. His arms circled Babe's neck, crushing the breath out of him. "Oh God," he muttered. "Oh, thank God."

The hunger came faster now, waves turning into a flood. Babe could hear his father's heart beating, blood rushing through arteries in his neck. If he tilted his head down, he could—

He yanked away. Ryan held him fast, but Babe surged with strength and pulled easily out of his grip. They stood there blinking, silent with shock. Babe had never refused a hug from his dad, much less pulled out of one.

Dude cleared his throat from the driveway. "He woke up in his coffin. I was walking by and I heard him shouting, so I helped him out."

"Mercy," Ryan whispered, and tried to drag Babe in again. This hug only lasted a few seconds before Ryan pulled back, wiping furiously at his own face. "I am going to *sue* that mortician out of everything he owns. Him *and* that chocolate company—they're both going to get it!"

Ryan ignored Dude and Babe's attempts to talk him down. "I put my boy in a box," he said. "I...I *buried*...How could they have let me do that?"

"It was a mistake," Babe tried. "It was just a mistake, Dad. It's not anybody's fault!"

"Not anybody's fault, my Aunt Fanny! Let me tell you, I'm going to march right down there and—" He faltered, gripped Babe at the elbows hard and then harder, as if trying to assure his fingers that there was something keeping them from closing. "Your glasses," he said doubtfully.

Dude rubbed at his nose. "I picked your pocket at the funeral."

Ryan groaned. "You little carnival freak!"

"Dad!"

"He had no right," Ryan told his son, and collapsed back into his arms. Babe breathed in and out, one slow breath following the last.

Muffled into Babe's shirt, Ryan said, "Ow."

Babe frowned. "What?"

"You're—digging into my back a little."

Babe's fingers were indeed digging into Ryan's back. He hadn't noticed. He tightened them into fists, apologizing fervently. When Ryan finally let him out of the hug and started into the house, Babe turned back towards Dude to find him at his side, about to follow him in.

The cops showed up while they were sitting in the kitchen, Ryan releasing a slow but steady stream of tears, Babe twitching and swallowing back saliva, Dude sitting straight at the end of the table.

Dude got up to answer the door and came back with Chief Higgins.

"Hey, folks," said Chief Kate Higgins distractedly, chewing nicotine gum and tilting her hat at the room. Her ill-fitting shirt was half-tucked into her belt, her unkept blonde hair shoved into a ponytail. "We got a call about a, uh…"

Her gaze fell on Babe. She raised her brows. She didn't look very surprised to find a recently dead kid up and walking around. The look turned into a stare, betraying nothing except the raised eyebrows. The back of Babe's neck prickled, and he gave her an innocent smile, only marred by a muscle spasming painfully in his cheek.

"Huh," Kate Higgins said. Her eyebrows came down. "Well, I can call Old Suzy back and tell her she doesn't need new glasses. That's Babe, all right."

Babe waved at her, sweating bullets. "Hi, Chief."

"Hi," Kate said. Her tongue flexed around her mouth, the way it did when she was trying to figure something out. Her smile was lackluster, as if she couldn't be bothered putting in the effort. This was not uncommon. Kate couldn't be bothered putting in effort for anything.

"Well, I hope this wasn't some dumb prank you two pulled."

"Damn, you got us," Dude said.

Ryan said, "My boy would never!"

"Right," Kate said. "So what did happen?" She looked over at Dude, who was his usual level of aloof. It was entertaining to watch her and Dude interact. An aloof-off, Babe once called it. It wasn't entertaining now, as Babe sat there with his hands in his lap, doing his best not to listen to everybody's blood rushing through their veins, just beneath their flimsy skin. *It's fine it's fine I'm fine. Nothing's happening.*

He held his breath, waiting for Dude's usual shtick. Every time Dude lied, the story got more ridiculous. It was surprising to hear Dude spout the same story he'd told Ryan: he'd been on a walk when he heard Babe call out.

"I was visiting the grave," Dude continued, "and I heard some shouts. He was digging himself up."

Ryan's hand squeezed around Babe's. It hurt.

"Uh-huh," Kate Higgins said. She'd been on the end of this innocent act since Dude was thirteen and experimenting with fake guns. This was right after he'd learned that propman and stuntman were two very different fields. But by then, he'd sunk too much time into both, so he decided to keep going. It didn't help that whenever Dude got the opportunity, he went for funny over safe. Combined with his usual flat drawl that made jokes sound like he was being serious, his talks with cops never went well.

Kate continued, "Is he okay?"

"He's fine," Dude said.

"'M fine," Babe mumbled over a thick tongue. Were his teeth getting heavier?

"It happened in Victorian times," Dude tried.

"'Scuse me?"

"They'd put a bell above the grave," Dude said. "Put a string down into the coffin. If somebody woke up, they'd ring the bell and someone would come and dig them out. Ding-dong."

Kate moved her nicotine gum over to the other side of her mouth. Kept chewing. "Lucky you were walking by."

"I'm a lucky guy."

"Uh-huh," Higgins said. She tipped her hat again, sparing another glance towards the sweaty, twitchy Babe, who was on the verge of lunging for her throat. "Well, I'm sure glad your boy's back, Mr. Simmons."

"Not as glad as I am," Ryan said, squeezing Babe's hand again.

Dude lingered in the house after the chief left. He picked up knick-knacks, examined them and put them back, ignoring Ryan's glare. Occasionally Ryan would turn his look on his son, the glare turning to light. He was doing a good job of ignoring the sheen of sweat drenching his son's body despite the air conditioner at full blast.

"Looks like they won't have to find someone else to play Founder Jim in the town play," he kept saying. "Looks like they'll have to take down that help wanted ad at the warehouse!"

Babe nodded distantly. He'd agreed to both of those because Ryan had suddenly brought them up like they were things Babe wanted to do, and he'd get confused and cross whenever Babe dared to hint otherwise.

You love that play, he'd say, when Babe suggested he wasn't over the moon about playing the town founder. And Babe didn't point out how the last time he got excited about it, he'd been eight years old. Ditto about working at the thornfruit factory, where Ryan was a supervisor.

Standing by the windowsill, Dude tilted a miniature deer statue too far. He caught it just before it toppled to the floor. Quick reflexes.

Ryan turned and glared.

"Sorry," Dude told him. "I've never been in your kitchen this long. I got excited. Is that a Monet?"

He pointed. Everyone turned to the painting above the

stove, which was going yellow. It was a watercolor of a nearby lake. Ryan had painted it, but neither boy knew this, and Ryan would never tell them.

"I think you ought to go," Ryan said.

Dude nodded, still rocking on the spot. "You got it," he said, and hesitated. "Do you think Babe could come with me to Anna's? Jules is over there, and—"

Ryan was already shaking his head, hands still over Babe's. "He needs to rest."

"Right," Dude said. He scuffed a boot against the linoleum. "It'd just be a short visit. Babe?"

Babe was wrenched further back to reality. It took him a second to remember how to speak. "Whuh," he said.

"Want to go to Anna's?"

Drool spilled over Babe's bottom lip. He wiped at it. He needed to get the heck out of this house.

"Yeah."

Ryan turned to him, betrayal making his eyes shine. "I just got you back and you want to go?"

"No," Babe said automatically. That one he could answer in his sleep. *No, I don't want to leave. Of course not. Why would I ever want to leave you?*

Ryan hadn't always been like this. If his wife hadn't left, he would have been more rational. But she did leave, and Ryan, mortally offended in a way that would become familiar, cut off all contact. *We don't need her,* he'd told his infant son that day, and many days since. *We don't need anybody but each other.*

"I just..." Babe continued. More drool. He wiped at it. "I..."

Dude handed him a dishrag. Babe put it to his mouth.

"You can see them tomorrow," Ryan said.

"But...can I at least call?"

"It's late. They'll be asleep."

"Dad—"

"I don't understand why you're pressing this," Ryan said, genuinely baffled. "Half an hour ago, I thought you were dead. How could you ask to leave?"

"I'm sorry," Babe said. "I..."

He trailed off. Babe apologized to his dad a lot, deserved or otherwise. Mostly otherwise. Not that Babe would admit this. *He's stressed*, Babe would tell his friends. *Dad has tender nerves. I shouldn't push back against him so much.*

Any pushing Babe did against his father was tentative or accidental. It didn't matter. Ryan always took it personally. And Babe would fold, if not immediately, then very soon after. He knew nothing else.

An itch arose in the back of his head. It wasn't words yet. Just one short, hard itch, a match striking against the flint of his skull. His jaw clenched. Something old and ugly reared inside him. He ripped his hands out from under Ryan's, the words coming clear and loud.

"My best friends think I'm dead right *now*," he snapped, in a tone his father had never heard out of his son, a tone even Dude was unfamiliar with, though he heard it once or twice a year. "I'm just asking for half a fucking hour to go over and—"

Dude and Ryan stared at him with a shock that was almost as blinding as Babe's. He'd never said anything worse than *goddamn* in his life.

He blinked hard, hand coming up to scratch at his face, his scalp, the back of his head.

"I'm...I'm so sorry," he said. He looked imploringly up at his father, who was still stunned to silence at not only being snapped at, but being *sworn* at. It was as much a surprise as finding his dead son standing at the door.

Babe touched his dad's wrist. For a second, he didn't even

hear the pulse under it. "Dad, I don't know where that came from—"

"You've been through a lot," Dude cut in, eyeing Ryan. "Right?"

Ryan finally closed his gaping mouth. "Right," he said, and then glanced over at Dude, annoyed at the agreement. He turned back to Babe, only hesitating a moment before taking his son's hands again. "I can't imagine what you've been through tonight. How about you go up to bed? I'll give them a call and let them know you're...around."

"Of course," Babe said automatically. He looked over at Dude to check if they were thinking the same thing.

They were.

chapter
four

BEHIND THE SHOP N' Save in the middle of town, Leroy Child scrounged through the dumpsters. He was trying to find another shoe, since some punk had stolen the right one while he was sleeping. Kids did that sometimes, stole things from him on a dare. They thought it was funny. Sometimes they threw things. Leroy tried not to feel angry at them, but after twenty years of townsfolk turning up their nose as he quietly begged outside the Shop N' Save, it was hard not to get a little peeved. This time, he suspected Hunter and his little gang. This meant he didn't get peeved, he got out of the way. Leroy was a Vietnam vet, but even he didn't want to tangle with that kid. Not after what he did to his teacher in freshman year. Old Mr. Jitterbug had left town pretty quick. After he was allowed out of hospital, anyway.

A shadow passed behind Leroy. He turned, mouth open on a swear word. He didn't like to swear. He thought it was base. But he'd had his shoe stolen and he hadn't eaten today, except a handful of bar peanuts given to him by Ben Hershim, a friend and local drunk. It was nine p.m. Hunger makes anyone act a little out of sorts.

The swear trailed off into silence. In front of him was

something that looked like a man. It had all the right features. Actually, it had almost identical features to Leroy's commanding officer back in the war, only its bones were sharper, its jaw and cheekbones and nose and brow all stretched out to a cruel edge. The figure was wearing neat loafers and an overcoat.

The back of Leroy's brain lit up. *Wrong*, it screamed. *This is wrong*.

The thing that wasn't a man smiled. Its eyes glittered. Behind them, something howled.

"Oh," said Leroy Child weakly. "It's true."

He'd lived in Bulldeen all his life. He could guess what would happen next. It didn't make it any easier.

Out of the six people who heard the screams, only one of them called the police. Her name was Milly Hart, and she lived in the basement of the fabric store next to the supermarket. She'd been trying to sleep. She had nightmares because of something that had happened when she was very young. She'd woken with a jolt, her hand already on her mouth before she realized the scream wasn't coming from her.

Over in Bull's Head, Babe Simmons suddenly felt like he'd eaten a three-course meal. This was lucky, as he'd been in the middle of charging towards Dude's truck after climbing out his bedroom window.

He slowed and stopped. Dude didn't un-tense in the driver's seat.

They blinked at each other.

"Uh," Dude said. "You... good?"

"I'm..." Babe said, and wiped at his forehead. No new sweat.

He'd climbed out his window while clinging to the shreds of his humanity. He'd straightened up and turned to the road, and by the time his gaze landed on Dude in his truck, Babe Simmons had been completely feral. Feral and *hungry*. Instinct—not his own, but instinct nonetheless—had taken over. He'd started to sprint.

Then, suddenly, he'd been himself again. No flood, no rush. Coming back to himself was like having a veil lifted. He could see clearly again. Dude was Dude, his best friend, not a sack of meat to sink his teeth into.

He stood in the driveway and flexed his hands, his neck. The hunger was gone, yes, but so was the exhaustion.

"I'm good," Babe said, and meant it. He could run a marathon if Dude asked him to.

"You sure?" Dude asked as Babe climbed into the passenger seat. "We could stop on the way to Anna's."

"Stop for what?"

"For...anything you need."

Babe didn't let himself think about what he might need.

"I'm good," he repeated. "Thanks."

Dude pulled out into the street. After Babe had gone to his room, Dude had run home and driven the truck here. It was a beat-up orange Chevy, and Dude loved it like a younger sibling. This meant he occasionally swore at it and told it to move, but he also kept it clean and safe and, when he could help it, on the right track.

"I can't believe you told him off," Dude said as they reached the end of the street.

Babe sighed. "It's not funny! I could've really upset him. I don't know why I said it."

"Hey, I'm just relieved to see you speak your mind around him for a change."

"Please just drive."

Dude drove. It was only four blocks to Anna's house. They were tucked in the middle of Bull's Head.

"Maybe her aunt will let Anna know before Dad does," Babe said.

Dude grunted. "Or neither of them will."

Babe tilted his head in acknowledgment. Ryan did love "forgetting" to tell Babe his friends had called, and Chief Higgins, Anna's aunt, was notoriously tight-lipped. It wasn't that she valued other people's privacy. She just kept to herself and wished others would do the same.

They drove two blocks in silence. Babe shifted relentlessly in his seat. Dude tapped on the steering wheel. Both of them were searching hard for something to break the silence.

Dude found it first, singing softly, *"Remember to shake, shake, shake, remember to take, take, take—"*

"Oh gosh," Babe said. "No."

"—your time after you pee, to shake it dryyyy—"

"Stop singing Scout Master Harwin's pee song," Babe said, grinning. "Stop it. I'm serious, I will yank the wheel and kill us both."

It rocked them both into surprised silence. Dude reached the end of a street and flicked on the indicator. The surrounding roads were empty. The indicator blinked lonely in the night.

Babe cleared his throat. "You know which Scout Master Harwin song I hated most?"

"The knot song."

"Not the knot one. I *know* how to tie knots."

"Obviously not," Dude said, holding up his handkerchief'd hand, keeping his eyes on the empty road as he turned.

"I know how to tie knots! It was a stressful situation! Are you gonna let me talk or not?"

"Is it the condom song?"

"The what? He did *not* have—"

"He did. You were away that week."

"Like heck I was!"

They fell into bickering like a drowning man coming up for air. Relief filled the truck so thick, they would've cried if they'd let themselves notice. So they didn't think about it too hard as they drove the remaining two blocks to Higgins Vet Clinic.

You could only tell Higgins Vet Clinic was a clinic thanks to the sign, otherwise, it looked like a perfectly normal house in Bull's Head. The vet clinic was out back. Dude volunteered there every weekend. Today was the first Saturday he'd missed in five years.

He knocked on the door.

A thunder of footsteps. Ryan hadn't called yet, and wouldn't call until the next morning.

The door wrenched open to reveal Jules Havelock, a Los Angeles fashionista who had joined the friend group in middle school. She had dyed purple hair, a messy green face mask and one hand of wet pink nails. Behind her, Anna Higgins—lifetime Bulldeen resident and friends with Babe since kindergarten—shoved into the doorway. She stared at Babe, her brown, bare cheeks tacky with tears, dark eyes shining with disbelief and hope.

Babe raised a grimy hand. "Hey!"

"Holy *shit*," Jules said. She lunged forward and kissed him on the mouth.

Babe spluttered as she drew back. "Jules!"

Anna darted forwards and kissed his cheek. "Oh god. We're *so* glad you're okay."

Babe nodded dumbly. He wiped Jules's lip gloss from his mouth. He'd never been kissed before.

He turned to Dude. "What, no kiss from you?"

Dude had been watching this with a smirk. His face went blank at Babe's words, looking down at his scuffed boots. "Ha," he said, voice low and flat. "You wish, bud." He clapped Babe on the shoulder, still not looking at him.

Anna's parents appeared down the hall in matching slippers and dressing gowns. Anna had bought them as a gift last year. Even Dude couldn't bring himself to make fun of them for it.

"Anna," Mrs. Higgins said. "Does someone need—"

"Oh God," said Mr. Higgins, who had better eyesight. He stopped halfway down the hall, goggling. Mrs. Higgins squinted.

Babe waved. "Hi, Mr. and Mrs. Higgins."

Mrs. Higgins screamed. Everyone jumped.

Her husband put a shaking hand on her shoulder. "You had an open casket this morning," he said weakly. "We saw...*How...*"

Babe regretted not changing out of his funeral suit. The night was still not cool enough for sleeves, and it was flecking dirt onto the welcome mat.

"It happened in Victorian times," Dude said.

"What?"

"Come in!" Anna told them, wiping her face with her sleeve. She put a hand on his arm, not noticing the grave dirt that crept under her nails. "I'll make you a hot chocolate."

The vet rooms were behind the kitchen. As soon as Babe sat down on a stool next to the bench, a cacophony of hissing rose beyond the wall.

He glanced over at the door that led into the clinic.

Mr. Higgins went to check. He came back out a minute later, puzzled. "Well, the cats are in a tizzy for no good reason. But the dogs are fine."

He went to stand next to his wife, who was lingering in the kitchen doorway. He put an arm around her shoulders and she absentmindedly reached up to take his hand. Babe averted his eyes like he was ten and still blushed when the princess kissed the prince at the end of the movie.

Anna stood next to the kettle, tugging at her tight curls, drumming her fingers on the counter. She kept glancing over at Babe, her relieved smile gaining momentum every time, and Babe ached with fondness for her.

Jules heaped hot chocolate mix into mugs, bumping the cupboard door closed with the considerable curve of her hip. "Wow, you guys must be tired," she told Anna's parents. "Just —so exhausted. It's past eight thirty!"

"Well," Mrs. Higgins started, but Mr. Higgins talked over her.

"We'll let you kids talk," he said, and glanced over at Babe so fleetingly that Babe thought he might've imagined it.

Mrs. Higgins tugged her husband down the hall. As soon as the door closed, the girls spun around to Dude.

"Holy shit," Jules repeated, and Babe noticed a speck of pink smudged under her chin where she'd unthinkingly scratched with wet nails. "I can't believe all that Bulldeen bullshit is real. Did you kill someone?"

"No!"

"Then what did you *do*?"

Babe turned in his seat. Dude was in the stool next to him,

swinging his legs slowly. His feet couldn't reach the ground. His legs were slightly bowed, which did not help his height.

"There's a ritual," Dude said. "Just…a word and cutting your hand. Easy-squeezy."

"That's it," Jules said uncertainly. She flipped her smooth, purple hair over her shoulder. It wasn't straightened tonight, frizzing out near her hairline in strange pale tendrils. "What, no side effects? Babe, you been jonesing for brains since you woke up?"

Babe blinked, remembering that clawing, overwhelming hunger that blanked out everything else. Not for brains. For *meat*. Live meat.

I wasn't me at first, Babe didn't say. Because then he *was* him. And Dude was Dude, not a meal. It was a lapse, that was all. A couple of lapses. But he was normal now. He felt good. He felt *great*.

"No," Babe said.

"He's fine," Dude said at the same time. He picked at the tied handkerchief, hesitating on the edge of speech. His mouth closed. Opened. "Are we going to school tomorrow?"

A chain of shrugs. Jules moved out of the way as Anna poured water into the hot chocolate mugs.

"Might as well," Jules said. "It's almost the last-ever day."

Babe fought down the usual panic that rose every time he remembered how close they were to graduation. Every day was a day closer to his friends leaving Bulldeen. Leaving him. After graduation, his friends were heading out to LA. They were going to college—at least, they'd start college. The only one sure she wanted to finish her degree was Anna. Dude wanted to get into stunt and prop work, and Jules wanted to be a songwriter. Or a DJ. Or a singer. Or a producer. *Something* in the music industry, she was sure. Babe was staying behind to work at the thornfruit factory, one of the only places that would definitely still be open ten years from now. He hadn't gotten into college and his dad had assured him this was for the best. Sometimes Babe even believed it.

Dude put his arm in front of Anna and her mugs. "New hot chocolate powder?"

She glanced back at the packet. "There are a few new ones at the supermarket."

Dude walked around her and grabbed the packet, tossing it up in the air and catching it with a flourish. He smoothed out the plastic and started scanning the back.

Jules looked up from scrubbing the green facemask off with a wet dish towel, fair skin turning red under the attention. "What's up?"

"Checking if there are any fun puzzles," Dude replied, still reading.

Anna held out a mug to Babe. He took it by the handle.

"Hey," Dude said, not taking his gaze away from the packet.

"There are no peanuts in it," Anna assured him.

Babe paused, mug halfway to his mouth. Dude used to check Babe's food when they were kids—he'd dubbed himself Babe's food tester. Babe would go for a bite of his sandwich only for Dude to fly in at the last moment and snag a bite.

Quit it, Babe would yell.

I'm a super taster, Dude had told him. *Any trace of peanuts and an alarm bell goes off in my head. I'll keep you safe.*

And he had. Just once. They were seven and over at Dude's house. Babe was about to eat a brownie when Dude swiped it. Babe shoved him and went in for another one, but Dude put a hand across his chest.

There are peanuts, he said, mouth full of brownie.

Babe told him to shut up.

No, I'm serious.

Babe had asked Dude's mom about it. *Those brownies? Yes, I put ground peanuts in them, I was going to take them to work.*

It was the only thing Babe's dad had ever thanked Dude for.

Babe put the mug to his lips and drank. Dude's heavy-lidded gaze flickered his way.

"Seeing any peanut products?" Anna asked.

"Nope," Dude said. "But the chocolate bar didn't have any info about peanuts either, and look how that turned out."

He met Babe's eyes and picked the mug out of Babe's hand. He took a swig and swished it around in his mouth. He swallowed. "No nuts in there."

Babe took the cup back, turned it so he wasn't drinking from the heart-shaped mark left by Dude's mouth, and sipped. It was perfectly fine hot chocolate, but it tasted wrong.

Not enough metal, Babe thought. His cheek twitched. The thought didn't sound like his. But where else could it come from?

Not enough copper, the thought continued. It wasn't his. The voice was too deep and too sharp. It tried to keep talking, but Babe swallowed mouthful after mouthful of sweet, wrong hot chocolate, listening to the wet glug of his throat until it drowned the voice out.

chapter
five

ALL ACROSS BULLDEEN, people lay awake.

Anna and Jules lay back to back in Anna's bed, as they'd done a thousand times before. After a few minutes, Anna would turn around and say, *should we keep an eye on him?*

In the room above them, Anna's parents lay facing each other. Their eyes were closed. They did not sleep. Near morning, she would reach across the bed and touch her husband on the chest. She would start saying, *do you want to talk about it,* and he would cut her off without opening his eyes. *Sweetheart,* he'd say, *I really, really don't.*

Across town, Police Chief Kate Higgins sat on her couch. She had a case file next to her, a suicide from fourteen years ago. On top of that was a glass of whiskey. In her hand, she held a photograph—her mom and dad, who had died six and sixteen years ago, respectively. Next to it was a photo of her grandparents, whom she hadn't seen since they fled the town in 1965, the same day the town hall burned down with eight people inside.

Something else was awake in Bulldeen. It looked like a person. It was wearing an overcoat. It was waiting outside Dude Marsh's window.

Dude sweated over his bedroom desk. He used it for homework and prop work. Usually prop work. He was scribbling on a slip of printer paper, occasionally stopping to flex his newly bandaged hand. The handkerchief had started to fall off on the way home. It really had been a flimsy knot.

"To Jules," he muttered as he wrote, "I leave my bench press and weights. You keep talking about wanting buff arms, now's your chance. To Anna, I leave my books. Hope they're useful in your English degree. To Babe…"

His pencil stopped. He stared at the paper, flexing his jaw. He didn't have *time*.

To Babe, he wrote, *I leave my college savings. Use it to get the hell out of here. And please don't feel bad. If you gave me the choice, I'd do it again. I always would. I—*

The creature knocked.

Dude shot up, the knock reverberating through his bones. "Coming." He went to the window and pulled back the curtains. He jerked at the sight of Hunter Creel, halfway through spitting out a curse when he realized it wasn't actually Hunter: the chin too narrow, the cheekbones too keen. This was someone, some*thing* else.

Dude made sure his voice was flat. "Is Babe okay?"

The creature didn't speak.

"Is Babe going to be okay?" Dude repeated. "He was weird until he got in my truck."

"Yes," the creature said from behind the glass. Its voice was smooth and hollow. "The hunger had set in. I fed, and he was sated."

Whatever *that* meant. Dude nodded. "Do you like chess?"

The creature's eyes were strangely shiny, like a poisonous frog Dude once saw in an encyclopedia. It didn't blink.

Dude did. Suddenly the creature was next to him in his room. Dude fought back a flinch.

"Little warning next time, bud," he muttered, sliding the window closed. He gestured towards the chess board he'd set up next to the letters. "So, what do you say? Winner gets it all?"

The creature scrutinized his room—dirty laundry piled in one corner, desk stacked with all his in-process props: half-painted rubber, a plastic blade, a chair he was gluing together so he could get someone to break it over him. A battered CD player with all those albums Jules made him listen to. The creature walked over to the bookcase and touched the corner of a book on dog breeds. It was falling apart. Dude had carried it around all through childhood.

Sweat trickled down Dude's spine. He ignored it.

"Or we can play Connect Four," he tried. "Or—"

"Are you trying to bargain with me?"

Dude shrugged. "I'd be doing it better if you'd tell me what kind of game you liked. Wait—you seem like a Twister guy."

The thing smiled. Its teeth were sharp, and then they weren't.

"What exactly do you think is happening here?"

"Uh." Dude wet his chapped lips. "I'm bargaining for my life?"

"Why would I want you?"

"Because...that's the deal. You bring Babe back, and you get me in exchange. Unless I beat you at Parcheesi."

The creature laughed. It sounded so much like Hunter's low scrape that Dude had to brace his wide shoulders to keep from wincing.

"This cannot be bargained. There is no escaping this."

"Right, but—"

"Fortunately, you are mistaken. I do not need your life for his. I need *many*."

Dude's throat went dry. "Run that by me one more time."

"If he was dying, then your life would have sufficed." The

creature still wasn't blinking. The smile remained. "But the effort required to bring him *back*..."

Dude scraped his bandaged hand through his messy dark hair and winced. He kept forgetting about the cut. The throb was fading. "What about that mom in the '80s?"

"She didn't kill just herself." The smile grew. Just a little.

The note sat unfinished on Dude's desk. He was going to find a draft he liked and write it out on a new piece of paper, just in case his plan didn't work, which it obviously wouldn't, but what was he supposed to do, accept death without challenging him to an egg and spoon race first?

"I really am gonna have to finish my chem homework," Dude said, dazed. He'd been putting it off in case he did have to die. Which, until thirty seconds ago, he was putting his chances at 90/10.

The creature waited.

Dude cleared his throat. "So, what do I do?"

"You don't do anything," the creature responded. "Leave it alone and the hunger will run its course."

Finally, Dude met its gleaming eyes. They weren't Hunter's, but they were familiar. They made Dude want to curl into a ball and never look at anyone again.

The thing sighed. "Babe will get hungry. He'll feed. If he can somehow hold back, then I will...take over, again."

It was strange watching this thing call him Babe. The only person who called Babe by his birth name was his father, but Dude expected this thing to follow suit.

Dude swallowed. Pulling Babe out of the ground. Dirt dripping off Babe's neat blonde hair onto Dude's cheek. Hot breath. For a minute there, after he'd brought Babe to life, and later when Babe had been running at his truck, he'd thought—

"Will he be able to hold back again? Like he did tonight?"

"Sometimes they do."

The crawling at the back of Dude's neck intensified. He brought up a hand to check, but there were no bugs. Just the creeps. He glanced at his bedroom door. His mother was working another night shift. He lowered his voice anyway. "What if I kill people for you?"

The creature didn't react.

"You have your debt paid," Dude continued. "And Babe doesn't have to, y'know, go beast mode and eat someone."

It stared down at him. Dude was very used to being looked down on. He came up to most men's shoulders.

"No," it said finally. "It must be him."

"Why?"

The creature blinked. Dude thought of camera shutters, saving a picture of Dude for later. Blinking was somehow more unsettling than endless staring.

"Hmm," it said.

"You already said Babe doesn't *have* to feed," Dude said, sensing a handhold. "So what's the difference between you eating some random guy and me bringing you someone half-dead?"

"Hmm."

"I'll do a great job," Dude said, solidly blocking out everything this would involve, lest his stomach start to roil. He tried to remember what he'd said at his one and only job interview at the Shop N' Save. "I'm dedicated, I'm hardworking, I'm a real go-getter—"

"The hunger would be sated," the thing said over him. "A violence committed by someone who belongs to the town. Yes, I think that would work. You would have to have them on the verge of death."

"I can do that! You'll arrive in time to...finish them off?"

"I will." The creature smiled again. "This is new. I almost hope Babe does hold back."

Dude blinked. He was standing alone in his room.

He let out a gust of breath, finally giving way to the shudder. It shook down his body like a tidal wave. "You and me both, you goddamn weirdo."

There was no chance he'd be able to concentrate on his homework. He crossed the room, stepping around the spot where Babe had died on his carpet, and lay down on his bench press, where he would lift weights until he was tired enough to sleep.

six

BABE TRIED NOT to take the staring personally. He would've done the same thing if they'd had an assembly about some kid's death and the next week the kid was sitting in homeroom.

He *did* twitch at the new nickname: Zombabe.

"A nickname on top of a nickname," he told Dude, after Buzz coughed it over Babe's name in rollcall. "This never would've happened if I wasn't friends with you."

"You love it," Dude whispered back a beat too late, eyes on the board.

Babe watched him as long as he dared. Dude was weird today. Distant. Babe asked if he'd gotten enough sleep and eaten breakfast, and Dude replied that he had, then went right back to picking absently at the bandage on his hand.

A *pssst* came from behind him. Babe didn't turn.

"Hey," whispered Buzz Kettering. "Freak. How'd that homeless guy taste?"

Babe kept his eyes ahead. Leroy Child had been found mauled to death on Sunday night. Wild dogs, the police were saying. They'd eaten his legs to the bone. Most of his face. Chunks of his torso.

Babe was trying very hard not to think about it. Just like he was trying to ignore the hunger creeping back into his gut.

The hallways were full of whispers. *Zombabe. You saw his body, right? At the open casket?*

But no one came up to confront him about it. Not until Zachary Litnus, who ambushed Babe as they were in line at the cafeteria.

Babe was standing with Dude and Anna when he heard the dread-inspiring sound of an inhaler, and a voice spoke up behind him.

"Babe! Hi!"

Babe held back a sigh. He turned, pulling up a smile. "Hi, Zachary."

Zachary beamed, pocketing his inhaler. He was a sophomore, slight and freckled, enthusiastic in a way that reminded Babe uncomfortably of his own mannerisms if he didn't rein himself in. Zachary was the head of the drama club and had directed the annual play since he arrived at Bulldeen High two years back.

Babe had a Pavlovian response to Zachary and his inhaler, since every time Zachary had talked to him this year, it was to bother him about the play.

"You're still doing the play, right?"

Babe kept the smile intact. "Well, I am the lead. It'd be pretty crummy of me to back out on you now."

Zachary clapped in that way of his that increased his chances of getting beaten up from fifty percent to ninety. "I knew you wouldn't let us down. And your friends will still help? Last I heard, Dude was pulling out of the effects team. I take it this won't be an issue now?"

He looked questioningly towards Dude, who rotated one big shoulder. "I'll be there," Dude said. "Jules too."

More clapping. Babe glanced around for anyone who might beat their faces in, but Hunter and his cronies weren't here yet.

"That's great," Zachary said, turning his bright eyes back on Babe. "Thanks again for organizing that fundraiser last year. I don't think I've said that enough."

Babe laughed stiffly. "Well, you just kept asking."

"Yeah, but everyone else told me to go away!" Zachary knocked him in the chest with a flimsy fist. "Not you. You're a good one, Babe Simmons. Even if you did agree to be in on that prank. I gotta say, I was at your funeral and you were *really* convincing! Was that actually you in the coffin or did Dude make a dummy?"

Anna gasped behind them. Dude coughed to hide it.

"Um," Babe said, glancing at his friends. They'd decided the official story and were sticking with it. "It wasn't a prank. I was in a coma that looked a lot like death."

"Wow," Zachary said, eyes wide. "Like Romeo and Juliet."

"Yes. Just like Romeo and Juliet."

Zachary squared his jaw, as if committing to something. His hand came up to Babe's chest again. Babe tolerated it.

"Don't pay attention to Mr. Jameson," he said. "He's just superstitious. He was really weird about Milly, too, remember? Though she *is* a weird one. Not like you. So, you'll be at rehearsals?"

"Do we need another one? The play hasn't changed since 1900."

"We *always* need another rehearsal. And with the new music and props—"

"Right," Babe said. "New props. Of course. Just let me know when to show up."

Zachary thanked him. He patted Babe's arm and bounced off towards the drama table, where his friends were guarding his seat.

"Mr. Jameson *was* weird," Anna said, as they sat down at their usual corner table in the cafeteria, trays laden with mystery meat.

Dude and Babe grunted. Babe was busy thinking about the play, Dude with wondering how he was going to almost-kill someone.

"It was like he really didn't see you," Anna continued. "But his forehead vein kept twitching when you didn't put your hand down. I thought he liked you, Babe."

Babe chewed determinedly at his mystery meat. In two weeks school would be over, and if he bumped into his old teachers at the grocery store he could avoid them.

A feedback buzz sounded from the PA system. Jules's voice rang out across the cafeteria. "Haaaappy Monday everybody! Hope everybody's having a great great great day."

A burst of static. The PA system was old. This was a common occurrence, and every other time this happened, it provoked a wince at best.

The static whined. Pain exploded in Babe's head. He yelled, jerking in his seat.

Dude said, "Babe, what's—?"

The static cut off. "Sorry about that, everybody! Anyway, remember to get your votes in for valedictorian. You have until the last day of school."

Babe unclenched slowly. What was that? The static hadn't even been that loud today. Both his friends had their hands up, halfway to reaching him. People from the surrounding tables turned back, uninterested now that Babe had stopped yelling.

Jules's voice continued to echo through the school. "I don't see why the teachers don't just pick an excelling student, but whatever! This is how Bulldeen High has always done it! And as everyone knows, 'what we've always done' is the best choice for everything. Oh, Principal Skinner wants the PA back. Bye!"

Cue guitar riff. Principal Skinner killed it prematurely. His dulcet voice bid them another happy Monday and the PA went silent.

Anna nudged her slim foot into Babe's. He pressed back. He couldn't imagine existing without his friends, but he'd have to learn. He wasn't leaving this year and he couldn't see himself leaving any time after. While Jules thought of her childhood in LA, and Anna half dreamed, half nightmared about life away from her family, and Dude looked forward to setting up roots in someplace that could love him back, Babe didn't think about leaving. Every time a thought began to manifest, he smothered it. It was easier that way. Easier to do what his father wanted, easier to convince himself it was what he wanted too. Easier to keep his head down and scream into his pillow late at night, just quiet enough for Ryan not to hear.

Another senior walked towards them. Babe pulled up a polite smile, foot dropping away from Anna's.

"KJ incoming," he told Dude, who didn't react other than to move his head very slightly.

KJ Duong arrived at the table with his usual perfunctory smile, like he was working a customer service job he didn't much care for. Some townsfolk thought it was like Dude's aloofness, but Babe knew different. Dude's aloofness hid a deep heart. KJ's disinterest was just that. It went all the way through.

"Hi guys," KJ said. He nodded at Babe. "Glad you're okay."

"Thank you," Babe said, as bland as he could manage, to match KJ's tone.

KJ cleared his throat. "Dude, you have a free period next? Want to study?"

"Sure," Dude said quietly. "I'll see you there."

The mystery meat was even more flavorless than usual. Babe worked his way through it, fork scraping hard against the tray. "Studying," when it came to KJ and Dude, meant making out in the basement. Which was fine. Good, even, for Dude to get that kind of attention. Babe didn't care that it was with a guy. He *did* care that KJ was so *boring*. And he never realized when Dude was making a joke. And he had never seen *The Lost Boys*, which was unforgivable.

"Honestly," KJ said lightly, "I'm glad you're okay, Babe."

"Thank you," Babe said again.

A low voice behind him spoke up. "Hey, dead freaks."

Babe tensed.

KJ turned and fled. Babe couldn't blame him. KJ was Vietnamese-American, which made him more of a target, due to existing while not white.

Death, resurrection, blind hunger for flesh—for a second, it all fell away. Babe had been tensing at the sound of Hunter since first grade when Hunter had chased him around the playground with a box of matches for a half hour, telling Babe he was going to light his head on fire. He'd burned the ends of Babe's blonde hair before Dude managed to tackle Hunter.

"You think he ate that homeless guy?" Hunter continued to his cronies behind him.

"Looks like a killer to me," Buzz sneered.

Moe laughed. Like all his laughs, it was high and desperate.

Babe glanced over at Dude, waiting, but Dude continued

silently separating his mystery meat into different sections—dark gray, light gray, regular gray.

Anna didn't look at them. "Go away, Hunter."

Babe kicked her gently under the table. Dude's gaze flickered over to him.

Hunter loomed. "How's it going, Zombabe? I was gonna go to your funeral the other day. Have me a good laugh."

"Please leave us alone," Babe said, and then wished he didn't. Fingers in his hair forced his chin up. Babe hissed. There was an unusual amount of pain this lunch period.

"I *said*—" Hunter started.

Dude cut him off. "Kinky."

A snatch of laughter from surrounding tables. Moe and Buzz whipped around to see who it was, and it immediately burned out.

Babe made warning eyes at Dude, but Dude was busy looking up at Hunter, his ever-heavy eyelids and flat voice alluding to boredom. "Go get your thrills somewhere else. Babe's not interested."

Hunter's jaw flexed. He stalked around the table and put his face up to Dude's, who looked up impassively. "Oh yeah, short stick? What about you?"

Dude's eyebrows raised slowly. "Are you asking me if I'm interested?"

Moe let out a giggle. Buzz socked him in the arm and Moe hastily rearranged his face.

Hunter took Dude by the back of the neck and shoved him down towards his mystery meat. Dude strained, a faint grimace twisting his otherwise blank face. Anna got up to run for a teacher like they were still in elementary school.

"Come on," Babe tried. "He's just mouthing off. He didn't mean it."

Hunter was busy baring his teeth, trying valiantly to shove

Dude's face in his food. "That's what you get. *Nobody* accuses me—"

"Nobody was," Babe said, the nervous smile taking over. "It was just a joke!"

"Just a joke, man," Dude said, elbows braced on the table, shaking from the effort of holding himself up as Hunter shoved. "We've been doing this since we were in diapers, Hunt, come on."

"Hunter! Let him go right now!"

Mr. Jameson limped across the cafeteria towards them. He'd been injured in a hoeing incident when he was a child. Anna was next to him. Hunter turned to watch them come, dragging his hand off of Dude's neck.

"*Thank* you," Mr. Jameson said. "Good to see you're finally making something like a good choice this close to graduating."

Hunter lunged. Before Dude could straighten up in his seat, Hunter smacked him in the face with a closed fist.

Babe stood, barely aware of the motion, the noise of the cafeteria fading away under the blood pumping next to his eardrum. He registered Dude's head snapping sideways, but it was suddenly much less important than the hypnotic throb of Hunter's carotid artery.

"Hunter! Goddamnit," Mr. Jameson yelled, and winced. "I mean, gosh darn it." He stepped forwards, then faltered, his eyes stuck not on Hunter, but on Babe. The side of his mouth was curled in mild shock and disgust, as if Babe was a strangely diseased dog. Like he might have rabies.

Babe sat down so fast, his chair screeched against the linoleum. He tried for a reassuring smile. *I'm fine,* the smile said. *Nothing to worry about here! No bloodlust, no sir! I didn't eat that homeless guy, who seemed like a very nice man and definitely had a name I can't remember right now!*

He swallowed the spit pooling in his mouth. When he showed his teeth to Mr. Jameson, it was all politeness.

Mr. Jameson noticed Anna looking at him strangely. He straightened his tie, which was the same brown as the rest of his suit. Mr. Jameson was the only teacher who bothered to wear a suit to work. "Here I was, thinking you'd avoid detention until graduation."

Hunter groaned. "Come on, he called me a—"

"I don't care what he called you. You should feel lucky you're graduating at all."

Hunter glowered until Mr. Jameson walked off, then he got right up in Dude's face, his breath strangely chemical, as if he'd been gargling with lighter fluid. "You're dead," he said softly, looking around the table. "Dead freaks."

He stalked away, his friends in tow.

Babe shoved the worry down. *If Hunter actually wanted you dead, he'd have done it already.* He'd told himself this many times.

Dude's cheek was already swelling from the punch, red and blooming redder. Babe winced at it.

"Anna," Dude said. "Probably shouldn't have gotten a teacher."

"What was I supposed to do, watch you get hurt?"

"Yes. Always yes. You let Hunter flop his tiny dick around until he gets tired and then you go off and lick your wounds."

"Says you. *Are you asking if I'm interested?* Come on, Dude!"

Jules strode over, plucked eyebrows raised. She dropped her tray down so it clattered, fork bouncing off the tray onto the table.

"Hunter flopped his tiny dick around?"

"Uh-huh," Dude said, poking cautiously at his reddening cheek with one blunt finger. Babe batted him away from it.

Anna leaned to whisper in Jules's ear. Jules's gaze flickered to Babe. "The static hurt?"

Babe shrugged tightly.

Jules opened her mouth. Anna nudged her.

"Uh," Jules said, derailing from what she'd been about to say. "Sorry about that."

No one was looking at their table now. Not many had been looking in the first place. People didn't look in Bulldeen, like they didn't look at the homeless man outside the Shop N' Save. What was his name? Babe should remember. They'd talked once, him and the homeless man. He'd been twelve and the man had seen him crying behind the video shop, which also doubled as a shoe repair shop.

What's wrong, the man had said.

Babe had been so surprised to be asked, that he'd stopped crying.

Because people didn't look in Bulldeen. And they certainly didn't stop to ask if you were okay.

Babe hoped the man, whatever his name was, had died fast. Then he got to thinking about flesh ripping. Skin giving way under teeth. Blood spurting.

"What's up?" Jules asked. She was chewing something, her compact mirror out as she reapplied her eyeshadow.

Babe zoned back in. "Sorry?"

"You look weird," she said, curving dark pink around her eyelids. It shimmered wetly, appetizingly, and Babe had to look away.

"I'm fine," Babe said, and repeated it in his head for the rest of lunch. *Fine. I'm fine.*

chapter
seven

CHIEF KATE HIGGINS had gone over the Hart case file a dozen times since Sunday. Where did Milly Hart work again? In high school, she'd worked at the bookstore, but that had closed down years ago. Which meant she was probably at the thornfruit warehouse. Kate made a note to check.

The other case file—the one about the town hall burning down in 1965—was more of a head scratcher. Nobody ever got all those details. Though it wasn't hard to guess.

A shadow flashed in the corner of her eye. She got her gun out of her bedside drawer and put it next to her on her bed, but there was no other movement.

Kate Higgins rubbed at her dry mouth. The kid had crawled up out of his grave. And this was Bulldeen. They didn't have long.

Still, she stared at her phone a long time before dialing the number. It didn't work, so she dialed the other one she'd found after weeks of searching on the internet. It rang fifteen times before a voice croaked over the line.

"Yes? Who is this?"

"It's me," Kate said, and had to clear her throat. Something had caught. "It's Kate."

Heavy silence. A kettle was boiling on the other end, and Kate imagined it: a small bungalow. A city apartment. No, he'd never live in a city. Too cramped.

"It happened again," he said. Not a question.

"Yeah."

"Is anyone—"

"One," Kate said. "Which is why you have to come this time. Okay? We have the advantage on this one. Found out the night it happened. The last case, she kept it under wraps. If you get here in the next few days, I think we can—"

"Think we can what?"

Kate swallowed. She reached for her water bottle, which she kept on her nightstand so she didn't have to dry swallow hangover pills. She unscrewed the cap and took a mouthful. Usually water made her feel refreshed. Clean.

"We can stop it," she said.

He sighed. It was one of the clearest things she remembered about him, that blustery sigh.

"Is it another child?"

"You heard about that?"

"Is it?"

Kate popped another hangover pill. "He's seventeen."

"God," he said. "Kate?"

"Granddad?"

"Don't go near him."

"Yeah," Kate said. "No shit."

The Bulldeen police station was two blocks over from the town hall. On one side was what used to be the bookshop where Milly Hart worked. Now it was a boarded-up rat nest. On the other side of the police station there was a bakery. About once a week, the baker, Mr. Hockstetter, passed out in his kitchen from whiskey and opioids, and a police officer would go around and man the cash register. They called it Hock Duty.

Hockstetter had started early today. When Kate went into the bakery for her morning coffee, her deputy was cleaning the display case. Deputy Lissiter snuck back around the counter, squeezing his massive frame through the narrow bar flap. Deputy Lissiter was approaching thirty. He was both fat and big boned. He was the nicest coworker Kate had, though this wasn't saying much.

"Hey, Chief," he said in his dusky, unaffected drawl. "You think of any suspects yet for the homeless guy?"

She held up a hand. "Does it look like I've had my coffee?"

He ducked into the kitchen. Kate surveyed the food behind the glass. Hockstetter had passed out before making the pies. Luckily, Lissiter was the only guy on the force who knew about baking. When he took over Hock duty, he filled in whatever Hockstetter had missed out that day. He wore an apron for it. It suited him.

Lissiter strolled back with a Styrofoam cup. No lid, no steam rising. He handed it to Kate, who took it and started to gulp.

"So I was thinking," Lissiter started again.

Kate made a noise into her cup. *Wait.*

"Yuh-huh," Lissiter said, and leaned against the counter. Kate stood there, slowly draining her coffee until the dregs were gone.

"So—"

"You were thinking," Kate finished. "I heard. Lissiter, even the coroner said it was dogs. Nothing else could tear a body apart like that."

"Yuh. But he said the teeth marks—"

"So the dog's got weird teeth." Kate saluted him with the empty cup. "See you when your Hock shift changes over at lunch."

She had her hand on the glass door when Lissiter said, "You haven't asked what I was thinking."

Kate paused at the door, bell just about to chime. Her hand rested on the doorframe.

"What're you thinking?"

Lissiter shrugged. His police uniform was tailored so it sat nicely on his large frame, but Kate missed the apron. It made her like him more. Lissiter was the kind of guy who didn't take an apron as an affront on his masculinity.

"Just thinking about the old town hall," he said casually. "Thinking about the Hart case."

He didn't say the Higgins case. Kate appreciated it, even if she couldn't help resenting him for bringing it up.

"What about it?"

He shrugged again. His face betrayed nothing. It stayed the same through every damn thing. "Some kid comes back from the dead."

"He wasn't dead."

"Coroner sure said he was. Same week, some homeless guy gets torn apart. Sounds familiar, y'know." A timer dinged in the kitchen. The pies were ready.

Lissiter started to move for the oven. "We don't get a lotta wild dogs out here," he called from the kitchen. "No sightings of 'em, either."

"I guess a couple drifted through," Kate said, and left.

It was a ten second walk to the police station, but by the time she pushed the doors open and smelt that stale air, her heart rate was falling back to normal. She liked Lissiter, but sometimes he disrupted her flow. Kid liked to dig.

Kate nodded at the part-time receptionist, a cute young thing doing community college in a nearby town. She was the most enthusiastic person in the one-story building. The rest of the place was filled with people like Kate: bored, and wanting to stay that way. She passed seven desks, all of them doubles for deeply uninspired men. Most of them weren't in yet. The ones that were had their feet up or a crossword out on the desk.

Kate headed over to the coffee station to fill her cup with a much more subpar coffee. She sipped at it, taking a more thorough lap of the room. Two of the officers were looking at something related to Leroy Child.

On the other side of the police station, a mutter. *Simmons.*

Kate rolled her tongue in her mouth. Took another gulp of coffee. Her head was starting to pound again.

"Alright," she said loudly. "Everybody look my way."

Their lone office chair swiveled. It was Officer Brennan's turn today. Everyone else turned around.

"How are we doing on the Leroy Child case?" Kate asked.

Silence. Officer Brennan, still swiveling side to side, cleared his throat. "Thought that got marked as wild dogs, Chief."

"It did, and it is," said Kate. "But I hear those whispers. It's all around town, people thinking one of our own did it. So, now's the time to air them out. Any leads?"

"Uh," said Officer Brennan, swiveling to a stop. "Nothing solid, Chief. Leroy was a leech, sure, but people's beef with him wasn't personal. He didn't get into fights or nothing. If it *wasn't* dogs, my best bet's that Creel kid. Little shit set fire to my tires last month after I busted him trying to burn another of those abandoned houses."

"Hunter?" Kate scratched at her scalp. "Doesn't sound like his MO. If the guy burned to death, maybe. Anyone else?"

A murmur of no's. The oldest cop, sixty-eight-year-old

Noah Dunwich, spoke up. "We should look at that undead kid," he croaked. "What'ssisname? Baby?"

Kate folded her arms tight across her chest. "Babe," she said. "Henry Simmons."

Dunwich nodded. His whole body shook. Kate didn't know if it was from age or drink. Could be a bad mix of both.

"That'ssim," Dunwich said. "Strange one."

Babe Simmons was an oddity in Bulldeen: a teenage boy who was unfailingly polite without getting swatted around the ears first. Babe didn't care about cars, girls, or their high school football team, the Bulldeen Bulls. In fact, all those kids were strange—Anna was too smart, too high and mighty, though no one dared bring it up around Chief Higgins. Jules was new, so even if she wasn't from the city, she'd stick out like a sore thumb. The ridiculous fashion and the prissy way she held herself, *especially* since she was fat, not to mention the *purple hair*—just made things worse. And Dude was always too laid back, hard to read. Made too many jokes but you could never tell when he was joking.

Besides Anna, Dude was the one Chief Higgins had talked to the most. Always walking on people's roofs to test his balance, going out into the fields to test some dumb prop he ordered from a magazine—or worse, ones he made himself. Kate saw him as harmless to everybody but himself. There had been a brief period where she thought she'd have to keep an eye on him—the night he turned fourteen, he'd had his very first drink at Jules's house. He'd ditched his friends and gone on a roaring bender, culminating in the destruction of the neon *Stars and Stripes* sign, a broken ulna, and six panicked calls to the cops about a kid climbing onto their roof and singing "Sweet Caroline."

It took Lissiter forty-five minutes to talk him down from

Old Suzy's roof. Then when he finally got down, he punched Lissiter in the face. Kate was there the following morning as Dude groaned himself awake in his cell. He hissed and clutched his arm. This was before they realized he'd broken it. He didn't tell them right away.

Kate asked if he'd had a nice time and he groggily said yes. Kate asked if he was planning on doing it again, the thing she asked all dumb teenagers they dragged in for a drunk and disorderly. Dude had looked up at her, hazy with hangover and pain, and said, "No, I don't think I will."

She hadn't banked much on it. But Dude had kept his word. You never heard about him stealing wine from the supermarket or loitering around Bull's Bottles trying to persuade adults to go buy him a fifth. On the rare occasion Kate broke up a party and Dude was there, he'd be holding a cup of water, sober as a judge. Kate couldn't understand it. He had a drunk for a mother, but Katherine Marsh was a quiet, sensible drunk who kept her head down and didn't bother anyone (other than the occasional DUI that got swept under the rug), so Kate couldn't see how that'd deter him. It was a Bulldeen miracle—finding something fantastic, something you knew would ruin your life, and then not doing that thing. Self-destruction was a town-wide hobby. What else was there to do?

"Again," Kate announced to the room of bored officers, "the official ruling was wild dogs. That's what we're telling people when they ask. But to keep you folks calm, I'll check Babe out. No one else goes near him, alright? Kid's been through a lot. He doesn't need cops piling on him."

A muted chorus of acknowledgment. Everybody turned back to their desks, to their coffee and papers and stolen bicycle cases.

Kate retreated to her office. She sat with the curtains drawn for a while, dust floating in the tiny room, settling on her hair, in her lungs. Then she got up and headed for the room where they kept their case files, which sometimes doubled as a laundry room in weeks and months when officers were kicked out of their house.

chapter
eight

KJ LEANED back in Dude's lap. "You know, I get the feeling you're not really into this."

A screw dug into Dude's hip. They were curled in the bowels of the Bulldeen High basement, hidden behind a colony of water pipes.

Structurally, this high school was a copy of the old one. Except for the boiler room. This school had no boiler room, just a concrete basement with cupboards of cleaning supplies, and pipes running along the walls and floor.

Dude and KJ didn't know or care that they sat inside a replica of a room that once exploded, killing over twenty people. Those people had died generations ago, and both boys shared the common and incorrect belief that history was something that happened in another building, instead of a long hallway they were trapped inside.

"You're the one who wanted to hook up a couple days after my best friend died," Dude said. "Even if he's alive now, it's kind of weird."

"Uh-huh," KJ said. His voice was light as it always was. "You looked determined. At the funeral."

"You went to the funeral?"

"Everybody went to the funeral." KJ put his hand on the ground to steady himself and grimaced, wiped basement gunk on Dude's best jeans.

"Hey." Dude thought about making a spunk joke, but he couldn't be bothered. He felt very disconnected from all of it—his body, KJ's body. Usually KJ's weight against him was hot. A turn on. Now it was just a weight. KJ scratched a single nail into the concrete.

"So," KJ said. "Was Babe in a casket-coma or was it a prank?"

"Coma. It happened in Victorian times."

"Huh," KJ said. "I was betting on a prank." He picked gunk out from under his nail. Wiped it on Dude's jeans, right next to the first grease spot. "I thought the stories were bull," he said. "Like, the girl who dropped out a few years back? And Anna's great-granddad—"

Dude dragged him forwards by his button-down. KJ made a muffled noise against his mouth.

Dude tried to fall into it: warm, soft lips. Hint of stubble. Broad shoulders under his hands, the slight bulge of muscle. KJ lifted weights too. They talked about it when they ran out of stuff to say, which was often.

KJ broke away with a sigh. "You *are* acting weird. In public, even."

"No one noticed," Dude promised. "And if they did, they won't link it to you."

"Good," KJ said. He leaned in, sliding his hands up Dude's skinny legs. "Hey, do you have my twenty bucks yet? I'm still waiting."

Dude was in the middle of saying *not yet* when KJ reached Dude's pocket and frowned, pulling out a lighter. It was small and silver and very familiar. Everybody in Bulldeen was wary of this lighter.

"What the hell?" KJ said, turning it to see the engraving. "Yup, there's the initials. You stole Hunter's lighter? His *dad* gave him that. He's gonna strangle you. Then he's gonna take the lighter back and set you on fire."

Dude reached up and flicked it on. Nothing happened. Hunter never let his lighter go empty.

It took several seconds of flicking for this to sink in with KJ. "Oh," he said in relief. "It's fake?"

"Ayuh."

"Why'd you make a prop of Hunter's lighter?"

Dude took it out of KJ's hand. "He's threatened to use it on me enough times." He flicked it some more. "I figured, why not have a safety net?"

KJ laughed. He had a short, stuttery laugh. Sometimes it was annoying. "What are you gonna do, swap it on him when he's got you backed against a wall?"

"Worth a shot." Dude put the lighter away and gripped KJ's thighs. "Let me show you my pickpocketing skills."

Another stuttery laugh. This one grated on Dude's nerves.

"You should come over after school."

Dude's hands paused at the back of KJ's knees. KJ hadn't suggested that before. *Too risky,* he'd always said since they'd started this arrangement last year.

"We're busy," Dude said. Everyone in town knew who *we* was when it came to Dude Marsh.

KJ rolled his eyes. "Right. Your mystery spot. Have fun."

Sometimes being with KJ made Dude lonely, more so than when he was on his own. KJ was a good guy, but they didn't click in any way beyond the physical. There were times when Dude would be exploring KJ's mouth with his tongue and find himself thinking that he'd rather be studying with Anna, listening to music with Jules, doing absolutely anything with Babe. Given the choice between riches, sex, success, and hanging with Babe, Dude would always pick Babe.

Juniper Lookout wasn't hard to find, and yet no living person in town knew where it was except Dude, Babe, Jules and Anna. Anna had found it first, walking around after elementary school. She'd been exploring the edge of the suburbs when she'd stumbled on a dirt path hidden behind a cluster of wild thornfruit. She'd followed it up to a hill. Just before the hill dropped off into nothing, there were two towering juniper trees, the only ones in Bulldeen.

You could see the whole town from Juniper Lookout. The sewer district was right down below, tapering out closer to Main Street. Then Bull's Head, the school tucked in beside it, and further on was the thornfruit warehouse. Then the fields, bigger than the whole town and stretching into infinity.

I felt very strange, she'd told Babe once, while they stood on the hill looking out over the town. *Standing there, that first time, when I was seven. I still get hints of that now.*

Strange how?

I don't know. Like...time unfolds on itself.

She hadn't said any more about it. She'd been embarrassed that she'd said that much.

She sat now on the hood of Dude's truck, staring out into town. Jules sprawled next to her, arm linked through Anna's, short heels bumping into the lights, head bopping in time with the music thumping through her headphones.

Dude lay above them on the roof, pressing at the scabbing cut on his hand through the bandage, and squinting up at the darkening sky. Babe was cross-legged next to him. He kept glancing out at Bulldeen, which was slowly turning its lights on. He kept looking up, then back down to his hands, like he didn't want to take it all in at once.

They came up to Juniper Lookout a lot. There wasn't much to do in Bulldeen. Sitting on a hill was right up there with throwing rocks at passing cars in the town square. Hill-sitting got you yelled at a lot less.

Jules paused her CD player. "You know the first thing I'm doing when I get back to LA?"

"What?" Dude said. So far, Jules had twenty things she'd do first in LA.

"Buy a cell phone."

Anna laughed. "Oh, to live in a place with cell service!"

Dude glanced over at Babe, trying to sense bitterness. It had been gutting, watching Babe go week after week without an acceptance letter. Not just to an LA college, but any college. It didn't make sense—Babe's grades weren't great, but they were better than Jules's, and her acceptance letter had arrived right on time. But the May 1 acceptance deadline had come and gone. Nothing was coming for Babe, who had his head tipped up at the sky.

One good thing about Bulldeen: there was no light pollution. Stars littered the sky every night. A few were already sprouting by sundown. Dude tried to remember the constellations his mom had taught him.

"Have you talked to your cousin yet?" Babe asked Jules.

"Yeah! He actually called the day—" Jules stammered to a stop. "Uh, Gabriel called last week. Left a voicemail saying that he'd be happy to have us stay in his living room for a few weeks while we find a place, as long as we don't mind sleeping on the floor."

"That's awesome," Babe said, his smile only a little strained.

Anna craned her head up at him. "You can still come, Babe."

"You should," Jules said fiercely. She pulled her head-phones down so they dangled around her neck. It was a frequent necklace. "After what just happened? Your dad will understand."

Babe's long throat worked. Dude watched it bob until Babe glanced over, at which point Dude pretended to be examining the sky behind his head. Another star winked into the night.

"I already asked," Babe said after a moment. "Well, I didn't ask, I just floated the idea, and he started going on about *why would you want to do that? You love Bulldeen. Where could you even get a job in LA—*"

"Where can you get a job *here*?" Jules interrupted. For a few years she'd had a job at the local movie theater, Bull Flicks. Thanks to some truly dubious stock market decisions by the owner, the theater had closed down six months ago. The only place you could trust to stay open was the thornfruit ware-house, and that was only as long as the toxins lasted.

Babe sighed. "I always have a place at the—"

"*Thornfruit warehouse,*" the others chorused. "*Nothing's sharper than thornfruit!*"

"Egg—xactly."

Dude held back a laugh. He loved the drawn-out drawl of the word coming out of Babe's mouth. He loved Babe's voice, period. He could listen to Babe talk for hours, and often had.

The sunset washed over the four of them. Dude felt surprisingly good for about ten seconds. Then he remembered why it was surprising: he had to almost-kill people and feed them to a monster. His smile fell away, his chest tightening.

Beside him, Babe did his high-pitched kitten yawn. Dude's smile crept reluctantly back.

chapter
nine

DUDE DROPPED Babe and Anna off first, then drove back to the sewer district and pulled in to his own driveway. Jules's house was a thirty second walk away, one of the five occupied lots on the block. The others were either torn down or marked with peeling CONTAMINATED stickers.

Before Dude could straighten out the car, Jules put a hand on his arm. "I changed my mind."

Dude paused, mid-turn.

"Let's go into town," Jules said.

Dude met her eyes. Ever since she'd arrived from LA, she'd always seemed larger than life. Too big for this town, with her dangly earrings and colorful eye makeup; with her clothing that townfolk swore would be "too much" even if she was thin; those bright blue eyes that always met him head on. It had been a relief, meeting her.

"You got it," he said, and put the truck into reverse.

They did this a couple times a month—park somewhere in town and go walking through the night. Last time was four days ago, before Babe's funeral. They'd walked in circles around the town square, not talking until Dude said, *I gave him the chocolate bar.*

You didn't know, Jules had said.

The packet said it might contain traces of peanuts.

A lot of them say that, Jules told him. *Dude, don't tell me you feel guilty.*

Alright, he'd said. *I won't.*

This time, they pulled into the McDonald's parking lot. It had been a new and exciting addition in the '90s, stuck behind the town hall.

Jules took the lead. Dude followed. Across the street from the town hall was a brown patch of grass with a metal mount and a plaque. The plaque read: ON AUGUST 3RD, 1965, THE OLD HALL CAUGHT FIRE. IT BURNED DOWN IN LESS THAN AN HOUR. EIGHT PEOPLE LOST THEIR LIVES. WE LIST THEM HERE:

And then a list of names. One of them was the grandfather of the local dentist. Then there were Hunter's great-grandparents on the Creel side. The Creels had been notorious ever since they arrived in Bulldeen.

Jules touched the date on the plaque. "Catch me up on Bulldeen lore. What was that story your grandma told? A woman rose from the grave. The night her and her husband left town forever was the night the town hall burned to the ground with eight people inside. Is that it?"

Dude nodded. He looked down the street towards the sewer district they'd just come from. A few closed-down shops away was The Horn and the gun store. You could count on those to stay open. But there were fewer shops every day, especially here at the edge of the town square. The patch of grass always seemed like a warning. A reminder of what was to come. One day, all of Bulldeen would be nothing but weeds.

"They were Anna's great-grandparents," Dude told Jules.

"What?"

"Yeah. Still might be. Maybe they're alive."

"You don't know?"

"I don't think Anna even knows."

Jules dug her boot into a crack in the sidewalk. There was a tree a few feet away, and roots were cracking the cement in swirling lines.

"I heard the bodies were strange," she said. "Did you hear that?"

"I guess."

"Strange like what?"

For the first time in his life, Dude was glad to see Hunter Creel. Buzz peeled by in his Pontiac Firebird, pulling close enough to the curb that Dude and Jules jerked backward towards the plaque. Hunter hung out the passenger seat window, yelling. His cackle echoed through the dark, accompanied by Moe's reedy laugh from the backseat.

"Hey, dead freaks!"

They screeched around a corner. Their laughter faded into the night.

Jules rounded on Dude. "You said there were no consequences for bringing Babe back."

"So?"

"So I don't buy it! All you had to do is cut your hand and chant? Please." She made a frustrated noise, kicked again at the root breaking out of the concrete at their feet. "A lot of people died when Anna's grandma came back. And the second... Milly's mom died, right?"

"Milly Hart is a rumor. All we know for sure is that her mom killed herself."

Jules rolled her eyes. "Okay. I'm new here, and even I know

that's bullshit. You've been so sketchy since Babe came back, it makes me think something's coming."

"Jules—"

"I can help," she insisted. When Dude opened his mouth, she talked over him. "Two heads are better than one! You want me to burn down the town hall with people inside? I'm in. Depending on the people."

Dude stared. Her broad jaw was set, determined. No backing down. *She doesn't have enough shame,* the townsfolk whispered. Dude loved that about her.

"Seriously? Just like that?"

She shrugged. "It's Babe. I'd do it for any of you."

Dude checked. No one was out this late. He lowered his voice anyway. "If you *did* have to kill people—like, more than five but less than ten, I don't actually know how many—who would you pick?"

Jules's answer came instantly. "The town Nazis."

Despite everything, Dude snorted. "You read my mind."

"Yeah? Who's first, then?"

Dude cleared his throat, shifting closer. "Buzz Kettering. He's still got two weeks left to make good on his school shooting jokes, and I don't wanna see how serious he is about it."

Jules let out a laugh that lost enthusiasm the longer it went on. It went on for a long time. "Yeah," she said after it finally died off. "So, what're you thinking? Do we buy a gun?" She had her whole body turned to him, her head tilted and waiting. Her eyeshadow glittered in the streetlight overhead, and Dude watched her fair face sparkle.

"You're really in this."

"If we gotta, then we gotta! We better be fast. We're out of here in a few weeks. Speedrun kill."

Dude nodded. He drummed his foot on the gutter

against the root that was forcing up into the street. He wasn't as fond of plants as he was of animals, but if he saw a tree being strangled by ivy, he'd cut it free. If he saw a plant that needed watering, he'd go get a water bottle. His mom said he got too attached to living things, but that wasn't true. Dude could develop a deep kinship with a rock. He just liked being kind. He had a lot of love in him and he wanted to put it somewhere, whether a dog or a tree or a friend. He didn't hate anybody. But he was fast growing used to the idea that he'd have to kill some people for Babe. When he cut the ivy away, he would throw it in the trash. If a dog was attacking his friend, he'd kick it away. Sometimes helping a friend meant hurting a dog. Sometimes it meant putting down a classmate.

"We have to...feed him to something."

Jules's eyes widened, blue irises framed by neon eyeshadow. "Babe?"

"No, no. Something else."

"Else," Jules repeated. She made a face, glanced over her shoulder as if to find the thing waiting there. "Dude, I gotta say —I hate this place."

"Yeah," Dude said. "Me too."

It was mostly true. He did hate it. But he loved it too. Bulldeen had raised him. He'd been beaten, sure. He'd been ridiculed and looked down on and told—not explicitly, but in every other way imaginable—that if he was open about liking boys, this place would go from dangerous to deadly. But he'd found all his best friends here. He'd climbed trees and dangled his feet off Juniper Lookout. Every good experience of his had happened here. So he loved Bulldeen a little, and sometimes he wished he could hate it like Babe and Anna did, a stifling hatred they both tried not to think about. Or Jules, who had arrived here five years ago and hated it with shiny newcomer eyes. Jules had an easy, city-born hatred. Bulldeen was a pit stop until her LA life could resume again.

But Dude looked up at the McDonald's sign glowing behind the town hall and all he could think of was—*beautiful*. It wasn't his fault. Dude found everywhere beautiful.

He pointed. His truck was there, and it was also the only place other than a bar that was open past six.

"Want to get food?"

"Yes," said Jules. "Yes, I do."

They set off towards it, night owls hungry for someplace to go in the dark.

chapter
ten

ANNA KNEW her Aunt Kate would usually eat a microwaved dinner in front of the TV, a glass of whiskey balanced on the arm of the couch. But it was the first Tuesday of the month, and that meant dinner with her brother's family.

Cats hissed from the back of the house all through the evening. Anna's dad kept getting up to check on them.

"They've been making a racket for days," said Anna's mom, spooning more peas onto her own plate and melting butter over them. "No reason for it. Just being dramatic."

Anna's dad sat down at the head of the table. Kate tried to meet his eyes, but he kept his gaze on his plate. They never talked about their grandparents—a tradition that had carried over ever since Kate was seven and her brother was nine, and their parents came home and told them that they wouldn't be seeing their grandmother again. But then they did. A few weeks later, they were told they wouldn't be seeing either of their grandparents again, and they shouldn't bring them up.

Anna's dad cut his potatoes into tiny, steadfast pieces until Kate looked away. Old habits.

On the other side of the table, Anna followed her dad's suit. She often did. Her dad was a good man, dependable and generous and kind. Anna strived to be all those things. He wasn't great at knowing when to put his foot down. Anna wasn't great at it either.

She allowed herself to glance at Kate. Aunt Cop, she called Kate when she was around her friends. She'd never say it to her face. Aunt Cop was being even quieter than usual tonight, and had barely touched her wine. The last time either of those things happened, she'd been recovering from a broken ankle. Kate kept looking at the door into the clinic, where the occasional yowl would seep through.

Anna could see Kate didn't believe her parents' story. That was fair. Anna wasn't sure *they* believed their own story, judging from how freaked out they'd been about Babe, all those worried looks they'd snuck at each other when they thought the kids weren't looking. The only one in the dining room who did believe that the cats were throwing hissy fits for no reason was Alicia, Anna's seven-year-old sister.

Alicia frowned down at her plate. She had bigger things to worry about than noisy cats. She clamped her teddy bear under one arm, struggling to break open a thornfruit. Today's project was refusing to eat anything savory. By dinner, her parents had given up and piled her plate with fruit. *Like it's the old times,* they'd told her. *They lived on thornfruit for years before the town made a profit.*

"Are you sure I can't help you with that?" Anna asked.

"Naw," Alicia said instantly. "I can do it."

A thorn stabbed under her nail. She shrieked, throwing the fruit down onto the table, and pulled her teddy bear up to her face. Her words were muffled with felt fur. "It cut me! Why do we always have to eat this stinky fruit?"

Anna's dad started, "You *wanted*—"

"Don't be ungrateful," Anna's mom said in unison. "It's the—"

"The fruit that saved the town," echoed Alicia, Anna, and, surprisingly, Kate. When Anna looked over, Kate met her gaze. She and Kate had similar-shaped eyes. It was one of the only things Anna inherited from her dad's side of the family, who were pale and dirty-blonde next to Anna's and her mother's rich dark hair and skin. Townsfolk had called the Higgins' side *unhealthy-looking*. Going off how smooth and shining Anna's dad's skin got after marrying, while Kate's only got greasier and more sullen, Anna bet it was a lifestyle thing.

"So," Kate said. "How's your friend doing?"

Anna thought about asking *which one?* "Babe's good. Thank you."

"Not too wild over what happened?"

Her parents traded a capital-L Look. Anna ignored them, chewing fast. Her words came out high and muffled: "What-doyoumean?"

Kate speared a single pea on her fork. Pincered it off with her teeth. "I mean," she said, "I might be a little shaken if I'd had an allergic reaction, been assumed dead, *buried*, and then had to climb my way up outta my own grave."

"*Kate*," Anna's dad hissed.

Behind the table, a cat screamed.

Alicia's eyes went wide. "Is *that* what happened?"

Anna's dad sighed. "Alicia."

"That's so cool," Alicia said. The thornfruit finally split in two in her tiny hands, flesh clinging between the halves. She put a piece up to her teddy bear's stitched mouth. "Wish I could do that. Anna, you wanna bury me later?"

"No," her parents chorused.

Anna squeezed Alicia's sticky hand. "Only if the grave is very shallow."

She cut another boiled potato in half, then looked at Kate

long enough that Kate raised her untidy eyebrows as she reached for her wine glass.

After dinner, Anna washed the dishes. It was a rush job, but she couldn't talk to Aunt Cop in the kitchen. Too many ears. She stacked the dishes in the drying tray and went out to the front porch.

Kate stood in the shadows, away from the glow of the kitchen window. She was leaning against the house smoking, picking at an old chickenpox scar.

She gestured at Anna with the cigarette. "Want one?"

"Love one," Anna said. She held out two thin fingers. Kate slotted nothing into Anna's hand.

Anna held her hand up to her face, mouth tensed in a circle, and breathed in air. This was their only inside joke. Anna was a devout nonsmoker.

She tapped her toes inside her shoe. This and pacing were her only nervous tics, and she hated to pace. It was too obvious. The toe-tapping was out of sight. If she was barefoot, she found a pocket to drum her fingers in. If she had no shoes or pockets, she tapped her tongue on her teeth.

Tell me what happened to Great-grandma and Granddad. It caught behind her lips. She'd dared to ask once when she was very small. She must have been small, because Kate had her on her lap. After she asked, Kate had put her down on the ground and walked off without a word.

Anna found out, of course. Bulldeen was a quiet town, but when it came to gossip, it was a whirlwind. The dressmaker's daughter went home with the baker's boy on Friday night and everyone knew by Saturday morning. She couldn't remember when she'd first heard the whispers, first got asked questions.

When she did get asked, she could honestly say she didn't know any more than they did.

Kate took another drag. "Did you guys do something to bring him back?"

Anna's heart skipped a beat. "What do you mean?"

Kate gave her a dry look. Almost disdainful. She breathed in and her mouth filled with smoke. "Anna," she said. "Don't bullshit me."

"I didn't do anything."

"What about Dude? Jules?"

Anna squirmed. "I don't know." She turned away, but the damage had already been done. Kate wasn't good at her job, but not because she was stupid. She just never put the effort in.

"Dude did it," Kate said, sounding certain. "Brought him back."

Anna tapped her toes so hard inside her shoes they started to ache. "People woke up in graves in Victorian times."

"I know," Kate said. "He borrowed that book from you. Remember where you got it?"

Anna had to think about it. Her ninth birthday, right? Who had given it—Oh. Right.

Kate tapped ash off her cigarette. It floated into the dark. "Grandma and Granddad are gonna visit soon," she said.

Anna blinked. Her grandparents were dead on both sides. Which meant that Kate was talking about her own grandparents, Anna's greats, whom she had never met and knew nothing about, except for the town gossip about resurrection.

A wave of impossibility washed over her. "It will be good to finally meet them," she said weakly.

Kate gave her another look. This one crossed into amused. "Don't mention it to your folks," she said, and stubbed out her cigarette on the wall of the house. It left a burn mark in the fading paint. She turned to head back to the light of the kitchen.

Anna took a bracing breath, tugging at a tight curl of hair which immediately bounced back into place beside her ear. "So it's true? What people say about her?"

Kate paused at the door. She didn't turn around. "I used to think it was just superstition. Bored townsfolk making stories."

"And then?"

"Then when I was about ten years older than you..." Kate rubbed at her mouth. She cleared her throat. Coughed. The cigarettes had been taking their toll for a while now.

Anna thrilled with it. She could only be talking about Milly Hart.

"See you around," Kate said, and walked not into the kitchen, but down the porch steps and into the night.

Anna poked her head into the living room and said something about homework, speeding up the stairs before her parents finished nodding.

Milly Hart had dropped out in her sophomore year, back when Anna was a freshman. She had no friends and sat in the toilets at lunch poring over the library's sparse Latin section. Everybody said she was into witchcraft. Anna had asked her about it once. Milly had startled. After Anna had specified yes, she was talking to her, Milly had admitted that all the Latin was for naming things in Dungeons & Dragons. She'd been explaining what a Dungeon Master was when someone knocked into her, sending her sprawling.

"It's fine," Milly had mumbled when Anna helped her up. She'd tried to say more, but her voice had gone strange and gaspy and then vanished entirely. She'd ducked her head and hurried down the hall. It was the only time Anna ever talked to her.

People who were brave or terrible asked her about her mother sacrificing herself to bring Milly back from the dead.

That didn't happen, Milly would say quietly. That was all she ever said about it.

Anna thought about calling Dude. *Hey, just checking in. Planning on killing anyone to even out bringing your best friend back from the dead?*

She almost didn't want to know. Because what would she do then? She wouldn't turn him in. She didn't want to think about what she'd do if she found out something like that was happening.

Thunder on the stairs. Her mother yelled, "Anna, Jules is —" and then Jules burst in the room, chucking her backpack in the corner and flinging herself down on Anna's bed in a super-model pose. "Hiiii!"

Anna swiveled her office chair around. "Hey. You know how adults are scared of Babe?"

Jules's pose wilted, manicured hand slipping off the pronounced curve of her hip. "Not all of them."

"Enough of them. Why would they be? In the stories I heard, it was the ones who did the resurrecting who were the dangerous ones. Great-granddad burned down the hall. Milly's mother killed herself. Also, why did it take eight people for Great-granddad, but only one for the mother?"

Jules shrugged. She had her thinking face on, her severe nose scrunching. "Maybe the mom killed more than just herself."

"If that's true, they covered it up."

"Yeah."

Anna sighed, getting up. Jules moved over on the bed and Anna climbed on, top-to-tail. Jules's feet wiggled in Anna's face. Her toes were painted bright lilac.

Anna batted them away. "Aunt Cop won't tell me

anything. But she does take case files home with her when she's working on them."

"You think she's dug these files up?"

Anna thought about Aunt Kate's probing gaze, the way she'd kept looking at her dad all through dinner like she was waiting for him to say something about Babe, about the grandparents.

"I think so," she said. She nosed at the downy hair on Jules's ankle. "So who are we keeping an eye on now? Dude or Babe?"

"Um," Jules said, strangely flat. "Babe?"

"I don't wanna wake up and hear Dude's burned down the gym with a bunch of people inside."

"Not a bunch," Jules said. "And if he *had* to do it, I bet he'd pick some real assholes. Y'know. If he *had* to."

Anna thought about asking. Jules was an okay liar, as long as she had a decent alibi. If she didn't, she'd stick with it until the lie became so obvious, it was barely any use to keep it going. No ability to make up stuff on the fly. Dude had the opposite problem—he could lie looking you straight in the eye and seem calm enough, but if he had to come up with something, it would be outrageous. Any questioning would make it more outrageous, because when given the choice between safe and funny, Dude went with the latter. Babe was the best liar in their group—real calm, not fake-calm-with-sweaty-armpits like Dude, plus the ability to make stuff up on the fly without bringing up UFOs or a fox running in and stealing something. Growing up with his dad had meant he'd had no choice but to become a good liar. His dad had a very skewed vision of his son, and he accepted nothing else.

Anna was an okay liar. She didn't like to do it much.

She pulled at Jules's leg hair. Her knee twitched.

"Want to do our chemistry homework?"

A beat. "What's the point? They won't fail us *now*."

"Still," Anna said.

Jules sighed noisily, then sat up to grab her backpack. Hand halfway around the strap, she bolted up. "Crap! I told my cousin I'd call him at seven!"

"Just tell him you forgot," Anna said, pushing away a prickle of annoyance. Jules had been on the phone with her cousin a *lot* lately.

Jules shook her head. "Gabriel was gonna ask out this girl, and I think he's going to bomb it. I *have* to hear the gory details. Sorry for loving and leaving you."

Anna tried to divine whether Jules was avoiding something, but there was nothing suspicious in her face. She *did* have a bad memory. Anna was just used to Jules blowing off school, jobs, and family, to hang out with her.

"You're not going to ditch us when we get to LA, right?" Anna laughed, but genuine worry crept into her voice before she could swallow it.

Jules glanced back at her, plucked eyebrows drawing together.

"You're my family," she said simply, and flicked a two-fingered salute. "Peace."

"Peace," Anna echoed. The door closed. Anna lay down, trying to tell herself the pit of worry in her stomach would be as intense if Jules was in the room, but at the end of the day, the matter still stood: Anna was an okay liar. Nothing more.

chapter
eleven

THE PHONE RANG. Babe put down a dish so hard it almost bounced off the sink, not bothering to check it as he raced for the hallway. His dad emerged from the living room.

"I got it, Dad. Thanks," Babe said, grabbing it from the cradle.

Ryan gave a *fair enough* sigh and turned back. When he got to the phone first, he liked to tell his son's friends that Henry was busy, and to call back later. Then he'd try to be the one to pick up when 'later' rolled around to tell them the same thing.

"Hello," Babe said.

Dude cheered. "Racing down the hall, he shoots, he scores! Babe gets the phone before Ryan! The crowd goes wild!" More cheering.

Babe bit his cheek to stop the grin, then let it loose.

"Guess who has the new *Friday the 13th*," Dude said.

"No way. It's out?"

"One night only, then it's back to the shop. Come over. I got that gross sweet popcorn you like so much. The new brand. I checked the ingredients. You're safe."

Babe laughed to cover the pleasant squirming in his stomach.

"Henry!" his dad called from the living room.

The squirming dropped. A rumble started. He'd eaten dinner, but it didn't reach deep enough.

"Come in here! You'll want to know about the different kinds of thornfruit packaging they'll have at the warehouse!"

Dude made a sound that was a lot like the word *awkward*. "Does he think you're still taking that job?"

Babe picked at his nails.

"*Are* you still taking that job?"

Babe pushed the receiver into the crook of his neck. "In a minute, Dad!"

"Seriously," Dude continued. "After last week? You're still obeying your dad 'cause you're too afraid he'll cry if you say no to one tiny thing?"

"It's not one tiny thing. It's *leaving*," Babe said quietly, lips barely moving. "Besides, it's good to save money."

"Before you come out to LA with us."

Babe picked at a chip in the phone cradle paint until the chip looked like a beetle.

"Before you go *anywhere* and do *anything*."

"It's not that simple," Babe tried. "I—"

Ryan emerged again from the living room, holding a notebook and looking expectant.

"I gotta go," Babe said. "Talk to you later."

"Babe—"

"Sorry." Babe hung up.

"Who was that?"

"Anna," Babe said. Ryan liked Anna the most out of Babe's friends. *Got a real head on her shoulders,* he liked to say. *And she's good to that family of hers. Always working at the vet, helping out. Loyal. That's what family should be.*

Ryan smiled. Handed Babe the notebook. "You'll want to take notes," he said, and headed back into the living room.

Babe followed, forever glad that they didn't own two land-lines. Otherwise he'd never have a private phone conversation again.

His stomach continued to rumble as he followed his dad into the living room. It wasn't an audible rumble. It sent vibrations through his bones, rattling through his teeth. He'd had two servings at dinner and it hadn't helped.

"Go get a pen," his dad said.

Babe went to the desk in the corner. Officially, his dad used it for filling out factory paperwork. Unofficially, it was where the Simmons family kept assorted useful objects.

Babe opened the first drawer, rummaged through the paper. Batteries, stamps, Babe's birth certificate, nail clippers. No pens. He reached for the second one—

"Don't open that!"

Babe's hand froze on the handle. He looked back at his dad, who was surprisingly panicked, rearranging his face into something more normal.

"Don't go through the second one anymore," Ryan told him. "I have private things in there."

Babe didn't want to know.

The third drawer was flush with pens. Babe took one and sat on the couch, broadcasting attentiveness.

"So," Ryan started, face bright and excited. His mustache quivered. "We have three kinds of packaging at the warehouse. You'll have seen the banana boxes around town, and we'll get to those. But right now, I wanna tell you about the mass orders. Those go in these waist-high plastic containers and get loaded into—are you writing this down?"

Babe scribbled. He held the pad up so his dad couldn't see he was writing *freckle eyelash neck blah night night cushion.*

Ryan kept explaining about the plastic containers. Apparently, there was a specific way of closing them, and doing it wrong could mean they spilled out during transportation. Transportation, of course, to other factories owned by the American company but stationed overseas, so they could make skin cream for cheap. Thornfruit wasn't sought after in recipes, but it was great for wrinkles. In Bulldeen, people cut them in half and put them on their eyelids.

Dude, Babe wrote on his notepad as Ryan explained which brands stocked skin cream made from thornfruit. *Movie Dude popcorn Eugene. E-U-G-E-N-E.*

His stomach growled.

Hungry, he wrote. The pen started to bleed and he lifted it up off the paper before it could spread.

"Wait a sec, Dad—pen bleed."

"Aw, darn," Ryan said, forehead wrinkling. "I'll have to explain again so you can redo those notes."

Babe ripped the note off, crumpled it up carefully so his dad wouldn't take it as an insult. "Dad, won't they give me training at the warehouse?"

"Of course! But you're getting a head start." Ryan placed his chin in his hand. "I'm so proud of you for continuing the family tradition. I did it, my dad did it, his dad...and one day your child can do this."

Babe laughed, loud and uneasy. "If I have kids!"

"Of course you'll have kids," Ryan said lightly, as if it was the height of stupidity to suggest otherwise. "You'll find a nice girl and settle down, don't you worry. Hey, see how I said *child* and not *son* back there? I don't care what you have, as long as they're happy and healthy."

He chuckled to himself. Babe joined in, a yell stuck behind his teeth.

"Now," Ryan said, clasping his hands together. "The *third* kind of packaging—"

"I'm gonna take the trash out," Babe blurted.

He dragged the trash bag out onto the curb, muttering all the way.

"Third kind of packaging," he said under his breath. "Come on, Dad, who *cares*?"

He heaved the bag in front of the trash bin, started to tie a knot in the top. Nobody was out at night, not alone, not since the homeless man had been killed. The neighborhood looked deserted. Out of the ten houses in the neighborhood, eight were occupied. This was good going for Bulldeen.

Babe struggled with the knot. It slipped through his fingers and he cursed quietly.

The bag fell open, exposing empty bags of frozen vegetables and potato skins and old meat. Earlier that week, Ryan had left a carton of chicken out to thaw on the counter and forgotten about it wedged behind the blender. By the time they found it again, it had spoiled.

Babe leaned down, sniffing. Gross. This raw meat was gross and nothing else.

"Gross," he said aloud, as if to convince someone who wasn't there.

And suddenly someone was.

"Nice night for it."

Babe spun around, startled. A man stood behind him, hands in his overcoat pockets. For a second, Babe thought his dad had followed him out. Then a second passed and he realized the angles were all wrong—his dad wasn't this tall, his dad didn't have sharp cheekbones or that jaw or those strange keen eyes, his dad would never wear a coat that went past his knees. He said those coats were for snooty people.

"Nice night for the trash?" Babe said, then he winced. He

couldn't make fun of some stranger. "Sorry. Yes, it's a nice night."

The man smiled. He had too many teeth.

Something itched at the back of his head. *Wrong wrong wrong.* Babe batted it away.

"You're the Zombabe," the man said, and his voice made Babe shudder. "Correct?"

"Yes, that's me. Sorry, but who are you?"

"I haven't been here in a while. But I know all the streets." The man's smile widened. "What's it been like?"

"What?"

"Being the Zombabe."

The itch at the back of Babe's head intensified. He could taste dirt in his mouth. When he'd gotten in the shower the night he'd come back, he'd rinsed his mouth out until his spit was all water. He'd scrubbed under his nails until they bled.

"I didn't actually die," Babe told this strange, familiar man, who seemed taller than he did when he first spoke up.

The man nodded. Looked out over the deserted neighborhood. Babe wished somebody else was putting out their trash too. Everybody was nosy in Bulldeen, but he'd take nosy Mrs. Smith over being alone with this guy.

Babe cleared his throat. "Well, I gotta get inside. My dad's telling me about my new job."

"Oh? What's that?"

Don't tell him, Babe's mind screamed. The back of his head tugged. He ran a hand through his neat blonde hair, hoping to quiet it.

"Uh, I'm working at the factory."

"Thornfruit. Good, honest work. I worked the fields myself in my youth."

"I won't be in the fields, I'll be in the..."

Packing district was lost in a mumble. Babe turned and fled into the house.

———

Ryan called for Babe as soon as the front door closed.

"Coming!" Babe yelled back. He gave himself a little slap and whispered, "Just a creepy guy, don't make this bigger than it is. Anyway, he's gone now."

He didn't look out the curtains to check. He walked straight into the living room, picked up the notebook and pen his dad had provided, and sat down next to him.

Ryan launched straight back into it. "So the *third* kind of packaging—"

Babe tried to look attentive. He scribbled more nonsense on his notepad. *Tall teeth overcoat itch itch itch dirt.* He nodded at the right times. But somewhere in between Ryan's explanation about the staff uniform and what to be wary of re: the other workers, something caught his eye.

There was a dark spot on the wall the size of a dime. *Mold*, Babe thought. They got it sometimes, mostly in the bathroom. What was a patch doing out in the living room?

He glanced around the living room walls. No other spots he could see, but what if it was in the walls now? *Behind* the walls. Waiting to bloom on the wallpaper, choke them slowly for years and years. What if it didn't bloom on the wallpaper at all, but stuck behind the walls? There'd be no sign, their lungs would just quietly go black. A decade, maybe two. Wait, how long was Babe going to live here? He wasn't going to LA, sure, but he had to move out of town sometime, no matter what he told Dude. He'd always believed he'd get out at *some* point. Before thirty. Definitely before forty. Maybe he'd wait for his dad to die, and then—

"Of course."

Babe jerked back to his father, thinking wildly of mind reading. Ryan's voice was bitterly disappointed. It filled Babe with a deep, primordial panic.

Ryan sat back with a sigh, staring at the floor. "You *always* do this."

"I don't," Babe said. He straightened his back, holding his pen and notebook steady. "Dad, that was when I was a kid, I'm not—"

"Anytime I get excited about something, you start rolling your eyes."

"I wasn't rolling my eyes! I got distracted!" Babe's pitch had gotten out of control. He dragged it back down. "I'm sorry. I'll pay attention."

Ryan raised his gaze from the carpet. He scrutinized his son skeptically.

"I don't know why you always shoot yourself in the foot with these things," he said. "This is *your* career. Maybe it's just listening to your father that bores you."

Babe always tried to wiggle out of blatant confirmations like this. He'd nod or hum or smile, but he wouldn't come out and say it unless he really had to.

"I wasn't bored," he said. "Tell me more about what coworkers I should watch out for." He smiled.

After a moment, Ryan smiled back, the excitement coming back into his face, his pencil mustache bristling. "As I was saying," he said. "There's this rude young man called Bryce, you'll want to avoid him."

Babe wrote down *Bryce* on his notepad. Next to it, he wrote *avoid*, and he kept writing notes for a full five minutes until he started to write *dirt* over and over, occasionally looking up to smile encouragingly at his dad, who smiled back every time.

chapter
twelve

BABE CARRIED a cafeteria tray with a wobbling apple and a bowl of sloppy joe filling. The kitchen had run out of buns. He was sluggish in a way that reminded him of the night he crawled out of his grave. He hadn't slept well. Bad dreams. *Strange* dreams, murky and confusing. It felt like if Babe tried hard enough, everything would fall into place. He couldn't figure out what he was doing wrong.

"You don't look so good," Jules had said as she met him in line.

"*You* don't look so good," he'd fired back at her.

Jules had tossed her shimmering violet hair over one shoulder. "You wish."

Now he was sleepwalking to his usual table. Dude and Anna were already there, Dude using a fork to explain the different types of reeling you can do after a punch. It made Babe more tired just looking at him. Maybe Dude would be okay with him not participating in conversation. Babe could just watch. He'd like that.

After he apologized to Jules, of course.

"You do look nice," he said as they made their way over to the table. "Obviously."

"I know," she said, shaking her wind chime earrings so they sang.

Babe slumped and zoned out of the conversation. He had his eyes fixed on Dude's mouth moving in front of him when he bumped into someone. The tray clattered to the floor, apple rolling away, joe slopping down a guy's jeans.

The cafeteria gasped. Fell silent.

"Gosh," Babe said. "Sorry—"

He looked into the guy's face. Hunter Creel glared back with an intensity that made Babe's bowels clench in fear. Hunter had put a teacher in the hospital in freshman year. He had set him on fire.

Now Hunter looked like he'd shit himself down his front somehow, thanks to the sloppy joes. Though he wasn't staring at his pants. He picked at his jacket, smeared with a finger of meat. His eyes watered. "This is my dad's jacket," he said, and it betrayed none of the tears and all of the anger. "He'll kill me for getting it dirty."

Babe swallowed. He knew the next words before they could make it out of Hunter's mouth. Across the cafeteria, Buzz and Moe had noticed the lull in cafeteria talk and were coming over.

Hunter bared his teeth. "Looks like you're gonna die twice in one week, freak."

Babe wished for a more mature reason to hate Hunter. Like Anna. She hated him because he was a bigot who "reacted to everything like a violent four-year-old." Babe just hated him because of all the times Hunter had beat the crap out of him.

"Hey, I'm really sorry," he tried. "It was an accident."

Hunter balled up his fist, pulled it back.

Babe flinched, squeezing his eyes shut so he wouldn't have to see it coming—the punch, or everybody's faces as they watched it happen.

He felt a hand around his shoulder, wide and solid and deeply gentle. Babe knew this hand. *Come on, Dude! What happened to letting Hunter flop his privates around?*

He opened his eyes. Sure enough, Dude was smiling demurely at Hunter, who looked about ready to kick both their asses all the way to Vermont.

"Hunter," Dude said. "Babe here didn't mean to wreck your fancy jacket. How about you just let him go with all his teeth, huh?"

Behind Hunter, Buzz grinned. He liked to draw it out. Moe was shifting from foot to foot, glancing excitedly at both his buddies, waiting to see what would happen so he could react to it.

"Get the hell out of here, Dude."

"My guy," Dude said, still smiling smoothly. "It's just a jacket." He reached out as if to tug on the zipper. Babe grabbed his wrists and yanked them back.

Dude paused. "Good call," he told Babe. Then, to Hunter, who was beginning to vibrate with fury: "Man, you already have detention. High school ends next week. How about we chalk this up to an honest mistake and all leave as friends?"

"Friends," Hunter said flatly.

"Ayuh," Dude said through his calm smile, not blinking.

Hunter's fist came back up.

"Wait a second," Dude said, rotating around to Hunter's side. He slid an arm around Hunter's shoulder. Hunter let him, too shocked to do anything else.

"Dude," Babe said, real panic cutting into his voice. "What the heck are you—"

"Shush," Dude told him. He had his determined face on, the one he used when he was constructing a risky, elaborate lie. He raised his voice like a carnival barker. "Ladies and gentlemen," he said blandly. "I can't keep it a secret any longer."

"I'm gonna turn you into a *paste*," Hunter said.

"Give it a second," Dude whispered. Then he leaned in and pressed a wet kiss to Hunter's cheek.

The cafeteria erupted in gasps.

Moe giggled. Buzz, when he'd recovered from gaping, shoved him.

"Our wedding will be in June," Dude yelled over the din of laughter. He tried yelling more, but Hunter socked him in the face. One good thing about getting beat up by Hunter was that Dude got to practice his falls. He hit the floor easily, rolling with the impact. This only pissed Hunter off more.

"Oh God," Babe said.

Hunter climbed on top of Dude and started whaling on him. Babe hung back, paralyzed with fear, fingers twitching towards Dude as Dude's face snapped back and forth under the punches. Dude twisted the right side of his face away so Hunter didn't catch his other eye, holding his hands up weakly. He did not fight back. There was no point.

Buzz and Moe yelled encouragement. The rest of the school just yelled.

Babe cleared his throat. "Stop it!"

His protest sunk under the yelling, under the wet sound of Dude's face being pummeled. The cheek that had almost healed from Hunter's punch several days back smacked against the linoleum and began to swell in earnest, blood pooling fast under the skin.

"Stop it," Babe said, and this came with a growl. Just the start of one, low in his throat and completely unbidden. Again, this went unheard. Or it went unheard by everybody but Hunter, who paused long enough to look over, his face contorted with sheer bewilderment.

"Did you just goddamn *growl* at me?" Hunter said. It, too, was lost in the jeering.

"Um," Babe said. "No?"

Dude snorted. He was lying crumpled on the floor, bleeding out of his nose and split lip.

The security guard descended then, yanking Hunter away. Hunter shoved, and the guard shoved back and gripped Hunter by the back of his neck. He held Hunter far away from him as if holding a wild dog by the scruff. Everybody knew about what Hunter had done to Mr. Jitterbug, and the guard didn't want to be next on the list.

Babe crouched down next to Dude, taking a hand. Anna was already there, holding Dude's other hand and pulling with Babe.

"You know what," Dude said, muffled over a bleeding mouth. His left eye was swollen shut. "This stings."

The nurse wasn't at all surprised to see them. She jerked her head towards the cot and told them to sit down. They did, all four of them on that crackling plastic sheet. Anna made pleasant small talk with the nurse, who was familiar with Anna because of the occasions Anna had to take a pain pill and curl up on the cot during heavy flows. Also, the nurse had gone to school with her parents. Also, she was the dentist's daughter, and every time anyone went to the dentist, they got updates on how Nurse Sliptick was going. There were no degrees of separation in Bulldeen.

The bell rang for next period.

"Come on," Dude said. "You guys can go."

After some cajoling, Anna and Jules left. Babe stayed and socked him in the arm.

"That was stupid," he told Dude. "Why'd you do that?"

Dude flexed his arm, the one Babe didn't hit. He'd moved

too much as he'd been holding the right side of his face away, and Hunter's punch had gone astray, catching him in the shoulder. A bruise was forming under his ripped sleeve.

"Old time's sake," Dude said. "One more for the road."

"Be serious."

"I am wild," Dude said, using his quoting voice. Babe didn't know what he was quoting.

Dude broke out in a toothy grin, teeth stained bloody pink. There was a clot of tissue in the gap between his two front ones. "Babe, I'm outta here in a couple weeks. This town's gonna be dust in my wheels. I'm not coming back."

"What, never? What about your mom?"

Dude shrugged. Grimaced at his hurt shoulder. "She'll survive."

"What about me?"

Dude looked at him with his good eye. The left was a puffy mess. Dude navigated the world with the tiny strip of eye available between his drooping eyelids. With any more swelling that strip would close up and he wouldn't see anything. In middle school, Buzz had punched him in both eyes and Dude had been blind for two days until the swelling had gone down.

"You gotta leave sometime," he said. "And until then, phones are a thing."

He felt cautiously around his blackened eye, skimming his eyelashes with the tips of his fingers. They were very long. He got teased about them. Babe had teased him about them, but that had tapered off as Babe realized how beautiful Dude's eyelashes were. Now he tried to pretend they didn't exist.

Babe picked at the plastic sheet between them, watching it crinkle between his fingers.

"What if I don't leave? What if I live here the rest of my life?"

Dude gave him an unimpressed look with his good eye.

"Babe, if you were actually happy living in Bulldeen the rest of your life, I'd buy Bulldeen Bulls merch and cheer like a maniac. I'd gladly listen to whatever boring gossip is going on around town. But you're not happy now and you won't be happy later. Some other tiny town in New England? Maybe. But not here." He crossed his arms and leaned back against the wall, back curving dangerously. He straightened up. Bad posture led to joint pain. Joint pain did not bode well for his stunt and prop man career.

Babe tried not to sulk. It was hard—he didn't like being told inconvenient truths, and he was already frustrated with hunger. It simmered deep in his gut, sparking out to the rest of him. His cheek twitched with it, a muscle fluttering in his jaw, as if trying to pry it open.

He could hear Dude's heartbeat. Was that normal? It beat slow and steady next to his own, which was growing erratic. Dude stunk with dried blood—crusted under his eye, blooming purple under his cheek. No, not stunk. He *glowed* with it. The glow sunk down into his veins, his pulsing veins, his warm, tight skin—

Babe's mouth filled with saliva. He swallowed it. His hands twitched. He sat on them.

He was very good at not touching Dude when he desperately wanted to. He had years of practice.

"What?" Dude said.

"What what?"

"You're sweating."

"I'm fine," Babe squeaked. His hands clenched around the plastic sheet. His head pounded. His blood howled.

Shut up, he told it. *You don't get to decide what I do. We're gonna sit here and suffer in silence and that's it, you hear me?*

A flicker in his head, annoyed. It didn't belong to him. It

was a very strange feeling being the vessel for an emotion that wasn't his. He frowned.

"Sure you're okay?" Dude asked, still leaning against the wall with a straight back. Brown curls tumbled over his forehead, boyish and lovely.

Babe got up and headed for the bathroom. He took slow, measured breaths. He splashed water on his face. Then he went back to the nurse's office and told Dude he was heading to class.

"Okay," Dude said. "Don't get into any fights on the way there."

"No promises," Babe said on autopilot. The hunger wasn't singing anymore. It had died down to a mumble. He sat down in class, unable to hear any heartbeat but his own.

chapter
thirteen

THERE ARE two filters in the human body: the kidneys and the liver. They filter blood, among other things. When alcohol is consumed, the liver and kidneys break it down until it leaves the system.

There are no filters for heavy metals. The body doesn't know what to do with them. When ingested, arsenic and lead —two of the metals found in Bulldeen soil—remain. They circulate within the bloodstream, around and around. After time, they build up. Prolonged exposure manifests in increased irritability, seizures, and brain injuries, to name a few symptoms.

In the old days, the issue was all the townsfolk eating Bulldeen-grown crops and livestock which fed on the Bulldeen grass.

By 2003, it was the water supply.

The Bulldeen sewer system was old. The pipes were lead. In small doses, it didn't do much. Over a lifetime the damage became clearer, but most of the town didn't notice or care about the pipes. They couldn't afford restructuring, and the effects weren't widespread enough to warrant panic.

The runoff, however, was a bigger problem. Over at the

end of the farming district was a river. Most of the townsfolk got their water pumped from a reservoir miles away. But the Creels lived half a mile from that river. They got their water from a well.

In some cases of heavy metal poisoning, during those endless cycles around the bloodstream, metal will pass the blood-brain barrier. This is hard to do. It can only happen with very fine particles. But with decades of slow, steady consumption, the body is unable to do anything but circle it endlessly inside, and erosion becomes inevitable.

The farming houses were the first houses in Bulldeen. Then everybody started to move inwards towards Bull's Head and the sewer district.

Townies, Hunter's mom called them.

Pussies, his dad said. Hunter preferred his dad's version of things. Ian Creel didn't eat fancy food or buy new clothes every year. Ian Creel sure as hell didn't use fabric softener. According to Ian, clothes should be hard and itchy.

Hunter dropped his backpack onto the floor and headed out onto the porch. He'd heard his dad from half a mile away, shooting cans off a fence.

"Hey, Pops."

Ian Creel grunted. His tongue curled down towards his chin as he concentrated. One eye closed. He squeezed the trigger. Twelve feet away, a can exploded off their fence.

Ian whooped. He was, like most of the town, born and bred Bulldeen. He had a beer gut and a receding hairline which he kept shaved down. He had lesions on his arms that had been showing up in the last five years. Ian wouldn't know about his cancer until it was too late, and he would never know about the arsenic in his water supply. The Creels didn't go to the doctor unless they were puking blood. Which Ian would, in time. The cancer was seeping into his stomach.

He coughed hard into his hands. "Not done yet?"

"Nope." Hunter leaned against the porch next to his dad, leather jacket spit-shined. He'd ditched the rest of school to clean it, wiping over every inch until it shone. "Wish I could just turn in now."

"Yeeeeap. Do that, and your momma's family won't give you money for a car."

"Bitch."

Ian cuffed him in the back of the head. Hunter took it in stride. Sometimes—usually after Ian finished his second beer—he'd laugh like Hunter said the funniest thing in the world, calling his mother a bitch. And other times he'd bring out his fist. Hunter craved his dad's laughter enough to risk it.

"It's useless, sure," Ian said, turning back to the gun and raising it to his eyeline. Two cans were left on the fence. "But her family cares about that stuff."

"Dumbasses," Hunter said.

"Dumbasses," Ian agreed.

You never knew what you were going to get with Ian Creel. Hunter prided himself on being the same.

Hunter settled in and watched his dad blow some cans to dust. He was a crack shot.

"Beat up some prissy little shithead today," Hunter said, leaning his chin hard into his arm. He liked to make his limbs go numb. His arm tingled as it was overtaken by pins and needles.

Ian grunted. "All those guys think they're better than us."

"Yeah," Hunter said. "Shitheads."

"Shitheads," Ian agreed. He eyed Hunter's jacket, which used to be his. Hunter sweated, but Ian didn't seem to notice anything new. He raised the gun again. There was an old oak tree just before the thornfruit fields. *Bang.* A branch went flying.

They laughed in time. Hunter cleared his throat, spat into the dirt. "Hey, Dad? You know that time you nearly burned down the school, but that teacher caught you?"

Ian barked a laugh. "Jitterbug. You got him good."

Hunter glowed quietly with the praise. "You would've done it, right? If he didn't ruin it."

"Sure," Ian said, his aim roving. None of the other branches were thin enough to go down in one shot. "Do this town some good. No one learns anything important there anyway. Nothin' about *life*. Fathers gotta teach their sons. Mothers teach their daughters. What'd you learn at school today, Hunt?"

"Nothing," Hunter said, which was what he always said when his dad asked about school. Ian threw back his head and laughed. Hunter watched it, hungry eyes on the joy in his father's wrinkled face, the crackle of his laughter.

Karen Creel emerged onto the porch, smoking a cigarette. She was a skinny, absentminded woman with a deep passion for gin, for pinning butterflies for display in the spare room, and for her husband and son. In that order.

She sidled up to her husband and leaned against his side.

He nudged the butt of his gun into her hip. "Move it, woman."

"Move me yourself," she said, and grinned.

Karen had told her son enough times that Ian hadn't been a good husband prospect. The Creels were too drunk, too white-trash, too dangerous. Karen's family had warned her off him, and she'd listened all the way up to senior year of high school, when her friend group had begun to orbit closer and closer towards the trashy side of town. The short story was this:

Karen's family never bruised each other, never shouted. They hurt each other in more subtle, intimate ways. Everyone Karen loved throughout her life had damaged her deeply. A lifetime of that can convince a girl that love and damage went hand in hand. Ian's family had a wildness that was refreshing, their savagery out in the open in a way Karen's family would never dare. Ian had shown up on prom night in secret, creeping up to her bedroom window with a fistful of flowers from her own yard. That was exciting. But later that night, when he got annoyed by her laugh and pinched the inside of her knee so hard it bled, *that* had been familiar. Do anything for a lifetime and it will become comforting. Later that night, he ripped her bra. She shoved at him, striking out too hard and breaking his nose. He stared at her, dazed with blood. Then he'd burst out laughing. They'd sat there in his car, half-naked and pained, giggling like kids. This was largely how their marriage had gone.

She dug her heel into his exposed toes. "What are you two talking about?"

He wrapped an arm around her waist with the hand still holding the gun. The barrel pointed up towards her face. He tapped her chin with it and she laughed.

Hunter watched, trying not to squirm. He was never entirely comfortable around his parents. Laughter could turn septic on a dime. He leaned harder on his arms until the pins and needles took over.

"Jitterbug," said Ian Creel.

Karen hummed. She leaned her head on her husband's shoulder, cheek resting on top of the scar she'd given him with a broken bottle halfway through their honeymoon.

"Tell me again," she said.

Gerry Jitterbug taught freshman gym for half his life. He'd taught Ian Creel one year after he got his first and only teaching job. Twenty years later, he taught Hunter Creel. Even if Jitterbug didn't know him around town, he would've recognized the Creel son on sight. He had the same eyes as his father. Those gray eyes screamed *if you mess with me, you'll regret it.*

Jitterbug didn't take the warning. He hadn't taken it when Ian Creel swayed on the spot, drunk and delirious, spilling lighter fluid all over the wooden floors of the gym. Ian was a small, scrawny thing with the cruelest right hook and even worse temper, turning in a second. He was too drunk that day to do anything but desperately try to stay on his feet as Jitterbug yelled at him. When Jitterbug came forward to take the kid's arm, Ian Creel slumped forwards and puked all down both their legs.

Three days later, Ian keyed Jitterbug's car. He spat at the back of Jitterbug's head every class. For the rest of his life, Ian Creel would jeer at Jitterbug in the street.

Jitterbug would ignore him. Inside, though, he'd gloat. *The Creels aren't so tough after all.*

This was what he was thinking as he dressed Hunter Creel down for forgetting his gym clothes. Jitterbug had had a bad day—he'd scratched up the car driving home from the bar, and his wife had noticed this morning. She'd cried over it. This was their new car. Jitterbug hadn't thought about it at all as his voice rose and rose, kids staring, and then trying not to look once they noticed who Jitterbug was yelling at.

Hunter stood there in his plain clothes, still and pale, hands clutched into fists at his side. He looked straight into the teacher's eyes. Never looked away once.

Jitterbug still didn't take the warning.

"Don't want to take a swing, huh? No? Guess you're just

like your daddy. 'Cept when I drug him away from this place, he was so drunk he couldn't have hit the side of a barn!"

Hunter blinked. His eyes shone. Jitterbug thought about bringing this up, but a chill went down his spine. He wavered. Came back to himself. If he'd stopped thirty seconds before, he could've escaped unscathed.

"What's everybody doing?" he said. "Get back to dodgeball."

The kids scrambled to comply, just how Jitterbug liked it. When he looked back at Hunter, the kid was already moving for the exit. That was the end of that. Or so Jitterbug thought.

What happened that night would be whispered in Bulldeen corridors for decades. Kids would swear they knew someone who saw the whole thing.

But nobody saw it. Even Jitterbug barely saw it. He heard a rustle out near the trashcans and went out to shoo away raccoons. He was halfway across his yard when something heavy hit him across the face.

He went down hard. His head bloomed with hurt, mouth open around grass and blood. His eyes streamed, looking up into the smeared, savage frame of Hunter Creel. Fourteen and wild, emptying liquid over Jitterbug's torso. It stunk. It made Jitterbug remember, dimly, that he needed to take his car in to get fixed.

"What?" Jitterbug said, slurring around his swelling tongue. It had sliced open on his own teeth when he hit the dirt. "What're you doing?"

Hunter dug a lighter out of his pocket. A cheap gas station lighter, faded orange. He flicked it on so the orange grew.

Jitterbug stared at it the whole way down. It hit him in the chest, just below his right nipple.

The flames ate up his shirt. After that, Jitterbug didn't look at anything. He squeezed his eyes shut, a noise like he'd never heard ripping out of his throat. He writhed on the grass and screamed as his wife found him, screamed as she beat the fire out with her own hands, screamed and sobbed as he was loaded into the back of his own car by his wife's lightly smoking fingers. A neighbor took over from there, giving Mrs. Jitterbug a bowl of cool water to dip her hands into as she sat in the passenger's seat.

It was an hour to the hospital. Jitterbug screamed the whole way.

No charges were pressed. The Jitterbugs got out of town the week after the attack, and neither of them said anything about who attacked this small-town teacher. It didn't matter. The next day, Hunter Creel strode down the halls and they parted to let him pass. He rolled a lighter in his hand, thumbing it on and off. When Principal Skinner noticed him holding it on campus, he'd avert his gaze.

Hunter thought about Jitterbug often. Mostly he thought about his dad barging into his room the morning after. Hunter had jumped, since Ian barging into his room could be very, very good (surprise trip out of town) or very, very bad (drunk and swinging).

But Ian Creel had been laughing fit to burst. He yanked his son out of bed into a hug.

"You beauty," he'd said. "You absolute beauty! You got that little shit! You let him know who's boss!"

Hunter had laughed, relieved at not getting hit, at the pure shock of a hug when his dad wasn't wasted. He'd hugged back so hard it'd turned into a wrestling match, and Karen had come to stand in the door, laughing, throwing cushions at them, and then knick-knacks off Hunter's bookshelf.

Later that day, Ian Creel had gifted his son his lighter. It had been his own father's, Isaac Creel, who had died in the fire that consumed the town hall. Before Ian bequeathed it to Hunter, he held it up to his own lips. The first and only kiss he'd ever give his son, passed through the lighter that Hunter would keep in his pocket until the day he died.

fourteen

LAST PERIOD WAS CANCELED. Mr. Clack didn't even drag out the VCR. He just said, "This is something my English teacher did for me in my last couple weeks at high school. Life is short, kids. Go out and live it!"

Jules piled her nail polish back into her pencil case, careful of her two wet purple nails. She'd only just started when Mr. Clack came in. She waved them dry.

Dude and Jules had a murder to execute.

"Technically we're not killing him," Dude said, as they huddled in one of the already-picked thornfruit fields on the edge of town. "We're getting him to the verge of death, then the thing's gonna take care of it."

Brambles rose around tall thin poles. The stalks, which absorbed all the poison and left the fruit free of it, were thick and barbed and covered in thin leaves. If you crouched down in these fields, you couldn't be noticed until someone was right on top of you.

Jules nodded seriously, blowing gum into a bubble and leaning sideways to pop it with a thornfruit barb. She'd picked purple gum, to match her hair. "What if he dies before the thing gets here to eat him?"

"It says that won't happen."

"So...what *is* it?"

"No clue." Dude fought back a shudder. "It's bad, is what it is."

"Mmmm." Jules's jaw cracked around a yawn. She'd been having strange dreams too, though not Bulldeen related. Jules dreamed of Los Angeles, lying down in the forest that bordered her house. Grass against her cheek. Stabbing pain. A hand, reaching. She always woke up before she found out if she managed to reach back.

Jules slapped her rouged cheeks, banishing the dreams to the depths of her mind. "Feeling great about this, Dude."

"You can always back out."

Jules rolled her eyes. "No way. Babe looked real pale today. Tired."

"Hungry," Dude supplied. "Yeah."

Jules hauled her backpack into her lap and unsheathed a CD player along with her giant, industrial headphones. She slipped them over her head.

"I made a mixtape," she told Dude.

He snorted. "A murder mixtape?"

She clicked the CD player open. KICKASS MIXTAPE was scrawled on the CD in blocky marker.

"Kickass," Dude remarked. He reached into his backpack and unearthed a hammer.

Jules tried not to think about what they'd be doing with it. "Rad."

"It's my mom's. Remember when she redid the back porch?"

"Which time? If it was the first time, I wasn't here yet."

"Oh," Dude said. "Right. Sometimes I forget you haven't been here forever."

Jules blew another bubble, chewed it flat, clicked the CD

player closed, and started the music. A rapid-fire drum beat. She closed her eyes and air-drummed along, trying not to think about her bare legs protruding out of her shorts and crouching against the dirt, about her heels growing roots deep into the soil she'd only been walking on for five years. *Sometimes I forget.*

Sometimes Jules forgot too. LA felt like a fever dream. She'd spent the first thirteen years of her life there under the smoggy skies, high-rise buildings, the sprawling forests. LA was life-sized. Bulldeen was a train set in comparison, a miniature she had to step carefully around. The train went around and around the track every day. Nothing changed. Jules hadn't bothered resenting her parents for anything since she was ten, but their decision to move here to hide from her dad's debt collectors was hard not to hate, just a little.

A tickle on her leg. Dude was drawing lines between the ingrown hairs on her leg, bright spots of inflammation. Jules had traced them with her fingernail this morning, forming a pentagram. With his ballpoint pen, Dude made a misshapen unicorn.

"She's beautiful," Jules told him over the music.

Dude neighed at her.

One good thing about Bulldeen: Jules had found a family leagues better than the one she had at home. She had a lot of friends in LA, but they were all party friends. Only sticking around for good times and fair weather. Not the kind of people you'd kill for.

That being said, she *was* looking forward to adding more people to her social circle. She would kill and die for her friends, but variety was the paprika of life. Or something.

Jules leaned her head back against the bricks, then reached out for the hammer on Dude's backpack. Her headphones vibrated with noise. *Hit me with your best shot!*

"Good choice," Dude said.

Jules grinned.

They didn't have to wait long. Buzz came striding out just beyond the fields, Moe in tow.

"Oh shit," Jules said, crouching lower. The brambles already stretched far over her head. She turned her music down, keeping it in the background. "Moe's here too. What if Hunter comes?"

"Well, we still can't do it with Moe," Dude whispered.

Buzz came to a stop just before the brambles. He had a strap around his chest and shoulder.

"Oh shit," Jules repeated. "He's got a—"

"I see it."

"I thought he came out here to practice with his nunchucks!"

"He usually does!"

Buzz lifted the rifle strap off his shoulder.

"Oh geez," said Moe. "Can I touch it?"

Buzz laughed at him. "Don't get drool on it."

"I won't," Moe said eagerly. He took the rifle like someone holding their grandma's china. He turned it admiringly around in his hands, keeping the barrel pointed carefully away. "Whoa. It's so cool."

Buzz took it back. "I can't believe your dad never took you out here to shoot rabbits."

In the winter, the brambles wilted and thinned. You could see the ground and, sometimes, rabbits gnawing at the dying leaves. The rabbits would die a day after. No one could figure out why the rabbits hadn't clued into this. They didn't eat the poison oak, they didn't eat stinging nettles. Just the thornfruit leaves. Even the birds wouldn't go near.

There wasn't much point to shooting the rabbits. They only got a day's worth of feeding. But it made for good target practice, which Buzz had gotten a lot of.

Buzz held the rifle up. The shaft grazed his shoulder.

"Wait," Moe said. "What're we shooting?"

Buzz shrugged. The rifle moved with the movement.

"I just wanna feel it kick," he said, and fired.

Dude and Jules jumped.

"*Shit!*" Jules screamed. It was lost in the gunshot blast. The bullet snapped a stalk in half and plummeted into the dirt a dozen feet away.

Dude stared, wide-eyed, through the brambles. "This is the dumbest way to die."

Jules turned off her Kickass Mix and stuffed her headphones in her backpack. "Throw your hammer!"

"Sure," Dude whispered back. "I'll just Robin Hood the hammer at him and get him right in the head, almost but not totally killing him. I'm sure Moe won't report this to the cops at all."

Jules curled herself in a tiny ball, backpack hugged close to her chest. Less surface area to shoot at. Dude quickly followed suit.

Another gunshot. Moe whooped.

"If we let them know we're here, will that make it better or worse?" Dude hissed.

"Go shoot at trees," Jules whispered. "Go shoot at cans outside your parents' house, you Nazi son of a—"

Another shot. Jules could see the dirt puff up from this one, barely five feet away. Her scalp sweated. She'd have to wash her hair again tonight, even though it got oily when she washed it two days in a row. Bulldeen dirt wedged under her nails. God, she hated this place. None of this was worth it, surely, nothing was worth her years stuck in this backwards shithole, where people glared at you if you dared to dye your hair or wear a skirt over thick thighs and the best live show was from a banjo player with eight fingers. If she'd stayed in LA she'd be at a record shop with cool people who had actual fashion sense; she'd be learning some strange art form from somebody's older brother, she'd have a towering world around her instead of dirt and thorns. Moving here was a mistake. Everything about Bulldeen was a mistake.

Dude's elbow dug into her ribs.

Jules blinked. Right. Not *everything*.

She wet her glossy lips. "We should crab crawl away."

Dude immediately started to inch sideways, away from the boys. Jules hooked her arm in his and followed. It made crawling harder, but it kept their spirits up.

The brambles rustled.

"Slow," Jules said.

Their crab crawl turned even crawlier.

Buzz and Moe talked in between gunshots.

"If I got enough ammo, I could take out half the school, easy."

Moe laughed uneasily, as he always did when Buzz talked about this. "You're not actually gonna go through with it, right?"

Buzz spat into the dirt. "Hunter'd do it with me." He raised the gun higher so the metal pressed against his cheek. "Well, he wouldn't shoot it up. He'd burn it."

Moe stayed quiet. He tagged along with his friends during their troublemaking, but he never instigated it. And he got very nervous when they started talking about shooting up and/or burning down the school. He was never sure which was a bigger possibility, though he thought burning would be more likely. Hunter cared less about consequences.

Moe sorely hoped they wouldn't invite him along, that they'd tell him to stay home that day. He liked to think he mattered enough to them for that.

He was looking forward to graduation. It meant he could stop worrying about it.

Buzz held out the gun to him. "Want a go?"

Moe took it reverently. His dad hadn't taken him shooting. His dad didn't talk to him except to tell him to get him more beer.

"Thanks," he said, and raised it. Buzz nudged it up more and Moe let him. Buzz was an expert, after all.

"Okay," Buzz said. "Fire."

Moe squeezed the trigger. It jerked in his hands, bullet exploding into the fields.

He yelled in joy. He had watched Hunter's face when they'd burned down that abandoned house last year out in the sewer district—a joy so big and excited, it had bled out of his eyes. This was what Hunter must've felt.

Twenty feet away in the fields, doing the world's slowest crab crawl, Dude and Jules flinched.

"Almost," Dude said.

This was a lie. It was minutes of crab crawling to the edge of the field. In those minutes, Moe and Buzz's talk faded away. But not before they overheard this exchange:

"Who would you get? If you were gonna do the shooting. Not me, right?"

"Ha! We'll see how much you piss me off. No, I wouldn't get you. I'd get all those too-good-for-town freaks."

Gunshot. Another stalk snapped. Tomorrow morning, Ryan Simmons would walk out into the fields and touch the broken edges of the stalk. He'd put his hands on his hips and glare out at the field.

"Goddamn kids," he'd say.

But that wouldn't be for sixteen hours. Now the sun was high in the sky and Buzz was running out of bullets.

"Freaks," Moe repeated. He knew who they didn't like, but he wasn't sure who they disliked enough to kill.

"Uh-huh." Buzz let off another shot, gun held steady against his face. "Y'know, I was thinking what a shame it is that Zombabe came back."

"He didn't...he didn't come *back*."

"Sure about that? Him and Dude were always creeps. Too close. *I* think maybe Dude did something unnatural. In more ways than one."

Down in the dirt, Dude crawled. Jules crawled beside him. Brambles tweaked their clothes, cut at exposed skin. As kids, everybody got dared to go into the fields. Dude went a bunch of times. Jules never had. She'd missed out on those dares, and she'd never been grateful until now. She was starting to think they'd never get out of there. They'd be crawling through the thorns forever.

The boys' talk faded. Gunshots echoed. Jules and Dude hit the end of the field and broke out into un-brambled air, sprawling out onto the dirt, covered in tiny cuts. Their muscles ached from crouching and crawling. A thin line of blood trickled down Jules's forehead into her mascara'd eyelashes. She wiped at it.

They lay there for a while, panting.

"Should we tell Principal Skinner about the shooting?" Jules said.

"No evidence," Dude said in a terrible approximation of Principal Skinner's bored drawl. "Nothing we can do."

"I just hate it," Jules said. "It never feels safe. What the hell did we do to him?"

"We exist," Dude said, even flatter than usual. He stood, brushing down his jeans. Only his arms and face were cut—his legs had been saved by thick denim. He wore jeans in all weathers unless he was working out. No matter what muscle he gained in his legs, they stayed toned and very thin. The contrast between his legs and his arms was enough to make him giggle sometimes—he didn't want to give others the chance.

Jules scowled down at her nails. Her two painted ones were scarred and chipped thanks to the fields. She shook them in disgust. "You going home?"

"Nope. I'm going over to KJ's."

Jules started picking dirt out of her hair. "You go over to his house now?"

"We leave in a couple weeks," Dude said. "What could happen?"

Jules brushed a thumb over one of the deeper cuts on her hand. It kept bleeding.

fifteen

AS DUDE and Jules hid in the thornfruit fields, Anna walked three blocks from the school to the library. The Bulldeen library was tucked between the pharmacy and a clothes store near Main Street. It didn't have a good selection, but it excelled in one area: copies of *The Bulldeen Post*. Newspapers were painstakingly preserved as far back as 1880, as well as building blueprints and farming layouts, and two books from local authors—*Sharp and Lifesaving: How Thornfruit Saved a Town*, by Barry Manning, and *An Extensive History of Bulldeen, 1860–1980* by Johnny Walks.

Anna started with the newspapers. She heaved down the books where they were collected together and laid them out on the small corner table. It was one of the two tables in the library. The other one doubled as a borrowing counter where you went to stamp books.

She flicked through the big years until she found the right date: *1965, TOWN HALL BURNS DOWN CLAIMING EIGHT LIVES! Early Thursday night, smoke was seen rising from—*

"Can I help you?"

Anna startled. Miss Henrietta stood behind her desk, her

librarian badge a dull shine on her vest.

She was the only librarian employed by the town council. She was the kind of person who should not have chosen a career that involved talking to people. The sides of her mouth turned down all on their own and she glared at people over whatever book she was reading.

Anna wavered. Miss Henrietta wasn't that old—maybe forty—but she'd been here since she was Anna's age.

"Um," she said. "I was wondering if you had any more information about the town hall fire?"

Miss Henrietta's eyes narrowed. "I'm sure I don't know anything new," she said coldly. "Why don't you ask your parents?"

"They don't, um—" Anna turned away, touched the photographed grainy husk of the old town hall. It was smaller than she'd always imagined when she walked past that empty space in the middle of town.

A shuffling from the stacks. Janitor Larry set his toolbox on the ground and began taking books off a shelf that sagged to the right. He was scary looking, waxen with a greasy mullet and almost no teeth, but harmless enough. At least that was what her parents told her when Anna had told them he creeped her out.

"Never mind," Anna said to Miss Henrietta.

Miss Henrietta nodded and went back to her book like Anna had never been there in the first place. Today she was reading a romance, the cover replaced by the dust cover of a science textbook. She was a sour asshole with a secret longing for passion she'd never find in Bulldeen.

Anna turned back to the article. The photo had been taken after the rubble had cooled, so there was no smoke drifting up from the charred remains. The bodies would've been removed by the time the camera got set up.

A prickle at the back of her neck.

"You think he did it?"

Anna turned. Janitor Larry was greasier up close. He also had shockingly nice eyes set deep in his worn face.

He nodded down at the photo, the burned-out hall. "Your great-grandpop?"

"I…don't know."

He hummed far back in his throat. "I knew 'im when we were kids. Good man. Sharp edges, though."

"Sharp?"

"Yeah. Him and that wife of his." He looked down at the photo, reached out and touched it in the exact same place Anna did. He would've known everyone who died in that fire. Even if he didn't know their names, he'd know their faces.

Anna edged away.

Janitor Larry didn't seem to notice. He stared at the photo, void of expression.

As Anna was about to turn for the door, he spoke up. "There were marks on the bones."

Anna stopped. "What?"

"'S what I heard." Janitor Larry took out a dirty handkerchief from his pocket, smeared dirt around his hands with it. "Nobody mentions it anymore. But back then, that was the whisper 'round here."

"Marks like…"

"Marks on Jessie Hart's bones too."

Jessie Hart was the mother of the four-year-old that had come back to life. Two weeks after the resurrection, Jessie had been found dead in her home, her daughter Milly wailing over her body. Cause of death had been suicide. Now that Anna thought about it, she didn't know how it had happened. This seemed like a glaring gap in schoolyard gossip.

"That kid that came back," Janitor Larry said slowly. "The

Babe kid. He's your friend?"

"Yes."

He gave her a long look, like he was trying to see something in her.

"He getting out of town after graduation?"

"No, he's staying here for a while. Working at the factory."

"Alright," he said. He didn't look too happy to hear it.

For the first time in her high school career, Anna cut class. It was coming up on the last week of school. Half the graduating class was leaving at lunch, if they came in at all.

She walked the five blocks through the town square to Aunt Kate's house. She sweated, but only because it was hot. She was surprisingly okay with breaking and entering into Aunt Cop's house.

Kate lived in a small, humid house on the corner of the sewer district. The house was a lot like her: shabby, but regular shabby. No care put into appearance, or into much of anything. The third stair up to the house had been broken for years.

Anna went around the back so passersby couldn't see her from the street. The laundry room window was open. Anna pushed until it was big enough to fit a seventeen-year-old girl, then she shimmied in. The laundry room was muzzy with cobwebs. A giant spider crept along the edge of the window as she squeezed in. Anna shuddered.

She got her feet into the laundry room and stood, brushing off dust and webs. She didn't come around here much, except for the year when she was twelve and came around on Saturdays to watch every season of *Zira: Fighter Queen,* Kate nursing a whiskey, Anna nursing a Kool-Aid.

It was hard not to panic while she was walking around in her aunt's house, even if she was only trespassing, no breaking in needed.

She checked the living room first. Kate spent a lot of time on that couch. But the only things on the empty cushion were pulpy romance novels, wilting in the heat.

She headed for the bedroom. On the nightstand were more books. Anna did a double take. Pulpy *lesbian* romance novels. She picked one up and studied the cover: two women drawn with pouty lips and skimpy clothes, one of them giving the other a longing look. *Forbidden Lovers!* declared the title in curling purple. Then, smaller: *Holly Hands walks the strange path of love… Will it free her? Or destroy her?*

Anna grinned, but her smile faded as she noticed the case files lying closed on Kate's single pillow.

She put the lesbian book down. It had a lot of folded pages, something which made Anna's head ping with interest, but she made herself focus on the files. It was an easy job once she got the first one open.

It was an autopsy. A black and white photograph of a woman dead on a silver tray. Jessica Hart.

Anna squirmed, looked quickly to the manner of death. SUICIDE. Okay, so that was true. What else?

CAUSE OF DEATH: BLOOD LOSS.

She kept skimming. MULTIPLE PUNCTURE MARKS. NECK WOUND WAS FATAL. What did she do, stab herself? She read on.

STOMACH AND HEART MISSING.

Anna read that over three times.

She looked back up to SUICIDE, blaring loud and bold.

She lifted the file. In the next collection of stapled papers, another photo of someone dead on the tray. This was a man, blonde and unshaven with a gory gash where his left ear should've been. Anna frowned. Was this in the wrong file?

VIKTOR CREEL, the paper said. MANNER OF DEATH: HOMICIDE.

Anna kept reading, a question blurring in her head. One of Ian Creel's cousins. He had the trademark Creel chin.

PUNCTURE MARKS, the autopsy said. STOMACH WOUND WAS FATAL. ORGANS MISSING.

Anna thumbed through the file. There were three more stapled papers. Three more bodies—a Jane Doe, then two more men with names of kids in Anna's school. All with multiple puncture wounds, all with missing body parts. No additional photos, at which Anna was disappointed and relieved.

Jessie Hart had left a note. Anna searched, but there was no other mention of it other than PATIENT LEFT A NOTE ON THE FRIDGE LABELED FOR HER DAUGHTER IN THE EVENT OF HER IMMINENT DEATH.

She was about to pick up the other file, the one with TOWN HALL on it, when there was a loud slurp from the doorway.

She spun around. Aunt Kate waved with her free hand. The other one held a sweating glass of Coke, a straw propped up in it. She was in jean shorts and a cut-off tank top, hip fat pushing out between them.

Lying felt useless. Anna sighed. "Why are you home?"

"I took a half day." Kate sucked at her Coke. "Want one?"

"No," Anna said. "Why the day off?"

Kate shrugged. Dirty blonde hair stuck to her forehead. "They didn't need me for the riveting case of Mr. Keener's missing bicycle. Or the case of those kids throwing rocks at Mr. and Mrs. Lockjaw's house again."

"How long have you been standing there?" Anna was

suddenly aware again of the lesbian books on the nightstand.

If Kate noticed, she didn't seem fazed. "Better question: what are you doing with those confidential files?"

"What are *you* doing? You're not allowed to take these home!"

Kate shrugged again. This one was more lopsided. She brought her glass up to her mouth and tipped ice between her teeth, starting to crunch.

Anna dropped the file onto the bedspread. "I never heard about those murders."

"Ayuh," Kate said. It echoed into the glass as she took a sip. "'Course you didn't. They covered them up."

Anna did the math. "*You* covered them up."

"I was just a rookie back then," Kate said. "But yeah. We got asked."

"By who?"

"Chief at the time. And the mayor."

"The—?"

"No more bad publicity for Bulldeen," Kate said. "The town hall was bad enough. We didn't need a repeat."

Anna opened her mouth. She closed it. Opened it again. "That's the stupidest thing I've ever heard," she said faintly.

Kate huffed a laugh. Her voice was scratchy from smoking. Her laughs came out differently nowadays. Rougher. She swallowed ice and said, "I thought so too."

"Then why..." Anna still felt calm, which was strange. Her voice was rising. "We don't get tourists anyway! All that thornfruit propaganda, it hasn't done anything! Why keep lying?"

Kate took another slug. There was a murky quality about the Coke that got Anna thinking there was something other than soda in it.

"Been like that long enough," said Aunt Cop. "Might as well keep going."

chapter
sixteen

BABE WAS ALREADY on his second glass of water in the Star and Shine diner opposite the thornfruit plant, the only diner in Bulldeen. It loomed big and square and gray through the window.

A tap on his shoulder. Babe turned.

"Gotcha," Dude said.

Babe turned to the other side. Dude settled into the seat next to him and stole his water glass.

"Hey," Babe said, but there was no heat behind it. The hunger had set in deeper. Bone-deep, not just gut. He was hyper-aware of everyone moving around him, the warmth of their skin radiating and pulling at him.

Dude chugged. His layered cheek bruise was fading purple, his swollen eye was almost back to normal, the slash on his hand was scabbing closed. The *cuts* were new: small and shallow, littering his face and hands.

"What the heck happened to *you*?"

Dude shrugged. "So, why'd Anna ask us to meet her here?"

"She didn't tell you either?"

Dude shook his head. Babe shifted to look at his watch. Dude held it up obligingly until Babe leaned back, sighing.

"We're gonna be late for homeroom."

Jules pushed open the door. She was also covered in small healing cuts. She fiddled with her faux-leather jacket zipper, sliding it halfway open, all the way closed. Repeat.

"Can I get a coffee?" she asked a passing waitress as she sat down at their table. "Thanks."

Babe nodded at her cuts. "Should I ask?"

"You should not," Jules said, and paused. "You look calm."

Babe glanced over at Dude, who looked just as clueless. He was slowly shredding a paper napkin into even strips, lining them up on the table in a circle with growing napkin layers.

"Calm about what?" Babe said.

Jules raised one eyebrow. Then, when it became clear he wasn't joking, she raised the other. "Talking with the resurrected baby?"

"Talking with *what*?"

The waitress set a cup of coffee down in front of Jules, who gave her a distracted smile and chugged half of it.

"This might just be the early hour," Dude said, "but did you say we're meeting a baby? A *previously dead* baby?"

"Yes."

Dude paused. "There are no high chairs here. Where will it sit?"

"I hate you," Babe told him.

Dude held his hand out for Jules's coffee. "Can I?"

She slid it over, a fleck of purple nail polish clinging to the rim.

Babe scoffed. "Oh, you ask *her*!"

The diner door swung open. Babe turned. Anna entered first, dressed in a bright yellow shirt she wore when she needed more energy than she felt. Behind her trailed a woman in the gray warehouse uniform. Anna had told Babe she was nineteen, but like many people in Bulldeen, she looked older than her age. Her skin was sallow, her forehead studded with the start of frown lines. There was something exhausted in her posture, like her body was tired from carrying her slight frame around. Her shoulders sagged. Even her long hair was limp. Babe hadn't seen her since she dropped out of Bulldeen High several years back.

Anna pulled two chairs out and sat down. "Guys, this is Milly Hart."

Milly sat gingerly in the other chair, smile tight. Her eyes lit up on Babe, but only for a moment. They looked away at the same time.

"Milly, thank you so much for meeting us."

"'S fine," Milly said. Her lips barely moved when she talked.

Anna held out her hand at Babe like a TV presenter. "Babe's going to be working in the warehouse next month!"

Milly jerked her head in a nod. "Which section?"

"Packaging."

"I work in labeling," Milly said. Each word had to struggle around her teeth. She reached up and tugged at her bangs. Milly didn't go to the town hairdresser. Babe got the feeling she couldn't stand someone touching her head long enough for a haircut.

"You'll be close by," Anna said. She looked at the others beseechingly. They looked helplessly back.

Anna waved the waitress down and everybody got a chipped mug full of instant coffee. Babe held his but didn't drink it. Ever since coming back, warm liquid tasted wrong.

Milly did the same, clutching her cup. This pissed Babe off so much, he held the cup to his lips and tipped it enough that it trickled against his closed mouth.

"Um," Milly said. She was looking at Anna again. "So, do I just…"

"Whenever you're ready."

Milly nodded. Her shoulders came up even further. This pissed Babe off even more, because he could tell this wasn't a situational thing. Milly Hart was constantly uneasy, eternally tensed. He wanted to shake her.

"Um," said Milly again. She tugged at her blunt hair. "I was a kid—like, a for real kid, I didn't know the alphabet yet—so it's all pretty hazy…"

She trailed off, like she was waiting for someone to interrupt. When no one did, she took a deep breath and started again.

"Um, I remember drowning. I think. Maybe I dreamed it after. But I think I remember how much it hurt. Water in my lungs. Then…then my mom. She had dirt on her. I think I had dirt on me too. All of this is just, like, flashes."

The waitress walked by. Milly shut up until she passed. Then she leaned in towards the table. "I was a kid," she repeated, her voice low. "I thought I made it up."

"Made what up?" Dude said.

"The—" Milly looked around again. There was a woman looking their way, but it was just the usual small-town glance of seeing people together who you wouldn't expect.

Milly hugged her own elbows. "The sharp… man. Whatever it is. With the old coat."

"Huh," Dude said. He let go of his coffee and put his hands under the table. Babe didn't need to look to know he was picking fast and vicious at his cuticles. Babe was always trying to get him to stop. He had nice nails, square and pale.

"I think it looked different to me than it did to my mom," Milly said, getting quieter and quieter.

She clicked her throat. Across the diner, a bell pinged,

signaling an order was ready. A cook called through the kitchen for more bread. The woman who had been watching them had given up and was now rolling a boiled egg with the flat of her hand, splintering shell over the table.

Milly wet her cracked lips and looked up. "Have...have you seen it?"

Her slate eyes went timidly from person to person. What kind of therapy did they send her to, after? Did they have therapists for kids that young? If they did, they wouldn't have any in Bulldeen. They'd gotten their first school counselor in 1996, and he was only there three days a week. The other two days, he helped out at the butcher.

Anna asked, "Could you describe it a little more?"

"Yeah," Jules said. "It looks different to different people? Who did it look like to you?"

Milly wilted.

Babe clenched his jaw against an annoyed sigh, even with all the hair on the back of his neck standing up. "What does it do?" Babe said. "Is it what burned down the town hall? Did it take your mother?"

Milly was so stiff it must've hurt. For a moment, Babe ached for her.

Then she made a noise, an almost baby-like gasp, and the irritation was back. *You always do this,* he thought, which was nonsense. He'd never talked to her before.

"I don't know," she said. "I don't know. No one ever told me anything. I just remember..." Her mouth twisted.

"Bodies," Anna said, barely a sound, as if she was trying to mimic Milly's method of barely moving her lips.

Milly's face went slack. Something fell in the kitchen, metal vibrating through the diner. Babe shuddered. Milly's eyes dragged to him, then back to Anna.

"I read the case file," Anna admitted in a whisper.

Babe blinked. What?

"It said there were other bodies? Along with your mother?"

A muscle fluttered in Milly's face. *It must hurt,* Babe thought. *It must actually hurt.*

"That's what I remember," Milly said, so soft Babe had to lean close. "I asked once. They said I dreamed it. It's true?"

Anna hesitated. The waitress passed. Anna nodded.

Another noise jerked from Milly's mouth. She hugged her elbows harder, shoving them inwards. Babe imagined her bones whining, jarring together. *Stop,* he thought. *It hurts.*

Dude picked at his hands under the table. His eyes were big and brown. The swelling from Hunter's punches was going down. Babe had done sketches of Dude's eyes back when he was trying to be an artist. They never turned out right, never captured that wry light, the deep moon that came out if you watched long enough.

Babe had been watching a long time.

"We can stop," Jules said, but Milly talked over her.

"You should get out," she told Babe. Not snarling, not unkind—just desperate. A need for him to understand what she was saying. She let go of her elbow, hand reaching like it was going to cover Babe's on his coffee cup, but then it bolted back to her own arm. "Go somewhere else," she continued, scratching her wrist, which was patchy with dry skin. "Like that old couple who burned the town hall down. Go somewhere you don't know anybody."

Babe's mind raced. "The *thing* you mentioned, the not-person—it kills people?"

Her mouth twisted like a train jumping tracks into a head-on collision. It moved, but no words came out of it. Just choked wheezes. "I—I have to get to work," she forced out. "I'm sorry."

She got up so fast, she stumbled. People looked over as she steadied herself on the table, still mumbling apologies.

Anna grabbed her arm. "Please, it's important."

Milly couldn't speak, didn't meet anybody's eyes, dressed in that awful bland uniform she'd been wearing for years, and Babe loathed her.

Anna rubbed her thumb down Milly's elbow. Milly flinched, but didn't move away.

"The autopsy said there were marks on the bone," Anna said, so fast and so hushed that Babe almost missed it. "On the bodies. Were they bite marks? Were they *your* bite marks, or the thing that isn't a person? What did the note say, the one your mom left?"

More people looked over. Babe felt his mouth pull into a tight smile in their direction. Milly was rigid, cowering, but still she didn't pull away.

"I...gotta...go...to...work," she managed, barely audible through her wheezing.

"Anna," Dude said. "Jesus."

At the next table over, the waitress overflowed a man's coffee as she watched. He slapped her in the arm with his newspaper. Her head whipped around.

Anna let go of Millie's arm. "Oh God. I'm so sorry."

"It's...fine," Milly gasped thinly, still not meeting her eyes. "Bye."

She kept her gaze on the ground and her shoulders at her ears the whole way out. Babe didn't know how she navigated the world like that, always looking down.

Anna sat miserably back in her seat. "Damnit."

"What the hell was *that*?" Jules hissed. "Anna! What were all those weird questions? What note? What *bodies*?"

"How about," Dude said, leaning into their space, "we go

have this conversation somewhere that isn't jammed with people?"

There were nine other people in the diner, not including staff. That counted as packed for the Star and Shine, the only diner in Bulldeen.

seventeen

THEY TOOK the long way to school, around the back of town. Thornfruit fields stretched halfway to Vermont. From here, they looked endless. Babe stayed away from the edges of town for this very reason—when he was a kid, he'd been afraid the fields would steal him away, that he'd be left wandering through the brambles forever.

Dude had the same fear. He had nightmares about it. He'd told Babe about it at a sleepover in fifth grade, tucked in next to him in Dude's bed. There was a sleeping bag for Babe, but they didn't start using it until they were nine, when they started to realize how strange it was for two boys to sleep in the same bed.

Dude walked in step beside Babe along the side street, kicking up gravel. He'd picked two of his cuticles bloody and was sucking on his bleeding fingers. Babe couldn't look at him. His skin itched, heat beating through his throat and down into his stomach. He'd eaten nine pieces of toast for breakfast and none of the slices had done anything to lessen the roaring hunger.

"I can't believe I was so hard on her back there," Anna stressed as the warehouse faded out of sight. "I was so *mean*!"

"Yeah, sure," Jules said. "I *guess* you pressed her pretty hard about the worst thing that ever happened to her. Now, what were you saying about the bodies? Did Aunt Cop actually have the case files lying around the house?"

Anna sighed. "Of course she did. You were right about them covering up the murders that happened with Jessie Hart's suicide."

"So," Jules said, kicking a stone so it went skittering ahead of them. "What, Milly Hart hulked out and ate them?"

"I know it's awful," Dude piped up, voice muffled around his fingers. "But is anyone else having a hard time not laughing at the image of a toddler going feral and eating people?"

Babe stared at him. Dude looked tired. His perpetually bedhead hair hadn't been washed in a few days, that greasy cowlick limp against his forehead. His big shoulders slumped.

The hunger wasn't just in Babe's stomach anymore. It was creeping into the rest of his body. Hungry veins, hungry bones. He looked at Dude and his mouth watered.

He tore his gaze away. "No, Dude, we're not laughing. It's not funny when I have this ticking clock above my head counting down to when *I'm* gonna go feral and start eating people!"

Everybody squirmed.

"Baaaabe," Dude said. He said it in his quoting voice. There was this bad '80s movie where the terrible Boston boyfriend kept getting into fights with his girlfriend and going, *Baaaabe!* when she stormed off.

"Don't *Baaaabe* me," Babe said, suddenly lit up with fury. He had to clench his teeth against it. His head itched. "I'm... what the heck did you *do*, Dude? You had to know something would happen."

"It'll be fine," Dude tried, dropping the Boston accent. "Babe, come on—"

Babe wasn't storming off. He was walking. He was walking very fast and very dramatic. Okay, he was storming off.

"I'm gonna just head away from a highly populated area where I might go manic and kill some students! Hope I don't kill my dad when he gets home, ha *ha*!"

"Babe!" Jules called.

Babe whirled around. "Why aren't you more *worried*?" he yelled at Dude, who was only a few paces behind. Dude always followed.

"I nearly *killed* you," Babe yelled. A truck thundered past them, kicking up gravel. Babe ignored it, raising his voice over the engine. "You could've died!"

Jules and Anna were giving each other confused looks. Babe barely noticed. He was too busy watching the vein pulse in Dude's throat.

Last year, they'd gone to a party and Babe had gotten drunk for the fifth time. Dude had been sitting above him on the stairs cradling a cup of water, and Babe had to look up at him. Drunk on beer and the throbbing music and the way Dude's low laugh pitched high at the end if Babe was funny enough, Babe had leaned into Dude's neck. He'd only stopped when Dude turned, hair brushing Babe's forehead.

What? Dude had said. He'd thought Babe wanted his attention. Which Babe did. He always wanted Dude's attention.

Nothing, Babe had said, throat suddenly dry. He still couldn't be sure what he had wanted at that party. Today, though, the desire was clear: he wanted to sink his teeth in.

Dude's face was grave. He'd been more serious over the past week than Babe had ever seen him.

"Everything's gonna be okay," Dude said, flecks of blood on his cheek left there by his cuticles.

Babe watched the flecks move with Dude's words. Soft

skin under that stubble. Dude had gotten stubble late, only starting in earnest last year. Babe had taught him how to shave. He dreamed of it sometimes, hovering over Dude at the sink, pressing a gentle blade along the foamy hollow of his throat.

Babe blinked. The itch under his skin was sharpening. He bared his teeth. "What if you brought me back wrong? Huh? What then?"

"Come on, you're—"

"Don't bullshit me."

Dude paused. Scratched at his cheek, slow, red flaking off under his nails. Babe watched his face, the unaffected mask slipping into something horrifyingly sincere. Babe expected him to stay silent—if Dude couldn't joke to diffuse this serious situation, surely he wouldn't say anything—but Dude's mouth opened slowly, haltingly, averting his eyes, and Babe was suddenly overcome with terror with what this strange, solemn version of his friend could come out with.

He looked away just in time for Dude to mumble:

"I'd take part of you over none."

Babe shivered. The itch grew until it was all he could do to turn around and walk in the opposite direction, his friends calling after him until their voices, too, were swallowed.

Babe lay on his bed with his headphones. His eyes were closed, knuckles white around his CD player. Music blared as high as it would go, but not high enough. It didn't drown out the howling in Babe's stomach, the howl that sometimes shrunk back but never receded, not since he'd climbed out of the ground and onto his best friend.

His dad came into the room. Babe didn't notice. Ryan

yelled something, but Babe was lost in a world of hunger that no amount of Red Hot Chili Peppers would satisfy.

The headphones were wrenched away. Babe's eyes flew open, and for a moment his body prepared to lunge.

"You didn't go to school today," Ryan said. He had his hands on his hips, and Babe hated him, hated everyone in this dying little town with all its sharp edges. "Mr. Jameson called me," Ryan continued, mustache bristling. "Well? What do you have to say for yourself?"

Babe simmered in the deep rage of every teenager who has been asked to speak, but knows that speaking will only make things worse. It was dwarfed by the much rarer all-consuming hunger.

"What if our bosses hear about this?" Ryan said. His voice rose. "You think they want someone who cuts school? *Losers* cut school, Henry! And then they cut work, they sit around all day drinking and spending taxpayers' dollars—"

A flicker behind Babe's eyes. He blinked hard. Something was growing roots inside him, growing *barbs*. And they weren't going to cut him up, because Babe was turning into a sharp thing himself. *I'd take part of you over none.* How much of him was left? He felt complete. He felt like himself, like he was all of him—*plus* this dark shadow.

He twitched like a bird under a cat claw.

"Are you listening to me, Henry?"

Henry. His name was Henry. What was the other one? *Babe.* The single syllable washed him in a thin layer of control.

"I'm... sorry," he said through bared teeth.

"Oh, you're *sorry*," Ryan sneered, which is what he said when he was in a very bad mood and wanted to goad his son into groveling. Then his face shuttered, winced into itself. He looked down at his son, clenched up on his boyhood bed.

Babe wondered what he was seeing. He was still glitching

in and out of a deep red haze. He could feel his own face twitching. How was his father not staring in horror?

Whatever Ryan saw, it wasn't horrifying. This made sense. Ryan had never seen his son for what he really was.

Music radiated from the headphones on the carpet where Ryan had yanked them from his son's head. Violins ramped up, exploding in a crescendo.

"It's fine," Ryan said, his voice thick in a way that had to mean he was remembering how Babe had died recently. "It's your last few weeks of high school. You should get this teenage hooligan-ness out of your system while you can."

His eyes filled with tears and they both looked away. Neither knew who hated it more when Ryan cried, though at the moment it was Babe, who hated everything. Ryan's tears made him gnash his teeth at his bedspread.

The voice continued above him. *Dad's voice*, he reminded himself, still tunneling in and out. *Dad Dad Dad.* Somehow, this only made the sharp worse.

Ryan's voice floated down through a pinhole. "I can't tell you how glad I am that those bad influences are finally going to leave you alone after this month."

Dad, Babe thought ferociously. *Dad. It's Dad—*

"I'll bet you didn't even want to cut school," Ryan continued. "I'll bet that Eugene boy—"

"Dude," Babe muttered.

"—*whatever.* I bet he talked you into it."

Babe lost time. Flurry of movement. *Oh God.*

Doorframe under his hands. He squeezed and wood splintered off. Ryan was behind him now, saying a name. *His* name, the wrong one.

Babe stumbled down the stairs. More wood came off under his fingers. A support beam snapped when Babe missed his footing and kicked it.

"Henry!" Ryan yelled behind him. "Henry!"

Babe shouldered through the front door.

"I'm going for a *walk!*" he screamed. It was muffled. His tongue was thick. No, his *teeth* were thick. It was hard to keep track of his body.

Get away from people you know, Milly had said.

Babe knew everyone in this goddamn town.

chapter
eighteen

BRIAN "BUZZ" Kettering was writing out a painstakingly neat card to his grandma. A thesaurus sat beside him at his kitchen table. He'd been looking up synonyms for "best" and was now on the second "e" of "supreme" in careful cursive. She always called to yell at him if he didn't write in cursive. *Is my son raising a barn animal?* It was the only time she yelled at him. She had very strong feelings on handwriting.

Buzz didn't mind. He loved his grandma. She'd taught him about their family's proud American history, showed him how to darn his socks, and given him his very first drink at the age of fourteen, a single shot of whiskey that made him go red trying not to cough. Buzz and his parents went out to visit her vacation house every summer. Their next visit was six weeks away. Buzz had it circled on his calendar.

He finished the second "e" and sat back, examining the lettering. Should he try on another card? No, this would do. He tucked it into an envelope and licked around the flap, sealed it, and placed a stamp on the front.

When they got to the vacation house, the first thing he'd do would be show grandma his new tattoo. *None before you're eighteen,* she'd told him, and he'd nodded. When his dad gave him a stick and poke with a sewing needle last year, he kept it hidden under his shirt. It was dumb anyway—a blotchy mermaid with tits that went in opposite directions.

This *new* tattoo, even grandma could be proud of, even if he was underage. He pocketed the envelope and stood in front of his mirror, pushing his left sleeve up to expose his shoulder. Hunter had done it last week and it was still raw: a small, dark swastika. He hadn't shown his parents yet—they'd be twitchy about it. His mom would worry about job interviews. *You know how sensitive those liberals are,* she'd tell him. His dad would hum and nod, but when they were in private, Buzz thought he'd get a clap to his good shoulder. His dad had one on his chest, fuzzy and faded.

Buzz pressed the skin around the tattoo, watched it go white and then red. Moe had fretted when he'd seen it and Buzz called him a wimpy little girl. Moe had gone bright cherry and Buzz jabbed him a little more. Moe was so easy to rile up sometimes. But he always forgave you, even that time when Buzz was too high and slipped during Knifey Fingers. It was nice having friends who forgave you. Not like Hunter.

Buzz shuddered, imagining what Hunter would do to him if Buzz accidentally swiped *him* during Knifey Fingers. Probably take Buzz's thumb off in retribution. The thing about Buzz was, he was mostly talk—nasty talk, talk that sometimes got him jazzed up enough to follow through. But Hunter wasn't interested in talk. Hunter was all action. If he was going to come at you, you wouldn't know it until he was already charging.

Buzz fluttered all ten of his intact fingers, patted the envelope in his pocket, and left to go find a mailbox. He was going to head to the one a block away, but as he turned in that direction, a voice spoke up in his head.

Go to the sewer district and put it in the one near Jules's house. The voice was familiar. Buzz couldn't pick it out from all his usual thoughts, and it was very appealing. It glowed.

The voice whispered some more, and Buzz grinned. He'd go to the one near Jules Havelock's house, then write a message on her garage, one he'd been wanting to write since she'd piped up during a class discussion on gay rights last month.

How can you guys be so hateful? she'd said, her double chin wobbling around her high, grating voice. *They aren't doing anything to you, so why are you so disgusted?*

This was what he thought about as he crossed town into the sewer district. He didn't remember if he'd replied—Moe probably did a fart noise, Hunter probably said something scathing that made her shut up—but he knew now what he should've said.

"We're not hateful," he muttered, scuffing his shoes against the road leading to Jules's house. "We're *proud*. We have something to be proud *of*. They don't. They have—they *are*—something to be gotten rid of, before they take us over."

Buzz thought about that a lot. About getting taken over. The video store had recently been taken over by that Chinese family, so now Buzz only went there to steal stuff.

He turned down Jules's driveway. He walked to the back of the house and around to the garage door, which was locked. He got out a knife from his deepest pocket and grinned. They wouldn't be buffing this one out anytime soon.

We can't let them replace us, his grandma always said. It was his first memory of her: sitting on her lap as she loomed huge above him. Her bald, cherished face saying, *we can't let them replace us. We have to take them out before they take us out.*

Metal groaned around an "F." Buzz glanced around, then started on the "A."

He was connecting the two sides of the "A" when he heard breath.

He turned around. Babe Simmons was standing at the end of the driveway.

Brief panic. Mild delight. What the hell was Babe gonna do about it except stand there all glazed and weird? He looked kinda like that dog with rabies that Buzz's dad had shot. Maybe he'd finally stopped being a pussy and gotten high for once.

"What're you gonna do?" Buzz said, trying to think of what Hunter would do in this situation. He nodded behind him at the garage door, the grooves he'd carved in. "Huh? What're you gonna do, fa—"

Babe rushed him. Buzz barely had time to hold up his hands. In the split second between Babe moving and Babe reaching him, Buzz had time to be confused. It was too fast, inhumanly fast, it didn't make sense—

Nails splitting into his shoulders. Fire in his neck.

Buzz tried to scream, but blood flooded his throat. He gurgled. His eyes widened with horror. The last thing he saw was Babe drawing back with vocal cords wedged in his teeth, their white roots still clinging to the inside of Buzz's throat.

***

Babe woke up. He'd been dreaming about one of those shotgun houses at the edge of the thornfruit fields. In the dream, there was a woman. A daughter. Her father stood in the doorway as she begged him to understand.

We're worse now, she'd told him.

His face hadn't given an inch. *Maybe that's the natural way of things.*

Babe blinked and the dream was gone. It was sunset. The ground was hard under him, all yellow grass and stones. He pushed himself up to his elbows.

"Oh God." His arms were drenched with blood. Pink

flecks stuck to his arm hairs. Babe's stomach churned. He sat up, rolling onto his butt.

Buzz Kettering's dead eyes stared up at him. He was propped up against the garage door, slumping sideways. His throat had been wrenched out. Bits of his jaw were missing, exposing his teeth. A chunk of leg and most of his left arm were gone, including the arm bone.

"Ohhhhh *hell*," Babe moaned, voice breaking. He rubbed his mouth on his shoulder. More blood. He could taste it in his mouth. It tasted...actually, it tasted okay. Nice, even. Better than nice.

He slapped himself hard.

"Focus," he hissed. He stood up on shaky legs. "Okay. Okay, where am I?"

He turned around. Jules's backyard. Why were they in Jules's backyard? At least they were away from the street. Had something happened to Jules? God, please don't let something have happened to Jules.

He glanced behind him. Dead body. Garage door with "FA" carved in it. Two guesses what *that* word was gonna be.

Babe considered the driveway. Then he went to the porch and knocked on the back door. He left red smudges, which he rubbed off with a clean bit of sleeve. As he rubbed, blood dripped off his fingers and onto the welcome mat. He swiped at it with one sneaker. It smeared.

"Jules," he whispered, heart thumping. Another knock. "Jules!"

Nothing. He went for the knob.

Jules's house was quiet and cool. Babe stepped in on tiptoes, every muscle tensed. As he closed the door behind him, Jules came back-first out of the hallway. Babe breathed a sigh of relief. Jules had headphones on, CD player in her pocket, wiggling her big butt in neon green boxers. She danced in a circle. Babe braced as she turned to him, but her eyes were closed. She was flossing her teeth and dancing and singing.

"Jules! Hey, *Jules!*"

More little circles. She was jumping now.

Babe waved his arms from the door. There was carpet in the hallway and he didn't want to drip on it.

Jules opened her eyes, mid-twirl. She came to a stop facing the door and recoiled, screaming, floss wedged in the back of her mouth.

"*I know I know! Please shush!*" Babe yelled back.

"Oh my God! Oh shit!" Jules ripped the floss out, took her headphones off. She made to drop them and then bent to carefully place them on the ground with the CD player. "What *happened*? Are you okay?"

She ran at him. Babe held up his hands to ward her off.

"We need to wipe the doorknob and the floor I'm standing on and also the porch and the yard," he said in a rush. "I got blood on it."

Jules looked him up and down, face twisting with horror. "Is it *your* blood?"

"No, I—I—" he dropped to a whisper. "Buzz is dead in your backyard. How did you not *notice*?"

"I was singing along," Jules said disparagingly, wringing her hands. Her gaze kept flitting away from Babe, as if not wanting to look at the blood for too long. She took several quick breaths, calming herself. "Shit! Okay, show me... ugh, show me the body."

Babe was turning towards the door before he remembered. "Where are your parents?"

Jules waved him down. "They're on a day trip. We have a couple hours before they get back. Go!"

Babe led her out to the backyard. Buzz was still slumped

underneath his handiwork. Babe averted his gaze and found Jules doing the same.

Babe swallowed. "I don't remember all of it. But I think I... saw him down the street and followed him here."

"And then ate him," Jules said softly. Her hand was over her mouth. "Are you, like...full, now?"

As soon as Babe thought about it, he realized what was missing: the cavernous, overwhelming hunger. It was gone. In its place was a deep satisfaction, a well of energy waiting to be tapped into, just like that first night.

They stood in the dying light, arms crossed, surveying the mess.

Jules inched around the body and felt at the grooves in the garage door. "This is going to be a bitch to fix."

"We have a buffer," Babe said. "You can borrow it."

"Thanks," Jules said.

They were motionless a while longer, thinking. Eventually Babe spoke up.

"Should we call somebody?"

nineteen

DUDE LOOKED up from the living room couch as the front door opened, a bag of corn chips in his lap and a hammer beside him. He tucked the hammer under a couch cushion.

Katherine Marsh came in the door and dropped her keys on the table like she did everything else: distracted and very, very tired. She was still in her hospital scrubs. The hospital was an hour out of Bulldeen.

Dude waited. Katherine headed into the kitchen and opened the fridge. Dude listened to the fridge door unstick. It was impossible not to: there was no wall separating them. The pop of a beer being uncapped. Glug of the bottle being drained.

Dude waited for the bottle to connect with the counter. This meant he was allowed to talk.

"Hey, Mom."

A spoon scraped. Katherine was eating yogurt out of the tub. "Did I leave enough money for food?"

"Yeah," Dude said, as he did every week.

The yogurt lid snapped shut, then the fridge. More glugging.

"Why didn't you tell me Babe isn't dead anymore?"

Dude froze, hand in the corn chip bag. He extracted one and crunched. "Did you just find out?"

"No, I found out on Sunday." In a truly uncharacteristic move, she rounded the couch and flopped down on the cushion next to her son. In a very characteristic move, she was holding a new beer.

"I was going to mention it," she sighed. She looked at him sideways, the only way she ever looked at him. "Do I need to worry about anything?"

Dude shook his head.

She cracked a smile. They had similar smiles, only hers had decades of weariness making it droop at the corners. "You won't burn down the town hall?"

"No," Dude said. He shoved another chip in his mouth. It made the conversation less heavy, eating corn chips, not looking at each other. "You don't have to worry about anything. Babe didn't come back, he was just—never dead."

She didn't say anything for a second. Dude was very aware of the hammer wedged between his thigh and the couch arm.

"Dude," she said. She hadn't called him Eugene for years. "I declared his time of death in the hospital. *That* was a dead body."

Dude's throat narrowed to a pinhole. He didn't ask why she hadn't told him. She didn't tell him anything. Not out of malice. They just weren't the kind of family that talked.

"Well," he said faintly, making his smile go toothy. "He got better."

She gave him an amused look. It had a hint of incredulity, the way she looked at him when he pulled some stunt as a kid. *Oh, you brought a running hose into the house? You painted the walls? Of course you did.*

There was something under the amusement, the incredulity. Dude didn't dig for it.

She shifted, as if about to sag into the couch. Dude waited. Maybe she'd lay her head on his shoulder.

But she only sighed and pushed herself to her feet like walking was a chore she was dreading. She took another pull of beer, four long swallows that made her gasp for breath when she came back up. She didn't have a lot of free time. She had to drink fast.

"I'm going to bed," she announced.

Dude nodded. It was seven-thirty. He ate another chip, sucked orange dust off his fingers. He winced on the ones where he'd picked too hard at the cuticles. He'd been meaning to stop doing that. Babe always hounded him about it, and it was one of their less fun fights because it wasn't a gag—Dude really did try to stop.

She padded down the hall, stopping to grab a six-pack. Her bedroom door opened and closed. There would be no noise from her room—she'd drink four more beers, hit the mattress, and be dead to the world. Sometimes she didn't even take off her shoes. Sometimes he would take them off for her.

Dude rolled the chip bag closed, dusted off his hands. He reached down to pull the hammer out into the open. It looked like nothing in his hand. Metal and plastic. He'd fixed the back porch with this hammer, his mom coming out and giving him lemonade. She'd been working part-time after an injury. Babe used to come around in the morning to watch cartoons. Anna would join in most days when she didn't have chores, and Jules would join when she wasn't searching for a job. That summer between freshman and sophomore year had been the best of Dude's life.

He got up. Thought about calling Jules. No, the fewer people he got involved, the better. She could help with the next one.

He stepped into his right shoe. The other one was suspiciously absent. He was nudging around the living room when the phone rang. He skipped, one foot bare, to the landline next to the fridge and took it off the hook with the hand that wasn't holding a hammer.

"Hello, this is—"

"You gotta come over to Anna's right now."

"Jules?" Dude flexed his fingers around the hammer. "What's wrong?"

"Uhhh." Jules trailing off into a high pitch. "I'll tell you when you get here. Come right now."

"Okay," Dude said. "Yeah, I'll be there. Seriously, what's—"

But he was talking to a dial tone.

"Rude," Dude said, and limped towards the front door to change into his sandals, of which he definitely had two.

He brought the hammer along in the glove box. He shoved a small, sharp vegetable knife in with it for good measure. Jules sounded the dangerous kind of stressed.

She flung open the door before his second knock. Her hand flashed out, grabbing his shirt and dragging.

"Whoa," he said. "Alright, I'm coming! What's up?"

"Dude's here we're gonna hang in the dog pen good niii-ight," Jules called to Anna's parents, who waved from the kitchen. Dude got maybe a second to wave while they were in view. He was still being dragged.

"What's in the dog pen?" Dude whispered.

Jules opened the back door into the dog pen. The backyard was half yard, half fenced-in area for the dogs to run around. Most of the dogs chewed eagerly at meaty bones. Anna was pacing in circles away from them, frowning, a golden retriever following her around excitedly. Babe was—

Dude snorted. "What are you wearing? I thought you were gonna go into packaging, not into the fields, Mr. Farmer Man."

Babe scowled. He was standing in the corner next to Anna, wearing jeans so baggy he was holding them up, and an equally baggy plaid shirt. Dude had never seen him in plaid before. Babe was strictly a T-shirt kind of guy.

"They're Jules's dad's clothes," he said.

"Why?"

"Because," Babe said, and hesitated. He looked down towards the dogs chewing on bones, pursing his lips. "Um. So, I...Buzz is dead."

"What?" Dude processed. "Wait, *what?*"

"Jules gave me clean clothes," Babe continued, thin arms crossed tight across his plaid shirt. "Since mine were—y'know, all bloody."

Dude swarmed with questions. "Did you *eat* him?"

Babe's worried eyebrows intensified. He adjusted his folded arms. "Some of him."

"Where's the rest?"

Babe looked at the ground. No, not the ground. The dogs were tearing meat off bones. Dude peered closer at them.

"Oh," he said, and swallowed against a sudden urge to vomit. He stepped towards his friends. *That* was why they were crowding in the corner.

Babe watched him anxiously.

Dude swallowed again. "Well, that's one way to do it. Why didn't you finish him off?"

Babe sighed. "After I came out of my—my fugue state, he wasn't that appealing."

"Fair 'nuff. He wasn't that appealing when he was alive."

A laugh slipped out of Babe's mouth. He swiped a hand

over it, pulling at his slight lips. They were pinker than the last time Dude saw him. He looked healthier. More alive.

"You're feeling better?"

"Yeah," Babe said quietly. "Much."

He didn't look happy about it.

The door opened. Everybody stiffened.

"Act casual," Dude hissed.

Chief Higgins stepped onto the grass. She raised her eyebrows at the teenagers clustered in the corner doing terrible casual poses, the dogs blissfully happy and crowding around a pile of meat in the other half of the pen.

"Right," Kate said, in her *don't wanna know* voice. She fixed her gaze on Anna, who hunched further into her casual pose. It involved her hands being on her hips, something her friends had never seen her do before.

"Granddad wants us to meet him near his motel," she said quietly, mindful of the parents back in the house.

Anna fell out of her casual pose. "What? He's here?"

"Just outside of town." Kate turned back. She stopped in the doorway, framed by the light, looking back at the teenagers standing shock-still in the night. "The rest of you coming or what?"

twenty

GRANDDAD MICHAEL HIGGINS looked like a corpse. It wasn't unexpected—he was ninety-four, after all. He had the trademark unhealthy Higgins pallor, slits for eyes, and he seemed very uncomfortable sitting up at nine p.m. in the twenty-four-hour diner ten miles outside of Bulldeen. It was right next to his motel, where his tiny Volkswagen was parked. Dude eyed it from the window. He'd done a bad parking job, all lopsided, but it wasn't like that parking lot was going to fill up anytime soon.

Dude sat up straighter in the diner booth. It was a tight squeeze; him, Babe and Jules crammed onto one side, Anna and the olds squeezed into the other. Dude kept a subtle eye on Babe, who had shuddered as they crossed the town line.

What's wrong? Kate had asked from the driver's seat.

Nothing, Babe had said, too fast. But he didn't look like he was about to snack on anyone, so Kate hadn't gone for her gun. She had a hand on it under the table.

Dude really hoped she wouldn't have to use it. He didn't want to jump in front of a bullet.

Dude was wedged in between Babe and the wall. The wood was unyielding on one side, the warm press of Babe was its usual level of overwhelming on the other. They rarely got this physically close after they turned eleven, when sharing a bed or play-fighting started to get dangerous instead of just frowned upon. The last time he'd had this much of Babe pressed up against him, other than when Babe was feral and snarling, was when Babe was drunk. Babe was a clingy drunk, and Dude had had to scale back his deep need into weary fondness.

Dude cleared his throat. "Your elbow's cutting into my spleen."

Babe moved it.

"It's still cutting. So deep, the cutting."

Babe threw up his arms. "Point to your spleen, Dude! I will get down on my knees and eat this entire table if you know where your spleen is."

Dude's finger roamed vaguely over his whole torso. "Spleen."

Jules checked Dude's watch. "Do we know how long this is gonna take? My cousin's at a gig right now, he was going to hold out the phone for me to hear."

Anna frowned. "This is important."

"I know. Just..." Jules folded her arms. "Just wanted to ask."

Anna kept frowning. Dude bumped her foot under the table and Anna looked embarrassed, as she always did when she thought she was being irrational. Dude didn't know how irrational she was being—Jules loved them, but she loved LA too. The gigs, the crowds, the people. She'd had a lot of friends back there. "Party friends," she called them, dismissive, but Jules was the kind of girl who made friends easily. Dude could picture her with a whole new group after a few months. She'd still be around, but the Bulldeen crew would no longer be her one and only.

Anna still looked troubled. Dude pressed hard into her

ankle, and Anna sent him an embarrassed smile. Dude smiled back.

He wasn't the only one smiling at her. Monica Higgins's eyes were soft, lined with age. The rest of her was severe, all hard cheekbones and slashing eyebrows. She had no makeup, no nail polish.

"So our boy married that Raeburn girl," Monica said to Anna. "Or did the Hallards have a daughter?"

Anna smiled, only a little strained. The Raeburns and the Hallards were two of the only Black families in Bulldeen.

"No, my mom is Lynn Raeburn."

"I remember her." Monica laid a hand on her husband's shoulder. He didn't look up from his coffee. "Mike, do you remember that little girl with all those library books? One time, Greg was crying over that baby bird he found in the park and she came over to help it. Poor thing still died."

She patted Anna's hand. "She was beautiful. So are you."

"Thank you," Anna said quietly, tucking a curl behind her ear. She was nervous, Dude realized. He didn't think she would be. She always seemed so confident. He sometimes forgot she was the same age as him.

Monica motioned at Jules. "And who are you, miss?"

"Me?" Jules was tearing half a napkin to shreds. "I'm new. I'm from LA."

"Always good to get new blood in town," Monica said, as if she still lived there. Jules sucked her lips back into her teeth. This was not a common opinion in Bulldeen.

"And you boys—Kate's already told us of you."

Moonlight struck the window, straight into Dude's eyes. He adjusted the curtain.

Michael spoke up, his voice thin and reedy. "Your father tried to steal shoes from my shop when he was half your age," he told Babe, who blinked. "Burst into tears the second I talked to him. I just said hello! Then I told him as gentle as I could to please put the shoes back, and he pleaded for me to not tell anyone, to just let him have them. He cried and cried until I made it clear he wasn't getting out of that shop with those shoes. Then, like magic, he stopped. Put the shoes back on the shelf. Slunk out of the store. Strange thing."

Babe's mouth opened and closed. He looked over at Dude, who took a handful of Jules's napkin shards and emptied them onto his wrist.

"Cut it out," Babe said, shaking the paper off and turning his face away. His smile was reflected back in the window, and Dude had to turn away to his own. Babe's leg was so warm against his, his elbow a hard press, their shoulders so tight against each other it made Dude think back to Babe rumpled and feral on top of him; the unrelenting, incredible press. Dude had had KJ's hands on his bare back, his thighs, and he'd never felt anything half as good as Babe pushing Dude into the dirt. In Dude's dreams the snarl was gone, replaced by a sly smile. *You love this, don't you?*

Yes, dream-Dude replied, every time.

Babe's smile would grow knowing. *Say please.*

Jules's foot knocked into his, eyebrows raised in question. Dude blinked. Right.

Anna cleared her throat quietly. "Speaking of parents, mine were very concerned to hear that I was heading out this late and they'd like me back before midnight."

"Of course," said Michael. He pushed his sleeves up to his elbows and Dude had a lightning strike of memory of Kate doing the same thing the morning after he got arrested, before she told him the story of her first time getting drunk. *Self destruction,* she'd said, *is a town-wide hobby in Bulldeen.* Dude had thought this was a strangely narrow view. The world was full of small towns.

"So," Michael said, and hesitated. His tongue pressed out over his wrinkled lips. God, he was old. Dude couldn't imagine ever being so old. He always imagined he'd die young.

"I apologize," Michael said. "This is not a story I've ever told."

"Take your time, honey," said Monica, her voice like balm.

Dude checked Babe's reflection in the window. No twitching so far.

"Actually," Kate said. "We're kind of on a time limit. We were hoping you could tell us how tight that limit is."

Michael shifted uncomfortably. "Well, I'm not exactly an expert."

"You and Grandma are the best experts we got."

"Right," Michael said haltingly. "Well—I still don't have the whole picture. I think we had the pieces—that brawl between the Rotguts and the Jessups, I'm sure that was part of it. And perhaps the boiler that exploded the high school."

Everybody stared at him.

"Wait," Anna said. "What does that have to do with the resurrections?"

Monica took his hand, weaved their fingers together. They were a different kind of wrinkled—his were coarse, deep, while hers had the quality of fine linen.

"Perhaps just stick to our story," she told him. "Rather than getting into the thick of things."

He nodded, face going determined.

"We were in a car crash. An animal—we never figured out what it was, it was so oddly shaped, like—"

"Honey."

"Right. It darted into the street. We swerved into a power pole at sixty miles an hour. I survived with just a broken arm. But Monica's lungs were crushed. She died before the ambulance got there."

The coffee machine bubbled behind the empty counter. Some shuffling in the kitchen. Dude wondered if he could excuse himself to sit in the car. He didn't want to hear the story. He knew where it ended.

Monica sighed, rubbing her husband's thick fingers. "Michael had found a ritual back when he was working at the library."

"We thought you started it."

Monica shook her head. Her husband gripped her hand and she gripped back, skin going even whiter. "The ritual mentioned a price," she continued. "But whatever it was, he was willing to pay it. So he brought me back."

"And then?"

Monica looked towards her husband.

He sighed, a heavy echo of her own sigh just a minute before. "There was this...creature," he began. "It came to me and explained what must happen."

Dude closed his eyes.

"What must—?"

"Death. Much of it. Monica would have to consume people."

"Eat them."

"Yes. We tried to leave town, but Monica didn't last a day before her heart started to give out. We barely made it back to town in time."

The rest of them looked at Babe, alarmed. Dude resisted the urge to take Babe's wrist to check his pulse.

"Um," Babe said, eyes wide.

Michael waved a hand dismissively, then placed it back on his wife's. "We'll only be here an hour, you'll be fine."

"The creature," Kate prompted.

"It will complete the killings if you do not," Michael said. "But it wants you to give in. To consume."

"So you burned down the town hall."

"We trapped them inside. We made up a fake story about —" he glanced at Anna "—about chasing the nonwhites out of town. But only to ten people. Eight showed up. I barred the doors and lit the flame as Monica..."

He trailed off. Music came on in the speakers overhead, playing a tinny love song Dude remembered his mother swaying along to, alone in the kitchen, a very long time ago. *Anything for you, my—*

"Ate them," Kate finished. "Right. Does it need to be eight people?"

He made a dubious noise. "It needs to be enough for fullness. To end the hunger."

"Which is how many people, exactly? Yours had eight. In the next case, we had six. We've only had one murder this time." Kate nodded at Babe. "By the way, Leroy Child—was that you? Don't give me that face," she said when he blanched. "I won't turn you in. I just need to know how deep to bury it."

"I didn't do it," Babe said, too slow. Like he had something else on his mind. He tugged at his baggy, borrowed shirtsleeves. His jaw flexed. "So...the ritual says you need to kill people to bring one person back? It's clear about that?"

Dude folded his arms tight across his chest. *Stop warding yourself,* his mother used to tell him, but he'd never grown out of the habit.

"Actually," Michael said, "It's quite vague about how many people. At first, I thought it required a trade. A life for a life."

"But it still said you had to kill someone."

"Yes."

Babe turned to Dude, eyes bright and very, very pissed off. "What the heck."

"I have terrible reading comprehension," Dude tried.

Babe slapped the table, making their cup of cutlery jump.

"Dude! You can't just—did you even think this through? Or did you just do what you always do—la la, everything will be fine, let's just do whatever we want and not think about the consequences!"

Dude couldn't look at him. He trained his gaze on Kate, who was eyeing the kitchen. The doors were still closed, but there was movement behind them.

Kate said, "How about we quiet down?"

Dude lowered his voice. "I did think it through. I thought it was only one person, like he said."

"So what, you picked out some guy—"

"What was I supposed to do?"

"Not pick a guy to murder! God! Who was it? Who'd you pick? Leroy Child? That's real nice, Dude. What were you gonna do when it became clear one wouldn't cut it?"

"Well, I was *gonna* kill Buzz, but it looks like you beat me to it."

Jules laughed, loud and fake. "There is a cop right here!"

"Hello, missus waitress," Anna yelled over everyone.

The table fell silent. The waitress shuffled towards the table, coffee pot in hand. She was old and had a bum leg. Her smile was warm.

"How are you folks doing tonight?" she asked, voice thick as molasses.

A mumble went around the table. *Good.*

"Your fries will be out shortly," she said, and held up the coffee pot. "Can I interest you folks in any more?"

"No, thank you," Anna said, trembling at a fever pitch. She tugged at a tight curl, let it bounce back into place, tugged at it again.

The waitress nodded. Dude checked her name badge. Penny. Dude used to call his GI Joe's imaginary girlfriend

Penny. His mom didn't let him get a Barbie, but he didn't like to picture his GI Joe alone.

Penny turned around and shuffled back to the kitchen. It took another ten seconds, during which Dude stared down at a scratch in the table. A circle, almost. Dude scratched until it was a whole one.

The kitchen door eased closed.

Babe's voice was low. "What were you gonna do, Dude? Once you knew?"

"I had a plan."

"What? What plan?"

"Maybe we should be quieter," Jules muttered.

Dude talked over her. "I had a deal with the—the thing, okay? I was gonna get people mostly dead and then the thing would eat 'em and you'd stop feeling hungry for man meat."

Babe stared. The rest of the table followed suit. Except for Jules, who busied herself with her glass of water, squeaking her finger along the rim.

"So—" Babe pinched the bridge of his nose. "You're just gonna murder people 'til the zombie in me goes to sleep?"

Dude thought about it. "Yeah."

"What the hell kind of plan is that? You're just gonna kill poor homeless guys until—"

"Jesus, I didn't pick the homeless guy." Dude went to cross his arms again, then stopped. Babe's elbow was a sharp point in Dude's side, their knees jumbled together as Babe twisted to face him. Dude wanted to keep that for a little while longer.

He took a breath. "I picked me. Okay? If I couldn't get out of it, it would just be me and then it'd be over."

Kate grunted. She'd been examining the windows since the waitress left. Dude couldn't blame her. Too much confrontation in this diner booth.

Babe's face wavered from anger to confusion to hurt. It

stayed in the hurt, bright and awful and so beautiful it made Dude ache.

"You—?" he said, in a very small voice. "What?"

Dude glanced towards the kitchen door. Come to think of it, he could really go for that cup of coffee.

chapter
twenty-one

THE FRIES CAME. They ate them in a dazed silence occasionally broken by Dude going, "Could everyone quit looking at me like that?"

Anna tried to start up a conversation about what work her great-grandparents did. Babe shut her down with, "Who cares where they *work*, Anna? God!"

Babe chewed strips off his nails. He didn't bother with the fries. Dude sat next to him, the tight space pressing their sides together. Their knees touched. Babe wanted to punch him. Babe wanted to eat him up. Babe wanted—

By the time they got out to the car, he was ripping out his cuticles with his teeth.

Dude noticed the three feet of distance he'd put between them as soon as they'd cleared the booth. He leaned against Kate's car and snorted. "How the tables turn."

Babe turned on him.

Dude raised his shoulders. For a moment, it only made Babe madder, then he was overcome by an emotion he didn't want to look at. He never did.

"Look," Dude started. "I wasn't gonna just lie down and

say *alright, put your teeth in me,* I had a plan to get me out of it."

"What was that?"

Dude hesitated. "Remember that scene where Bill and Ted play chess with death?"

Babe climbed in the cop car and slammed the door.

Dude stayed outside. Babe pressed his forehead up to the window, forcing back tears and watching the Higgins family. They were standing around the only other car in the motel parking lot, Grandpa and Grandma Higgins clasped together, and the other two standing a safe distance apart from them and each other.

Kate's stiff arms took a second to come up and pat her grandparents on the backs. Babe wound down the window and Kate's voice floated through.

"Why not get in touch?"

"We thought it was safer," Grandpa Higgins wheezed. "And even if we'd tried, your parents cut us off after what happened."

"They thought it was an aberration," added Grandma Higgins.

They were standing shoulder to shoulder now, knotted into each other, her arm around his elbow. He held her close by the waist, his fingers pressing comfortably into the material of her dress, fabric and skin bending under his light pressure.

Babe's throat clicked, the sound echoing around the empty car. The miracle of putting your arm around someone's waist.

He wound the window up and rubbed his forehead against the glass. Weariness was really setting in now. Sweat pooled at his temple, his knees, the base of his neck. His heart beat slow and then slower still. He thought of checking Dude's watch.

Dude still hadn't gotten into the car. When Babe checked through the tinted, warped screen of the back window, he was unmoving. Was Dude looking at him? He wondered if the warped glass made Babe look like a strange creature, body jutting out in inhuman and unnatural ways. *They thought it was an aberration.*

The back seat door opened. Jules climbed in and budged over to the middle seat next to Babe.

He kept looking out the window. Jules was his friend and he'd miss her terribly when she left for LA, but they didn't spend a lot of time together one on one. They didn't have many deep talks. That happened with Anna or Dude.

But when she reached out and took his hand, it felt like the equivalent of an hour of late night talking he'd never forget. He squeezed on her hold and she squeezed back. He didn't look away from the window. Eventually, Kate and Anna started walking back to the car. They got into the front seats. Dude got into the back.

A knock on Babe's window. Monica waved.

"I'll be seeing you," she said.

Babe frowned. "Sorry?"

She stepped away from the car, walking back to her husband. Babe watched them wave from the asphalt, smaller and smaller until they vanished into the distance.

The glass was cool on Babe's forehead. He drifted, warm and tired, towards sleep.

"How're you feeling?" Anna asked, and he assured her in a slurred voice that he was fine. Midnight crept close and his heart beat slower. Slower.

They ripped through the town lines. The town sign declared, *WELCOME TO BULLDEEN.*

Babe's eyes jolted open, heart rate kicking back into gear.

"What?" Kate said from the driver's seat. She was watching him in the rearview mirror.

Babe gritted his teeth. "Stop the car."

"Why? What's wrong?"

"Stop the car!"

They skidded to a stop. Everyone jerked forward in their seatbelt except Dude, who rarely wore one despite all his safety talk when experimenting with stunt work. He slammed into the back of Anna's seat and fell back, groaning.

"That's what happens when you don't obey basic car safety rules," Babe fumed. He unlocked his seatbelt to climb out into the dry grass, stalking away from the car.

Dude followed. Anna got out of the car, too, but she lingered at the door.

"What's up?" Dude called. "Babe, you feeling okay?"

Babe turned on him. Dude flinched, and Babe couldn't blame him. His shoulders were down like he was about to charge, and he had no idea what his face looked like. If he did, he might've tried to hide the angry tears which had surged back up.

"How could you DO this?" he yelled. "You were gonna just —what? I'd wake up and find you dead? How the heck would I live with myself?"

"Babe..." Dude's hands opened and closed. His cuticles were bleeding again, just like Babe's. Twin wounds.

Babe couldn't meet his eyes. "I can't be in a car with you! I'm going home." He started to storm off, then he spun back. "I don't have to eat anyone for a few days, right?"

Kate craned her head out the car window, chewing nicotine gum. "Ayuh."

"Great," Babe said, and turned around to storm some more.

"Babe!" Kate called. Babe stopped. "All of y'all gotta come over to mine tomorrow. Midday."

Babe laughed, a little hysterical. "Are you gonna kill me?"

"Nah. That wouldn't do anything. Energy's already been used to bring you back, more people would still need to die. We're gonna kill *other* people." She spat the gum into the grass, a spot of gray against the yellow.

Babe stared at her.

She lifted her eyebrows. "You still walking home?"

"Yes," Babe said lamely, his voice squeaking, and he set off into the night.

The thornfruit brambles stretched out into oblivion. Babe used to think they were the whole world, those fields. That Bulldeen was the only real place and everywhere else was just thornfruit.

He walked alongside the wire fence. Reached out and snapped off the top of a plant. Or, he tried to. The stem clung. Babe yanked. It peeled down, but didn't detach.

Babe threw it out of his hold, disgusted. Of course the fruits below it didn't dislodge. They stayed stuck to the stem, growing fat on Bulldeen poison.

"I hate you," Babe told the field. "You taste like dirty underwear."

The field was silent.

Babe screamed. It echoed out and out and out.

Behind him, a laugh. Babe whirled, thinking of creatures and teeth.

Hunter leaned against a lamppost, arms crossed over his *Evil Dead* shirt. "Hey, dead freak."

Babe's first instinct was to pull himself in, make himself a smaller target. His second was to look around, check if anyone was there. As he was pulling in his elbows, about to glance around, his head itched. An odd calm washed over him. It was a satisfying calm, the kind right before the storm.

Babe's shoulders settled. He met Hunter's gaze solidly.

Hunter's smile twitched. He cocked his head. Babe was behaving uncharacteristically unlike a prey animal.

When Babe spoke, his voice came out just as calm as his eyes. "Beat it, Hunter."

The smile came back, spreading oil-slick slow across Hunter's face. It wasn't tremble-excited, like Moe's would have been. It wasn't delighted, like Buzz's. Hunter's smile was quietly curious, ready to turn to a snarl at the slightest provocation. Ready to lunge. "Yeah?"

"Yes," Babe said.

"Gonna make me, Zombabe?"

Another itch. Babe's mouth opened, twitching, exposing his teeth. A voice not unlike his came out razor sharp. "Why don't you push me and see, Hunt?"

Hunter's head cocked further. For a moment, he leaned forwards, trying to glimpse something familiar. His heart beat faster, preparing for the fight—

And then squeezed, stuttered, began to beat slow again.

"Not yet," he said.

Neither Babe nor Hunter were sure who was more surprised.

Hunter raised an unconscious hand to scrape at the back of his flaring head. "Me and Buzz will see you soon, freak. Then you're back in the ground."

This cut through the calm. Babe frowned. Buzz? Did Hunter suspect?

"That's what you *get*," Hunter continued, and turned to

head into the thornfruit fields. He vanished instantly into the stalks.

Babe watched him disappear. He looked down, almost expecting his body to look different, but there he was: skinny chest, long thin arms, gangly legs. He flexed his hands at his sides, power surging through him. So at ease, so confident, that he didn't even think to be scared at the sudden appearance of the feelings.

He took a bracing breath. Suddenly the thornfruit fields surrounding him didn't look so bad.

As that thought settled, something deeper broke through. Babe from an hour ago reared his head—Babe who would've turned tail from Hunter and run. Babe who had never met Hunter's gray eyes on purpose, not once in all his life.

That power flooded out of him, replaced by a shaky confusion. He was so busy being confused, he didn't notice the figure behind him until it spoke.

"Looks like I might not be necessary."

Babe shrieked, spinning around.

The sharp, elongated almost-Ryan smiled down at him. "If you do it in enough time," it continued.

Babe pressed a hand to his racing chest. "Why—why the time limit?"

It gave him a puzzled look. Like Babe was supposed to understand. "Hunger can't be ignored," it said. "Wait too long and it takes over."

Babe licked the back of his teeth. He'd scrubbed for ten straight minutes and he could still taste copper. Sometimes it made his mouth water.

"I almost got in a fight with Hunter."

"You've fought him before."

"No, *he* fought *me* before. I just lay there and got hit." Babe was shaking again, an all-over quiver he tried to clamp down on, to control, but the fear from his confrontation with Hunter was finally trickling in. Hunger wasn't the only thing that took over if you ignored it for too long.

It took all Babe had to look the creature in the face. He wished it didn't look so much like his dad.

"What did you do? This—it's not me."

"It could be," the creature said quietly. "I don't invent. I just...emphasize."

Babe swallowed. "Well, quit it!" It came out like a snarl, the sharpness from before leaking back.

The creature grinned, exposing all its teeth. "There. Isn't that satisfying? Wouldn't it be so much easier to give in?"

Babe didn't answer. He started to walk away, backward, so he could keep an eye on the thing. It stayed where it was. After a few steps, so did Babe.

"Were you here before the town?"

A slow head shake.

"What...birthed you, then?"

It tilted its head, considering. Held up its hands as if checking its nails. "Bulldeen is a bad place," it said. "Some places, they get bad enough to make something out of it."

"Something like you?"

But Babe was speaking to empty air. He checked over his shoulder and then all around, but neither the creature nor Hunter were anywhere to be seen.

Babe stood there until he stopped shaking.

It was almost two by the time he got in the front door. Ryan, of course, was sitting on the couch with the living room light on. He followed Babe down the hall, yelling about how worried he was, how he'd called the police, how could Babe do this to him?

Babe mumbled apologies and waited for him to tire himself out. After Ryan got to the crying stage of anger, he told Babe he hoped Babe was happy and that he didn't want to look at him right now. Babe went gratefully into his room and collapsed into bed. He fell asleep with his shoes on.

A baby was yelling. As the light spot faded, Babe took in the room —he was standing in a narrow, grimy hallway.

The cries were coming from the living room.

Full of dread, Babe walked in.

Blacked out windows. Moth-eaten carpet. Small mattress next to the dead TV. The baby—no, a small child—stood up in the crib, sobbing. Its wails were strange. The way it stood was strange. Babe couldn't work out what it was.

"It's okay," Babe said.

The child's cries hitched. It—she, the child had a bow in her scraggly hair—looked over at him. Her shoulders were oddly stiff.

"You're alright," he told her, coming forward. He stopped at the side of the mattress. He'd never been good with kids. "You're..."

He trailed off. Took another look around the room. Had he been here before? He didn't think so. But it tugged at him, at his heart and his brain and his deep hunger.

The toddler sniffed. Its lips came together.

"Babe," she said. No childish babbling. A child who had been speaking for a lifetime.

"Oh God, that's weird," Babe heard himself say. He squinted. The way she held her mouth, her shoulders, unnaturally tight—

"*Milly?*"

Milly wiped at her face. She was standing too easily, that was what it was. An adult in a child's body.

"*Sorry,*" *she said quietly.* "*I'm really overwhelmed.*"

"*That's okay,*" *Babe said.* "*I mean, it makes sense. Is this your mom's house?*"

Milly nodded.

"*Okay,*" *Babe said, voice cracking on the end of it. A memory formed at the edges of his mind.* "*I met the thing you talked about. The...wrong thing.*"

Milly's small throat worked. She wore a faded purple onesie with a Teletubby on the stomach.

"*What did it say?*"

Babe struggled to remember. This was a dream. The rules still stood.

"*Bulldeen is a bad place.*"

"*Yes,*" *Milly said.* "*We know.*"

Babe's hands twitched anxiously towards her. "*Should I get you out of here?*"

"*No. I don't know.*" *Down the hall, the front door opened. The sound of a struggle. A man's muffled yelling.* "*Mom's coming. She has someone else for me.*"

"*Oh God,*" *Babe said. His nostrils flared. The man in the hall was bleeding heavily.* "*Come on.*"

He started to scoop her up, but she backed away.

"*That's not how it happens,*" *she said.* "*I don't...we shouldn't...*"

"*It's a dream,*" *Babe said desperately.* "*It doesn't matter!*"

Everything in him screamed to get out. Everything except something that existed inside him, but was not him. It was small and sharp but sometimes it got very, very big, enough to block out the rest of him. That part told him to stay.

"*Go,*" *Milly said.*

"I can't just leave you here!"

"You aren't here," Milly said, sad and earnest and deeply wrong, holding a child's body the way an adult would. She trembled.

The scuffle in the hall grew louder. A harsh bang. The yells faded into moans and Babe was hit by a wave of nostalgia: had he been here before?

"She doesn't come in if you're still here," Milly told him. "I want...I want my mom."

Babe had never felt nauseous in a dream before. He started backing up. "I'm sorry," he said. "I'm so sorry."

"I want my mom," she repeated.

Babe stepped out of the living room just in time to see the back of a woman's head. Messy brown hair, cut with a knife. She was dragging somebody by the shoulders, grip slipping, hands wet with —

— sweat.

Babe wiped at his forehead, his cheeks, tasting salt. He pushed himself up and stripped for a shower. It was three a.m. It took him two tries to undo his fly. His hands were shaking, his mind across town fourteen years ago in a dingy little living room, waiting with deep love for something terrible.

twenty-two

DUDE WOKE up to someone poking him in the spine. He turned over. A poke to his ribs.

"Quit it," Dude mumbled.

"You gotta go," a voice said. Dude jolted—for a second, he didn't know where he was. He rolled onto his back to see KJ leaning over him, panicked.

"You gotta go," KJ repeated, in a hurried whisper. It was the most panicked Dude had ever heard him.

Dude nodded. Rubbed at his face, slapped his cheeks, trying to wake up properly. He hissed in pain as he remembered the fading bruise, his healing eye, his newly bruised torso. KJ shuffled to the other side of the bed and started pushing Dude's clothes into his hands.

"You shouldn't have slept over," he said, low, like he was lecturing himself instead of Dude. "What if my mom came in to clean my room?"

"Well, the room's still gross." Dude jumped up and down to pull his jeans up. They settled around his slim waist. "So I think you're safe."

"Shhh."

"I'm talking as quiet as you!" Dude took his shirt from KJ's outstretched hands. KJ winced at the bite marks blossoming over Dude's chest. Angry purple bruises.

"I think I went too hard," KJ said.

Dude buttoned himself up to the neck. "I asked."

Like you're trying to eat me, he'd said.

He shoved down a hot wave of emotion and focused on tugging his socks on. "Hey, thanks for, y'know. Having me over."

KJ shrugged. Dude had knocked on his window at midnight last night. "You seemed freaked out. As freaked out as you get, anyway."

He hadn't asked what was wrong. Dude appreciated it.

He climbed out the window with one shoe on. KJ threw the other one out after him and Dude waved a thank you, pulled it on, and headed for Higgins Vet Clinic.

Saturday morning meant volunteering. Last Saturday was the only time Dude had missed it in five years.

Mr. and Mrs. Higgins were at the kitchen table when Dude arrived, wearing matching bathrobes. They waved their bagels at him. They still didn't know who Anna went to visit last night. Jules had told them it was a "personal issue." She'd implied it had something to do with her parents, and Mr. and Mrs. Higgins hadn't asked. They didn't like Jules's parents.

"Hey, guys," Dude said.

"Hi, Dude," they chorused. It was comforting at the Higginses' house. They talked to each other here. They spent time together and even enjoyed it.

Dude went for the door at the back of the kitchen, the one beside the backyard door.

"Hi, guys!" Cages were set into shelves in the wall, metal

coated in soft blankets and newspaper. A cacophony of meows started up, but the interested kind, not the terrified kind. The cats had calmed down the past couple of days, minus last night when Babe had shown up.

Dude started opening cages, exchanging the newspapers and putting fresh food and water down, scooping poop into the trash. If a blanket was soiled, he found a new one. He kissed noses and stroked heads. Most of the kept animals in town came through here at some point. All the cats in here knew Dude enough to be at least grudgingly affectionate, and he found himself on the good end of many head-bumps.

Next was the kennels. There were only five dogs today, kept overnight for observation or recovery, or because the parents were out of town.

Dude did the same as in the cattery. He scritched necks and flanks and kissed more noses. He ended the way he always did: sitting on the floor and letting the dogs walk around the room. Most of them came up to him, wagging their tails and sniffing.

One of them hung back. This guy was new, barely out of puppyhood. A mutt, definitely some Staffy in him. He trembled in his cage.

"Hey, buddy," Dude said gently, scooting forwards. He checked the name tag. "Jazz? Hi, Jazz. I'm not gonna hurt you. Are you scared, being in a new place? All these new smells?"

Jazz whined. His tail wagged timidly.

"Aw, look at you," Dude said. "You're gorgeous. Aren't you gorgeous? Look at that big smile."

He held out a hand. Jazz trembled at him, then leaned up and sniffed.

"There you go," Dude said. Other dogs bumped his legs, nosed at his hair. He patted a Labrador absentmindedly, waiting.

He had other chores, but he didn't have to be at Kate's 'til midday, and it was only eight a.m. So he sat there and waited until Jazz emerged, still shaking, and butted his nose into Dude's elbow.

"Hey, bud," Dude whispered. "Good job."

Jazz climbed into his lap. Dude laughed, keeping it quiet so he didn't freak him out, and let Jazz lick his chin. After a while, Jazz dropped his muzzle onto Dude's shoulder with a huff.

Dude waited. When Jazz didn't move, he slowly brought a hand around Jazz's body and hugged him close. He pushed his face into Jazz's neck, happy to hold something alive. His hidden bite marks stung, not entirely pleasurably. His bruised eye throbbed, not at *all* pleasurably. He clung softly to Jazz until the dog started squirming. Then he kissed the dog's temple and pushed him carefully off his lap, standing up to finish his chores.

Around ten, he went into the kitchen for a snack. Mr. Higgins was still at the kitchen table doing a crossword puzzle.

"Want a toasted waffle?" Dude asked him.

He shook his head, frowning down at the crossword. "What's a nine-letter word for a snake eating its own tail? Ends with 's.'"

Dude paused, frozen waffle in hand. Anna had told him about the concept a few years back, trying to make something interesting out of their history assessment. "Don't know," he said finally. He slotted the waffle into the toaster and pressed down, leaning against the counter to wait.

"How was last night?" Mr. Higgins asked, still frowning at the crossword.

Dude crossed his arms. "Fine."

"Yes?" He glanced up.

Dude tried to look innocent.

Mr. Higgins ducked down again. "What did you get up to?"

"Nothing interesting."

"Mm. How's the gang doing?"

"They're fine."

"Good," Mr. Higgins said. His lips tightened into a thin line.

Dude scratched at the insides of his arms rhythmically. Index one, thumb two. Middle finger. Repeat.

"Ouroboros."

Dude continued to scratch. "What?"

"A snake eating its own—"

"Right," Dude said.

Mr. Higgins wrote the letters painstakingly in the tiny squares. He hovered on the edge of speech, wanting to ask about his daughter, he'd spoken to so little this morning; about Kate, who was obviously involved in whatever was going on. He wanted to ask *what*, exactly, was going on. But he trusted his daughter. He trusted she'd lead her friends and her aunt to do the right thing. And more importantly, he was a coward. He was terrified of the answers he'd find.

He nodded at Dude. "Put your waffle up before it burns."

Dude reached for the toaster and pushed CANCEL. The waffle popped up, steaming and perfect.

Kate's living room was a lot like Dude's—empty food wrappers, carpet that needed to be vacuumed. Hers had the addition of the old whiskey stench. He'd never been in it before.

He sat on her couch, Jules and Anna on either side. Kate

moved things around in the kitchen, fridge opening and closing, ice clinking. She hadn't offered them a drink.

Anna reached over and twisted Dude's watch towards her.

"He'll be here," Dude told her.

Anna rubbed at her arms. It was another hot, humid day, and rubbing only made the heat worse.

"I don't know," she said. "The way he stormed off yesterday—"

"He freaked out and ran away. He does that sometimes. He always comes back. That's Babe."

The worried dent in Anna's eyebrows didn't smooth. On Dude's other side, Jules picked at her striped pink nails. On her middle fingers they were studded with plastic diamonds.

Anna sighed. "That's Babe maybe once or twice a year. Never twice in one week!"

"He's stressed."

Jules latched onto a chipping diamond and started to pull. "Also, there's a monster in his head."

They turned to stare.

"What?" Jules said. The diamond snapped off. "You guys haven't noticed the twitching?"

There was movement from both doorways into the living room—from the kitchen and the front door. Kate appeared with a glass of Coke, ice already melting. Babe came through the front, wiping his sneakers on the welcome mat. The mat had been a gift from Anna's father to stop all of Kate's dirty footprints, ghosts of which were still visible in the living room carpet.

Babe waved at the gang on the couch. They waved back. Babe's face was open and apologetic, slightly scared. Dude didn't know what that fear was about. It wasn't like they were going to shun him for getting pissed off.

Dude nodded. "Hey."

"Hi." Babe's gaze caught on Dude's shirt, buttoned up to the base of his throat. The only time Dude buttoned it up all the way was for formal events: school photos, prom, middle school graduation.

Babe frowned, teasing. "Are you getting ready for a dance, or—" He stopped, the playful expression falling off his face as he remembered he was busy being awkward.

"Sure am," Dude said dryly. The bite marks itched underneath his collar.

Kate lit a cigarette one-handed. She blew a plume of smoke, which drifted towards the ceiling. "Sit," she said.

Babe perched on the edge of the couch next to Anna.

"Now," Kate continued. "About the murders we're gonna commit—"

Dude snorted, startled.

Anna dropped her face into her hands.

Jules laughed, undercut by Babe muttering, *oh gosh*.

Smoke wafted into the side of Dude's face. He coughed.

"As I was saying," Kate said. "Last night, they mentioned a ritual. It might be able to stop the creature, put Babe back to normal without killing a few more people. Anybody up for a library trip?"

Miss Henrietta was on a break. Janitor Larry was reading behind the counter. He looked up, unconcerned. Then he saw who it was.

He shoved back his chair and grabbed his broom.

"Hello," he said, holding the broom across his body like it might protect him.

Kate rolled her eyes. "We aren't gonna sic him on you, Larry. We're looking for the second ritual."

"Wait," Babe said. "What's happening?"

Dude pointed at Janitor Larry, who hadn't relinquished his death grip on the broom. "He's the one who helped me find the summoning ritual."

"What? *Him*?"

Janitor Larry eyed Babe warily, as if he might leap for his throat any moment. He smelled like the library—dust and old books and older carpet. The carpet smell was the most prominent. He kept his eye on Babe the whole time he made his way to the ceiling duct, which he removed. He reached in and came out with two thick rolls of paper.

"I don't want nothing to do with this," Larry said as they gathered around the table. "Don't tell me nothin'. Alright?"

And he hobbled off, leaving the rituals on the table. The paper was feathery, crackling as Kate unfurled the pages. Babe leaned over them and blinked.

"These are in Latin?"

"Yup," said Dude.

"You know *Latin*?"

Dude pointed. Along the bottom of the summoning ritual, there was a messy clump of English.

"Granddad Higgins circa 1965," Dude said. "The second one looks, uh, bit more difficult."

There was no English in the banishment ritual. Worse, it was blotted with ancient stains. Blood? Coffee? It obscured about half the document. Even if any of them could read Latin, he'd have trouble deciphering this.

Dude looked over at his friends. They all looked suddenly unenthused.

Kate rolled her tongue in her mouth. "We're on a time limit. Until we figure out what this means, Babe's gonna have to find some people food."

Anna spoke up. "We're really—"

"If you've got an alternative, I'd love to hear it."

She squirmed. "Does Babe have to *eat* them? Dude said he was going to bring people to the creature and—"

"Good point."

Anna made tight circles in the gray library carpet, pacing. "This is wrong. This is so wrong."

"Ayuh," Kate said. She took out a packet of cigarettes and lit one up. "I'm still gonna do it. If you can't, that's—"

"No," Anna said, coming to a stop in front of the table. "I'm still gonna."

"Yeah?"

"Yes." Anna lifted her face up, her eyes bright and determined. "I think it's morally repulsive. But...it's Babe. I'll hold the knife myself if it saves Babe."

Dude had the bizarre urge to smile. He ducked his head. The moment felt big and inappropriate. They were planning to do something horrible. He chanced a look over to Babe to find Babe already looking at him. As soon as their eyes met, Babe startled and looked away.

"Don't think you'll have to do much knife holding," Kate said after a moment. Another cloud of smoke rose slowly towards the ceiling. "I was thinking we lure them somewhere. Let Babe at 'em. What do you think?"

They all looked at each other. It was as good a plan as any.

"Also," Kate said, "Buzz's parents reported him missing this morning. I'm on the case. Did you eat all of him or is there a partially digested body to hide?"

They shifted awkwardly.

"We fed him to the vet dogs," Babe mumbled.

Kate inserted her lips in between her teeth, sucked, released. "Bones? Clothing?"

Anna winced. "We burned the clothes. Bones are at the bottom of my garbage."

"Right," Kate said. "Okay, then."

Dude touched the corner of the banishment ritual, folded it. The corner broke off, luckily a corner without anything on it.

"Guess we're learning Latin," he said.

Anna made a noise.

"What?"

"We know somebody who knows Latin."

They confronted Milly Hart after work, all except for Kate. Police showing up wouldn't put Milly at ease, and they agreed they shouldn't be seen in public as a group. Milly was in her gray work uniform, clutching her timecard with one hand and letting her stringy hair out of its messy bun with the other. Her fingers froze mid-comb as she saw them.

"We're not here to bother you," Anna rushed. "I mean— maybe we are. You know Latin, right? For Dungeons & Dragons?"

Milly looked thrown. She'd been expecting probing questions, not someone bringing up the hobby she'd only talked to one person about in real life. "Uh," Milly said, looking around them, searching for a trick. "I guess?"

Anna fished out the copy of the ritual from her pocket. They'd copied it before heading their separate ways. "We need your help deciphering this," she said, and held it out.

Milly eyed it, even sniffed it a little, before taking it. "What is it?" she asked, face already opening with understanding, even as she asked.

Babe said, "It can kill the thing that killed your mom."

"For good," Anna said.

Milly's head snapped up. For a moment, her pale eyes

blazed, chin higher than any of them ever saw it. But with the lifted chin was a terrible dread, and soon her chin was back down and so were her eyes. "You're sure?"

"Yes," Anna said.

"Mostly," Jules added.

Milly's jaw fluttered. She looked like she was about to cry, but a moment later, the wet sheen was gone. Her head jerked in a nod. "I'll help," she said.

They watched her walk away. It was a long time before Babe spoke up.

"So," he said, only a little awkward, "anyone wanna go hang at Juniper Lookout?"

They set off towards Dude's truck, the four of them stepping in time.

twenty-three

ANNA FOUND Janitor Larry in the stacks the next morning. He was leaning against a shelf, flicking through a book on gardening. They didn't have many of those in Bulldeen. Anna had to stand in front of him for three seconds before he looked up, his shuttered face closing off even more.

"Said I didn't want anything to do with it," he mumbled.

"That's fine," Anna assured him. "I just need you to point me in the direction of someone who can tell me what I need to know."

Janitor Larry shifted on the spot. He rotated one shoulder, then the other, jerky gears that needed oiling. "Whadda you need to know?"

"I want to know about the shootout in 1940. And the boiler that took out the old high school."

His face creased inwards. All this access to newspapers and gossip, and he hadn't even started to connect the dots. Anna couldn't bring herself to be surprised. It wasn't that he couldn't put it together, it was that he wouldn't. Every Bulldeen citizen who had started to see the edges of the big picture had immediately shoved it in a drawer to rot.

"Boiler happened too long ago for anyone to tell you

about," said Janitor Larry. "There's a book around here that—"

"I've read it."

He nodded. A short, sharp jerk of his head. "Right," he said. "Well, s'pose you'll wanna see Ben, then. He was around for the shootout."

"Where's he?"

"Ben?" Janitor Larry rubbed at a stray speck of dirt on his thin nose. He tilted his wrist up to check his watch. "It's going on eight a.m. Reckon he'd be at The Parrot."

The hospital was an hour out of Bulldeen, but there were three bars within the town limits. The scummiest was The Parrot. Anna's parents had warned her not to go inside. Her father had gone in one time around her age and didn't remember much after the third drink. He'd spent the next two days puking over a cut lip.

Anna loved that story. She'd gotten him to tell it many times. It was an exciting, appalling peek behind the curtain of the infallible man she'd always known.

She hesitated at the front door. There was a hole near the doorknob, some remnant of a fight.

You won't get in trouble, she reminded herself. *Mom and Dad will never know. You're not drinking, just talking. And Aunt Cop will get you out if something does happen.*

She gripped the doorknob. Grease imprinted itself on her skin. She wiped it on the underside of her dress and pushed the door open with an elbow, walking in fast so as to not lose courage.

It was dark. Anna's eyes took a moment to adjust.

The Parrot was just as dingy as she'd been promised. There

was a photo of it circa 1940 in *An Extensive History of Bulldeen, 1880–1980* by Johnny Walks. Nothing had changed: the same rickety wooden seats up by the bar, same peeling leather booths shoved in the corner. Maybe it was even the same men—two of them sitting on opposite sides of the bar, hunched over glasses of amber liquid. A bartender leaned behind the counter, polishing glasses.

Ben's got the crookedest nose in town, Janitor Larry had told her. *Can't miss him.*

That's not a lot to go on, Anna had said.

He'd laughed. *Trust me, kid.*

Thank God there were only two men in the bar. Anna walked up to the first and said, "Excuse me, sir?"

He turned. His nose bent so far to the right, it was nearly on his cheek. He had to be in his eighties. He looked older.

"Oh," Anna said. "Ben?"

He frowned, not meeting her eyes. He gave her a look from her hair to her shoes. Anna wished she'd worn pants and sneakers instead of a dress and sandals, but his gaze wasn't creepy, just confused that a respectable-looking underage girl had willingly walked into The Parrot to talk to him.

"Sorry," Anna said. "Janitor Larry—I mean, Larry who works in the library as a janitor—maybe we should call him Library Larry—he said you were at the Rotgut and Jessup shootout in 1940?"

His thumb worried at the edge of his smudged glass. "This for...a school report?"

Anna nodded wordlessly.

Ben gave her another look down to her toes, still frowning. He took a slug of whiskey and nodded at the seat next to him.

Anna climbed on, keeping a safe distance from the bar. It was greasier than the doorknob. Decades of dried spirits layered on top of each other. She got out a notebook and pencil from her pocket.

Ben eyed them warily, then went back to his glass. He didn't look at her for more than a few seconds at a time. He didn't look at anybody for long stretches. Ben was a gruff, monosyllabic old man who'd spent most of his life drinking away his unemployment money in The Parrot. He'd been one eviction away from joining Leroy Child behind the Shop N' Save. He'd talked to Leroy often, giving him bar snacks he smuggled out in his pockets. He'd cried after finding out he'd been killed.

"I was a kid," he warned. "Memory's a funny thing."

"That's fine."

He grunted. Took another mouthful of whiskey. His fingers trembled slightly around the glass. "Know the basics about the Rotguts and Jessups?"

She shook her head and readjusted herself on her chair, dress sticking to the wood.

"Well..." Ben said, trailing off. It had been a while since he'd told this story. He had to remember the ropes. "Before we had Miss Petty and her daughters, there were two tailor shops in town—the Rotguts and the Jessups. Rotguts were more down to earth types. Jessups, you went to them if you wanted something fancy done. Some fiddly ballgown lace fixed, that sort of thing. Both of them good in their own rights."

Anna scribbled and squinted. It was hard to see clearly in this bar. There was one window behind the counter, and the rest of it was lit by a trio of bulbs hanging over the booths.

"How I heard it," Ben continued, "was that they already hated each other when they got here in the 1800s. They definitely hated each other when they settled in here—Granddaddy Jessup and Granddaddy Rotgut always stealing each other's customers and mumbling under their breath when the other spoke up at church. One day, Granddaddy Rotgut was walking along Main Street and Grandaddy Jessup said, *stupid son of a whoreson bitch.* Uh, 'scuse the language."

"It's fine," Anna repeated. "He swore at him?"

Ben shifted his skinny elbows on the bar. "'S what Rotgut would tell you. Other folks said that Jessup stepped in dog shit, didn't even know Rotgut was there. Don't matter which was true. After that, they were at war."

"But—it might've been an accident."

Ben shrugged. His body was too small for his clothes, it was like watching someone move inside a bunch of sheets. "Don't take much to fire some folks up."

Down at the other end of the bar, the second man broke into a coughing fit. Hard, wet hacks. Colds were common all year 'round in Bulldeen—only the new houses had insulation, and only the rich could afford to build new houses. Most of the people who lived there were not rich.

"Then the youngest Jessup boy got himself into a bar brawl," Ben said, voice growing steadier, more confident. He nodded towards the front door. "One of Rotgut's boys stabbed him with a corkscrew. He bled out right over there."

Anna turned in her seat. Her hand, still sticky with doorknob residue, twitched around her pencil. "What was the fight about?"

"Same thing all bar fights are about between young men, I'd guess," Ben said. "Pride, girls, or both."

Anna busied herself with writing so she wouldn't have to look his way. She needn't have bothered—Ben busied himself staring into his glass, swishing liquid around.

"Anyhow," he continued. "Only a matter of time before things got bloodier."

"How did the shootout start?"

Ben signaled the bartender, who put down the glass and rag

and came over. He poured two fingers of whiskey into Ben's waiting glass, and Ben downed half of it in one swallow.

"Thanks, Rick," he said. He scratched at his nose, which had been smashed in 1972 during a bar fight. Both girls and pride had been involved. "I was a kid," he repeated. "I didn't see much. But I heard things."

Anna waited, keeping a straight face.

"From what I heard," Ben said slowly, as if prying the words from somewhere he'd forgotten, "Jason Jessup, the middle kid, he went around to the Rotgut family house and let the air out of everyone's tires the night before they're due to head out of town to see some relatives. So they're stuck in town. The morning of the shootout, Reggie Rotgut, nephew of the head tailor, is fuming, saying they gotta get revenge. So he heads over to the gun store to buy ammunition. Now, the man who runs the gun store is shacking up with Lilian Jessup, tailor Jessup's granddaughter. And he hears a Rotgut raving about the Jessups, stocking up on ammo, so he sends a messenger to tell his sweetheart's family what's going down. And the Jessups start getting worried. Things have been getting less heat-of-the-moment over the years. More planning— egging the houses, sabotaging an outfit for an important client, letting air out of tires, that sort of thing. And now the Rotguts are buying ammo and talking about revenge."

A light flickered above them. Anna glanced up, stiffening.

Ben didn't notice. He was too deep in the story.

"A few of the Jessups want to call a town meeting, make sure nothing wild's gonna happen. Other Jessups, mostly the older ones, want to take the fight to them. A few of the Rotguts try to talk Reggie down, but others are riling him up. By midday, nobody's bothering to talk anyone down. The Jessups head to buy more ammo and—"

"—and they run into the Rotguts in front of the store."

Ben nodded.

"You were there?"

"Backseat of my dad's car, parked across from The Horn. He'd gone in for a drink." Ben tilted his glass, looking into the comforting whiskey glow. His father had drunk whiskey. And his grandfather. There were more whiskey drinkers before his grandfather, but Ben didn't know about his relatives past Granddad Jimmy, who had given Ben his first taste just after the shootout. To Ben, whiskey tasted like relief, a sign that a bad thing had finally finished for good. He took another long drink, motioning to Ricky the bartender, who filled his glass again.

"I was in the backseat," he repeated, "playing with some toy soldiers. Not those plastic ones, real tin ones. It was hot and I had the windows down. I was making blasting noises—and then the yelling started."

"What did they yell?"

"Same stuff those families had been yelling at each other for years. *Thieves, liars, no good rotten bastards*—'scuse the language."

"Who shot first?"

Ben slid his thumb up and down the glass. He'd only had two so far, and the shake in his hands was only just beginning to settle down. Anna did her best not to watch it. Sometimes Kate's hands shook around her first cigarette of the day.

"Rotguts," he said. "Don't know who in particular, but it came from their side first. Both the families were standing on the sidewalk, kind of spilling out onto the road. Once the shooting started on the Rotgut side, it started on the Jessup, the womenfolk screaming and running, ducking behind cars parked on the side of the road."

"Did they duck behind—?"

"Almost. Jason Jessup squatted behind the car right in

front of me. Met my eyes through the back window. Smiled too. Not a reassuring smile, the kind you give a kid when something dangerous is happening—no, this smile was all excited. This was after the shots started actually hitting people."

"They didn't hit at first."

"Nope. All of them standing out in the open, not six feet away from each other, but not one bullet out of that first round made it into anybody. Went into cars and buildings instead. Anyhow, everybody took cover behind cars, 'cept Granddaddy Jessup and Granddaddy Rotgut. They took cover behind the steps leading up to the town hall. This was before it burned down. Rotgut ducked down on one side, Jessup on the other. And their sons and sons in law and nephews, they all opened fire."

"And they died."

"Yup," said Ben. He rubbed once again at his smashed nose. "Every single one. Both families wiped out. Women too. Caught in the crossfire—or so they say."

"You think they were shot on purpose?"

"Not on purpose," Ben said after a moment. He took another drink. A stray drop chased down his wiry chin. He wiped it away with the back of his slowly-steadying hand. "Everybody was firing blind and stupid, and those women were in the wrong place at the wrong time. 'Cept for Agatha, who was right where she wanted to be."

"Agatha?" She hadn't been in the history book.

Ben nodded. "Only a few years older than me. Agatha Jessup went right up behind Granddaddy Rotgut and smashed his head in with a rock."

Anna laughed, shocked. She covered her mouth. "I'm sorry. That's awful."

"Yeah, 'specially since he didn't die right away. Had just enough time to turn around and shoot the poor girl in the stomach. She tried to crawl away, but another bullet caught her on the sidewalk. That one might've been by accident. I didn't see who did it. I was too busy watching Granddaddy Jessup run out into the firefight trying to get to her."

"Did—"

"Right in the head. Exploded like a Halloween pumpkin kicked on Thanksgiving."

Anna scribbled. Ben watched her pen move, admiring her neat handwriting. She reminded him faintly of Agatha Jessup, though he didn't realize this. It was her sweetness, her determination. Goodness radiated out of her, but a particular kind of goodness, the kind that did not shy away from doing terrible things if it was to save someone they loved.

"Whole thing took less than five minutes," Ben continued. "Felt like a lifetime."

Anna finished the bullet point. *Agatha Jessup.* "Was there anyone else around during the shootout?"

"Sure, we were near the town square. For about a week after, everybody said they saw it. Then, just as quick, everybody shut up about it. You know Bulldeen. But the people I saw for sure—the butcher watched from his shop. Some people from the supermarket watched from there. The newspaper boy, Farley Uris, he almost got his head blown off. Hid behind a lamppost across the street. Lucky to make it out alive."

He hesitated. Anna pounced on it.

"Anybody else?"

"Sure," Ben said, with a noticeable decrease in enthusiasm. "Me and Farley, plus this high school girl who worked at the checkout counter—we all agreed there was somebody from out of town standing near the firefight. Not in it, but too close. Strange thing was, he looked calm."

The light above them pulsed. This time, Ben looked up with Anna.

"Calm," Anna prompted.

"Well, he had bullets flying near him. Anybody else would make a run for it, or at least panic."

"He was from out of town?"

Ben hesitated again. "Well, that's the thing. We all recognized him from somewhere. But none of us could come up with a name. Farley knew everybody in town. If that man had an address here, Farley would've delivered newspapers to it. We supposed he must've passed through sometimes."

Another flicker. Ricky the bartender muttered, annoyed, about *what was wrong now, goddamnit?*

"What did he look like?" Anna asked.

"Aw," said Ben. "This was a long time ago. I haven't even thought about that man in decades."

This was a lie. Ben thought about the man about once a month after waking up sweating from dreams he couldn't remember.

"Strange thing," he continued. "We all recognized him, like I said. But I could've sworn he looked like my old teacher, 'cept sharper cheekbones and jaw, all that. Big coat. Farley said he looked like his boss. That checkout clerk even thought he could've been a *woman*. We all agreed he was tall. And sharp. Sharp cheekbones, jaw, nose. Even his *teeth*, a little."

"That sounds about right," Anna said hoarsely. She cleared her throat. "Do you know anything about the man several children saw outside the school just before the boiler exploded?"

Ben blinked. He looked her full in the face, caught up in the moment, the third drink seeping into his bloodstream.

"Now," he said, "there's nothing behind that. That boiler explosion was a tragedy, clear and simple. Can't find no one here who can tell you what it was like, but my grandma was a teacher there. Side of her face got burned up in that explosion.

She had nightmares all her life. Never talked about 'em, but that woman screamed us all awake."

"What did she scream about?"

Ben made a noise in the back of his mouth. "This is for a school report, you said?"

"Yes. Did she scream about anything?"

He opened his mouth, breathing in and out without saying anything. He was missing most of his teeth.

"*Somebody stop it*," he said eventually. "Look, those kids who think they saw somebody...maybe they did. But I can tell you right now, there was nothing suspicious about that explosion. Those kids, they probably just wanted to make sense of it."

"Right," Anna said. She made herself smile, though a sick feeling was taking over her stomach. "Of course. You're right, I'm sorry for bringing it up."

"'S no problem," Ben said, eyes down at his drink. He thumbed at the rim, tacky with spirits. It had been a while since he'd held anybody's gaze for that long. It would be the last time. Ben would die two months later choking on his own vomit in the bathroom of The Parrot. He'd be spitting distance to where he'd sat and told Anna what had happened when he was a kid in the backseat of his father's car.

Anna climbed off the stool and started to thank him.

"You shouldn't go around alone," Ben told her. "Stick with your friends. There are wild dogs about."

"Yes," Anna said. "Of course. Thank you."

She walked out into the blinding summer light, trying not to cry out of sheer anger and dread. *Somebody stop it.*

Once, she'd asked her dad why they still lived here. Why they didn't move to a city, somewhere more accepting, somewhere they wouldn't call her 'high and mighty' for holding her chin up and meeting people's eyes? He'd been silent a long time, and then he'd said, *people grow where they're planted.*

Anna headed towards Bulldeen High feeling like a mouse in a maze. *We're trapped,* she thought. All of them had been trapped in this thing that had been happening since before they were born and would be here long after they were gone.

Somebody stop it, she imagined Ben's grandmother yelling, about to be shaken from a dream she would never talk about for as long as she lived.

We will, Anna promised.

chapter
twenty-four

WHILE ANNA GRILLED BEN, Kate Higgins dealt with a different drunk.

Hockstetter snored on Kate's shoulder as she dragged him into the back of the bakery and let him slump against the industrial fridge. He snorted, made some hopeful noises that approximated wakefulness, and then tilted forwards.

"Rest easy," Kate told him.

Out front, Deputy Lissiter eyed the pies. They were sloppily done. It was most obvious in the crusts, which hadn't held together properly, but the filling was just as lackluster. Since Lissiter had started making them during his turn in the bakery, people around town had clued into why the pies were only good on days when Lissiter was on Hock Duty. Nowadays, he sold a couple pies a week out the back of his house—cherry for Miss Petty on Saturdays, and a pumpkin pie for the Bull's Head branch of the Smith family on Thursday mornings.

Kate emerged from the back, apronless. Lissiter was the only one who wore it.

"Morning," he said.

She nodded at him, going for the cabinet. "Usual?"

"Ayuh."

Using tongs, she dropped a cinnamon doughnut into a brown paper bag and handed it over. He rolled the bag up, dusted the cinnamon off his fingers and tucked the bag into his pocket.

"Thanks," he said, and waited.

Kate met his gaze head on. Neither of them spoke for several seconds. Both of them were very good at silences.

Kate bit the back of her tongue. Another thing the chief and deputy were good at: keeping their faces empty. It was a natural state for them both.

Kate broke first. "Something to say, Lissiter?"

"Thanks for asking," Lissiter said in his long, flat drawl. "Just wanted to say we've seen you hanging around with that Babe kid."

"Hanging around?"

"Driving him places."

"I gave him a ride."

Lissiter nodded. He had this calm, kind demeanor that made perps open up to him. If you got arrested, Lissiter was the cop you wanted to put you in handcuffs. He was the one they sent if someone was causing a disturbance. He had the best track record of talking them down, and he was the only one who would always try to talk. Even Kate rode up to a lot of scenes and pulled out her gun before bothering to open her mouth.

Kate chewed some more on her tongue. She was not about to spill her guts because Lissiter was being patient. It had never worked on her during his seven years on the job.

Lissiter cleared his throat. "So, is he up to anything?"

"Not that I can find."

"You'd tell me if he was up to something, right?"

She pinned him with a look. He squirmed. It was satisfying to watch.

Lissiter wasn't superstitious, but he knew there were things about Bulldeen he couldn't—and didn't want to—explain. He wanted to be as far away from those things as possible. When Milly Hart worked at the bookstore, Lissiter had made his wife go in. If Babe Simmons really had come back from the dead, he didn't want anyone he cared about anywhere near him.

"Just—" he said, and paused to smile politely at a woman who came in the door. He got out of her way and leaned towards the counter, lowering his voice. "Know you've got a soft spot, Kate."

Kate didn't dignify that with an answer. She stared at him a few more seconds, then nodded at the woman, Mrs. McKay, an eighty-year-old who often wandered into shops in the middle of town thinking she was at the doctor's.

"Mrs. McKay," Kate said. "Going to have to ask you to leave. I'll be back in five."

"I have these moles on my back," Mrs. McKay croaked, fumbling ineffectually with her shirt.

Deputy Lissiter sighed. "Chief, it's just hit opening. There are customers."

Kate was already heading out from behind the counter. "Gonna stop that woman from flashing us?"

Deputy Lissiter put a hand on Mrs. McKay's back. She looked up at him, hands pausing on her top button, which she still hadn't managed to open. "This way, ma'am," he said, and guided her out. "No, you can just keep your shirt on for the moment."

Kate poured herself a coffee. She scraped the BACK IN 5 sign out from behind the slot machine in the corner, taped it onto the door and closed it behind her.

Half a dozen feet away, Officer Lant was crossing the road towards the police station.

Kate shouted at him. "*Lant*! Take over Hock Duty 'til I get back!"

Lant wavered in the middle of the street. A car came up and honked. He waved at it to give him a moment.

"Go," Kate told him, and Lant diverted his course towards the bakery.

Lissiter followed Kate to her squad car parked across the road. They climbed into the front seats, Kate chugging half her coffee before giving it to Lissiter to hold. He took it. He didn't ask why she hadn't gotten him a coffee. He was that sort of guy.

They drove out of the center. When he'd brought up her soft spot, Kate had decided she was going to take him for a drive. While Mrs McKay had tried to take off her blouse, she'd decided where to take him.

They drove towards the hills, the only side of town not surrounded by thornfruit fields. Halfway up the left side of the hills, about a mile away from Juniper Lookout, there was a baby cliff. In the '50s, it had gotten the nickname Makeout Point, and the name had stuck. Teenagers drove their cars up here to kiss and sometimes more. Cops got called out there sometimes by a worried parent. Kate's only memories associated with this place were of shining a flashlight into cars and watching teenagers untangle from each other, blinking in the light like deer.

Lissiter associated this place with his own teenage make-outs. He'd only ever kissed one person: Greta Harwig, his high school sweetheart and now wife. They'd ended their first date here, the car fogging up with their hot breath. They'd also taken a three a.m. trip here on their honeymoon, nineteen and giggling like much younger kids.

Kate had also only kissed one person: Gemma McKay, Mrs. McKay's only daughter. They'd never dared meeting at

Makeout Point. Their kissing happened in Mrs. McKay's basement every weekend for three years of high school. Then Gemma moved to Cincinnati. Ten years ago, when Gemma was home for the holidays, they had an awkward encounter at the Shop N' Save. They'd pretended not to notice each other in the frozen food section. Gemma left a voicemail on Kate's answering machine a year ago, but Kate hadn't yet mustered the courage to check what it said.

Kate drove up to the edge of the tiny cliff, dwarfed by much higher summits, and idled the engine.

Lissiter handed her back the coffee. "You're a handsome woman, Chief, but I'm a happily married man."

Kate allowed herself a gruff laugh. She chugged the rest of her coffee and shelled two cigarettes out of her pocket. She handed Lissiter one and kept the other, lighting both of them.

Lissiter rolled down the window. Smoke drifted out into the morning air.

Kate put her cigarette to her lips and breathed deep. Her last doctor had made concerned noises during her examination and told her to cut back. Kate had agreed, but she'd also agreed she'd cut back on alcohol. Neither of these things were happening, even with the nicotine patches on her arm and the water she made herself swallow between drinks, trying to make herself slow down.

Self-destruction was a hobby in Bulldeen. Kate didn't have anything else to do. At least that was what she told herself.

"Remember when we came to see your brother up here?"

Lissiter winced. "Yeah," he said. "I remember."

Kate hummed into her cigarette. Blew more smoke. "Remember how we didn't arrest him? Should've gone to jail for what he did to that freshman."

Lissiter shifted uncomfortably in his seat. He looked over the town, which they could see most of from this vantage point, and tried to think himself back to times there with his wife. Greta was his sweetheart, but also his best friend. She always made him feel better, and she'd made him feel fine about what they'd done about his little brother.

Family's family, she'd assured him, arms tight around him the night they'd come up to Makeout Point to find Johnny Lissiter doing bad things to that teenage girl. *Anyone else would've done the same.*

"But you didn't wanna ruin his life," Kate continued.

Lissiter sucked smoke. He squeezed his free hand in his lap, trying to conjure Greta's slim fingers slipping through his. *Anyone would've—*

Kate took his half-smoked cigarette so she was holding two in one hand. She took a double-drag and flicked them both out the window, still glowing.

"We make the law around here," she told Lissiter, who hadn't commented on the cigarettes. "If we say it's right, then it is. If I tell you to stay out of Babe Simmons's business, you stay out of it. You hear me?"

"Yes, Chief," Lissiter said. "I hear you."

"Good. Don't make me tell you again."

She reached down to the keys, but she didn't turn them yet. She'd looked out at the town for too long, and the hooks it had in her were starting to twist. Sometimes she'd look out over the familiar streets and get so full of emotion, she couldn't stand it. The strange thing was, most of the time, she'd be full of love. She'd lived in Bulldeen all her life. Even in her early twenties, when a few of her graduating class were escaping to other states or even other countries, somewhere they could have a vegetable garden, Kate would wake up in the morning and look out at her barren yard and think: *I could stand another sixty years here.*

Of course, there were times when she wanted to scream.

She'd stand in the break room, listening to her coworkers laughing over a dyke joke, and hate this place with an intensity that made her stomach churn.

She gazed out over the town for a long moment. Beside her, Lissiter waited. He had things to do. He thought he might have a lead on that stolen bicycle case.

Kate breathed out, thinking of smoke and doctor's visits and the first cigarette she ever had with Gemma McKay down in her parents' basement, and tried to figure out whether this fullness was love or hate. Three more seconds passed. Kate still didn't know. She turned the key. The engine kicked into life and she reversed out of Makeout Point like a bat out of hell.

chapter
twenty-five

ZACHARY LITNUS STOOD in the middle of the gym, surveying his lands like a hawk. For two hours a week, the gym was the drama club's domain, which meant it was Zachary's. He pointed towards the extras fake-walking in place. "Fake-walk better," he instructed.

He pointed towards Dude, who was fiddling with the props they'd dragged out from the prop closet. "Dude, you're absolutely *certain*—"

"It'll work," Dude assured him. He tugged at the rope, which pulled a long line of cardboard plants up one by one. Usually, they got extras to stand behind the stage and lift cardboard cutouts, but this year, Dude had suggested they try practical effects.

"It's just a pulley, real simple—"

"Great," Zachary said, waving him off. He clasped his hands, pointing all his fingers towards Babe, who sat next to Dude in his usual clump of friends. Babe sat cross-legged with a script in his hand, though he didn't need it. Jules sat across from him, with a radio in her lap and the script, which she *did* need, to make sure she knew the musical cues. With Dude revamping the effects, it wasn't a hard job to talk them into redoing the music. They used to have people playing a triangle and guitar, but of the only three people in Bulldeen who knew how to play guitar well enough to provide background music, one was dead, another was out of town visiting their godmother, and the third was experiencing opioid withdrawal with an intensity that meant they couldn't play guitar if they wanted to.

Anna sat a short distance away, chewing on her thumb knuckle. This was uncharacteristic of Anna, who did not usually partake in mouth-based fidgeting. She'd been distant since she'd arrived at school that morning, the way she got after they had to put an animal down at home. They had to say her name twice to get her to zone back in.

"Babe," said Zachary, with the smile of someone grateful for what he's received while still hoping for more. "How's my Founder Jim?"

"He's fine," Babe said. "I mean—I'm fine."

"I just asked because I don't hear any lines being read."

Babe gave him a tight smile. Every year, the high school seniors put on this play. Babe had seen it seventeen times. He cleared his throat, reading the first line he saw.

"I will give anything."

Dude spoke up, still tying the pulleys to the props. "Will you really?" He didn't need the script either. He nodded over at Anna. "Hey Anna...Anna! Keep it going."

Anna's head came up. Her knuckle dropped from her mouth. "What?"

"I will give anything," Babe prompted.

Anna blinked. "Will you really?"

Dude leaned over towards Babe. "You got some tape I could use?"

Babe dug in his deep pockets. He sifted past small scissors, band-aids, and cat food, and revealed a roll of tape.

"Thanks," Dude told him. He snapped off a line and secured the thin rope onto the ground so it had no slack, keeping the cardboard upright. He got up and moved over to Anna, dropping into a crouch in front of her. He jogged his closed fist a few times and flattened it out.

"Paper," he said.

Anna's eyes lost some of that faraway sheen. "Are you going to play fair?"

"Always."

Anna eyed him. Held out a fist. When their fingers released, Anna threw paper. Dude threw a finger-flickering motion.

"What's that?"

Dude continued flickering his fingers. "Fire. Burns paper and metal."

Playing hand games with Dude never ended with any winners. In freshman year, he'd invented fleshed-out personalities, backstories, and death scenes for every finger in Chopsticks.

Jules snapped her fingers in front of Babe's face, one headphone tilting away from her ear, pressing into her cheek. "Hey! I'm supposed to be pushing the musical cues. Keep going."

Babe shook the smile off his face. "I swear."

Jules pressed a button. Sparkly dark music leaked from her headphones. *Sparkly dark music* was what she'd written on the music sheet, and it was just about right.

She held up her script. "What about your family?"

"Take them."

"That is not your choice to make. They must give themselves over to the town."

"They will," Babe said. "All of us, we will do anything to survive."

Something flashed at the back of his mind. Not an itch, but something close. It felt familiar.

Jules went to press a different button, but her finger fumbled. Static rang out through the gym.

Babe cried out in pain.

Jules blinked, startled. "Right, sorry!"

"It's fine," Babe said, smiling as hard as he could to put off all the weird looks he was getting.

Jules pressed a button. The music turned eerie.

"The family stops toiling," she read from the script directions. "They come to center stage where Founder Jim and Bulldeen are standing. Bulldeen holds out a hand and Wife takes it, smiling. She takes Daughter's hand, Daughter takes Son's hand. One by one, they walk into the dark."

She picked up the script to slap it back down against her knees. "I am going to be so glad to get out of this place. Who has a town origin where the founder's family gets sacrificed?"

"It's a metaphor," Babe said, scratching his head. "That family all died of natural causes. They gave themselves to Bulldeen by working really hard to establish the town. Building, sewing, cooking."

"What's that?" Anna said from her spot a few feet away.

Dude undulated his hand. "Tar. It smothers."

Anna chopped her fingers at it. Dude made burbling sounds, fluttering his hand over hers. His messy hair looked good—he'd obviously washed it. It curled over his forehead, hanging in his eyes, light brown brushing his lashes. It was a school night, one of the last ever, and Babe ached in a way that had nothing to do with hunger.

Dude looked up. For once, Babe didn't look away, their grins not yet solid on their face when Zachary clapped his hands.

"Alright," he yelled, voice echoing off the tall walls. "Everybody get into your places. Let's do this from the top."

Babe took his place in the imaginary wings, that curious familiarity still hanging around the edges of his skull. It niggled at him. It scraped. The script bent in his fist, fingers clenching around paper. It bothered him. Not the contents of the script, but the script itself—they'd grown up watching the older kids act it out, and now *they* were the older kids and they'd stepped right into those roles. It was like the roles had been waiting for them.

Babe's cheek twitched. He stilled it.

"Action!" Zachary yelled.

Babe walked with the extras into the space they were pretending was the stage. Zachary spoke, narration washing over Babe: pilgrims arriving, farmers toiling, barren fields. Struggle. Poison.

Babe acted it all—optimism, then desperation. Lingering on the desperation.

"Founder Jim begged," Zachary narrated.

Babe swallowed. Turned to the empty gym wall where an audience should be.

"Please. I must save the town. I will give anything," he said, and shuddered.

Zachary lowered his megaphone, which was actually a piece of paper rolled into a cone.

"Babe?"

Babe cleared his throat. "It's nothing," he said.

Zachary wavered. Yancy Land, world-class stoner and notorious ditcher of everything but drama club, waited next to him. Yancy was playing the voice of Bulldeen, but not the figure itself. On the night of the show, they'd have a shadow appear on stage. That was also a new addition. Every year before this, they'd had an actor. Dude thought it'd add to the atmosphere if they just cast a huge shadow across the stage. *Makes it less human,* he'd said.

Yancy Land deepened his voice. On the night of the show, he'd stand behind the stage, a thin sheet between him and the hulking shadow of Bulldeen. "Will you really?"

"I swear," Babe said. The words caught in the back of his throat. He cleared it again. "I swear," he repeated, but his voice was still curiously deep, as if mimicking the shadow.

The girls went up to Juniper Lookout. Dude and Babe cruised into Shop N' Save, waving at the greeter. Last year, that guy had been in their art class, and now he was on track to become the manager. He'd still be there when the shop closed down five years later.

Babe pushed the cart. Dude chucked food into it, his mother's weekly cash deep in his pocket. They bypassed the fruit and veg section, heading straight into the breakfast aisle where he restocked on Wheaties. In the next few aisles, he collected chips, rice, cans of peaches, and tomato sauce. The real motherlode was the frozen food aisle: frozen fries. Frozen meat. Frozen pre-chopped vegetables, which mostly tasted the same as fresh ones once he heated them up. Dude liked them in the warm, comforting way of childhood meals. He did, however, get tired of canned fruit.

As they slouched down the sweets aisle, Dude threw in a couple of Coconut Wonder bars with a decent act of nonchalance. They'd eat the chocolate on the way home, Babe advising Dude to keep his darn hands on the wheel until Dude inevitably obeyed and started teeth-shimmying the bar into his mouth. Babe cried laughing every time. It was their favorite part of the week.

Babe reached down and touched the Almond Delight. It had been a new addition next to their old favorites. They didn't get a lot of new stuff at the grocery store. He'd been excited to try it. "Hey," he said. "What was my funeral like?"

Dude snorted, examining the ice-cream cones stacked above the sodas. "What?"

"Come on." Babe scooted the shopping cart gently into Dude's hip. "Did the teachers cry? I know they're all avoiding me now, but did they cry?"

"Uh. Some of them."

Babe fixed him with a look.

Dude sighed, reaching out to flick at the ice-cream box corners. They had three kinds.

"I don't know, I wasn't paying attention."

Babe spluttered. "*Pardon* me?"

"I was—" Dude cast a look around. They were nearing the end of the aisle. Ahead of them were the milks up against the wall, and a woman sneaking cream into her pocket. Ms. Davis had been their kindergarten teacher before falling deep into addiction and losing her job. Her weekly supermarket trips involved a lot of sneaking things into her coat, which she only wore for stealing things. Everybody in town knew about the stealing coat, but Ms. Davis was very polite and had a cousin in every store she stole from, as well as in the police. Other than that one time she broke the pharmacist's nose, she didn't bother anyone. They returned the favor.

Dude busied himself in the ice-cream cone boxes, picking them up and turning them around. "I was thinking about the ritual," he said quietly. "By then, I had it in my pocket."

They weaved silently towards the checkouts. The Bulldeen Shop N' Save would not survive long enough to get self-checkouts.

Dude and Babe didn't talk again until they reached the

Chevy. They loaded the groceries into the trunk and got in the front seats. Dude held a Coconut Wonder bar, trying to be subtle about checking the ingredients. Babe clicked his seatbelt into place and Dude threw the chocolate into his lap.

"EpiPen's in the glove box," Dude said.

"Thanks," Babe said, unwrapping the bar.

Dude started the engine. They pulled out of the parking lot, Dude holding the bar in the one hand he kept on the wheel. Once in a while, he'd take a bite and place his hand back.

Babe missed the teeth-shimmying. He finished his bar just as they pulled into Babe's driveway in Bull's Head.

Babe crumpled the wrapper in his fist. "Did you bring me back because you felt guilty?"

Dude wasn't surprised at the question. He'd been expecting it. "No," he said. The truck idled in the driveway.

"Because you don't need to feel guilty. It could've happened anytime, I wasn't ever careful enough with food—"

"It wasn't because I felt guilty."

Dude's chocolate bar wedged half-finished between his hand and the wheel. It was beginning to melt against the plastic, against flesh. As Babe watched, Dude brought up his hand and scraped the chocolate from his palm with his teeth.

Babe looked away.

"You're my best friend," Dude said. It contained worlds. He flexed his hurt hand against the steering wheel, bandage straining against his skin.

Babe nodded. The enormity of his situation had rarely hit him in those first few weeks. It made him shake. He wanted to tell Dude everything he'd been holding back, all those things he never let himself think. But all he could manage was, "You're my best friend too."

He reached for the door handle.

"Hey," Dude said. "Look, I should've—I should have told

you what was going on with you. The hunger thing. It must've been really scary for you, not knowing."

Babe held the handle, eyes on his house in front of him. It was old and familiar. And it loomed.

"I knew," he admitted. "Deep down. We all knew the stories. I just—I hoped that if I didn't think about it, if I shoved it down, it'd go away."

He climbed out of the truck. He started up his driveway, not looking back, hands sweating at his sides. He wiped them. They kept sweating.

twenty-six

THE DEAD FREAKS were up to something. That much was clear to Hunter. He watched them in the cafeteria talking like a bunch of spies, heads bent together.

"Those sickos," Hunter told Moe.

Moe looked over at him. He'd been picking at his meatloaf for ages, not eating, with that annoying worry screwing up his mousy face. Hunter wanted to punch it. Sometimes he even did. Moe took it well, even if it could make him cry.

"Who?" Moe asked, all thin and sulky.

Hunter jabbed his finger towards the dead freaks. Dude balanced a fork on one finger. Jules was laughing, Anna was smiling, and Babe was hitting him in the shoulder.

"What the hell are they up to?"

"Don't know, Hunt." Moe rubbed at his neck. Hunter had punched it this morning when Moe was being annoying.

"I hope Buzz shows up," Moe continued. "He still has my copy of *On The Road*. Why would he ditch without telling anyone?"

Hunter shrugged. But he knew: Buzz was finally doing what he'd always talked about before he'd moved onto waxing poetic about a school shooting. He'd "gone out of town," which meant he'd gotten a cousin to make him a paper trail somewhere. Soon the freaks of the town would start going missing. Buzz would come back eventually. If there was any suspicion, Buzz would point to the paper trail. *But I couldn't have done anything! I was in Portland/Chicago/New goddamn York!*

Not that there'd be much suspicion. Most of the cops would congratulate him. It was just a precaution.

Hunter smiled to himself. Buzz was *dedicated*. He hadn't even dropped by to talk to Hunter. A little disappointing. Hunter would love to help get rid of some freaks. Maybe Buzz would clue him in when the time came.

"You goddamn better," Hunter muttered.

"What?"

"Was I *talking* to you?" Hunter kicked Moe in the shin. "Shut it."

Moe hung his head. "Sorry."

A peal of laughter from the dead freaks table. Jules, the fat, prissy LA girl, cried laughing. Next to her was Anna, too good for anybody, never knowing her place. Dude folded in half with the force of his laughter, Babe leaning towards him almost enough to graze his forehead. Freaks.

Hunter's lip curled. Buzz had better come soon.

A low whisper: *You should burn them.*

Hunter jerked around. Nobody was behind him. Nobody would dare sneak up on him, not in Bulldeen.

Moe asked, "What is it?"

"Nothing," Hunter said.

The itch at the back of Hunter's brain had been there for days. Weeks, if he thought about it. Maybe longer. But in the last few days, it had been turning into words. He'd be walking around school, filled with the usual brimming anger at the wood and brick walls, and a voice not unlike his own would whisper, *it deserves to burn.*

Hunter had been freaked out at first. He'd even pushed a sophomore up against some lockers, demanding why he was talking to him. But it wasn't the sophomore. It wasn't anybody. It sure wasn't *Hunter*, though the voices sounded increasingly more like him. Sometimes, anyway. Some days, they sounded like his dad.

When Hunter pushed open the front door to his house only to hear a frenzied whisper, he thought it was his head voice going off again. Then he pushed off his shoes—he wasn't bothering with a backpack anymore—and walked deeper into the bowels of the house. The whispering was coming from the living room.

Hunter hesitated, then went around the hallway, into the kitchen. His mother was de-boning a chicken. Her fingers shook around the throat. Sometimes she'd forget to make food for days and everybody would survive on crackers, bread, and anchovies.

"Don't bother your father," she told him without looking up. "He's busy."

Hunter grunted, heart sinking further. His dad had been having a bad day too. A lot of the time they matched up. Hunter would come home in a rage only to find his father yelling to himself up in his room.

He wasn't yelling now. He was whispering, whispering with enough force that they could hear him through the wall. Hunter held his breath, came as close to the living room doorway as he dared.

"Son of a bitch son of a bitch son of a *bitch*—"

Hunter rolled his shoulders anxiously. *Someone must've*

pissed Dad off at work. Or maybe they made him take another break. Ian had worked for the thornfruit warehouse for decades. Every few years, he'd switch roles—from the fields to packaging, from packaging to labeling. The latest change was eight years ago, triggered by Ian throwing a wrench at his boss's head. They couldn't fire him. Where else would he go? Nobody wanted to endure Ian Creel's wrath. Or worse, his son's. Maybe Ian would set Hunter on them. So they kept Ian on, shuffled him around somewhere new until he screwed that up, then shoved him away from whoever he hurt or whatever he broke.

Between every role change, they'd have him take a break. A few weeks, maybe a month to "get his head right." And it worked. Ian would come into work fresh and bright-eyed. Then the years would pass, his fingers would shake more and more, he'd get closer and closer to an incident. The longer Ian stayed around thornfruit, the worse he was. The fields had been his first and shortest role. This latest one was janitor, and it was his longest. But they still lived in Bulldeen. Thornfruit grew on three sides of the town.

The truth was this: it wasn't just the chemical runoff in his water supply. Ian Creel would have deteriorated if he moved to Timbuktu, but it would have happened more slowly, and only in his mind.

Hunter listened for a while longer. The mumbles stayed on the same track. Quietly, carefully, Hunter went upstairs into his room. He stood there, opening and closing his hands. He trembled.

Something strange was happening at the very back of his head. It felt familiar. He didn't like it.

A thunder up the stairs. Hunter jerked. He ran for the open window, hooking one leg out just in time for his dad to burst through the bedroom door. It cracked off its hinges and hung there. Ian barrelled in, making an immediate run for Hunter, who only had the top half of his body showing above the window.

"*Son of a bitch!*" Ian bellowed, grabbing. Too late—Hunter dropped two stories onto the yellow grass. He fell on his feet, then down onto his ass. Pain sparked up his legs, but he didn't notice. He got up and started limping, then running, then sprinting, away from his father's repeated screams. He got to the edge of the property and looked back over his shoulder to see Ian Creel shambling out of the house, still screaming at him, his mother hanging back at the door, wringing her raw-chicken hands.

He ran until his lungs ached. He ran until he got out of the fields district, through the rich asshole neighborhood, and towards Main Street. He ducked into the alley behind the liquor store and braced himself against the wall, chest heaving.

He took three gasping, hitching breaths. Then he realized what wall he was leaning against and straightened up, whipping off his dad's leather jacket and patting it all over for grime marks. The liquor store alley was dirtier than the basement floor at school. That homeless guy used to live there, the one who got eaten by wild dogs. Whenever he'd been asleep on the sidewalk, Hunter had kicked him in the head as he'd passed. The guy woke up flustered, mad, but he'd always shrink back when he noticed who it was.

Hunter closed his eyes, feeding on it—the fear in that man's face. The grudging hatred. Sure, he'd gotten kicked in the head, but he'd put up with it. Nobody wanted to tangle with Hunter Creel.

You're just that tough, whispered the voice in the back of his head.

He pulled his dad's jacket on with quivering hands.

"I *am* just that tough," he told himself. Maybe the voice wasn't so bad.

He left the alley, still sweating from his sprint. He'd rob the corner store, he decided. Nothing drastic—slip some chocolate bars and a carton of cigarettes into his pockets. There'd be someone there he could shove around.

The store was depressingly empty. Hunter slid cigarette carton after cigarette carton into his pockets, staring down the clerk, who tried his best not to meet his eyes. Hunter was about to go over and steal a lollipop, just to screw with him, when the bell above the door pinged.

KJ slouched in, hands in his pockets.

The voice stirred. *You could follow him. He spends time with one of the dead freaks. You can get Dude alone.*

Hunter turned. Waited.

KJ went over to the drinks first. Opened the fridge and stared in. He took out an orange juice. Put it back. Picked up a soda. By then, Hunter was getting more than a little frustrated.

He marched over and stood next to the fridge.

KJ glanced. Then he jumped. "Hey! Hi, Hunter."

Hunter nodded. He didn't speak.

KJ watched him cautiously. He reached to put the soda back.

Hunter's jaw twitched.

"Uh," KJ said. "Can I help you?"

Hunter stared him down, knowing his silence was more worrying than his usual routine of calling KJ racial slurs. Hunter would go to the grave believing KJ was Chinese.

KJ laughed nervously. "Alright." He headed for the door.

Hunter followed him out. He glanced back at the store

clerk, who instantly buried his face behind an *Archie* comic. Hunter let himself smirk, but he didn't really feel it. It wasn't enough.

KJ walked normal enough at first. Then he picked up the pace. Hunter started to jog. KJ, hearing heavy footsteps, tried to sprint. He never got the chance.

Hunter grabbed him by the back of the shirt and shoved him into the sidewalk.

KJ whimpered, holding up his hands. "Whatever I did," KJ said, "I'm sorry, okay? I swear, I'll make it up to you—"

"Where can I get Dude alone?"

KJ trailed off. "What?"

Hunter shook him. "You two sneak off together, where do you go?"

"He's—we hang out in the basement sometimes!"

Hunter grinned. The guy was almost in tears. "Next time you guys arrange a basement hangout, you tell me about it."

"I will!"

Hunter leaned in until his teeth skimmed KJ's ear. His mouth watered. For some reason, he wanted to bite it, bite and keep on biting until his teeth met through the flesh. He sucked back saliva. "If you try to warn any of them, I'll cut off your balls. That's what you'll *get*."

"I won't," KJ croaked. "I won't tell them, I promise."

This all happened on Main Street. Their old elementary school teacher started to walk towards them, then crossed to the opposite sidewalk. Three cars drove past as Hunter held KJ to the ground. The drivers looked out their windows 2nd then back at the road. Because they were scared of Hunter, sure, but also because people didn't get out of their cars for this sort of thing. If you lived in Bulldeen, you were left to deal with your own business.

For better or goddamn worse.

As Hunter held KJ on the ground, he had an idea. It was all his. Nobody needed to nudge at him.

A few years ago, his father had told him a secret. It had to do with Mr. Jitterbug. All those years ago, before Ian Creel got too drunk to light the gym on fire, he'd crawled underneath the floorboards and stashed five cans of gasoline. The plan had been to light the floor on fire, and the sparks would fly down into the cans and explode them. He'd had to break some panels to get in, then nailed them shut when he'd returned the next day.

If only they'd built another boiler after the last one exploded, Ian Creel had told his son. *That would've made things much easier.*

Last year, Hunter had found the spot his father had nailed sloppily shut, and broken it back open. He'd crawled the same route his father had done. All five cans of gasoline were there and accounted for. Stale, sure. But they'd still burn.

Hunter shoved KJ harder into the ground, grinning. KJ shrunk into himself.

"It's your lucky day," Hunter told him. "I was gonna beat you up, but I got stuff to do."

"Okay," KJ said, nodding furiously. "Thank you."

"You're goddamn welcome," Hunter spat, and stomped on KJ's groin. He walked away to the satisfying song of KJ's screams.

chapter
twenty-seven

MILLY HART'S basement apartment had no windows. It was one big room with a toilet in the corner, dark and dismal despite all the attempts to lighten it up: posters displaying colorful TV shows and movies, a shelf full of bright books and figurines in armor; maps on the wall with places Babe had never seen before, places with mystical names like *Mistdoor* and *Kilimoor* and *Glorfunshelk*.

"I play a lot of Dungeons & Dragons," Milly admitted, with a nervous laugh.

Anna perked up. "Right! Who with?"

"Um," Milly said. She was as stiff as ever as they clustered on and around her couch. It only fit two people, so Kate and Babe had taken the cushions. Anna, Jules and Dude sat on the carpet.

"I play it over email," she said. "It's...very slow going. But it's been going for ages now, so we've really constructed a good campaign."

Babe nodded politely. Anna had tried to get them into D&D a few years ago, but she and Babe were the only two with the attention span for it. You couldn't play D&D with two people.

"It's actually why I started learning Latin," she said, coming to stand in front of them, fidgeting with her sleeves. "I wanted to make a language for my character."

Anna shone with excitement. "That's so cool!"

Babe's stomach growled audibly. Everyone eyed it. He resisted the urge to close his arms over his torso.

"So how's the ritual going?" Kate asked.

"Right," Milly said, and ran to her nightstand. It was a short run. The basement was big, but it was still a basement. She took the ritual carefully, unfurling it as she walked back close enough for them to see it. There was transparent paper clipped over it, the thin sheet riddled with scribblings and corrections.

"So," she said, and Babe blinked in surprise. In that one word, her voice was more solid than Babe had ever heard it. "First off, this isn't ancient Latin. It's...kind of pidgin Latin? Written by someone who doesn't know a huge amount about Latin. We have the first instructions—there's no diagram for the spell, we just draw a circle and make sure it's linked up. The invocation to start the spell was mostly intact. I think I have it figured out: *Bulldeen, I invoke you. Come and feed.*"

Kate huffed a laugh. Babe craned his head to look at her on the ratty couch. She had a cigarette in her mouth, its smoke curling up to the ceiling.

Milly didn't notice. She was too deep in it. "Then there's some chanting—*we revoke your power*—basic stuff. And after that, we run into some problems. Um." Her fingers curled around the transparent paper. She glanced down at them, remembering her audience.

"Problems..." Babe prompted.

Milly gasped in a breath. For a second, no words came. "Sorry," Milly said, and shoved her bangs out of her face with one hand. She nearly dropped the papers. "Right. Um, so we don't have the full incantation for the banishment. There's something about a water source, and poison, but the rest of it..." She sighed. "I'll work on it. And the location is important. We need to go to where the ritual was first performed."

Kate asked, "Where's that?"

"That's our next problem." Milly pointed at the bottom, where the stains were worst. "I think this word is *cēlans*—that's the present participle of *cēlo*. It means hidden or secret. So the ritual needs to happen in 'the hidden place.'" She gave them a hopeful look. "Do we know where that is?"

A wall of blank faces.

Milly's shoulders went up around her ears again. "Sorry I haven't been much help."

"Done better than any of us would've," Kate said.

Babe's stomach growled again. This one gurgled on and on.

Dude laughed.

"What?" Babe said, rounding on him. "Huh? What's so funny?"

Dude shrugged, still smiling. "Nothing."

Milly raised a hand like she was still in school. It wilted back down to her side when everyone gave her an incredulous look. "If we don't figure out the ritual in time, are you going to eat someone?"

Everybody looked at each other in silent agreement: they were *not* going to tell Milly their plan to kill Nazis.

Anna piped up. "Hopefully not."

Milly nodded. "If you do," she said quickly, "you should plan it? Make it a bad person instead of, of...someone you're in front of at the store."

"We've been thinking about that," Babe admitted, after a pause.

Milly nodded, started furling the ritual back up. "I can leave if you guys need to talk about that stuff."

"This is your house," Kate said. "*We'll* leave."

"Thank you so much," Anna added. "You'll try to work on the incantation?"

Milly's face went hard and determined. "I will."

"We'll work on the location," Jules said, and struck a Superman pose. "Hidden place! Here we come!"

Anna led the way out. Halfway up the stairs, she whirled around, stopping everybody in their tracks. "Milly!"

Milly jerked upright. She'd started to put her tablecloth back on the table. "Yes?"

"Do you know much about that boiler explosion that took out the old school?"

Milly opened and closed her mouth. She looked questioningly at the others. "I don't think so," Milly said. "Why? Does that have something to do with this?"

"Maybe. I don't know. Do you know much about the first thornfruit workers who froze to death?"

"Um. No more than anybody else? Sorry—"

"Alright. Thanks anyway! And thank you for letting us use your place! It's so nice."

Milly's voice caught, unable to struggle up her throat. She made some strained noises and shot them a thumbs-up.

Babe glanced over his shoulder as Anna started to move again, letting everyone else trail up behind her. The room was still depressing. But, watching Milly as she painstakingly adjusted her yellow tablecloth, one of many splashes of color lighting up the dark room, he couldn't make himself be appalled.

None of them had ever seen Kate so excited as she was when discussing which townsfolk Babe could kill. They gathered around the hood of her car up on Juniper Lookout.

"Didn't even know this place was here," she said, and shook a piece of paper from her jacket. It was done on cheap notebook paper.

"Since I'm Chief," she started, "I have a decent idea of the bad shit happening in this town. So here are some options."

She spread the list out on the hood. Dude climbed onto it and scooted over. It was hard for all of them to gather around and still have room.

"So obviously we got our pick of Nazis," Kate said, "but here are the worst ones. I can never get enough dirt on these guys to do anything about them."

Babe raised his eyebrows at Anna. It was news to both of them that Kate wanted to do anything about anybody.

"Take your pick," Kate said, and started reading out the list. Babe's face pinched and didn't smooth out until she finished. A laundry list of child molesters, wife beaters, rapists, and hate crimers. Babe hadn't known about all of it, but he wasn't surprised. A lot of stuff happened in this town behind closed doors.

"How hungry are you?" Kate asked once she'd finished.

Babe considered. It was becoming constant. Heavy. "Pretty hungry."

"Which means what? A couple days?"

"Yeah. Maybe."

Kate snapped her nicotine gum. She'd chucked one into her mouth right after she stubbed her cigarette out on Milly's concrete wall.

"We stretch you out to the end of your rope, we get more time to figure out your ritual. But I don't want you going feral again like you did with Buzz. We'll feed someone to… whatever that thing is, before you get that bad. Alright?"

"I guess."

"How's tomorrow before school?"

"*Before* school?"

"You wanna go feral during fifth period?"

"…No."

She clapped him on the shoulder. He almost expected an ash handprint.

"Good man," she said. She was grinning. It looked dangerous. "I know just the meal."

chapter
twenty-eight

JULES PUT on her ass-kicking outfit: tiny denim shorts, red tights, and a pink crop top made out of an old hoodie. Combat boots she saved for occasions that might need punching, to suit the mood. Her purple hair was up in a stylish yet functional knot at the back of her head, with some butterfly clips thrown in for flavor.

She clipped her CD player to her belt and put on the ass-kicking mixtape she'd made. As always, the tunes required air guitar and kicky dance moves in front of the mirror, after which she paused to redo her eye makeup, which she'd noticed was lopsided.

"I envy everybody who sees me today," she told her reflection, and sashayed out of her bedroom with her music on full blast.

Her parents were in the kitchen. Her mom was making bread, her obsession of the month. Her dad read a monster truck magazine at the table.

"Heeeey," Jules sang as she walked through the kitchen into the front hall.

"Heeeey," her dad sung back.

Her mother grunted, too busy kneading dough on the countertop to concern herself with words.

Neither of them looked up at their daughter as she strode past. They rarely bothered with their daughter and she rarely bothered with them. When she was a kid, she used to cry for their attention, make messes, or scream. When that hadn't even earned her the bad kind of attention, she'd decided the best way to deal with her parents' disinterest was to be just as disinterested. Her parents didn't dislike her—they were actually known to get along very well in the rare occasions the three of them were all in the same room—but they didn't care much about her, either. Jules didn't mind. If she ever found herself feeling otherwise, she quickly talked herself out of it.

Dude was waiting in his truck. Babe was in the passenger seat, as usual. Jules climbed into the backseat with Anna, leaning over to kiss her on the cheek. Anna smiled, surprised and pleased, and Jules panged with guilt. She hadn't been that physically affectionate lately, too busy on the approaching promise of LA to put her usual focus on her friends.

"Guess who has a kickass playlist ready?" Jules drummed the headphones that ringed her neck.

Dude sang it. "I guess Juuules."

"You're...flashy," Babe said, in a tone that suggested he didn't entirely disapprove.

"Those really aren't murder clothes," Dude agreed.

Babe sucked in a tight breath through his nose, but it was annoyance, not hurt. Jules had been quick to catch up on the group dynamics when she'd joined in middle school. It had been hard to be concerned about Babe and Dude bickering—they both enjoyed it too loudly. She loved to watch them. Those *boys*.

Jules rested her chin on Dude's shoulder, waiting to see if Babe would take the bait.

"Murder clothes," he repeated.

Jules glanced at Dude triumphantly. He flashed a distracted grin at her and said, "Yeah, with the all-black and the gloves and the plastic."

"You're in jeans."

"*You're* in jeans," Dude shot back.

Anna piped up, clutching her seatbelt. "Am I the only one who wants this over as soon as possible?"

"Right," Dude said, putting the truck into gear.

Both he and Babe spoke at once: "Wouldn't wanna be late for homeroom."

Jules smiled. She wasn't thinking about what was going to happen. She was thinking about her music, which came back into focus as she slid her headphones back onto her head, careful not to mess up her hair.

Kate leaned against the guy's fence, smoking a cigarette. She tilted her head at them as they pulled up.

"Mornin'," she said, squinting hard into the sun.

Jules beamed. "Ready to go!"

Kate grunted, glancing down her clothes. "Flashy."

Jules planted her hands on her hips. "It's my ass-kicking outfit."

"Alright," Kate said, and pinched her lips around her cigarette. Sucked it down to the filter and crushed it under her boot. Jules didn't have to get close to smell the stale whiskey under the smoke. Hungover was Kate's natural state.

Music drifted up from Jules's headphones, now around her neck. Jules hummed along, did a little dance, shook her hips.

It was maybe seven a.m., warm but not yet hot. Cardigan

weather. Not that people in this town wore cardigans. Jules rubbed at her arms.

"Go around the back," Kate said. "Wait in the yard. I'll open the back door after he's finished."

"But not *finished*," Babe prompted. "Right?"

"That's what I meant," Kate said. She nodded at him. "So, the thing will just show up once he's close to dead?"

Babe looked over at Dude, who was busy picking splinters out of the fence.

Dude bit a shard of wood from under his nail. "'S what it said."

Another nod. "Anyone wanna come as backup? In case he catches me by surprise."

Anna took a step back. Dude resumed splinter-picking. Babe looked away.

Jules stuck up a hand, Milly-style. "I'll do it." She'd brought a playlist for kicking ass, after all.

Kate gave another pointed look at her crop top and tights. But she just said, "Alright," and jerked her head for Jules to follow. Jules bounced into place behind her, shooting her a salute.

"Music off," Kate said.

Jules reached to her hip where the CD player was strapped. The music around her neck cut in mid-guitar riff. They walked side by side up to the front door, where Kate knocked.

"Don't say anything."

"Got it." Jules winked.

The door swung open. An old man in a woolen shirt peered at them. His eyes widened.

"Higgins!" he cried. "How the hell are ya?"

"Hi, Marcus," said Kate, standing still for the hug. She raised one hand to clap Marcus on the back, staring straight ahead.

Jules stood to the side, drumming a tune on her shorts.

Marcus pulled back from the hug and gestured at her. "And who's this lovely young lady? Not another recruit, I hope? You're woman enough for the force in this town!"

"I'm Jules," said Jules.

Kate gave her the side-eye. Jules ignored it, holding out a hand that Marcus shook enthusiastically. His hand was wrinkled and clammy and Jules had to wipe her own hand when he let her go.

"I'm driving her to school," Kate said. "Passed your place. Thought I'd drop in. You gonna invite me in or are we gonna stand out here growing roots?"

Marcus laughed. "Sharp as ever, I see! Come on, you two."

He took off down the hall, surprisingly fast for an old man with liver spots on his balding head. His place was musty, water stains on the carpet and wall. Photos lined the hall: family photos and a line-up of cops standing outside the Bulldeen police station. And there was Marcus, uniform and full head of hair glowing in the sun.

Present-day Marcus, wearing loafers and a toupee, sat them at the kitchen table and started bustling around, bringing out cookies. A Confederate flag hung over the oven.

"How's retirement?" Kate asked him.

"Boring," he replied. "Coffee?"

"Sure."

He poured some instant. They hadn't caught up to espresso machines in Bulldeen, even in their lone diner. Jules longed for a mochaccino, but wrapped her hands obediently around the mug he pushed in front of her.

Kate swallowed a long mouthful. "How's the family?"

A pause. "Ah, you know," Marcus said as he poured his own coffee. "Don't see 'em much."

"Heard anything from your daughter?"

"Bethy? No, not recently."

"Mm," Kate said. She took three long gulps. Jules kept sipping even as Kate got up, chair scraping back.

Marcus turned, coffee in hand. "So what's it like being Chief Higgins?"

"Exciting as ever," Kate said. She leaned on the counter, hand curling around the coffee brewer. "Jules, if you wanna look away, now's the time."

"I'm good," said Jules.

Marcus looked between the two. His smile still hadn't faded when Kate took a handkerchief out of her pocket and jammed it into his mouth, then picked up the coffee pot and slammed it into his head. It shattered, glass going all over the linoleum or embedding in Marcus's face.

Jules jolted, a gasp punching out of her.

Marcus let out a muffled scream. Another hit, this time with the plastic base of the coffee maker. Marcus hit the floor.

It was violent. It was really violent. Jules averted her eyes, hunching into her shoulders. What had she been thinking? She'd barely been able to deal with Buzz's body, why did she think this would be different? She had thought it'd be like a movie, but movies had that safety of the screen. There was no safety here. It was happening right in front of her.

Nope, thought Jules. She shuffled her chair around, pulled her headphones over her ears. Kate kept hitting him. Jules didn't know what with. Marcus tried to yell words around the handkerchief, but they dissolved as Jules turned the CD player back on.

Soothing guitar riff. *One, two, three, four!*

Jules hummed along. Sometimes there were gaps in the song and the noises filtered in: grunts, moans, the impact of Kate's hits. As the song faded into the next one, there was silence apart from ragged breathing.

Jules chanced a look. Kate was crouching beside Marcus, who was wheezing weakly.

"This is for your daughter," Kate said softly. "And every other little girl you took with you into that woodshed."

She stood. Jules turned back hastily, let Kate come over and touch her shoulder. Kate didn't linger, didn't even look at her, just tapped her arm and then walked to the back door off the kitchen.

"You can come in," she said into the backyard.

Jules sped to Anna's side as they filed in, linking their elbows together. Anna gasped, turning her head away from the bloody man on the tiles.

"So it just shows up?" Kate says.

"'S what it said," Dude said, quieter than before. He wasn't turning his head away, but he didn't stare. Just glanced at and then away from the old man, who was still twitching and groaning.

Babe did stare. His pupils filled in. His mouth twitched open.

"Babe," Dude and Kate said in unison.

"What?" Babe said dazedly, and then blinked hard, looking away from the blood spreading towards them on the floor. He snapped back to himself. "Oh. What?"

Jules stared determinedly out the window. He had a nice garden. An *impossibly* nice garden, considering where he was. Was that an azalea bush?

"So," she said, "are we just standing around this dying guy until—"

Babe shuddered. Jules opened her mouth to ask what was wrong when a figure came in from the hallway.

"Hello," it said to her.

Battered leather shoes. Big overcoat. A shiny spine of buttons. The creature smiled down. It took a second for her to realize that it looked like a strange amalgamation of her parents, only sharper. Everything in Jules's brain screamed at her to run.

"Hi," she squeaked. She pointed at Marcus on the floor. "We have something for you."

She stepped out of the way. It watched her for another second, then looked around at everyone's faces. Down to Marcus, groaning and bleeding out.

Jules held her breath. But the thing just looked for maybe five seconds. Then it looked over at Babe, who was staring resolutely out the window. Jules made a note to mention Marcus's azaleas, their strange color, how they almost pulsated.

Dude said, "Aren't you going to..."

The creature's arms hung at its sides. "No."

"No," Dude repeated. "Huh. Well—"

"But you said you'd do it," Babe said. His gaze flickered to Marcus—to the blood that stopped before his own shoes—but only for a moment.

"And I will," the creature said. Its voice was smooth, rich. It would've been pleasant if everything else about it didn't make your skin crawl. "When we get hungry enough."

"But—" Dude started.

Babe talked over him. "He's going to die! He doesn't have *time*."

"Yes," the creature agreed. "A waste."

And it pulled out the seat Kate had been sitting on. Her coffee was still there. It reached out one long finger and rotated the mug by the handle, as if readying to pick it up.

Anna's grip tightened. Jules looked over to see Anna looking desperately at her, like she might do something. When Jules just stared, Anna said, "We can't just let him die. I mean, not without—"

"It *would* be a waste," Jules tried.

Babe glared. Jules held up her free hand in defeat even

though it wasn't an angry glare—it was a panic glare, his big eyebrows pulling inwards in worry.

They turned to Kate, who shrugged. She had a spatter of blood on the curve of her chin. "Gotta eat," was all she said.

Babe's shoulders twitched forwards, then back.

Marcus moaned. They were coming weaker from behind the handkerchief.

"Time limit," Dude reminded them.

"I *know*," Babe snapped, and braced himself. "Fine, I'll... Everybody get out, I'm doing it."

Jules tugged at Anna, who stayed rooted to the spot. "Are you sure?"

"Yes," Babe said, rushed. His pupils grew and grew until his eyes became dark pools. He wasn't looking at them now, he was staring down at Marcus's faint, paling skin. "Get out."

Kate made for the door. Dude made to clap Babe on the shoulder.

"Dude," Jules said.

Dude aborted the motion mid-swing and gave a thumbs-up instead. "We'll have fresh clothes for you to change into when you come out, buddy."

Babe didn't answer. The last thing Jules saw before she dragged Anna out the door was Babe finally looking up, meeting the eyes of the creature with an expression Jules couldn't begin to read.

Jules sat under the azaleas and thought vaguely of a Lovecraft story she'd read in freshman year. The Colour of Something Something. She plucked a furry petal off, held it up to the light. Iridescent purple.

"How the hell did he manage to grow something like this in Bulldeen?" she asked.

No one answered. Anna was pacing again, flattening a tiny circle of grass as she went over it. Kate flicked through her police radio. It hadn't chimed all morning.

Just outside of Jules's range, Dude sat with his legs crossed, facing the back door to the kitchen.

Jules scooted over and leaned her head on his shoulder. "Howdy."

Dude nudged her with his chin. "How long does it take to eat someone?"

"A normal person? I don't know," Jules admitted. "A feral Babe? I also don't know."

"Maybe we should check on him," Anna said.

Jules glanced over to the other yards. If you stood on your toes in the neighbor's yard, their group would look like specks in a sea of flowers. Her butterfly clip was starting to loosen in her bangs. She tightened it, plastic scraping her scalp.

I shouldn't have gone in with Kate, she wanted to say, but wouldn't say with Kate still there. *I thought it'd be cool. I thought it'd have a soundtrack.*

She sniffed, turning her mind to nicer things. "Milly seems cool."

Anna hummed in agreement, eyes on the grass as she paced.

"I know she's older," Jules continued, "But she gives me little sister vibes. I always wanted a little sister."

Anna looked over. "What am I, chopped liver?"

Jules beamed. "You're my twin!"

The back door creaked open. Babe peeked out, face and hair dripping with water. His shoulder, the only other part Jules could see, was also damp. He was shirtless, towel clutched around his waist. He didn't meet anyone's gaze.

"I took a shower," he said. "You promised clothes?"

Dude shot to his feet. "They're in the trunk."

"Why are they in the trunk?" Jules asked from the ground.

"So he wouldn't get stuck in your dad's old jeans again!" Dude called, already jogging for the car.

It took Jules a second to realize she should make a joke, try to lighten the mood, but by then Dude was already gone.

chapter
twenty-nine

IT COULD BE ARGUED that the valedictorian should not be chosen like homecoming queen. It could be argued that historically, speaking in front of the graduating class was a privilege that should only be awarded to the scholar with the top marks.

Historically, Bulldeen High found that deeply boring. What had started as a joke in 1848 quickly snowballed into an earnest tradition. The top student got *valedictorian* squirreled away on their records, but it wasn't widely talked about. What *was* talked about was who would be the most interesting senior to send off the graduating class every year.

This year, the vote had been skewing towards Vicky Valdin, who did have the best grades in all her classes. But in the last two weeks before classes ended, the vote took an abrupt turn. Students dropped by the voting box to ask if they could change their vote to Babe Simmons.

Neither Babe, nor any of his friends, noticed this, until the day they killed the old man. Freshly fed and freshly showered, Babe walked with Dude towards the football field, where they would sit during free period. Strung up at the back entrance was a banner, the letters done in duct tape.

ZOMBABE FOR VALEDICTORIAN.

Babe came to a stop in the hallway. Dude, who had been trying to perfect the art of rolling a coin along his knuckles, stopped with him.

"What?" Dude said.

Babe pointed.

Dude looked. "Ah."

Joseph Blythe, football star and low-key asshole, careened past and slapped Babe on the shoulders.

"Zombabe for valedictorian!" he yelled, in the grunting tone he'd normally yell, BULLDEEN BULLS FOR LIFE.

"Ha ha," Babe said automatically. "Thanks."

Joseph walked off with his arms raised, still crowing.

Babe and Dude watched him go, students parting to walk around them. Since the funeral, most of the student body took care not to bump into Babe Simmons.

"Zombabe for valedictorian!" called April Tanner, high-key cheerleader and low-key asshole, as she turned the corner. If April made it to her twenties, she would pluck out her fangs and turn into a genuinely decent human being. Glimpses of it shone through sometimes, glimpses she tried hard to smother. These glimpses were the reason she wouldn't make it to her twenties.

April flashed them a wave and Babe had to focus on keeping the polite smile. Who would be next? Hunter Creel? Would Moe tell him *he* was rooting for him?

Babe thought about the voting box sitting safely at the entrance to school, just after the metal detectors. "It's too late to change the vote, right?"

"Uhhh," Dude said. He scratched his nose with the coin he was holding between his knuckles. "Sure."

"You don't sound very confident."

"Nope," Dude said, popping the *p*.

Babe groaned.

"What? Everybody saves their vote for the last couple weeks. Never know what could happen." Dude drummed his fingers on his backpack straps. "Think they're gonna use the field? I wanna lie on the grass."

Babe sighed, still staring up at the banner. "If they *are* using it, you can lie on the sidelines."

It was one of those rare periods that the field wasn't being used by a P.E. class, the cheer squad, or the football team. Babe and Dude sat in the middle of the grass, practicing fake punches.

"You gotta come in faster," Dude told him. "Come on, how many years have we been doing this?"

"If I come in faster, I end up actually punching you!"

Babe couldn't count how many times he'd ended up accidentally punching Dude during these sessions. When he was eight, he'd broken Dude's nose. He'd sobbed over Dude, apologizing wetly as Dude lay dazed on the playground bark, blood leaking down his chin.

I'm fine, Dude kept telling him, muffled through the blood. *I'm good, I'm fine. You didn't get me that hard.*

On the field, Dude beckoned at him.

Babe rolled his eyes. Then he shoved a fist at Dude's face. Dude jerked backward, leading with his cheek—the place Babe would've punched if his fist had connected. He braced himself on the grass, moaning.

Babe hummed approvingly. "I still think you're getting better at it."

Dude snapped back into place. "I'm not letting the punch carry me enough."

"You're good!"

"I—" Dude squinted past him. Babe turned.

KJ stood at the edge of the field, hunching. He was always cautious when talking to Dude in public, but now he looked almost scared. He took little paces just beyond the grass, reluctant to step onto the field, eyeing Dude like he wanted to signal something.

Dude cupped his hands around his mouth. "Hey, KJ!"

Babe curled his hand into a fist, catching grass between his fingers and thinking about punching, wishing KJ was the kind of offensive he'd want to punch. Why did KJ have to be so damn bland?

KJ wavered at the sidelines. Then, as if walking across coals, he sped across the grass and stopped right in front of Dude, mumbling something unintelligible.

Dude shielded his eyes from the sun. "What?"

"We should meet up," KJ said. He glanced over his shoulder and blanched. "Shit."

Moe was lurking around the edges of the field. As bullies went, he wasn't one to worry about. Babe frowned up at KJ. He had only seen him this panicked at a house party last year. KJ had eaten half an edible and spent the rest of the party curled up under the stairs, ears blocked and eyes scrunched shut. At school the next week, Dude had gone to talk to him about it. They'd had a good talk about their relationship with substances—namely, how they didn't take them. That was how they'd come up with their boiler room arrangement, heads bent together in the library talking in hushed tones about how weed turned KJ's brain into a hellscape, how it lit up Dude's brain in ways he didn't want to get used to. KJ's foot had bumped into Dude's ankle and stayed there. Dude had let himself get caught looking at KJ's mouth. He'd been the one to suggest they go somewhere more private.

Dude had told his friends about it a few months after it

started happening, his voice low and rushed, and not looking at any of them as they sat under the stars on Juniper Lookout. Jules had giggled a lot, Anna made surprised, supportive noises, and Babe had stayed silent, also not looking at any of them, yanking grass out of the hill with such ferocity it hurt his fingers.

At the edge of the field, Moe noticed someone was scared of him. He stopped in surprise, then wiped that expression off his face and tried to dig up Hunter's terrifying glare. On Moe, it came across as indigestion.

"I—I should go," KJ stuttered, and sped back across the field. The long way, so as to not cross paths with Moe.

Dude and Babe watched him flee, mystified.

"Guess he pissed off Hunter," Dude said.

"Guess so," Babe said. There was no other reason why anyone would be scared of Moe. They waited, but Moe just stood there at the edge of the field, slumping in disappointment at the retreating KJ. Still, there was the faint excitement of someone being afraid of him. It gave him the boost of confidence to call, "On a date, boys?"

"You know it," Dude replied immediately. "Wanna join us? We were hoping you'd show up."

Babe laughed, giving Dude a warning push. Dude rocked with the impact.

As Moe always did when confronted with something without Hunter or Buzz to back him up, he wilted. He mumbled for a moment, trying to come up with something, but his heart wasn't in it. Moe didn't have that deep hatred that churned in his friends' chests. He had resentment, sure, but in the moment, it was always overshadowed by panic.

"You guys are sick," he said, cheeks bright with embarrassment. He walked off, angry with himself, pretending it was directed at those sick boys. He almost believed it. It was always easier to blame somebody who wasn't you.

Back on the grass, Babe and Dude chuckled to themselves as they watched Moe's vanishing back.

"That's gonna come back and bite us in the butt," Babe said.

"You, maybe," Dude said easily. "I'm outta here." He lay back against the grass. His long lashes brushed his cheeks. Babe let himself look until he heard footsteps treading behind them on the grass.

Yancy Land, voice of the Bulldeen shadow, was coming back from a weed-induced nap around the back of school. He tossed the boys a peace sign as he passed. "Heyyyy, Zombabe for valedictorian!"

"Hell yeah," Dude echoed, eyes closed.

Babe sighed. "Thanks," he said resignedly, but Yancy didn't hear. He was already past them, off to cast his vote.

chapter
thirty

BABE WAS STANDING *in the middle of the road in Bulldeen square, watching the old town hall burn down. People screamed, crowded, threw buckets of water. Most of them watched.*

"Here we are," said a woman next to him.

Babe turned. She was maybe thirty years old, thick black hair. No makeup.

In front of them, the fire roared.

"Monica Higgins," Babe said, recognizing Anna's great-grandmother.

She nodded. Firelight reflected in her eyes.

"I was wondering when this would happen," she said. "For me, it was earlier."

"Earlier?" Babe stepped out of the way of a man charging with a small, useless bowl of water. "Was it just you?"

"No. There was a daughter. You'll see her soon." Monica sighed, shook out her hair. It was thick and wavy. She twined it in her fingers. "My, but I miss this. Tell me, how is Milly Hart?"

"Did she come here? After she came back?"

Monica nodded. "Poor thing. Too young to know what was

going on. I held her as the fire ate up the town house. She cried the whole time."

Babe shivered. In the distance, someone was sobbing. He couldn't see who it was.

The hall roof began to cave in. It was completely blackened.

"Are you still in there?" he asked.

Another shake of the head. "By now, we're piling our luggage into our car. Setting our sights on Chicago."

Getting out. Babe ached with it: careening past the welcome sign, never looking back. I'm gonna leave this town in the dust. *Babe didn't know if he was capable of leaving anything.*

A piercing scream from the grass outside the town hall. A woman ran for the burning front door and got tackled to the ground. She stayed there, pinned and wailing.

"He must love you very much," said Monica Higgins.

Babe looked over. She was old again, silver hair trailing past her shoulders, wrinkles pulling her eyes down. She smiled. Her eyes gleamed in the firelight. If Babe looked

if Babe looked close

if Babe looked close they were almost —

— wet.

Babe clenched his fists in the sheets, which were once again soaked with sweat. For a second, his body didn't feel like his own, like he was a stranger moving someone else's limbs. Then the feeling was gone, and he was himself again, panting in his bed, skin crawling.

He sat up. Moonlight streamed through the open window. He got up and pulled it closed. Stood there waiting for his breath to even out, thinking of Monica. Did she just wake up, shaking in a motel bed, her husband sleeping peacefully beside her?

He stayed with that for a moment: Monica reaching out and smoothing a hand through her husband's hair. A smile so fond, so full, it made Babe's chest clench, bringing him back to himself with a dull crash.

———

Anna's voice came sleep-muzzy over the line. "Hello?"

"Hey. It's me."

"Oh. Hey." Sheets rustling. Anna had a landline in her room, next to her bed. If there was a vet emergency, she'd wake up her parents. If not, they didn't want to be disturbed.

"What's wrong?" she asked.

"Nothing." Babe wrapped an arm around his knees. He was sitting on the floor, cord limp above him. He rubbed his bare feet into the carpet, focusing on the roughness. *Me. I'm me. I am in this body and it is me.* He should've put on his glasses. The world's fuzziness didn't help ground him.

"How's the reading going?"

More sheets rustling. Anna was getting comfortable for a long call.

"It's...interesting," she said. "You know our school is almost an exact replica of the old one?"

"Yeah?"

"Yeah, they made it with the old blueprints. Same material, same builders even. They used different paint though—grays instead of whites. The paint is cheaper, but a little lead-y and more flammable. And they used different wood for the gym. And they put fire axes around the school in the 1900s."

"They did?"

"Two of them are still there."

Babe tried to think where the heck he'd seen a fire ax. He hadn't even seen a hose. It was tempting to let Anna keep talking, but she didn't continue. She knew why he'd called. And because she knew, she would answer if he asked her more about the reading she'd been doing on Bulldeen. But Babe was tired and wired and nighttime always felt like limbo. Unreality. You could say anything sitting under your phone at night, your oldest friend on the other line.

"Anna?"

"Yes?"

"Do you think I've changed?"

"Not in any way that's important," Anna replied instantly, and he loved her for it. "Other than eating people. And you've been, um. Irritable."

"I'm sorry."

"I know."

"Do you think—do you think it's been in me the whole time?"

A pause. "Do you?"

Babe swallowed. It was impeded by nothing. These days, he'd be walking around and he'd remember swallowing flesh. It didn't disgust him.

"I always felt like something was rotting in me," he said slowly. "That one day, it'd kill me."

Anna laughed. She didn't do bitter, but this came close. "That's not the creature. That's just Bulldeen."

Babe leaned his cheek on the wallpaper. Anna didn't join in on the tirades every teen experimented with after a lifetime in Bulldeen, about burning it down or never coming back. Babe used to think it was because she *did* plan on coming back. Now he knew it was because if she let loose about how much she hated Bulldeen, the flood would never stop. It would come and come, and the hate and bitterness would consume her.

"What if," Babe said, and swallowed, "what if it's *not* better out there? What if the poison isn't Bulldeen, it's me? And we go to all these places, but we don't ever flush it out?"

Anna's answer was immediate. "You aren't poison. No matter what your dad says."

"What? Dad doesn't say that."

"He makes you feel like there's something wrong with you, right? Deep down."

Babe didn't have anything to say to that. He wrapped an arm around his knees.

"We aren't poison either," Anna continued. "We're...we're good. We're good to each other. And we'll keep being good to each other when we get out of here. Maybe that's all that matters."

Babe closed his eyes. The fuzzy world turned black. He could never look at the important things. He took a breath. "It's late. I should go."

"Babe—"

"Bye."

"Do you remember dying?"

Babe stopped. He'd been reaching the phone towards the receiver, about to hang up. He held the phone back to his mouth.

"You don't have to answer," she said.

Babe took a shaky breath. He didn't speak for a long time.

"I remember Dude," he said finally. "His face over me. I remember this feeling of...calm. He told me everything was going to be okay."

"You believed him?"

"No. But...I don't know. His voice..."

It made dying not so bad. Actually, it was kind of nice. Him so close, saying my name. Looking at me like I was the only thing.

He didn't say it. But Anna's silence was knowing.

Babe bumped his hand on the wallpaper, three long taps, three short, three long again. Dude had tried to teach him

Morse code when they were younger so they could talk during class.

"Dude loves me too much."

"Too much?"

"Yes." Barely loud enough to hear. "And I can't...he deserves more and I can't give it to him."

"What does he deserve?"

Babe thought back to Anna's great-grandparents, their casual closeness. Their deep, obvious love. The miracle of meeting someone's gaze and holding it. Of not looking away.

He started to fake-yawn. It turned real halfway through, his jaw cracking around it. "I should go back to sleep."

"Right," Anna said, lit with realization. "You have the play tomorrow."

It took a second. Babe let his head fall into the wall.

"Damnit."

chapter
thirty-one

THE ANNUAL BULLDEEN play took place in the town square. A miniature stage was dragged out from the church basement and erected on Main Street, in between the new town hall and the plaque for the old one. It was a night to reflect on their town's history. A chance for the soon-to-be high school graduates to contemplate their future by looking back on the past.

For most residents, it was an opportunity to get stinking drunk in the middle of town square.

Babe stood on the stage, script in his back pocket. Just in case. He could recite the thing with his eyes closed, but there was a lot to be said about blind panic. He was dressed in "farmer clothes": the same old overalls and shirt and boots from 1977. The previous costume had fallen apart during a monologue the year before.

Dude sat on the corner of the stage, making last minute adjustments to the prop plants. Crouched behind the stairs up to the stage, Jules slotted a CD into a radio and tweaked the dials. Static raged over the speakers and Babe yelled in pain.

"Sorry!" Jules called, switching the static off. She stood and gave Babe the thumbs-up. Babe returned it, one hand holding his ear cautiously.

Jules turned the thumbs-up on Anna, who sat in a folding chair in the audience. Anna gave a tiny cheer. She was moral support. She hated this play and hadn't been to it in years.

Behind the folding chairs, Kate stood with her hand on her gun. Big gatherings always made her skin crawl. This gathering was making her glance over to the plaque commemorating the old town hall and shift her shoulders nervously.

Away from Chief Kate's radar, Hunter stalked around the chairs, impatient. Buzz still hadn't shown himself. *What are you waiting for?* Hunter thought, as he watched Dude poke Babe in the neck with a fake crop.

It was 7:55. The play started at eight p.m. Bulldeen residents slowly filled the chairs.

There was a jumble of noise behind Anna, a familiar croaky voice saying, "Sorry, sorry—"

Anna turned. Milly Hart was trying to get to a chair far away from anyone else, hair hiding her face.

"Milly!" Anna lifted a hand. It took a few more calls before Milly realized it really was her name being called.

Anna gestured at the empty chair next to her. "Come sit!"

Milly hesitated. It felt dramatic to say *who, me?* even if that was what she was thinking. She *sorry*'d her way out through the aisle and up to Anna's row, near the front.

"I think I've figured out the incantation for banishment," she said. "But I'm not totally sure, I didn't want to call until—"

She fell silent at Anna's hand on her shoulder. She couldn't remember the last touch she'd had beyond an accidental bump in the supermarket.

"Milly, you can have one night off!"

Milly blinked. "We're on a time limit," she said weakly. She looked at Babe up on stage, standing around awkwardly. "Is he—"

"He's fine," Anna assured her. She coughed, shifted her crossed legs. "For the next few days, anyway."

Right then, Milly decided to work on the ritual late into the night after the play. Keeping her tone as quiet and polite as she could manage, she said, "So the boiler explosion wasn't an accident?"

Anna glanced around. Milly did the same, though her eyes didn't take anything in, so she didn't notice Deputy Lissiter watching them from a corner seat. He made eye contact with Anna and smiled blandly.

She smiled back, safe in his distance. Nobody else was paying attention: two strange girls being strange together. Who would care about that?

"I think it tore apart families," Anna said softly. "Fruitless blame, grief. All that pain. Where do they put it? They shove it into each other."

Milly nodded slowly. She'd always thought Anna was very smart.

"I don't know, maybe I'm doing all this reading for nothing," Anna continued. "I just don't want to miss anything."

Milly nodded more vigorously. Her eyes hurt from staring at the ritual during breaks at work.

"So," Anna said, drawing herself up with a bracing breath. "Enough about that—tell me about your Dungeons & Dragons campaign! Who's your DM?"

Milly's eyes lit up. It was an exceedingly rare opportunity to talk about this in real life. "Um," she said. "I am, actually."

"Yeah? That's so cool! What's the world like? What characters do you have in your group?"

"Um," Milly said again, and, slowly at first, described her game.

Anna leaned forwards on her hands to listen. Milly Hart could talk a mile a minute when she got the chance to do it about something she gave a shit about. And she gave many, many shits about her D&D campaign, a seven-year long steampunk campaign with her internet friends. Both of them were annoyed when Zachary Litnus stood in the middle of the stage, took a suck on his inhaler, and began to clap. Between claps, he announced, "The play is starting! I repeat, the play is starting! Everybody to your seats!"

"We'll continue this later," Anna whispered.

Milly nodded excitedly, then tried to tone it down into a normal, measured head bob.

The stage lights dimmed, another innovation from Dude, who gave a thankful look to the guys in charge, both of whom had only shown up to rehearsals just once.

The music hummed with bright violins. Babe took on an excited air, walking across the stage with his fellow farmers. When they hit the middle of the stage, they began to walk on the spot. Some of them were better at it than others.

Zachary Litnus yelled from behind the stage, "The town of Bulldeen was officially established in 1870. A farming town. They began to set out farmland and dig crops—"

The farmers on stage swung hoes towards the wood, stopping just before they hit. Up and down.

"—and after some struggle, the crops bloomed. Families grew roots and settled in for a long stay. Suddenly, illness began to take the town. The land was poison!"

Sad violins. The farmers fell about, clutching their stomachs. Sympathy from the audience. Milly fought not to echo them.

"What to do? They would not leave. This was their home. All hope was lost—until one man decided to take things into his own hands. Founder Jim begged."

Lights on Babe, rising upright in the middle of the stage. Determined look into the distance. Then, for a moment, a confused look. This was not in the script.

I've been here before, Babe thought. Then it was gone. He was standing on a stage—it was all a story. He turned to the back of the stage, every light going out except for the one making him sweat down his spine.

"Please," he said. It came out two shades deeper than his normal voice. He coughed and it returned to normal. "I must save this town."

Nothing. Then, emerging into the light: a huge, jagged shadow. The audience broke into gasps, whispers.

Babe suppressed a shudder. He turned to look out over the audience, all those eyes on him. He landed on Milly, who was holding herself as tightly as ever. A frisson of understanding sparked between them.

It's a metaphor, Babe told himself. *He made thornfruit by fusing some weird plants. This never happened.*

The audience stirred, looked at each other. Behind the stage, Zachary Litnus dug his nails into his hair. The shadow was waiting and so was Yancy Land, who was smoking a blunt behind the stage. He held off on the next puff. It was Babe's line.

Babe cleared his throat. "I will give anything," he said, voice steady and clear and deep, generations lining up behind it.

The rest of the play unfolded. Babe sweated through it. Dude and Jules watched in the wings, aware something was wrong but hoping it was stage fright. Only Milly Hart had an inkling of what was really going on.

Jules played them out with a triumphant orchestral track, and Babe lurched off the stage, barely sure where he was putting his feet.

Anna came out of the audience just in time to catch him as he stumbled. "Are you okay?"

Babe didn't look at her. Milly came up behind Anna, unsure about how close she could get, but very sure of what was happening. Every year, she would get itchy during this play, like she was wrong in her own skin. Every year, she'd go to bed and have strange, murky dreams. When she was eight, she'd burst out of her chair and run down the road into the super-market. They'd found her an hour later, hyperventilating behind a display of chocolate bars.

What happened? they'd asked her.

Milly hadn't replied. She didn't quite know herself. She still didn't fully understand, but she got the gist.

"It goes away," she told Babe. "You just got too close to something."

Babe wiped at his forehead with his sleeve. "Close to what?"

"I don't know," Milly said. "I only ever get flashes."

The townfolk milled around them, chatting, getting refills. An occasional glance over their way made them lower their voices: no one was excited to see the two resident zombies talking in hushed, worried tones.

Dude and Jules converged on them, Kate coming up the aisle, as Milly worried her hands together.

"You're still in it," she said. "So maybe it'll be clearer for you."

"*What* will be clearer?"

"I don't...um." Milly bit her lip. She hugged her arms, face stuck in a wince, like she didn't want to say what she was about to say.

Anna touched her elbow. "What is it?"

"Just..." Milly sighed. "Have you tried a cat?"

chapter
thirty-two

"THIS FEELS WRONG," Babe announced.

The others didn't look at him. They were sitting on the floor in Anna's dark kitchen, cats hissing behind the wall that separated the vet and the house. Dude and Jules were in a whisper-argument over the best dog breed. Anna frowned at the cat medication list over by the back door, muttering about incorrect dates. Milly Hart was holding a cat in front of Babe's face. It was dangerously old, suspiciously calm, and felt like a skeleton cling-wrapped in fur.

Babe sighed. "She's gonna go feral and scratch up my face."

"Hey," Dude said. "Be nice to Ms. Kissy."

"Yeah," Anna said from the door. "She's being nice to *you*."

Ms. Kissy stared unblinking, her yellow eyes wide in the moonlight. She was faded white and shot through with gray stripes. Her ears ended in long trails of fur, giving her the illusion of horns.

"I don't think that's what this is," Babe said. He leaned to one side to meet Milly's eyes. "Why doesn't this cat hate me, and why is that so unsettling? Wait, why do cats hate us in the first place?"

"They can tell we're wrong."

"And this one?"

"This one's close to death. It's occupied with bigger things than us."

Anna and Dude turned to stare at her. Babe started stroking Ms. Kissy's bony head, appalled.

"Excuse me? Ms. Kissy is *what*?" Anna said brusquely.

"Ignore them," Milly said, with that narrow focus that had surprised Babe back at her basement house. "Look into Ms. Kissy's eyes."

Jules sighed. "She's a million years old, guys! Sometimes cats die!"

"Poor girl," Babe said, stroking her head with one careful finger.

"Look," Milly insisted.

Babe sighed. He lowered his face so he was nose to nose with this old, apparently dying, cat, the only feline in town who didn't want to rip him to shreds. Ms. Kissy's tiny, sandpapery tongue darted out and licked him on the cheek.

"Aw," said Babe and Dude.

"Focus," Milly said. "Both of you."

Babe mumbled, "Yeah, Ms. Kissy," and fixed his gaze on hers. There were specks in her eyes, yellow against the dark iris and pupil. After a few seconds, Babe could tell the slight difference between the two shades of black.

His bones began to grow heavy. His eyelids followed. They drooped. He was falling asleep. No, he was falling—

"Alicia!"

He jerked up. Alicia, Anna's seven-year-old sister, stood in the doorway sucking on a juice box.

"Whussgoinon," she said, in the slur of the very sleepy. Her teddy bear trailed at her feet, clutched in the hand that wasn't squishing the juice box. "You guys saying hi to Ms. Kissy?"

Babe took one of Ms. Kissy's tiny paws and waved it in her direction.

"Yes, we are," Anna said. "Go back to bed." She ushered her out of the kitchen. Alicia whined, the noises fading and then vanishing down the hall.

Milly didn't tell Babe to focus again. She'd gone stiff when she saw Alicia. She wasn't good with kids unless they were talking about something she was interested in, then she was great with kids to the point that parents thought about asking her to babysit, until they remembered who they were talking to.

Babe asked, "You've done this before, right? This isn't some Dungeons & Dragons thing you're hoping will work?"

"I've done it before," Milly said. "You just need to focus."

"What did you see?"

Milly squirmed. "Flashes. It's murky. I don't think it will be murky for you."

Babe thought of those first dreams after he came back, all mist and frustration. "Cross your fingers, I guess." He put his nose to Kissy's a second time.

This time was slower. First the yellow specks. Then the irises, the pupils. Endless black drawing him in. Babe resisted.

Fall, said a voice. It wasn't the creature. The voice sounded a lot like Dude.

No, Babe told it. *I don't know where I'll end up.*

Fall, it said again. It wasn't Dude. But it wasn't anything else, either. Nothing pulling his strings. It was something Babe made up in his head to make him feel brave.

Babe took a breath. It smelt like Dude's room. He'd died there, but it still didn't scare him. He'd spent the best times of his life in Dude's room, watching TV and reading books and talking about stunts, laughing so hard it hurt.

Babe took another breath and —

— lets it out, sucking another one in immediately. Caroline rushes into the house and slams the ritual on the table, the table and chair set she made with her father and mother and brother when she was very small. In the corner of the room, a cat hisses, hackles shooting up.

Caroline is twenty-eight years old. She is engaged to be married. Her mother passed on her old wedding dress. It sits in Caroline's closet across town, waiting to be worn in church next week. There is a rip in it, but Caroline tells herself it is from wear and age, not because her mother put it there, right at the breast where the mending will be obvious.

She pulls a steak knife from the drawer.

A creak from behind her. The cat screams.

She grabs the ritual, shoves it into her pocket, and turns. Her father stands in the doorway, face pulled tight. He wears an old, neat coat that makes him look even bigger, more imposing.

"Don't do this," he tells her.

She doesn't look at him, holds the knife at her side. "It's a cursed existence, Father! Even now that we have money and food, the townspeople rot!"

"We survive. We live well—"

"We do not live well," she spits. "We are terrible. I am terrible. The things I said to my fiancé last night, he...he will never forgive me, and I will deserve it. As much as he doesn't deserve my own forgiveness for what he said to me when we first met. Father, when was the last time you talked to your son? He locks himself in that room with his drink. And Mother, she's a pillar of the community, but everyone avoids her eyes when she walks in because of that barbed tongue, that barbed tongue I'm sure she didn't have before we moved here!"

"You were young."

"I remember," she says. "I remember you too. You were

more...alive, then. Now you're a ghost." She comes forward, grips his shirt. "We can stop it."

"Can't stop it," the man says, voice cracking with age. He gently untangles her fingers. "It was born of this town. It is the way it is 'cause we are the way we are."

She shakes her head, wrenches her hand away. "We're worse now."

"Maybe that's the natural way of things," the man says slowly.

The daughter stares at him. Tries to see the father he was before they came here so long ago. She'd come up to his knees then. Even after they came to Bulldeen, he had those rare good moments. Even terrible people can't be terrible all the time, and there are good memories in this family, even as they drag each other down into the brambles.

Between them, the cat yowls.

"I'm going to go," she says. "I am going to put an end to it."

He shakes his head. "Where's that ritual, Caroline?"

"I...I don't know what you mean."

He sighs. Squares his jaw. He walks over to a kitchen chair, the one they made together, and picks it up.

"What are you doing?" she asks.

After that, it's just screams. The cat streaks out of the house and is never seen again.

I don't want to be here, Babe thinks with the part of him that is still present, but it doesn't matter. He watches as the daughter stops twitching, as her body is thrown into a hole under the house and covered. Thornfruit grows over her grave, rots without anyone to pick it, then grows again out of its own waste. The town creaks along, surviving but never thriving, its occupants living their lives with no knowledge that this thing in the soil is the same thing in their veins. Sometimes a townsperson will be filled with a deep dread, sure that something is wrong and no one

can stop it, but then that fades and they go about their day, the
knowledge buried deep, reappearing only in dreams from which
    in dreams from which
    from which they wake
    reappearing only in dreams from which they wake —
— gasping.

Babe tried to bolt up, but stopped at the furry weight on his chest. Ms. Kissy meowed down at him.

Milly leaned over him. "You crumpled over like that. We thought it was best to let it happen."

"Thanks," Babe croaked. He cleared his throat. His heart beat hard inside his chest. His face was wet. He wiped at it.

Ms. Kissy meowed.

"I know," Babe told her, then held out his dry hand for her to butt her head into. She did, squeezing her bony body down his palm. He could feel every knob in her spine and all of her ribs.

His friends came over as he sat up. Dude had been walking on his hands. He was rolling his wrists in a way he only did after that stunt.

"What happened?" Anna asked.

"You were out for an hour," Dude added, still wrist-rolling.

Babe frowned. "What? I was gone for a few minutes, maybe."

They shook their heads. Babe ducked his own, remembering the daughter's determined fear. *I am going to put an end to it.*

"What did you see?" Anna asked again.

Babe swallowed. "You know how Founder Jim's family died of natural causes?"

"Sure."

"I don't think the daughter did."

thirty-three

FOUNDER JIM'S house was a shabby shack on the outskirts of town.

"Why does he get an annual play," Jules asked as they stood outside the rotting house, "but his house doesn't even get a plaque? The old town hall got a plaque. And you're all supposed to love this guy, so why's this out here getting termites?"

Babe didn't answer. He was standing in the doorway, feeling time dissolve into itself. He touched the doorframe. There were notches with the children's ages. He wedged his thumbnail into *Caroline, age 12,* which came up to his chest. The house looked the same as he'd seen it in his vision, just a lot older. There was a hole in the wall where a plank had been torn off. It lay on the floor, next to the table. The whole place was the kitchen and two bedrooms—one for the parents, one for the kids. A few feet away from the house was an outhouse, which Dude was standing in.

"I'm so glad I don't have to go outside to pee," he called, muffled, from inside. He'd closed the door on himself. "I don't know how Australians do this."

"They don't *all* have outside bathrooms," Jules told him.

She was hovering awkwardly outside the front door like everyone else.

"No," Dude said. "Pretty sure they do."

Babe shuddered.

"What?" Anna said.

He shook his head. "Nothing. This place gives me the creeps. Let's get this over with."

At the back of the group, Milly raised her hand. She was carefully holding a copy of the ritual, crossed out and rewritten and crossed out again. She shuffled towards the front of the group.

"There are a few variants of the incantation we can try," she said. "Surely one of them will be the right one."

Kate spat ash into the dirt, narrowly missing Jules's foot. "Are we sure this is the place?"

"*Cēlans!* The hidden place!" Milly called from inside the house. She sat down on the floor hard. Babe winced, but she didn't seem to notice the thud of her butt on the wood. She looked up at him, eyes bright with excitement. "Because of the body under the floorboards."

"If you can think of another hidden place," Jules said, stepping away from the spit, "we can go do the ritual there."

Milly unsheathed a marker from her pocket and began to draw a circle. She crawled along the kitchen floorboards until it encompassed all the available space, then sat in the middle.

"Bulldeen, I—" She paused, looking up at everyone standing carefully beyond the circle. "Sorry, does anybody else want to do this?"

Kate shrugged. "You translated it. Go nuts." She shook ash onto the floor. Anna reached over with her foot and stamped it until it stopped smoking.

Milly cleared her throat. Her voice shook slightly. "Bulldeen, I invoke thee. Come now and feed."

"Jesus," Kate said under her breath.

Milly looked up at them. "The next bit might need all of us?"

"Great," Dude said. "What do we do?"

"Just—" Milly nodded around at the clumsy circumference. "Stand around the circle and repeat with me: 'We revoke your power.'"

"We revoke your power," they chorused. Some of it was mumbled, as if Principal Skinner had said *good morning, kids* and the assembly had to say *good morning* back. But Milly had enthusiasm to spare, growing stronger the more she repeated it, and it was infectious.

By the fifth go around, they were even and in time and strong. Just like the sixth time. The tenth time wavered.

The sixteenth time, Dude dropped out entirely.

"How long do we keep doing this?"

"Until something happens," Milly said, rushed, in the space between incantations. "We revoke—"

Dude joined back in. On the twenty-third time, Babe said, "Nothing's happening."

Milly coughed, trailing off. "I guess we move on to the next part." She got the copy of the ritual out of her pocket, smoothed it out on her lap.

"'There will be no more poison in the water of this well,'" she read.

Nothing.

Milly cringed inward. "I don't think...the format of the words, the Latin, it's irregular..."

Babe was flushed with irritation. He used to do that as a kid, that terrible cringe whenever he felt uncomfortable, which was most of the time. Why did Milly still hold herself like a distraught child? Did no one get her to snap out of it? It was one of the only things Babe truly thanked his father for. Ryan used to berate him every time he saw Babe's shoulders come anywhere near his ears. Eventually, Babe had learned to control his body, make his voice come normally. Watching Milly fall into his old habits was like watching a videotape of him at age nine. It filled him with shameful rage. He could hardly look at her.

His head itched. He raised a hand to scratch absentmindedly at it.

Anna was already consoling her. "It won't be your translation. You're the only reason we even made it this far."

"Oh my god," Babe burst out. "Could you be an adult for five seconds?"

The room stared at him.

Milly cringed further. "I'm sorry—"

"Quit apologizing," Babe spat. "It's not a big deal! Quit making it one! I mean, yes, it's a big deal the ritual didn't work, but it could be a hundred things! Maybe you got the words wrong, but maybe we're in the wrong hidden place! Maybe the second ritual was never supposed to work! Maybe we're just doomed! Whatever it is, it's not gonna be helped by you folding in on yourself like a baby."

Milly blushed all the way down her neck. Ugly blotches. Her head was turned down, her slate eyes wet. Babe wanted to shake her. He wanted to cry. His head was still itching, but so little he barely noticed it.

"Babe," Dude said. Not surprised. A little appalled.

"Don't," Babe told him, and left. There was a moment in the doorway where his chest tugged, a strange déjà vu, like he'd walked out of this doorway many times before. He didn't look back.

His blood ran high all the way back to Bull's Head. It was only when he closed his front door behind him and stood in the hall that he stopped, reality crashing in.

"What the heck am I *doing*?" he whispered to himself. Milly's hurt face came floating up and he winced. He'd been so mean! How could he have been that mean? Why was he yelling at his friends, at people just trying to help?

He turned around, reaching for the doorknob.

"Henry?"

Babe held back a sigh. Hitched up a smile. His hand dropped down to his side. "Hey, Dad."

Sure enough, Ryan came in from the living room. "How was your day?"

"Fine," Babe said. "Yours?"

Ryan groaned. His pencil mustache was tousled. He'd been rubbing it stressfully. "Still trying to find ways to keep those hooligans from doing target practice in our fields. I can't believe how inconsiderate they are, those little punks."

"Punks," Babe agreed, thrumming silently with nerves. "Hey Dad, I'm actually kind of tired. I'm gonna go take a nap."

"Oh, I see. You don't want to hear about my day."

"No, Dad, that's not—" Babe bit his tongue hard. Squeezed until he almost broke the skin. "How was your day?"

Ryan folded his arms defensively. "Yeah, you're *really* interested."

"Dad! Tell me about your day or let me go take a nap!"

"Well," Ryan said, taking on a hard edge, "with *that* attitude—"

Babe stepped past him towards the hallway.

"Why are you being *so*—" Ryan said, and then stopped. Took a deep breath. "Whenever you want to talk about how you've been lately, I'll be right here."

Babe paused, one foot in the hall. Sometimes Ryan came

out of nowhere with some genuine sweetness and bowled Babe over. He knew how it would go: he'd go in with some problem and Ryan would find some way to make it about him. Comfort was never just plain comfort, it had to lead back to him somehow. Half the time, it'd lead to Ryan accusing Babe of calling him a bad dad for not being able to fix a problem. God forbid Babe approached him with the problem being that Ryan kept pushing him into things he didn't want to do. He'd only tried that once. It had ended with Ryan crying and Babe coming to his room hours later to apologize.

Parents didn't want to know when they were the problem. Babe felt stupid for even trying. He'd known that in his head, but for some reason, his heart had insisted that Ryan would understand and put his son's needs first.

The old anger rose in him. It solidified into an itch.

You should hurt him. He deserves it.

Babe's cheek twitched. He bit the inside of it, that smooth flesh. It would be easy. His dad wasn't old, but he was frail. Even if he were a strongman, Babe would be able to take him. All he had to do was turn around and—

What the heck am I doing?

Babe ran to his room. Closed his bedroom door and leaned against it.

"I'm not hurting him," he said aloud. "I'm not hurting anybody."

Milly's face, again. Dude's eyes tightening as Babe stormed away from Kate's car near the Bulldeen sign.

Babe sat on his bed. He thought about crying. A single tear slipped out before a thought struck him: *Oh God, I'm just like him.*

He scrubbed desperately at his face. He'd been cruel to his friends and then gone and cried about it! What a jerk!

He squirmed, got up, sat back down again. The idea was so uncomfortable that Babe couldn't think about it alone.

———

Babe tapped gently but insistently on Dude's window.

"Come on," he muttered. "Be home."

Dude appeared warily in the window, hands hasty on his collar. Buttoning up again. The tension bled out of his wide shoulders upon seeing his friend. He pushed the window open. "Get in here."

Babe clambered in. It was much easier since he'd hit his growth spurt in tenth grade. Before that, they'd had to use a stepladder.

"What's up?" Dude asked once Babe had both feet on the carpet.

"Nothing," Babe said. He wiped his slick forehead. "I just—"

He stopped. In the middle of the room, where Babe had climbed off Dude's bed to choke to death, the carpet had been cut out. On the exposed wood sat an exercise bike.

Babe pointed. "You hate exercise bikes."

"With all my soul," Dude said. "It's mom's. She's gonna turn my room into a gym. She doesn't wanna use my bench press, so."

Babe couldn't look at the exposed wood under the exercise bike for too long. It was in such a stupid place—to get to the door Dude would have to walk around the bike. And there was no reason to pull up the carpet.

Babe swallowed. "What? Your mom doesn't want to accentuate her extreme shortness with some buff arms? Weird."

"They don't accentuate—"

"Oh, damn. Has nobody told you? That's so harsh."

Dude flicked him in his hollow cheek. Babe batted his hand away, his smile fading, adrenaline smarting in his veins.

"What is it?" Dude sat down on his bed. The springs creaked. Babe eyed Dude's covered neck and wondered for half a second if KJ had sat on these creaking springs, before he jerked his thoughts away from them. He didn't want to think about KJ and Dude together.

"Am I like my dad?"

"'Scuse me?"

Babe wiped again at his face. He'd walked here so fast it had almost turned into a run. "It's not all the monster. It just emphasizes. It emphasizes *me*. So, am I?"

Dude rubbed at his nose. "Look, if you're thinking about growing a mustache—"

"Come on! Just—"

"Sometimes."

Babe's jaw closed with a click.

"It's not that bad," Dude hurried to say. "Everybody has a little bit of their parents, you know?"

"You're not supposed to say that!"

Dude laughed, low and uncomfortable. "Do you want me to lie?"

"*Yes*," Babe burst. "Apparently, you're good at it! *The ritual's just a hand cut and a chant, no price needed! No deaths here, no sir!*"

Dude made a face, wisecrack incoming. Babe cut him off, smearing a third time at his face, but the sweat was gone. The heat was inside him, itching at the wrong side of his skin.

"God, you're so...what, it's fine if you die, but not me? You don't get to die!"

"I'm not gonna die!"

Babe talked over him. "How could you do that? It's insane. YOU'RE insane. You'd just...you'd do anything for me, who does that? I don't even have to ask, you just...you'd do anything."

His chest heaved. He'd gotten closer as he spoke, only realizing it when Dude had to look up to meet his eyes, worry creasing his forehead.

"Are you okay?"

Babe felt great. Babe felt amazing, but the kind of amazing that reminded him hazily of that time he got drunk and tried to clear the stairs with one jump: messy, bright exhilaration before the pain set in.

Babe stepped closer. Dude, still sitting on the bed, tilted his head back even further. Automatic. Unconscious. The slope of his neck was so lovely, even covered with his shirt collar. The carotid above it, yes, but also the familiarity of it. How many times had Babe zoned out in class staring at the back of Dude's neck?

"You would, right? You'd do anything?"

Dude blinked as if waking from a dream, disappointed by reality. "Okay. This isn't you."

He shifted as if to get up, but Babe put a knee on either side of him on the mattress, penning him in. The closeness was intoxicating. Babe had been holding back for so long.

"No inventing, remember? It just emphasizes." Babe leaned in, squeezed a hand around Dude's upper arm. He loved Dude's arms, the faint bulge of muscle, the veins wrapping proudly around. He traced his thumb up a thin blue line and said, "You know how I get when I'm wasted? All clingy and pathetic? It's only with you. I don't drape myself all over Anna, I don't get mad at people for trying to talk to Jules. It's just you. That time on the stairs, I kept getting so close, I know you noticed something."

He wavered down towards Dude's upturned face. Dude

was still trying not to meet his eyes, and still failing. His heart-beat thudded staccato, lips parted, eyelashes trembling.

Babe grinned. He'd never felt so powerful as he did putting his lips against Dude's ear. "I really wanted to bite you. Not to hurt. Just..."

He opened the first two buttons of Dude's shirt, exposing the bruises he could faintly smell now, blood pooling under the flesh. New hurts. Babe opened his mouth against the brightest bruise.

Dude's breathing was loud in the silent room. Babe bit down, soft blunt pressure, and a gasp punched out of Dude's throat. Half-fear, half-arousal. Babe drew back to watch his eyes, pupils blown.

"You shouldn't be that surprised," Babe told him. "Look at those wide eyes under those big eyelids. Lemme see."

He pressed Dude's eyelids up with his fingers. It wasn't hot, Babe knew this in the quiet part of his head that was still whispering that he was being goddamn weird right now, but that part was so quiet and the hunger was so loud. *Consume.* Babe wanted to paint over KJ's bruises, mark Dude as his own. He wanted all of Dude, the sexy and strange and mundane—his veiny arms and his skinny chicken legs, his shaggy hair and heavy lids, the rank musk under his arms. The soft pink under his tongue. Spit and acid, sinew and tendons.

As if from a long distance: "Babe. Cut it out."

The voice was pained. No teeth in Dude's neck, no knee digging into him. The pain was from wanting. Babe was all too familiar.

"I want to," Babe's nose roved Dude's scalp, his cheek, his neck where the bite-mark bruise gleamed red with fading pressure. "I promise. You love me, right?"

"You're my best friend," Dude whispered.

"I know. But you love me like—"

Dude caught his hand. Babe had been about to touch his face.

"Not like this."

Babe stilled. Dude's hand was shaking around his wrist. His pupils were still blown, but wet. His mouth was tight.

Babe pulled back, the fog lifting. "I'm—"

"We should call Kate. Get you another Nazi to eat." Dude pushed him off with big, gentle hands. Babe sat on the bed, struck dumb as Dude stood and put some distance between them.

"I'm fine," Babe heard himself say.

"You're not." A smile jerked over Dude's face. "Go home."

"Dude—"

"If you eat somebody on the way, make sure they're an asshole."

"Eugene."

Dude stopped. He'd been heading for the door. His hand flexed on the knob.

"I'll see you tomorrow."

Babe ran. He made it halfway home before the roar in his chest started to turn dangerous and he slowed to a walk, fists clenched at his sides. What the hell was *that*? He'd suspected for years Dude had feelings for him; he'd known it even longer than he knew he felt the same way.

A cat ran across the road, freezing when it caught sight of Babe. Its teeth flashed, a yowl rising into the night.

Babe hissed back. The cat flinched, darting away with its ears flattened back against its head. Okay, maybe Dude had been right to reject him.

Not like this. Did Dude mean he didn't want it while Babe

was liable to rip his vocal cords out, or that he didn't feel that way? Could Babe have been wrong for years? He'd been so sure. The terrified kind of sure, a certainty he never looked at too closely, because then he started thinking ridiculous things. Things like *you could have this,* which only made him more scared. He wanted it too much. He didn't know what would happen if he gave himself over, other than that it would shake him like nothing else was capable of. It was always safer to push it down, drop Dude's gaze, pretend not to notice. He thought he was in control. He really believed he could ignore the hunger that rose in him when he saw Dude walk in a room.

Babe laughed, a trembling noise in the dark.

"Yeah," he said to himself. "Good goddamn luck."

chapter
thirty-four

BABE WAS STANDING IN A FIELD. *The thornfruit had been harvested for the year and he could see for miles. He squinted around. He couldn't see town, which meant he'd gone further into the fields than ever before. It meant he was outside Bulldeen limits.*

"You do not get out."

Babe turned. The creature stood in front of him, all sharp edges. It looked almost like his dad. No, it looked like Hunter, like Buzz. It looked like the late-night TV presenter who had warned about homosexuals.

But mostly it looked like his dad.

It smiled softly. "Give in, Babe. It's too deep inside for you to do anything else."

Babe swallowed. He put a hand to his chest as if he could feel the barbs shifting inside him, but there was nothing.

"I'm not yours," he said.

The smile widened. "Of course you are. You're Bulldeen through and through."

"That doesn't mean anything," Babe spat. "Bulldeen is just —it's where I come from."

"It's more than that." The creature took a step closer, shiny

shoes sinking into the dirt as if it weighed much more than it looked. "Your roots are deep in this place, and this place is poison. It's all you know. It weaned you and now you secrete it."

"I don't," Babe said, but it sounded unconvincing. He cleared his throat, spit rumbling in his throat. "I'm not poison. I'm...I'm good to people...my friends. My friends aren't poison. Dude and Anna are Bulldeen-grown too, and we're good to each other."

"Are you?"

"I don't know. We're teenagers! We do our best!" Babe cast a look around, trying for an escape, but it was just fields. The stubby thornfruit was sleeping through the winter, ready to burst forth when the heat turned up again.

The dirt under Babe started to sag. His bare feet sunk into the earth. A stirring in his gut, the stir spreading to his chest, his groin, up his throat into his head. Mouth filling with saliva.

"We're not poison," Babe said, teeth wet with spit and blood. He spat it into the dirt, which gave way to even more. Babe dropped in up to his waist, flinging his arms out to catch himself. His elbows thumped into the dirt, stopping his momentum.

The creature stood over him. The dirt began to pull.

"No," Babe said. "No, wait, I don't—"

He sank. Dirt up to his nipples, his neck, his chin. Dirt rising over his head. Babe strained for the surface, gasping in a mouthful as he was swallowed up by the —

— noise.

Babe jolted up in bed, heart pounding.

The phone rang a second time. Footsteps down the stairs, Ryan muttering about early morning calls.

Babe lurched out of bed, stumbled, fell, caught the door and ran for the stairs.

Ryan was already at the bottom, phone up to his ear, frowning. "Why do you want to talk with my son?"

"Igotitthanksdad." Babe grabbed the phone out of his

hand. He walked as far as the cord would allow, ignoring his dad's offended look. "Hello?"

Kate's voice was even more gruff than usual. "I'm coming over."

"No." There was an itch at the back of Babe's head, so small he didn't notice it was there. He lowered his voice, even as Ryan walked reluctantly into the living room. "I can last."

"Yeah?" A slow exhale. Babe imagined the first cigarette of the day between her fingers. "How're you feeling?"

"I'm..." Babe trailed off, thinking this through. The irritability was still there. The more he focused on it, the emptier he felt. And the more something lined up behind that emptiness, waiting.

"I'll be there in twenty."

"N—" Babe clenched his jaw, thinking of Dude's shaking hand around his wrist. "Alright."

Babe checked. Ryan was still in the living room, shifting things around. "Any calls about the old man going missing?"

"Not yet." Kate yawned. "Might be a while. That guy didn't have people over and he didn't go anywhere."

"Hopefully they think he crawled off somewhere to die. Like a cat."

"Meow," Kate said dryly. "Hold tight."

"Holding. See you soon." Babe hung up. Ryan, shockingly, did not appear immediately in the hallway entrance. Before Babe could reach the doorway, Ryan's voice rang through the hall: "What did the Chief want to talk to you about?"

"Nothing." Babe leaned on the doorframe. Ryan jerked up, slamming the desk drawer closed. It was the recently forbidden one. "What's in there?"

"None of your business." Ryan smoothed down his mustache, still wet from the shower. "I was just about to clean it out, anyway. Nothing worth keeping."

Babe smiled, thin-lipped. It was that or baring his teeth. "Have a good day at work."

"Uh-huh," Ryan muttered. Then he perked up. "Have we measured you for your work uniform yet?"

"Uh. No."

"Great! We can do that this weekend." Ryan came forwards and slapped Babe's shoulders. "Wish granddad could see you. He only worked there for a decade, but he'd be so happy to have you on board."

Babe doubted it. Granddad wasn't happy about much, least of all his relatives.

"I should shower," he said, fighting back the urge to wrench his father's hands off.

Ryan took a second to let him go. His gaze had turned contemplative on Babe's shoulders, as if trying to guess their width without a measuring tape.

Babe didn't think much of showers. He didn't like being naked. Showers were done as fast as possible. This time, however, he stood under the hot spray and tried to discern how hungry he was. He wasn't out of control yet. But he was definitely getting close. His skin felt too tight. Getting dressed, a broken shoelace almost made him throw the offending shoe against the wall. He caught himself just in time, slowing the momentum to a stop.

He fit his shoe back on and walked carefully and deliberately to the drawers. They kept all their spare knick-knacks in here. The first drawer was unremarkable, all tape and paper and safety pins. The second drawer was their sewing drawer, for mending clothes. The third drawer was Apparently Forbidden, and Babe took a vicious pleasure at opening the stupid thing.

Envelopes. Large and white. He was about to close the drawer when he noticed the addressee. Henry Simmons. Why did his dad have a bunch of letters addressed to him?

He looked at the back of the first one. Then, still not registering, he read the second envelope. By the third, a sensation like an egg breaking on top of his head, trickling yolk down his spine.

Colleges. They were all from the colleges Babe had applied to. They'd arrived months ago.

He tore the first one open, unfolding it with shaking fingers.

On behalf of California State University at Long Beach, I am pleased to announce your admission—

"What the heck?" Babe croaked.

He opened the second one.

Congratulations—

The third, the fourth. Babe sat there, staring dazed at every torn-open envelope scattered on the carpet. He'd gotten into UMaine. Oregon State. *UCLA.* He could follow his friends into their new life together.

Except he couldn't. The reply date had come and gone. He couldn't get into any of these colleges now, not if he begged.

Babe's cheeks flushed hot. His eyes filled. Most of the anger was aimed inwards. *Why are you surprised?* he berated himself. *Of course Dad did this. If you're surprised, you're an idiot.*

But Babe couldn't help it. He still had that stubborn voice in his heart, the one that insisted that when it came down to it, Ryan would put his son first. Children want to believe in their parents. Some of them never give up, not entirely, even as their parents prove them wrong over and over again.

Babe grinded his teeth. He was tired of being proven wrong.

There was an itch in the back of his head. This one, he

noticed. He scratched at it. With his hand, yes, but also with his mind. There was something right there, whispering. There was—

He pressed.

It split open, whispers spilling through.

He wasn't meant to hear the creature whispering to Hunter, wasn't meant to hear the dangerous curl of Hunter's thoughts as they took root.

Babe only listened for a few seconds, enough to realize what was going on. Then he was up and running, broken shoelace flopping in the breeze, bolting for school as fast as he could.

chapter
thirty-five

HUNTER CREEL STOOD in the school basement, twitching. The voices were coming faster now. The faster they became, the more in control Hunter felt, which was strange. When they'd started, he'd felt bizarre, disastrous. Now he felt powerful. Powerful and sharp, like people could cut themselves on him if they dared come close.

Beat him, the voices said. *Burn him.*

The bell rang. It vibrated down the pipes. Hunter leaned into it. Anytime now.

Yesterday KJ had come to him after homeroom, eyes averted, voice a gutted whisper. He'd revealed to Hunter what time he'd told Dude to meet him, then he'd turned on his heel and left without looking back. The fearful line of his retreating back hadn't been as satisfying as Hunter had hoped.

This would be. Hunter was sure of it. He reached into his pocket and toyed with the lighter trigger. Buzz would laugh so hard when he told him. Where the hell was he?

The pipes hissed. Hunter hissed back at them. "Shut up," he told them. "I'm waiting."

The door opened. Hunter retreated to the shadows. There

was a narrow set of stairs down into the left half of the base-ment. You couldn't see the whole room until you got to the bottom.

Dude appeared in inches: first his feet. Then his legs, his skinny little legs. Narrow waist. Big shoulders. His mess of hair, which Hunter had rubbed gum into in second grade. The school nurse had cut it out. Dude had a giant bald spot in the back of his head for months after, and Hunter had pressed his thumbnail into it every time he got close.

He flexed his hand around his tin of paint thinner. Waited for the moment of recognition. His heels flashed with adren-aline, like standing somewhere very high, about to step off.

Dude looked around. His gaze landed on Hunter's dark form, face hidden in the shadow of the pipes. He took a step towards it.

Hunter moved forwards.

Dude's foot faltered.

Hunter grinned. "Hey." He jerked the can forwards, drenching Dude with paint thinner.

Dude froze as it ran down his pants. Then he turned. He made it up two steps before Hunter got to him. He grabbed Dude by the back of the shirt, the back of his neck, yanking.

Dude struggled, fell back against the steps. Hunter climbed on top of him, nose wrinkling.

"God, you *stink*," he said. "What do you two get up to in the basement? Huh?"

He shoved his arm up against Dude's throat.

Dude, the boy who usually went for funny over safe, said something very surprising. "I don't know what the hell you're talking about." Then he slung his forehead up into Hunter's nose.

Snap. A horrible howl echoed around the concrete. Hunter

clutched at his bloody face, tears blinding him. Dude was a blurry shape crawl-running up those damn stairs, back up to the light.

Still howling, Hunter followed.

He caught Dude by the ankle. Dude, who was stretched into the hallway from the waist up, shouted *"HELP!"* at no one in particular. Students veered around, staring. A guy from English walked over to help him up, saw who was clawing his way up Dude's soaked leg, and ran in the opposite direction.

Hunter hung on, clutching Dude's thighs now, as Dude crawled out onto the linoleum. He kicked, skimmed Hunter's gut, kicked again.

Hunter detached himself and lunged.

Dude held up his arms in a Wonder Woman position in front of his face, already bruised from Hunter's attack last week. Hunter rained blows down on his arms. Students milled a safe distance away on both sides, some of them watching, some of them trying to think of an alternative route to get to their next class.

"Stop hiding!" Hunter yelled, yanking at Dude's arms. "Lemme—"

Dude kicked uselessly. Hunter scrabbled for his lighter, unsheathed it from his pocket. Clicked it open.

Someone screamed.

Hunter grinned. There was the fear he was looking for. Right there in Dude's eyes.

He triggered the flame—

And then he was tackled around the middle. He was ripped off of Dude and thrown onto the floor, head bouncing on the linoleum, lighter skittering away. Hunter thought of line-backers and lions. He pushed himself up just in time for Babe Simmons to kneel down and punch him in the face.

Hunter hit the linoleum again. The lighter bounced away. His head rang.

Bother, said the voice over the ringing, colored with surprise.

Hunter sneered. He really didn't like the voice saying *bother*. It made him think of Winnie the Pooh. The voice continued, saying something like *should have used Buzz*, but it was so distant Hunter must've misheard it.

Babe hit him again. He was on top of Hunter now, still punching.

"*What the fuck*," he bellowed as he punched Hunter in the cheek, the forehead, the neck, "*were you trying to do to Dude?*"

Hunter laughed through blood. "Thought it was pretty obvious—"

Smack. His eyebrow opened under Babe's knuckle. *Smack*. His lower lip split. He groped for his lighter. Too far away.

Dude appeared above them, pulling at Babe's shoulder.

"Babe, he's down, he's *down*—"

"I'm gonna goddamn *kill* him!"

Hunter didn't hear any of this—he was too busy swimming in and out of consciousness. Babe's face rushed down at Hunter's, and then Hunter's ear was on fire.

He screamed. Other people joined in. Principal Skinner stood above them now. Babe pulled back, something stringy in his teeth, dripping red.

Blood ran down the side of Hunter's neck. Hunter groped at it.

"You bit off my goddamn *ear*," he managed.

Principal Skinner reached for Babe. Dude stopped him, put a hand on Babe's shoulder, and Babe stood under Dude's gentle pull.

Hunter gasped on the floor. He rolled onto his belly and crawled for his lighter lying over near the lockers. He shoved it into his pocket and pushed, unsteady, to his feet. Nobody approached him. Principal Skinner was talking, but Hunter didn't know or care if it was at him.

He stumbled away, ear burning, head tunneling, waiting for the voices.

chapter
thirty-six

PRINCIPAL SKINNER SIGHED. "I don't know what I can do here."

Ryan trembled in his tiny wooden seat. "*Expel* him, like you should have done in first grade when he set my son's hair on fire! Or in sixth grade, when he bashed my son's head into the water fountain! Or—"

Principal Skinner sighed. Picked up his snow globe and tilted it back and forth, watching the plastic snow. He had a collection of snow globes, all the major cities in the world. It used to fill Babe with longing, a desire to explore. Now it just made him sad. Skinner hadn't traveled out of Maine either.

Babe twitched in his seat, licked at his back teeth where Hunter's blood was caked. He pried a shred of skin out from between his teeth and started to chew.

Okay, he thought, *I really have to skip next period and go eat someone.*

"Again, Mr Simmons, it is the *last* day of school. The fact that Hunter is graduating is a miracle in itself. If I expel him now, his family will come down on me as a matter of honor."

"Who *cares* about that!?"

"Might I remind you that your son bit a man's ear off?"

They looked over. Babe stopped chewing.

"Just the lobe," he said.

"In self-defense," Ryan spoke over him. "That madman was going to set someone on fire!"

"I don't know what you want me to *do*."

Ryan stood up, swiped his jacket from the back of the chair. "Useless," he spat. "Henry, we're leaving."

Babe swallowed the shred of ear and got up. He nodded awkwardly at Principal Skinner, who nodded back tiredly and held his snow globe up to the light.

"Useless," Ryan repeated as he slammed the door shut behind Babe. He almost caught Babe's elbow in the slam, but Babe didn't mention it.

"Just sits there and does nothing for decades," Ryan hissed as he stormed down the hall, Babe trailing along after him. "Hunter could've killed you, and Skinner would just sit there with his damn snow globes and just do—nothing! Why, I should—"

"Dad," Babe tried, his voice much calmer than he felt. He always had to keep his voice calm around Ryan, unless Ryan wanted a reaction. Then Babe would tailor himself to whatever the situation called for. "It *is* the last day."

Ryan ignored him. "I'm so glad that boy is getting out of Bulldeen soon."

"Hunter isn't going anywhere."

Ryan looked up. Babe didn't usually disrupt him during his tirades. There was a flash of confusion, then Ryan arranged his face in an innocent expression. "Right. Well, that's—"

"You mean Dude," Babe realized. His mouth twitched. He stopped in the middle of the hallway.

Ryan was almost around the corner. He turned around, eyes wide and wounded when he noticed his son was no longer following.

He marched back, pencil mustache trembling. "How many times has he almost gotten you killed?" he hissed. "Those stupid stunts he's always dragged you into? All those times he caught Hunter's attention and got the two of you beaten to a pulp—"

"That's not his fault," Babe said quietly.

"You could have been hurt, you could have died, you *did*—"

Babe clenched his teeth. "*Dad.*"

"He's a bad influence."

Don't bite Dad. Don't do it. Babe's breath came shakily. "*You're* a bad influence."

Genuine confusion flashed over Ryan's face. He prided himself on being the best parent in town. Attentive, loving. So many parents in this town let their kids run wild. Not Ryan Simmons. "How could you say that?"

"*Dad.* I found the acceptance letters."

Ryan's jaw snapped shut. Time folded in on itself. Something soft gleamed in his eyes, then it was gone, replaced by righteous pain. Jesus Christ couldn't hold a candle to Ryan Simmons.

"I told you not to go in that drawer," he said softly. "You had no right."

Babe wished he still had Hunter's ear shred. He opened his mouth. Maybe this time, he'd scream.

"It's what my dad did for me," Ryan said.

We're trapped, Babe thought, shaking with rage. *We're all trapped in it.*

"You'll be happy about this one day," Ryan promised. "In

ten years. Heck, in twenty it might be the best thing that ever happened to you!"

It was the joy that did it. The genuine excitement in his father's voice.

Babe felt his upper lip curl. His teeth parted in a snarl. The next thing he knew, he had Ryan up against the wall, feet dangling in the air as Ryan spluttered.

"Henry! What—"

"How," Babe spat, barely recognizing the sharp grate of his own voice, "can you be around every day of my life and still think something like that can make me happy?"

His knuckles were white in his dad's suit jacket. Ryan stared at his son, uncomprehending.

"How could you be so STUPID?" Something was happening to Babe's face, something unnatural. His eyes, his teeth. He could tell, because Ryan's indignation was giving way to horror.

Babe grinned. "See me now, Dad? Huh? You see me?"

"I—" Ryan gaped, face blanching, eyes filling with tears. "You...Henry...what *happened*—"

"I DON'T WANT TO BE YOU," Babe roared. "LIVING IN THIS TOWN MY WHOLE LIFE, WORKING AT THE FACTORY, IS THE WORST THING I COULD POSSIBLY IMAGINE! I HATE YOU!"

Ryan shrank against the wall. Babe tried to feel satisfied, like the itch in his head urged him to, but all Babe could think of at that moment was how old his dad looked.

"Babe."

Babe jerked. Kate Higgins stood at the end of the hall, dressed in her cop uniform, gun out of its holster. Dude and Jules followed quickly, momentum halting as they saw Babe.

"Uh," Dude said. "Hi, Ryan."

Ryan whimpered.

Kate raised her eyebrows towards Babe expectantly. The safety on her gun was off, her voice wary. "Need some help there, kid?"

Babe swallowed. "No," he gritted, forcing his fingers to loosen.

Ryan dropped to the floor, knees folding out underneath him. He gaped up at his son, tears streaming freely.

"I gotta go," Babe mumbled. He opened his mouth to say something more, an apology, an explanation. How could he begin to explain to his father what had happened to him, what he'd become in these past few weeks?

"Henry," croaked Ryan. He tried to reach for him, but Babe pushed him out of the way and followed down the hall, where the others had disappeared around the corner.

chapter
thirty-seven

CROUCHED in the place where Dude and KJ used to kiss, Hunter flicked his lighter open and shut.

Kill them. The voice was sounding more like him with each day that passed. *They killed Buzz.*

"Nobody can kill Buzz," Hunter said. "Buzz is in hiding. Gonna...gonna let me in on the plan soon."

A flash of irritation. Not his. It *could* be his—his ear throbbed. Blood crusted down his neck. Son of a bitch took his ear. He was gonna kill the dead freak.

This whole place should burn.

"Yeah," Hunter said. He looked around at the grimy metal nest. He used to talk with Buzz about how they'd shoot this place up. Hunter never cared much about that. Annihilating the student body wasn't enough. The whole place should get razed to the ground. Like his dad had tried to do.

Yes.

"Yes," Hunter said softly. He pressed his thumb into the lighter trigger's sharp grooves until the skin broke.

Kate took her gun from her holster and started to load it. "How much should we be worrying about this Hunter kid?"

Babe looked over at Dude, who was sitting on the table in the otherwise empty lab. Dude paused in unscrewing the knob from the cupboard. "He seemed pretty determined this time," Dude said. He shifted uncomfortably, pulling his shirt away from his skin. His clothes clung, his front drenched in paint thinner. There had been a moment after Hunter slinked away, when Babe was fussing over Dude's clothes and trying not to bite him.

Sorry, Babe had said in the hallway before he was led into Principal Skinner's office.

Dude had shaken his head. He knew what Babe meant. *You're fine. Everything's fine.*

The gun magazine snapped back into place. "Just spitballing. How do you feel about snacking on Hunter?"

"I don't feel terrible about it." Babe jiggled his knee. He was sitting in a tall lab chair, wedged in between the wall and a table. He flicked his tongue around the inside of his mouth. It tasted like spit. "This feels a little public, though. We're at *school*."

"Nazi it is, then." Kate shelled out a cigarette.

"Fire alarm," Dude reminded her.

Kate eyed him. She went over to a window and propped it open. "So *you* bit Hunter's ear off, fully you. All Babe."

"Mostly," Babe mumbled. "I wouldn't have done it...before."

Kate fixed him with a look. Cigarette smoke leaked out the window, but traces of it stayed in the room.

"He was hurting Dude!"

The door to the science lab opened. Jules spilled through, Anna close behind.

"Found her," Jules said. She collapsed into a spindly chair next to Babe. "How much longer do we wait?"

Kate checked her watch. "Milly's got another ten minutes before we call it a day and go kill ourselves a Nazi. Got one picked out for you, Babe."

"Gee," Babe said. "Thanks."

Anna paced. Kate lit another cigarette off her first one, other hand around her holster.

Babe, the adrenaline wearing off from the fight, put his head down on the table. Another itch at the back of his head. "I think I can tune in."

"Explain," Kate told him. She thumbed her gun safety on, then off. On again.

"Like I did with the cat," Babe said. "I did it this morning, with Hunter and the creature."

"Do it."

Babe followed the itch in his mind. He picked. He shoved. He had to reach out to something, find a barrier and fall through —

— the door.

A few dodgeballers looked up and then immediately looked back as Hunter sneered at them. He straightened up, slinking in, carrying a bulging shopping bag.

His eye was swollen from Babe's punches, his smile brittle and bloody. He got some more looks from the kids playing dodgeball, but he didn't care about them. He marched over to Moe Stafford.

"Whoa," Moe said, ducking out of the line of dodgeball fire. "What happened to you?"

Hunter came in close. Moe flinched.

Hunter's voice shook. "It's time, bud. You gonna help me out?"

"What're we doing, Hunt?"

Hunter grinned. His eyes were bright, excited, near tears. The only other time he'd been like this was just before he lit Jitterbug on fire. "Finishing what my dad tried to do, Moe. We're gonna burn this place down."

Moe's face turned disbelieving. He waited for the punchline. It didn't come.

"You're in, right?"

Moe shook his head, slow and reluctant. "What? N-no."

Hunter's grin faded.

The teacher yelled from across the gym, "Hunter! Is this your class? No! Get outta here!"

Hunter didn't look at her. His jaw fluttered, his eyes threatening to overflow. "Just hold this," he muttered, and shoved a beer can into Moe's hands. Hunter had found it in the corner of the boiler room. He'd filled it with paint thinner. It sloshed over Moe's fingers, spilled down his wrist.

"What?" Moe said. "Hunt, what?"

Hunter pulled him over to the back of the gym and stood him over the place where his father had hidden the gasoline. He jogged the can so it drenched Moe's shirt, soaking the front of his gym shorts.

Moe wrinkled his nose. "Ew! Why'd you do that?"

Hunter got the lighter out from his jacket.

"Hunt," Moe said, voice rising higher and higher. "Wait, no, what're you—" His mind blurred with panic. He didn't think to drop the beer can, now half-full of paint thinner.

Hunter put the lighter to the hem of Moe's P.E. shirt. It went up like a bonfire.

Moe shrieked in agony. Hunter turned away as flames raced down Moe's pants, scattering up towards the can, which exploded in Moe's hand, sending sparks down towards the gasoline under the floorboards.

His classmates screamed. April Tanner ran forwards to help, stripping off her shirt and beating at Moe's writhing, fiery body. Everybody else froze in horror or ran for the doors. The runners weren't fast enough. Hunter already had the doors closed. He unspooled a chain from his shopping bag, knotting it around the handles until the door was barred shut.

He pressed his face in the glass window, trying to see Moe. He couldn't, not past the students clamoring at the door, but he could see the tiny explosions from the gasoline cans. They came up from under Moe. Just one at first, and then another, a chain of explosions reaching to touch —

— Babe on the shoulder.

"Babe."

Babe gasped himself back to the lab room.

Jules dropped her hand. The others stood around him, waiting.

"We—" Babe said, and gulped another breath. Kate's cigarette smoke had thrown him off for a second. Where was the nearest fire alarm? Everyone's heartbeats were very loud. "We gotta get to the gym."

Jules pushed herself off the rickety chair. The others milled around, waiting.

Babe's cheek twitched. He forced the muscle still and stabbed a finger at Kate's cigarette. "Kate—"

"It's near the window."

"You gotta put it up near the alarm. Hunter just lit the gym on fire and he's not stopping there."

Kate stared. Then she launched herself up onto the lab table, scrambling up to her knees and then to her feet. "Little shit," she hissed, straining her cigarette as close to the fire alarm as she could get. "When I get my hands on that kid—"

A red light blinked on. The alarm blared through the halls of Bulldeen High.

Kate climbed down.

Dude asked, "Does the gym have sprinklers?"

"It was sprinklers or goalposts for the football field," Anna said. "Guess what we went with?"

"Go," Babe said, but the others were already gunning for the door.

Students emerged from classrooms into the halls, confused. They parted in even more confusion when they noticed Chief Higgins storming the halls, Zombabe and his friends at her side.

"Out!" Kate called. "Everybody *move!* Somebody get the fire department down here!"

Not many students were running. Not yet. Only the ones who were closer to the gym. They'd heard the screaming. A few of them had seen Hunter Creel dancing wild, spraying paint thinner.

Babe rounded the corner that led them to the gym. The gym doors quivered with the weight of dozens of high schoolers throwing themselves at them. At the far end of the hall, Hunter emptied another paint thinner onto the floor and threw it down the next hall.

He looked up. Grinned.

"Get the doors open," Kate instructed, and unsheathed her gun.

Hunter disappeared around the corner.

Kate followed.

Everybody else ran to the gym doors. People were screaming behind them, screaming and choking, clawing at the tiny windows. A sheet of fire climbed the far wall.

Jules tore uselessly at the chains around the door handles.

"We need something that can cut these," Anna said. "Or—"

Babe curled inwards, gasping.

Dude touched the middle knob of his spine. "What? What?"

Babe jerked. A growl ripped out of his throat. Anna and Dude looked at each other, Dude's hand flinching on Babe's back.

Inside the gym, another scream. Louder than the rest, more terrified.

"It's inside with them," Babe said, through gritted teeth. "It's—"

The terror inside the gym multiplied. Babe felt it through the creature's eyes. Blood filled his mouth. A girl with no shirt and burned hands. April Tanner had tried to save Moe. She'd cried as his screams got weaker and finally silent. The tears weren't dry on her face when a sharp hand clamped around her middle, dragging her backwards onto the floor. The arm held her down as a creature who looked inexplicably like her dead aunt ripped out her stomach.

"Oh God," Babe said, and straightened. His head wasn't clear, but he was in control. Dude gave his back a pat and dropped his hand.

"Shit," Jules echoed, and started sprinting down the hall. "*I'm on it!*" she screamed as she tore around the corner.

"She's on it," Dude said. "Hey, she knows she's running in the opposite direction, right?"

Beside him, Anna gasped and began to run after her.

"Okay!" Dude called after her. "We'll just be here!"

While Dude and Babe fumbled uselessly at the chains around the gym door, Kate caught up to Hunter. She grabbed him and threw him up against the wall, putting the gun to his gut just in time for him to douse her with paint thinner.

"Careful," he said, teeth bared and bloody. His eyes were all pupil. "Shoot me and the spark will light us both up."

Kate stared him down. Fluid dripped into her shoes. She clicked the safety on.

"Good choice," Hunter said.

"Thanks," Kate said. She brought up the butt of the gun and smacked him across the face.

Hunter groaned in pain. He reared up and grabbed her wrist, sinking his teeth in.

"Shit," Kate hissed, and clocked him again with her free hand.

Hunter, now bleeding profusely from his head, brought his knee up and kicked her in the groin. Once. Kate's face tensed in pain. Twice. Kate yelled.

On the third hit, Kate shoved away from him.

"God*damn*—"

Hunter kicked her in the knee. Lucky shot. She wobbled. Hunter rabbit-punched her in the face until she went down, groaning. He whooped at her as she hovered groggily above the ground, blood oozing from her split lip.

"That's what you *get*," he told her.

The PA stuttered on. Hunter took off for the gym.

Principal Skinner had taken his snow globes. No records, not his diploma framed on the wall, just his snow globes thrown into a bag as the fire alarm went off.

Jules knocked his lamp off his desk as she lunged for the

PA. She switched it on, blasting through the channels. The fire hadn't melted the speakers yet.

Dude and Babe were still yanking at the chains when Anna ran up behind them with a fire ax.

"Move," she told them, and swung it into the wood. She gestured at the students behind the tiny windows. "Out of the way! I'm bringing it down!"

Another blow. A tiny cut in the door. Anna cursed.

"Where the hell," Dude said, "did you find that?"

"Janitor's closet," Anna panted. "Before 1940, it used to be part of the cafeteria. They walled it off. Careful!"

She brought it down an uneasy distance from Dude's shoulder. He sidestepped away.

"Thanks," she said, and brought the ax down again.

It took eight chops before Dude took a running leap and broke down one of the doors, which had grown flimsy with cuts. Babe pulled him out of the way just in time for the smoke to burst out. Teenagers followed.

Babe, Anna, and Dude pressed themselves back into the wall as their classmates poured through, gagging and screaming. Over it all was the crackle of fire, which was now reaching the ceiling at the back of the gym.

The inside of the gym was choked with smoke. The wall of fire penetrated the smoke with a terrifying glare. Moe's body was a blackened husk by the back of the room. The creature hunched over April Tanner, eating her kidney. April had been dead since Anna's first ax strike. Her torso was in ribbons. Her eyes stared unseeing into the ceiling where the smoke formed a deadly, choking blanket.

Anna retched at the sight.

"Geez," Babe said weakly.

The creature rose and charged at Zachary Litnus, who clutched uselessly at his inhaler. He'd passed out at the back of the fleeing crowd. Half-conscious and exhausted with smoke, he crawled feebly towards the exit.

"Shit," Dude said, and started for him.

The speakers came on.

Static screamed through the school.

The creature keened, folding inwards. Babe did the same, their yells bouncing off each other.

Anna grabbed Zachary Litnus by the hands and pulled, nudging Babe to follow. Dude took his wrists and suddenly the pulling got a lot easier.

"Give him to me," Dude said as they cleared the door, Babe stumbling out with them, blind with pain and barely able to walk. He was doing better than the creature, who couldn't unclench from its knot of pain.

Dude continued, "I can carry—"

Hunter hit Dude at a sprint. He smacked into Dude from behind, sending them skidding into the gym. Zachary tumbled to the floor, wheezing. Dude's nose cracked against the wood of the gym.

"Christ," he gurgled, blood in his throat. He struggled onto his back.

Hunter knelt over him, knee against his stomach, grinning and sweating. It was hot in here. The gym fire was a dozen feet away, too far for Hunter to drag him without his friends getting to him. He dug into his pocket, unsheathing his lighter.

Out in the hall, Babe kept screaming, eyes streaming with pain. The scream didn't have words.

Hunter did.

"You're dead, freak," he said, and flicked on the lighter.

Dude flinched. It was instinct, even as the homemade

BLAMMO sign popped into place where a flame would be, just the way he'd crafted it last week. Hunter's real lighter, the one his father had kissed before giving to him, was bunched deep in Dude's back pocket.

Hunter's smile flinched with him. He stared. "What—"

Babe slammed into him.They rolled off Dude, keeping under the sheet of smoke which continued to rise and fill the gym's high ceilings. They gasped for clean air. Searing heat emanated into the hall where Anna was struggling to pull Zachary to safety.

Babe growled into Hunter's face, fighting the urge to curl in on himself as the static relentlessly shrieked through the burning gym.

"Wait!" Hunter said.

Babe lunged down and bit the rest of his ear off. Hunter's plea turned into a howl, a song to match the static still raging over the PA system.

Babe spat out the ear and took another bite. This one from Hunter's neck, Hunter writhing underneath him. Babe's teeth began to close, frenzied with blood—

He reared back. Blood oozed from Hunter's throat as he lay paralyzed with shock, both of them choking on the smoke.

I am not—

Babe turned. Dude stood behind him, holding out a hand. Babe grabbed it, shoving the pain from the static behind a very thin wall. He twisted back to look at Anna struggling to help Zachary stand. Babe hauled himself to his feet, gaze looping from Dude to the creature still bellowing in agony a few feet away.

He took one stuttering step towards the door before sighing. "Goddamnit," he said, and turned back to extend a hand towards Hunter.

Hunter slapped it away.

"We gotta get out of here," Babe said hastily, eyeing Hunter's bleeding neck. A leak, not a flood. "Come on, you little creep, get up!"

Hunter bared his teeth. "Get away from me," he said. Then he yelled the word Buzz had begun to carve into Jules's door.

Dude pulled at Babe's shoulder. "We gotta go."

The PA stuttered. The static cut out for seconds at a time.

The creature uncurled jerkily from its bow of agony. It took one limping step towards them.

"Damnit," Babe said. He didn't look at Hunter again.

Dude jogged to the doorway, hefted Zachary onto his shoulder. The three of them hurried into the hall, coughing, the monster picking up speed behind them. Babe chanced a glance over his shoulder. They weren't going to make it. After all this goddamn effort, they weren't—

"Move."

Babe looked up to find a bloody Kate Higgins standing there with her gun raised.

They moved.

Kate shot the creature twice in the head. It slumped to the side, limbs spasming. Its leg moved half a step forwards. Kate shot it again and reloaded her gun. As she clicked the magazine into place, the creature took another shuddering step and vanished.

"Asshole," Kate spat, and limped around. "Let's go."

Jules nearly ran into them as they rounded a corner. They stumbled out the high school doors to find that the fire department still wasn't there, but everybody within ten blocks had shown up to gawk. The fire had spread past the gym, eating up the lines that Hunter had sprayed across the halls.

Hunter would never know that he almost succeeded at burning down the school. He lay in the burning gym, sucking in smoke and trembling with shock. Blood pulsed sluggishly out of his neck. The wound wasn't fatal, but the smoke was. His lungs filled with fluid. His vision pinholed.

The PA system faltered to a stop. The wires to the gym had finally melted. Flames took over the gym ceiling.

Hunter tried to smile. He couldn't remember why he was happy. It had something to do with his dad. But all he could think of in his heat-struck, smoke-filled mind was how much he wanted to touch those flames above him.

A figure blocked the raging light. For a second, it looked like Ian Creel.

Hunter opened his mouth. He didn't know what he'd say, but it didn't matter. In fifteen seconds, he would die, still wordless, choking on the fluid building up in his lungs.

The figure walked away. Hunter tried to turn his head. His neck didn't hurt anymore, nor his chest. He tried to turn his head some more and it fell to the right. April Tanner lay dead a few feet away. The shirt she'd tried to save Moe with was draped over her chest. Her guts were a bowl of red, all scooped out.

Hunter gurgled a laugh. Last year at a party, he'd squeezed her ass. She'd called him a jerk. Then, noticing who he was, she'd left the party and avoided him for the rest of their lives.

That's what you get, he thought, and choked for the last time.

There wasn't a lot of joy in watching your school burn down. Babe would feel cheated if he wasn't putting most of his energy into fighting down the monstrous force rising through his body.

Another flare. He clenched his teeth and swallowed it down, eyes on the smoke pillar billowing up from the school. The fire was consuming the cafeteria now.

Consume, the voice echoed.

Shut up, Babe told it.

Next to him, Anna kept glancing over at the kids being loaded into cars and driven towards the hospital an hour away, Zachary Litnus among them. Jules chewed on her nails, spitting out purple polish. Kate wiped at the bite mark on her wrist. Dude turned his own wrist to check his watch. They were still on a time limit.

"*Babe!*"

Babe turned. Milly was running at him, drenched in sweat, chest heaving. Even her running looked uncomfortable, pinched, stiff. Babe flared with annoyance, but it wasn't his. Babe was deeply relieved to see her.

Still running, she yelled something at him.

Babe strained, trying to hear over the yelling and sirens and bursts of fire. "*What?*"

"—ced—not cēlans!"

She dodged around Deputy Lissiter, almost fell over, kept running after his failed attempt to steady her.

Babe yelled, "*What?*"

She slammed into him. "*Cedrus!* It's not a hidden place, it's *cedrus!*"

"Cedrus? What is—"

"Juniper!"

Babe stared. She was shaking, and they'd shared a dream together, and she'd done all this translating for him, and he couldn't—he *couldn't* hate her. He kept imagining Milly Hart pinning up those posters, painting the tiny details of those figurines, meticulously crafting those maps, filling up that dark little room with her very own light.

"Juniper?" he repeated. "Does that—"

She nodded frantically. Her eyes streamed, not from the smoke. She reached into her pocket and crammed a piece of paper into Babe's hand.

The others were gathering round. Milly leaned closer, mouth shaky against his ear. He blocked out the cacophonous noise of her heartbeat, homing in on her words.

"I didn't kill my mom," she said. "The others—I ate. I bit her in the back of the neck and then I stopped. She couldn't move, but she wasn't dying. The... the *thing* had to come in. It took a long time."

She dragged in a ragged breath, squeezed the hand which held her note.

"You can have it," she said. "The police chief back then gave it to me. I thought about burning it, but—"

She didn't finish. She pushed back, wiped her face with the backs of her hands.

"Milly," Anna said. "Are you alright?"

Babe held the note up. The handwriting was unsteady, the paper ripped off a grocery list. Old blood dotted a corner.

I DON'T REGRET IT. I'D DO IT AGAIN AND AGAIN AND AGAIN

Pained swearing. Babe looked up to see Dude righting himself after tripping over a crack in the asphalt. Ash streaked one cheek. He stunk of paint thinner. His hair was singed and his eye was bruised and his nose bled bright crimson down his mouth and chin. Nobody had ever been more beautiful.

Dude limped up to stand in front of Babe.

"Babe," he said. "What's up?"

A warm wave of affection blocked out the flares of hunger.

I'd take part of you over none. Babe sucked in a breath. "We gotta get to Juniper Lookout."

Kate nodded, short and sharp. She cast a look around the parking lot. Her squad car was surrounded by onlookers in their own cars. "Everybody in Dude's truck. I'm driving."

Smoke drifted overhead. More sirens. The fire department was finally arriving.

Milly started towards the truck. Babe put a hand on her arm and she paused. "Thank you," he said. "We wouldn't—we *couldn't* have done this without you. *Thank* you, Milly."

She stared at him, wet still cascading down her face. Slow, halting, she reached up and covered the hand that touched her shoulder, nodding tightly.

"Let's end this."

***

Kate had a hand on the driver's door handle when Lissiter came up behind her.

"Chief," he said, eyes flickering nervously to Babe who was twitching in the backseat. "What're you doing?"

"What does it look like?" Kate said, and tried to climb in. Lissiter grabbed her shoulder, turning her around. She let it happen, then shoved his hand off.

"I don't know what the hell it looks like," Lissiter said, frowning at her bruised cheek. He glanced back at Babe buckled up in the passenger seat, Milly squished in beside him, and dropped his voice. It wouldn't have mattered—there was enough crackling flames and chatter and sirens to fill the ears of whoever might've been listening.

"What're you up to?"

Kate glared. For the first time in decades, she took someone's face in her hands. "If I don't get in this car and go where I need to go, more people are gonna die. That's all you need to know. Now you get on your speaker and tell those dumbasses parked in the middle of the road watching the light show to get the hell out of my way, alright, Lissiter?"

He stared at her, cheeks squishing in her forceful grip.

"*Alright*, Lissiter?"

"Alright," Lissiter said. Kate dropped her hands. Lissiter hesitated, and then he was ducking through the crowd to his car, leaning in to get to the speaker. "CLEAR THE ROADS! IF YOU GOT A CAR IN THE ROAD, MOVE IT OUT OF THE WAY! THAT'S YOU, MRS MCKAY, PLEASE MOVE YOUR STATION WAGON! MR KEYES! I SEE YOUR VAN! PLEASE MOVE IT OUT OF THE WAY!"

"Good kid," Kate said, and got in the truck.

thirty-eight

IF WE LIVE THROUGH THIS, Babe thought as they tore through the town in Dude's truck, *I'm getting the heck out of here.*

Another flare of sharp. It invaded Babe's head, tried to flood him out.

"Shut up," he told it.

His friends glanced over.

"Not you," Babe said.

They careened away from the smoking high school, past the plaque and the new town hall. Past the sewer district and up into the hills. Very few townsfolk had ever been up to Juniper Lookout.

Anna had been the first of their friend group to find it, the first in generations. She'd immediately gone to find Babe. He'd stood on that hill, looked down into the town, and felt something he would never be able to describe. Later, he'd say it was dread.

They drove up the hill to the lookout, where, hundreds of years ago, Founder Jim had planted two seeds from his hometown. Juniper seeds. He'd brought his daughter up to watch them grow. It was their secret. One day, he'd come up there alone with a ritual. And now they were barreling towards it, Chevy kicking up dust as they wound towards the jumping off point crowned by two juniper trees.

There wasn't much good about Bulldeen. It fed on toxins. But the land doesn't make all of a town—the people help. And some people tried to be good. That seeped into the soil too. The force was weak, but there. Caroline had started it when she was a child, and it had waited for a long time before it finally found Anna Higgins. Of course, Anna brought her friends, her friends who did their best to love each other in a way that nourished instead of poisoned.

The truck screeched to a stop. They piled out, Anna taking Dude's knife from the glovebox and heading over to the gap between the juniper trees. She got down on her hands and knees and began to cut a circle into the grass.

The others hung back. Kate asked Babe, "Anything?"

Babe struggled to keep the hunger at bay. Blood coated his teeth, down his neck. His mouth watered. He spat red out into the grass.

"I don't know," he said, shaking. "I think—"

Anna crawled to a stop, joining the ends of the lopsided circle and scooting into the middle. She wiped the knife on her skirt and sliced her palm open. Blood dripped into the dirt.

"Bulldeen, I invoke thee," she said in a rush. "Come now and feed!"

Babe jerked. Anna's head flew up. Kate got out her gun.

Babe ground his teeth. "Keep going."

She set her worried eyebrows in determination. She nodded. Anna had never been anywhere else. Her roots were thick in the ground.

"We revoke your power," she said. "We revoke your power. We revoke—"

Milly stepped up to the circle edge. She was shaking almost

as much as Babe, crying openly. "We revoke your power," she said, the words half-gasp.

Jules stumbled into place beside her, voice joining the chant. It rose like the wind suddenly whipping around their heads. There was never a wind so strong in the small town of Bulldeen, Maine.

Babe and Dude stepped forwards as one.

Kate was last. Anna had to look over, still forming the words. Her eyes questioned.

Kate shivered. Then, like stepping off a cliff, she took the last place around the circle.

"We revoke your power. We revoke your power. We revoke—"

The wind howled. Babe sucked in a breath as it echoed down through his toes, into the line cut through the soil. Past the soil. Deeper, deeper.

A familiar voice spoke in his head. *Give in,* it said, close to panic. *Give yourself over.*

Babe raised his voice over the wind. "We revoke—"

The wind yanked at him so he stumbled sideways.

"It's too strong!" Jules screamed.

Milly held out her hand. "Grab hold!"

One by one, they clasped at each other. In the middle of the circle, Anna squeezed her eyes shut as the dirt flew around her face.

"*We revoke your power!*" they yelled, dirt in their mouths, lancing between their teeth.

Behind them, the creature emerged where Founder Jim had once put a knife to his starved hand. It staggered, then lunged for Babe.

Kate strode back from the circle and shot it in the head.

It roared. The wind roared with it.

"*I'm in you. You want to give in. To consume.*"

"Fuck off," Babe told it.

The wind stuttered. Something in Babe chipped, a leak began to trickle. Then it began to flow. The hunger left him in a flood.

The creature panted. *"If I die, Bulldeen dies."*

"Good," Kate said, and shot it again. It reeled back with the impact.

"Holy shit," Dude said. Babe squeezed his fingers. He'd never felt more alive. The miracle of holding someone's hand.

Milly was the only one who hadn't stopped chanting. She stopped now to yell, "Anna, the incantation!"

She fumbled it from her pocket, held it out. Anna stretched.

The wind caught. The paper whipped away, over the hill.

The creature tried to straighten up. Kate shot it again. Two bullets left.

"Shit," Jules said, watching the paper spiral. "Shit, shit—"

Milly fell forward onto her knees. Anna crawled, grabbed her wrist. Milly said something, but it was unintelligible over the wind. Her voice kept dying, breaking into quivers.

"Milly," Anna said, but she was too far away. Even with Anna clutching her, even with people standing around, they were too far away.

Babe pushed forwards. Dude followed, always. They got on their knees next to Milly.

They tried so hard to be good to each other, and they mostly succeeded. Destruction was a hobby in Bulldeen, but not for them. One by one, they'd made a choice: they wouldn't hurt themselves. And they sure as shit wouldn't hurt each other. Babe knelt in the grass and something stirred in the ground, a force as old as humankind, as much a part of the town as the wrecked creature limping towards them.

The force climbed up into Babe. It whispered the words.

From somewhere deep inside of him, Babe said, "The well runs dry."

Milly lifted her face. Grime and tears, wind whipping their hair around their heads, clawing at Babe's glasses.

The creature staggered forwards one step. Two. Kate stepped back with it until her heel grazed the circle.

"The well runs dry," Babe repeated.

Milly nodded. She'd dreamed about it so many times. A woman trying to save the town, to save herself and her family. The dream was always gone after she woke.

Her palms pressed into the grass. "The water runs clear."

The creature dragged itself forward, head dripping.

"You love this place," it called to Kate, blurring at the edges. *"You love it more than you hate it. You don't know what you would be without it."*

Kate readjusted her grip on her gun. "Guess it's time to find out."

The creature's mouth twitched. A drip of its cheek stung the grass, face flickering into a million masks— an aunt, a teacher, a TV presenter, Hunter Creel, Ian Creel, Ryan Simmons—as Babe and Milly spoke as one:

"There will be no poison here."

The creature froze, wind whipping at its overcoat. The wind began to drop.

"But..." it said, and staggered. Fell to its knees. The wasted soul of Bulldeen raised its face to the sun.

"But I love you," it said, soft.

Babe wet his lips. "Choke on it."

It blinked. Its jaw crumbled inwards. The face followed, flowing down its neck and body until all of it disintegrated into the grass. Skin bled over the dirt and turned to waste. From this compost, a single thornfruit vine shot up. Fruit swelled on the tip and rotted in front of their eyes. The stem followed, and all that was left of the creature was a pile of dark sitting on a hill.

Babe smacked his tongue around his mouth. Suddenly, he had the strongest urge to wash it out.

The silence grew. Babe asked, "Does anybody have water on them?"

Dude got up wordlessly, heading to his truck. He rummaged in the glove compartment and came back with a small bottle of water, the label long gone. He'd started storing it there last month. *For our trip to LA,* he'd said, and then changed the subject. No matter how hard Babe tried to broadcast happiness for his friends leaving, Dude always saw past it.

He held the water out to Babe, who stood and took it. He swilled water around his mouth and spat away from their feet.

Dude watched him. There was no mistaking the tender look in his eyes. "You still hungry?"

Babe did another swish and spit. His stomach growled. Now that he thought about it, he was ravenous. "Just the usual kind," he said, and pulled Dude in by the back of the neck.

Dude made a noise into Babe's mouth.

Jules gasped from back in the circle where the girls were still sitting. Anna shushed her. The click of a gun's safety going on, Kate pushing herself to her feet and brushing herself down.

Babe didn't notice any of it. The world narrowed down into Dude's chapped lips tasting faintly of nose blood, his rough hands gentle and hesitant on Babe's waist.

Dude stared at Babe as he drew away, eyes wide and dazed in a way that had nothing to do with the ritual that had just condemned the town to death. Babe watched his eyelids shudder with the familiar urge to make a joke. But when Dude spoke, it was the most sincere word Babe had ever heard from him.

"Yeah?"

Babe nodded.

"Okay. Good." Dude's tongue darted out to touch his bottom lip. The miracle of heat transfer.

Jules asked, "We don't have to go back to class now, right?"

Anna laughed, relieved and loud. She leaned into Milly, who only hesitated a moment before leaning back against her. Over at the cliff edge, Kate squinted out at the smoke still rising from the high school.

"We don't," Babe agreed, and kissed Dude again.

Off in the distance, the burning high school began to dim, from a flame to an ember to a spark that struggled for several minutes. They stayed there for a long time at their spot on Juniper Lookout as the spark dissipated into black smoke, then gray smoke, and then, finally, nothing.

chapter
thirty-nine

THE WEATHER on graduation day was mild. Sunny skies. Not too hot. Gentle wind.

Babe sweated through his robes in five minutes.

"I'm going to throw up on stage," he told Dude, who was zipping up his suitcase on the bed.

"That'll be something to remember." Dude slid his toothbrush into the suitcase pocket. Babe's luggage was already out in the Chevy. They'd waited until Ryan was at work, then snuck through Babe's bedroom window, stuffing his clothes into a suitcase the Higginses had bought for him the day before. There were no suitcases in the Simmons house. They didn't go anywhere. On that one trip to see Granddad Simmons in the hospital, Babe had used his school backpack.

Dude reached for the tracing paper on his desk. Babe handed it to him thoughtlessly, still stressing. "Did they pick me just to spite me?"

Dude slotted his pad of tracing paper in with his toothbrush. He came over and put a solid hand on Babe's shoulder. "Definitely."

Babe flicked at Dude's hand. Then, because he could, he

linked their fingers together and leaned up to kiss him. Dude smiled into it.

"You'll do great," he assured Babe, and went to do up his shoes. He braced his boot on the bed, batting away the long robes that tangled over his laces. "If you do puke, make sure to get some on Skinner."

Since the gym had burned down and taken half the school with it, graduation would take place on the field. Parents sat on folding chairs under the shade of the oak trees and students crowded around the miniature stage they'd used for the play, sweating and eyeing their parents' chairs enviously.

One good thing about small towns: graduations are a fast affair. It only took fifteen minutes to go through the list of names, and soon, Babe was being called back on stage.

He had no idea how valedictorians did it in big cities. He was standing in front of maybe a hundred people and sweating bullets.

"Uh," he said. "Hi! I'm...I'm Babe Simmons. Henry. I'm your valedictorian today."

Dude cheered. Jules and Anna joined in. After some nudging, Milly let out a tiny cry of support.

"Thanks," he told them. He didn't look off to the left, where the parents were sitting. His dad had been one of the first ones to show up today. At least he hadn't tried to talk to Babe before the ceremony. Or maybe he had—Babe thought he'd seen Kate moving menacingly in Ryan's direction before he sat down. She sat off to the side, flashing Babe a thumbs-up.

Babe got his speech out of his sleeve. It was one page long.

"First off," he read out, "thank you for choosing me as valedictorian. I didn't see that coming! So—thanks."

He cleared his throat. Kate had suggested this next bit to throw off suspicion. "Secondly, I think we should have a minute of silence for the members of our community who have gone missing. We hope to find you soon. And this minute of silence will also be for Moe Stafford, April Tanner, and Hunter Creel, who tragically died in the fire that took half the school."

A murmur ran through the crowd. Everybody knew that Hunter had set the fire that killed him. They knew what he'd done to Moe and April. Some of the older members in the crowd also murmured at the mention of disappearances, since many of them were still wary around their resident Zombabe. Janitor Larry sat in with the parents, narrowing his eyes up at the stage. But not too narrow—everybody also knew who had broken down the gym doors. They knew about Zachary Litnus, who would've died if they hadn't carried him out of the gym. He was coming home from the hospital today. He'd already called Babe to thank him three separate times, only hanging up when his croaking gave way to a coughing fit.

The crowd all bowed their heads along with Babe, who counted along on Dude's watch.

"Alright," Babe said once the minute was up. "So, I...I wasn't one of the people thinking to prepare a speech for when I get this gig. I got all those votes in the last couple weeks of school, so I wrote all of this yesterday."

He adjusted the speech paper. It was a page ripped out of an exercise book.

"I'm really nervous," he began. "Not about the speech— well, yes, about the speech—but more about leaving. I'm heading to LA. A few of you are getting out of town over the next few years. I'm sure you're just as freaked out as I am. You've grown up here too. Bulldeen is the world. We don't know what it'll be like after we pass those town limits."

The crowd shifted. Tassels tilted sideways, graduates

leaning over to whisper to each other. Most of them would have never left. They would have stayed there, married, had children, and died in Bulldeen if not for the failing crops. Word was already getting around about the wilting stalks, the rotting fruits. If it continued—which it would—the harvests would stop. Bulldeen would have to pack up and move. Some of the town was still in denial, but as the months and years passed, reality would set in: there would be no more thornfruit. Bulldeen was dying for good.

The graduates looked up at Babe almost as anxiously as their parents watching from the folding seats. The parents had been here longer. They were just as scared as their children of living somewhere else.

Babe looked over the crowd, towards his friends. They smiled at him. Babe smiled back, letting himself meet Dude's gaze, who held it just as steadily.

"Not long ago," Babe continued, "I asked my friend—what if it's not better out there? What if, wherever we go, we take ourselves with us? And she said—yeah, that's what happens, but that doesn't have to be bad. We don't have to be poison. We can be good to ourselves, good to each other. And we can keep doing it when we get out of here. Maybe all that good can infect the next place we live."

He chanced a look over at Ryan. His dad was staring, expression unreadable, down at his own hands.

Babe looked back at his paper, relieved. He would look his father in the eye again, but not for a long time. Ryan had to change first. That would take time.

"Anyway," he said. "That's it from me. Happy graduation, everybody."

Babe wobbled down the stage stairs into a graduate group hug. Everybody's hats bumped. Dude reached into the middle and tugged on their tassels.

"That was beautiful," Anna's father said as he came up with the rest of the family, Mrs. Higgins crying at his side, Alicia staring determinedly at her feet with her teddy bear in a stranglehold. Kate stood back at a safe distance as all the hugs went down. Alicia clung around Anna's neck long enough that everybody cooed.

Mr. Higgins stayed quiet, but when Alicia let go, his eyes were shining too.

His wife handed him a Kleenex.

"Outta heeeere," Jules sang to a made-up tune that changed every time she sung it. This version vaguely resembled "Closing Time" by Semisonic. "Outa outta outta here, so finish your whiskey or beer!"

The others echoed it. Jules linked hands with Dude. Her parents weren't here, but neither was Dude's mom. Katherine Marsh had to work. Jules's parents didn't know she was graduating today, though they were aware she was leaving this week. They'd left for Vegas two days prior.

Mrs. Higgins patted their cheeks one by one. "Let us know how the move goes, alright? If you have any questions—"

"Your phone will be clogged with calls from us hapless teenagers," Dude assured her.

She dropped his face. "We'll check up on your mother."

"Thanks," Dude mumbled. He was very glad when Alicia shoved her teddy bear up at Anna and everybody broke out into *aww*'s again.

Anna took it gingerly by the front paws. "Are you sure?"

Alicia nodded, eyes on her little boots as they kicked at the dirt. "You're gonna need him more than I will."

Anna nodded seriously, hugging him close. "I'll take good

care of him," she said, and looked up at her parents, reminded by the hug. "You won't cancel on Grandma and Granddad again?"

Mrs. Higgins looked at her husband, who sighed. "No," he said. "I think...I think we're long overdue for a meeting."

"And you'll—"

"I'll give them a hug from you," he confirmed, smiling with a warmth that he'd passed right down to his daughters.

Kate slid her sunglasses up into her hair, squinting into the crowd. "Ryan's making his shot."

Babe spun immediately. His friends followed. They headed for Dude's truck, Ryan on their heels.

"You didn't have to come and get your stuff while I was at work," Ryan called. "I wouldn't have stopped you."

Dude cursed, robe twisting around his feet. He hadn't adjusted for length. "Shit. Go on without me."

Babe nodded at the others. "It's fine. It's fine," he repeated to Dude, who gave a dubious look to the approaching Ryan.

The girls closed the distance to the Chevy, the truck bed overflowing with everybody's bags, which bulged against the bungee cords holding them down. Dude untwisted his robes from his shoes, Babe holding them out of the way just in time for Ryan to stop in front of them.

"You can't just not come home," he said desperately.

Babe gave him a thin smile. "Hi, Dad."

Dude waved. "Hi, Ryan."

Ryan ignored him, grabbing his son around the shoulders. "Are you okay?"

Babe eased him off carefully. "Your dad stopped you from going to college?"

"What?"

"You didn't finish the story."

Ryan frowned, lost. Parents milled around them, hugging their children, tousling tassels, straightening caps.

"I...was going to go to art school," he said slowly. "I know how upset you are—I felt the same thing. I wish my dad was around now—I could tell him I forgive him. That I love him."

He smiled sadly, full of hope. His eyes were the same brown as Babe's but not the same shape, and Babe looked into them with rage and a slow understanding that crept close to disgust. But not too close. For the first time, Babe looked at his father and saw a man. Someone utterly separate from him.

Most days, Babe had no idea what he wanted to say. He'd say something and later he'd puzzle, confused and frustrated, because none of it got at the crux of what he meant. The problem was that he didn't know what he meant, so of course expressing that was going to be a mess.

But sometimes, we know exactly what we're thinking. Sometimes the meaning comes and the words arrive neatly, right after. These words came easily, as if Babe had known them a long time.

"I love you, Dad," he said. "But I don't think you know me that well."

Ryan stared. He couldn't understand. Babe didn't know if he ever would.

"I..." Ryan started.

"See you later." Babe turned towards the truck, bumping Dude's shoulder to feel his solid, steady weight beside him.

Ryan trailed after them. "Thank you."

They kept walking.

"For bringing him back," Ryan continued.

Babe stumbled. Ryan was looking at Dude, his eyes wide and wet. "Even if he never talks to me again, I'm glad he's in the world."

Seconds passed. Dude jerked his head in a nod. He looked

towards Babe, who thought about saying something more. But his friends were waiting in the truck, Milly squeezing into the middle with Anna and Jules, Kate ready to follow along in her cop car. When Dude got in the driver's seat, Babe busied himself examining his nails so he wouldn't have to look at his dad's reflection, small and pathetic in the rear-view mirror.

Dude hit the gas, driving away from Bulldeen High for the last time.

They stopped before the sign. YOU ARE NOW LEAVING BULLDEEN. COME BACK SOON!

Milly climbed shakily onto the asphalt.

"You should come with us," Anna said.

Milly laughed, brushing her stringy hair out of her face. "I'm gonna have to go somewhere! The town's going to be dead soon."

The road out of town was lined with thornfruit fields on both sides. If they were to walk over and touch a fruit, the skin would give under their touch. Workers came in each day with less and less untainted fruit. Soon, the stalks would collapse into themselves. They'd never grow back.

A cop car pulled up. Kate got out onto the road, sucking on a cigarette, nicotine patches littered under her rolled-up sleeves. Her sunglasses stayed on top of her head, but she still squinted hard. She had not woken up without a hangover in over a decade, and this morning was no exception.

Dude gave her a salute. "Chief."

Kate nodded at him, lighting another cigarette from the one in her mouth. Around them, the stretch of road lay empty. No one else was getting out of town today.

Anna pulled Milly into a hug, which Milly returned

fondly. She was getting better at hugs. She'd incorporated Anna's method of adding a squeeze at the end.

"Send me a reminder about our D&D session," Anna said into her shoulder. She squeezed.

Milly laughed, giving a returning squeeze and drawing back. "I will! I can't wait to meet your character. Email me whenever you can." She turned timidly to Babe. "Do you still—"

"Of course," Babe said, smile breaking out warm across his face. "Send me a reminder too. I'll be online." His smile twisted. "Anything I should watch out for?"

"Nothing dangerous. It will take a very long time for any non-dying cat to trust you. Sometimes you'll have strange dreams, but you'll forget them when you wake." She met his eyes with that thread of understanding he used to hate. They would email about more than D&D. Milly would follow them out to LA the coming year, right when the bad things started up again.

But that was later.

Babe hugged Milly a second time. Then he hugged Kate, who was almost as unused to hugs as Milly. Her arms were stiff. She clapped him once on the back and pushed him away, holding his arm with a firm hand. "Gimme a call if you start getting hungry."

"I will."

"He won't get hungry," Milly said.

Dude, Babe, Jules, and Anna climbed back into their seats. Kate and Milly stayed in the middle of the road as it shimmered in the heat.

"Outta here," Jules whisper-sung to the tune of "Ob-La-Di, Ob-La-Da." "Outta here, life goes on, *bra*—"

The Chevy rumbled to life. Babe took one of the last looks he'd ever give Bulldeen, and thought about shuddering. It was hard to do with his friends next to him, a packing job waiting in LA before his classes started in the second semester. Suddenly, everything in Bulldeen seemed like a nightmare, one that lingered after waking. None of them would forget. But the day lay ahead, things to do and people to do them with, and Babe was more than ready to open his eyes into the morning.

The truck took off. The sign flashed past.

Babe watched it go by. "Wait!"

Dude stomped on the brake. Babe opened the passenger door.

"Forgot something," he said, climbing out onto the cracked, gleaming road. He went to the trunk bed and fished out a tire iron, thin and unyielding under his fingers. He strode back to the welcome sign and swung. Kate and Milly stood back as Babe smashed the sign once, twice, three times. It clattered to the road with a resounding cheer from Jules hanging out of the backseat window.

Babe gave the others a nod, then he got back in the truck. It took off away from town, fast and then faster. The sign rocked lightly on the asphalt, still quivering from the contact. As Kate and Milly watched, it rocked to a stop and was silent.

"I gotta admit," Dude said, glancing over at Babe as he entwined their fingers together between their seats, "that was kind of hot."

Babe grinned. "Eyes on the road."

"Right," Dude said. "Guess you want me to have both hands on the wheel too."

He tried to pull his hand back, but Babe held it fast, raising Dude's hand to his face and kissing his second knuckle.

"Let's not go that far."

Dude laughed. Babe twisted in his seat to look back at Jules with her head back and her music on, Anna holding her little sister's bear under her chin, Bulldeen fading into nothing behind them. Around them, the thornfruit fields blurred past. At this speed, you couldn't tell they were dying, but the knowledge was there.

Babe took a shaky breath, flooded with a relief so intense he felt like he might cry. He turned back to settle into his seat, smiling, trembling, squeezing Dude's hand and getting the pressure right back.

After a while, the thornfruit fields fell away. The highway out of Maine came into view, the world opening in front of their truck.

They drove right in.

END.

babylove preview

Even with the blood, rituals and resurrections, the most surprising thing about the summer of 2003 was Ivy Wexler.

Frankie Tanner was in her usual lunchtime haze when Ivy marched up. It took a second to realize Ivy was, in fact, looking at her, and not just leaning her hip against Frankie's table for a place to rest.

Frankie blinked up at her through clumpy mascara. The pleasant blur from smoking up in the bathrooms faded into the background, the real world coming into sharp, irritating focus. Meatloaf stench from the tray in front of her. Low hum of Bulldeen High, all whispers and unkind laughs.

Ivy motioned for Frankie to remove her headphones.

With a scowl, Frankie did. "What do you want, princess?"

Ivy gave a short and surprised chuckle. They'd talked before—in a small town like Bulldeen, it was impossible for them not to—but this was the first time they'd spoken directly since first grade, when Ivy found her crying behind the swings. Frankie had a faint, improbable memory of Ivy's arm around her shoulders, her soft voice in Frankie's ear. *Everything's going to be alright.* Sometimes Frankie thought it was a dream. It was difficult to reconcile that gentle version with the girl who stood in front of her now, shiny and intimidating, the first freshman they let onto the cheerleading team in decades.

Ivy beamed, flicking her straightened hair away from her heart-shaped face. "Your sister says you're going to have to do summer school if you don't pass a make-up test for Mr. Clack."

Frankie looked across the cafeteria to where April Tanner sat. April tipped her head back to laugh at what Frankie assumed was a bad joke, since that was definitely her sister's fake laugh.

April wasn't looking their way. She never looked at her little sister while they were at school. Why would she? They were in entirely different social circles. As in, April Tanner *had* a social circle. She hung with the other cheerleaders and, on occasion, Bulldeen Bulls footballers.

Frankie was a one-woman band. She preferred it that way, and if anyone tried poking holes in this theory, she just said it louder.

"Well?" Ivy cocked her head expectantly. More pale hair fell into her face. "Are you failing or aren't you?"

Frankie reached for her headphones. "Go mess with somebody else, Ivy. I promise I'm very unsatisfying to taunt."

"I'm not *taunting* you. God." Ivy rolled her eyes. "I'm asking if you want help."

"Help," Frankie repeated, unable to stop the incredulous smile. "*You* want to help *me*."

"For a favor, of course."

"Oh! Here I thought you were doing this out of the goodness of your heart."

Ivy's next laugh cut off abruptly. She rubbed the corner of her mouth, slim fingers twitching as if resisting the urge to cover it. *That would be a shame*, Frankie thought, and then squashed that thought into a manageable size to store away and never look at again.

Frankie rested her chin on her hands, rings digging into her jaw. "So what is it? Drug deal? Oooh, do you need me to kneecap someone? I don't hurt kids. Well, maybe for the right price."

"Good to know," Ivy said, bright and only a little mocking. "Look. I'm a good tutor. Do you want to help, or do you want to be stuck listening to Mr. Clack talk about Moby Dick for the rest of the summer?"

"You still haven't told me what it is I'm helping with, princess."

Ivy's mouth pulled under her twitching fingers. She was still rubbing, red gloss glinting at the corner of her pinkie where she'd swiped her lips by accident.

"I need—"

An arm looped around Ivy's shoulder, cutting her off. Marvin Martin, mediocre footballer and perpetual polo shirt wearer, grinned at his girlfriend's shocked gasp.

"Whoa, hey! Something got your tongue?" He pinched her chin.

Ivy smiled, so wide and so fake Frankie didn't bother hiding her scoff.

But the smile didn't even falter. "Just fulfilling my end of a bargain. Is there a seat over there for me?"

He frowned. "Yeah, babe, always."

Yeah babe, Frankie mouthed mockingly, rotating her fork in her meatloaf. *Always!*

Ivy twisted to look behind him at the cheerleader table. "Mine looks a little cold. Mind warming it for me?"

She lay a hand on his skinny chest. His confused expression softened.

"Alright," he said, obviously not fooled, but not prying. He lingered by the table long enough that Frankie shot him a dangerous look. Why didn't the black lipstick, piercings and knife tricks in the parking lot make people leave her the hell alone? It made them ignore her, sure. But it didn't protect her from this shit.

Marvin's annoying grin slid back into place. "Hey, Loser Tanner. Coming to the party next weekend?"

"You know me," Frankie deadpanned. "I am the party queen."

"I bet." Marvin's squinty dishwater eyes got even squintier. "You totally should. It'll be fun."

"Marvin," Ivy said. "My chair."

"Right, yeah." He didn't look at her. "Come on, don't be like that. We're inviting everybody. We're inviting, uh—" He looked around for more undesirables, gaze landing on the dead freaks—so named due to a certain bully always leaving them with a menacing *you're dead, freaks*—clustered around their usual table.

Marvin cupped his hands around the yell. "HEY DEAD FREAKS! WANNA COME TO MY GIRLFRIEND'S PARTY NEXT WEEKEND? HER PARENTS ARE OUT OF TOWN!"

The dead freaks jumped. There were four of them, all seniors on track to graduate next month: big, outgoing (and in Frankie's opinion, weirdly fashionable) city kid Jules Havelock the only one Frankie found interesting. Then they had haughty, smart Anna Higgins who could have been interesting if only she was haughtier; polite, quiet "Babe" Simmons who was probably a *little* interesting behind closed doors; and, of course aloof, burly "Dude" Marsh, who might be interesting if he was faking all that aloofness, but somehow Frankie bet he wasn't.

Anna's smile was tight as she replied, "Thanks, Marvin. We'll see how the night goes."

"Everybody's coming," Marvin repeated. "Shit, even loser Tanner is coming! Right, Tanner?"

Frankie weighed up her options. Option one: say nothing. Chance being seen as pathetic instead of distant and cool. Option two: come up with something snarky, which was harder with the weed fuzzing everything up. Chance sounding pathetic. Option three: walk away. Chance looking cowardly. No matter what Frankie did, she was still Loser Tanner: stark opposite of her older, cooler, athletic bitch of a sister, who in that moment was examining a nonexistent chip in her nail.

Frankie decided to sneak dye into April's shampoo later. She opened her mouth to go with a snarky comment—always the most dramatic option—but Ivy talked over her.

"Marvin. My chair."

Marvin waited for Ivy to relent. When her smile only got bigger and shinier, he sighed.

"Yeah, yeah. Going to warm up your chair." He rapped his knuckles on the side of Frankie's tray, making it rattle. "Come hang, weirdo. It'll be fun."

He grinned again, broadcasting to the cafeteria how outside of the joke she was, and Frankie resisted the urge to slam her lunch tray into the side of his head. She wasn't an idiot. She knew when she was being made fun of.

Ivy waited until he was out of earshot before taking a scrap of paper from her pocket. "Come over to mine after school, alright? I'll make it worth your while."

"I know where you live, you're like three streets away from me." Frankie leaned back in her chair, away from the paper Ivy had placed on the table. She meant it as a teasing tactic, something to make Ivy actually explain what was going on, but all she got was the swish of Ivy's cheerleading skirt as she turned towards her gang. Ivy was, much like Frankie's sister, one of those desperate girls who wore her outfit outside of practice. Like it mattered she was cheerleader on a small-town team that only people who would grow old and die here would remember. Okay, so a good portion of the high school population.

Frankie raised her voice. "Hey! You haven't told me what we're doing yet!"

Ivy glanced back, blue eyes flashing. "See you later, Frankie."

It was the eyes, pale and haunting. No, it was her name. Classmates called her Loser Tanner. Teachers called her Francesca. Her parents called her *you. You, turn the music down, I had a late shift last night.* When April deigned to talk to her, she called her sis.

No one called her Frankie. It stunned her into silence long enough for Ivy to sit down in the chair Marvin pulled out and bowed over, provoking another fake laugh Frankie didn't have the energy to scoff at.

Frankie uncurled the paper, still expecting a joke she wasn't in on.

But there was the address, sitting pretty in Ivy's loopy handwriting. *For Frankie,* it said at the bottom.

Frankie touched the *i*. Instead of a dot, there sat a small inky heart.

Thank you for reading this preview of BABYLOVE.

thank you

Thank you so much for reading Zombabe! If you want to support me, please leave a review on Goodreads, Amazon or any social media of your choice.

You can find out about my next fiction projects and other exciting updates by subscribing to my monthly newsletter! Sign up by visiting my website at isbelleauthor.com.

You can also follow me on Tiktok @i.s.belle_writes and Instagram @isbelleauthor.

acknowledgments

I'll keep it brief: thank you to Jessica McKelden, Rachael Herron, Catriona Turner, Edward Giordano and my old Masters class for your editing work! I couldn't have done this without you.

Thank you to my dear friend Aster Santiago for the beautiful cover art. I am in constant awe of you.

about the author

I. S. Belle is a Young Adult author who lives in New Zealand. She has a Creative Writing Masters from the International Institute of Modern Letters. She works in a bookstore and stops to pat dogs in the street. If you have a dog and your local bookshop allows pets - for the love of booksellers, please bring them in.

also by i. s. belle

BABYLOVE SERIES

BABYLOVE

SUGARSNAP

SWEETHEARTS - Coming Soon

ZOMBABE

ZOMBABE

GIRLS NIGHT

GIRLS NIGHT - Coming April 2024

9 780473 656645